THE SILVERFISH

A Story of the United Star System Postal Service

EMILY FISHER

First Stillwater River Publications Edition

ISBN: 978-1-965733-42-4

1 2 3 4 5 6 7 8 9 10

Publisher's Cataloging-in-Publication
Provided by Cassidy Cataloguing Services, Inc.

Names: Fisher, Emily, 1994- author.
Title: The Silverfish : a story of the United Star System Postal
    Service / Emily Fisher.
Description: First Stillwater River Publications edition. | West
    Warwick, RI, USA : Stillwater River Publications, [2025]
Identifiers: ISBN: 9781965733424
Subjects: LCSH: Postal service—Fiction. | Space ships—Fiction.
    | Stowaways—Fiction. | Soldiers—Fiction. | War—Fiction.
    | LCGFT: Science fiction. | Action and adventure fiction. |
    Humorous fiction. | BISAC: FICTION / Science Fiction /
    General. | FICTION / Science Fiction / Action & Adventure. |
    FICTION / Science Fiction / Humorous.
Classification: LCC: PS3606.I7724 S55 2025 | DDC: 813/.6—dc23

Written by Emily Fisher.
Cover illustration and interior design by Elisha Gillette.
Published by Stillwater River Publications, West Warwick, RI, USA.

Messenger of Sympathy and Love
Servant of Parted Friends
Consoler of the Lonely
Bond of the Scattered Family
Enlarger of the Common Life
Carrier of News and Knowledge
Instrument of Trade and Industry
Promoter of Mutual Acquaintance
Of Peace and of Goodwill Among Men and Nations.

—"The Letter" Dr. Charles W. Eliot

Acknowledgments

Thanks to my parents, who always encouraged big dreams, and to my siblings, the best of critics and fans. Thanks to the friends who read the first drafts (and asked for more). And thanks to my husband Dan, my own heroic postman.

❶ Signature Required

United Star System Postal Code, Chapter 1, Section 7: Whoever knowingly obstructs the passage of any courier and/or sanctioned airship carrying mail shall be fined by the planetary government originating the obstruction.

"Excuse me, I need someone to sign for this."

A distant explosion rumbled through the loading dock. Debris sprinkled down from overhead, coating Horris Jensen and the panicked security clerk in a fine layer of dust. Horris paid the debris no mind; he simply tapped his pen against the tablet in his hand. The clerk, however, looked between the ceiling and Horris with a horrified expression.

"The Idolers will be here any minute! I don't have time for this!"

Even as the clerk spoke, spiderwebs of cracks appeared in the ceiling and walls around the little docking depot. Another rumble shook the loading deck, and this time, some of the docked ships groaned in response. Horris glanced over his shoulder before looking back to the clerk.

1

"It's regulation," Horris said with an accepting shrug of his shoulders. "No oversized package goes off-world without an authorized signature."

The package in question was a large metal box, sealed tight with multiple clasps around the lid. The box, already sitting on a hand trolley, nearly came to Horris' abdomen. Shipping it wasn't the issue: oversized packages like these were the reason Horris kept the hand trolley ready. But without a signature, the package would get flagged at the depot and returned to sender. The sender, in this case, was the tax office of the Imperial City of Creedence, located on the planet Creed. The Imperial City of Creedence, at the moment, happened to be under siege by an army known as the Idolers.

It would have been a hassle for everyone involved. So Horris rounded his shoulders and tapped his pen against his tablet once more.

The Imperial clerk gaped at him. "Who cares about some stupid package? Just take the thing and *go*! Can't you see we're under attack?!"

"Signature," said Horris quite firmly.

The clerk cursed, leaned across the depot counter, and scrawled a hasty signature at the bottom of the paperwork. His duty complete, he ducked beneath the counter—and just in time, as an explosion shattered the bay doors into pieces.

Horris turned to watch a group of Idolers spill into the loading dock. One spotted him and raised his gun, only to be caught by the wrist by another. A woman, ruggedly gorgeous in the way all rebels were, looked Horris up and down. "Careful! He's USSPS."

Perhaps it helped that the USSPS uniform was a particular shade of cerulean, which stood in sharp contrast to the crisp black uniforms of the Imperials and the mish-mash of browns and reds the Idolers wore. At any rate, most of the Idolers relaxed back.

The one with the gun scowled. "What the hell are you doing here?"

"Retrieving one last package," Horris said, nodding to the hand trolley.

The leader, who wore a heroic red scarf around her neck, glanced around the docked ships. Satisfied at the relatively quiet state of the bay, she turned back to Horris. "Is there anyone else here?"

"No," said Horris, perfectly aware of the Imperial clerk cowering beneath the depot counter.

"Then you should take your package and get out of here, friend," the Idoler replied. "Fireworks are going to begin soon."

Horris nodded. He slipped his tablet back onto his belt, pushed the package onto the hand trolley, and started for the little speeder marked with the USSPS logo. Behind him, the Idolers fanned out, making for the biggest and most impressive ships. One made a beeline for the docking screen, barking orders about so-and-so taking such-and-such ship, to be used at this-and-that coordinates.

The Idoler with the twitchy trigger finger frowned as Horris and his hand cart trundled by. "WAIT!"

Horris stopped to look at him. So did many of the other Idolers. The twitchy Idoler gestured to the box with his gun. "Open it."

"Can't," Horris said. He used his very best Customer Service voice, which didn't let his irritation show.

"Why not?"

"United Star System Postal Service Code, Chapter One, Section Three. All mail is to be opened by the recipient or a representative party. Unlawful opening of mail could result in a fine from your local USSPS representative."

"A *fine*?" The Idoler barked a laugh, and several of his fellows echoed it. "Who's going to fine us? The Imps?"

Horris' lips drew together in a tight line.

"Alexios," said the Idoler with the scarf. "Let him pass."

"Could be weapons," said Alexios, eyeing the box with interest. "Or intel. Things the Imps didn't want us to get our hands on."

He stepped forward, only to be blocked by the scarf-wearer and Horris both. The scarf-wearer gave Alexios a sharp look before turning to Horris. "Where is this going?"

"This package is bound for Apollonia."

The scarf-wearer stepped around Horris to inspect the label on the lid.

To: Sophia Warden
Condo 13A, Halcyon Living Community
138 Broad Garden Road
District 7, Kalikos, 18308
Theron, Apollonia
USSPC 222645-A7

The scarf-wearer shrugged as she turned back to Alexios. "Don't think they have much use for weapons in Kalikos. It's a gray-hair community. Go on," she gestured to the blue USSPS-issue speeder, already piled high with mail. "Don't let it be said the Idolers stood in the way of a man's duty."

Horris set his foot against his hand truck, pulling it back onto the wheels. He glanced around at the assembled Idolers before nodding to the scarf-wearer. "Have a good day. Stay safe."

"You as well, friend."

■

"You're *late*."

Basah folded her arms over her chest as Horris' speeder came to a stop in front of her. Her ears flattened against her head as he cut the engine and slid off. His passenger car was piled high with parcels and packages; the oversized one was lashed to his speeder with several bungee cords.

"I had to get a signature," Horris replied, trying not to be annoyed. He undid his helmet and held it against his hip. "I don't want us to have to double back when they close the gates."

A distant explosion and the peppering of gunfire echoed the sentiment. The *Silverfish* had landed in a recently abandoned mail depot just outside of city limits. The regularly-stationed postmen had already left Creed. Posties didn't receive *that* much in hazard pay, and the union would have objected in any case. A ground postman wouldn't stick around when the starcraft roared and wheeled overhead in epic battles.

There was no mistaking USSPS 131-C, the *Silverfish*, for one of those war dogs. She was a Grummon-class cargo vessel commissioned for express interstellar deliveries; she had a shield but lacked cannonade or any other means to wage war. Anyone would recognize her purpose at a glance.

The crew of the *Silverfish* lay scattered around her. Roddy sprawled out on his back on the bow. He had a pair of binoculars in hand, watching the steady stream of ships leaving Creedence for the atmosphere. Fives sat by the gangplank, drawing in the dirt with a stick. And Basah stood at the end of the gangplank itself with a peeved expression.

Horris elected to ignore her expression in favor of powering down his speeder. "Did you manage to hit the neighborhoods around here?"

"Not much to canvas," Basah replied. "Everyone's evacuated these parts. Didn't want to stick around when the Idolers rolled through."

Another explosion confirmed the observation. Basah and Horris exchanged nods before unhooking the sidecar from the speeder. The packages had to be scanned a final time onboard the *Silverfish* for confirmation, but they could do that once they were off-planet.

Fives got to his feet to help unload. That left Roddy as the holdout: he remained on his back, watching the war dogs dip and wheel, binoculars whipping from fight to fight as he tried to keep pace.

"Rod!" Horris called. "Rod, c'mon. We need to get back in the air."

"Five more minutes," Roddy replied.

"No more minutes," Horris said firmly. "Cockpit *now*."

The pilot rolled off the bow and onto the ground with a groan. He straightened, grabbed a box of envelopes off the speeder, and stalked up the gangplank. Horris pretended not to hear the muttering under Roddy's breath. Basah had no such pretensions and fixed Roddy with a dark look as he made for the cockpit.

Fives, meanwhile, stared at the oversized box strapped to the speeder. Horris handed off a package to Basah. "Fiver? Are you all right?"

"Yes." Fives continued to stare in that wide-eyed, unblinking way of his. Then he slipped the oversized headphones around his neck over his ears. "It's just loud."

Horris nodded. Lots of things were loud for Fives, only most of which could be blocked out with his headphones. And given the chaotic state of Creedence, he'd had more noise to deal with than usual. Even from here.

Fives had his attention wholly fixed on the box. It took Basah tugging on his jumpsuit to get him up the gangplank and into the ship to prep for launch. That left Horris to load the packages and the oversized box into the cargo hold. The belly of the *Silverfish* was made of rows and rows of shelves; all jammed with packages sorted according to priority and planet. Horris secured the oversized box in place so the contents didn't shift during takeoff and double-checked that similarly-sized packages hadn't jostled during atmosphere entry.

The United Star System Postal Service provided service to the twenty-one planets and forty-three principalities, colonies, and other independent satellites of the USS. The pay was good, but the hours were long, and the accommodations aboard mailships left something to be desired. The *Silverfish*, a typical two-deck Grummon, was no exception. The lower deck was taken up entirely by the mail hold and the engine. The upper deck housed three crew cabins, a mess, two supply closets, a water closet, and the cockpit. As the sticker Basah slapped onto the cargo door read: *you don't have to be crazy to work here, but it helps!*

Horris tilted his head to the side as he boarded. The engines were running, but he didn't hear the distinctive purr that indicated they were about to make for the outersphere. Why hadn't the main thrusters been activated?

He got his answer when he stepped down into the cockpit: Roddy had gotten distracted again. This time, he was leaning forward in his pilot's chair to watch the sky battle overhead.

"Rod." Horris collapsed into the pilot seat beside Roddy's and buckled in. "Let's go."

"Yeah, yeah. We're going. Haven't you ever wanted to fly one of those beauties?"

Horris followed his gaze skyward. "No."

"Why not?"

One of those beauties was shot clean through and blasted out of the sky, careening down to crash into one of the city's towers.

"Just a hunch," Horris said dryly.

"Imagine how fast those ships go," Rod murmured. He tore his gaze from the sky long enough to start flipping switches and pressing buttons, preparing the *Silverfish* for launch.

"The *Silverfish* is fast," Horris said, immediately defensive. Speedy deliveries were their bread-and-butter after all.

Roddy gave him a look. "Sure. For a mailship."

She was able to get skyward, and that's what really mattered. Amid the battles of faith, the small vessel achieved liftoff and launched smoothly into the atmosphere. The *Silverfish* built the necessary speed and momentum to break through the atmosphere, jettisoning up and up and up–

–until they hit the dark blue-black of outer space.

Horris engaged gravity. Roddy charted a course for their next stop–it would probably take the better part of a day to get there–before leaning over and cranking up the ship's radio. His jazzy playlist drowned out the hum of the engines and the soft clicks of gravity's engagement.

Horris waited until the music began to speak: "You could get killed trying to fly one of those war dogs. And I'd much prefer you didn't. Get killed, I mean."

"I know, I know," Roddy sighed. "It's just–I don't want to be a mailman forever."

"It's *safe*," Horris said.

"*Safe*. We land in the middle of an active warzone, hold out our forms, and ask if anyone has anything they'd like shipped before they're blown to kingdom come. And maybe sell some stamps while we're at it."

"We don't sell stamps." Horris snapped. "Besides, it's important. What *we* do is important. If Creedence falls tomorrow, to either side, these packages could be the last thing people off-planet receive from their loved ones."

Roddy gave Horris a critical look before punching in coordinates to the nearest jump point. "What took you so long at the depot?"

"I had to get a signature."

"Fine. What took the signature so long?"

"The depot was being stormed by Idolers."

Roddy slammed his hand against the *Silverfish*'s console. Something in the depths of the ship beeped, followed by sudden cursing from Basah. Roddy shouted an apology before twisting to glare at Horris. "And you're going to lecture me about being safe? Why didn't you get the hell out of there?"

"Because Chapter One, Section Three states–"

"Oh, to *hell* with regulations!"

Horris' eyes flashed. "Don't say that. Besides," he jabbed a finger at the brim of his postman's cap, "the United Star System Postal Service is a neutral entity in all inter- and extra-star conflicts. Everyone knows better than to interfere with a postman at work. Otherwise–"

"Not everyone appreciates rules like you do, Horry," Roddy said. "And not everyone is terrified of USSPS sanctions either. Creed is about to go into lockdown. They're not going to give a damn about extra sanctions. You may not be so lucky next time." His voice softened as he turned back to the console.

He didn't add what Horris knew he was thinking: *if you're gone, what do I do without you?* It was the same fear he battled whenever Roddy fixated on those war dogs. It was the deep-seated, stomach-tugging fear of losing your brother to something pointless.

And he and Roddy were brothers, as close as two men could get short of blood. They'd grown up in the sprawling metropolis of Grand York, war orphans clinging together for survival and companionship. Bold, brash Roddy had kept them fed; Horris, polite and introspective, had kept them on the good side of the law.

Even their looks complemented each other: Roddy was fair while Horris was dark; Roddy was tall and gangly, while Horris was muscular and broad-shouldered. Roddy's hair was a sandy tangle of curls with the pointed ears of an Elentee poking through. Horris kept his curly black hair in a tidy fade, and his ears were properly human. No one would ever mistake them for brothers. But nevertheless, they were.

And out of love and respect for Roddy, Horris decided not to follow the thread of contention. The deep abyss of space moved around them at a steady clip. It would be a day before they reached their next destination. Imperials and Idolers were behind them now and would remain so with the trade routes closed. So he stood, stretched, and casually leaned forward to study the *Silverfish's* console.

Too late, Roddy saw what button Horris was going to push.

"Oh, no, Horry, you asshole—!"

BLIP is now online!

The cheerful, slightly-tinny voice covered the sound of Roddy's groan. The pilot threw his head back against his seat. "Oh, fuck off, BLIP!"

BLIP is an autonomous artificial intelligence. BLIP is incapable of fuck.

Roddy's groan lengthened as Horris quietly slipped out.

Do you need assistance navigating to our next destination?

"NO!"

It sounds as though you are in distress. BLIP will play calming music to lower your epinephrine levels.

The brassy tones of Herb Alpert and his Tijuana Brass Band rang throughout the *Silverfish*. Roddy's frustrated screaming complemented *Love Potion No. 9* quite nicely.

Stepping through the panel doors into their tiny mess muffled both Roddy and Herb Albert. Horris allowed himself one small smirk before looking around for Basah.

The Mefana was searching for a snack. Her ears flattened against her head, and her tail thrashed as the brassy trumpets blared over the intercoms. Her eyes—slit like a cat's, orange and always calculating—narrowed as Horris came to join her.

"Hey, Bah," he said, trying to ignore her piercing look.

"Horry." She replied. "What's wrong?"

"It's nothing," Horris said. He yanked the snack cabinet open, hoping against hope that someone hadn't already eaten the last peanut butter granola bar. He groaned when Basah squeezed in beside him. She didn't need to say a word to make her disapproval known. "Fine. It's Rod."

Basah snorted. She scanned the contents of the cabinet before helping herself to a sleeve of crackers. "Thinking about ditching us to die in someone else's war?"

"The usual daydream," Horris sighed. "I just wish he weren't so eager to go out in a blaze of glory."

"I don't know. Maybe his replacement would actually listen to me when I give recommendations about upgrading the ship."

"We don't have the funds to upgrade the ship." The quest for snacks thus unfulfilled, Horris straightened. He rubbed his face, suddenly looking forward to a nap. "But our next destination is outside the warzone. It's not going to matter in the long run."

"Where're we due? It's a jump, right?"

"Hm? Ah–" Horris pulled his tablet from his waistband and pow-ered it on. He opened their itinerary and flicked through it quickly. "Delta Io. It's the next arm over in this pinwheel and then a straight shot to Franklin-Two and Hayabusa Base. After that, it's the Brose Front, and finishing up in Apollonia. We'll have a new run in two weeks. Hopefully, nowhere near here."

Basah nodded in agreement. She made note of something on her own tablet before offering some of her crackers to Horris. He smiled and murmured a thanks. "Where's Fives?"

"Engine. I'm bringing him a cookie."

The engine room was last on his post-liftoff rounds. 'Engine room' was a generous term, in truth: it was more accurately an engine pit, at the center of which the motor hummed away. Modems and routers and all manner of machinery blinked green and occasionally beeped.

Benches had been built into the circular engine pit. Fives sat on one such bench, staring at the floor. His overly-large orange headphones rested against his neck; Herb Alpert seemed to agree with him for the time being. He lifted his head when Horris and Basah entered.

His wide, too-dark eyes fixed on Horris. "You and Roddy were disagreeing, and you made Roddy upset. Roddy hit a button so he wouldn't hit you."

"Got all that from down here, did you?" Horris sighed. He did his best to ignore the look from Basah.

"Yes," Fives said. "You two are very loud when you don't get along."

"Well. We're not going to argue anymore…about this, anyway," Horris said. "Sorry you had to hear all that, Fives." He waited for Fives to nod before turning to Basah. "Did Roddy hit any really important buttons?"

"Nothing we can't adjust for," Basah replied. Her ears had lifted back to their usual position. "Did you need anything else, Horry?"

"No. Just doing rounds. Making sure everything is okay." He looked at the engine.

So did Basah. "Well, it hasn't exploded yet."

They both chuckled. Horris turned to leave, but Fives' soft voice stopped him short:

"Captain?"

Horris half-turned back. "Yeah, Fives?"

"Your last package is currently experiencing hallucinations brought on by oxygen deprivation."

"...*what*."

"Your last package," Fives repeated slowly, "is currently experiencing hallucinations brought on by oxygen deprivation."

Horris and Basah locked eyes. A moment of horrified realization passed between them.

Fives jumped as Horris and Basah bolted out the door and down the narrow hallway to the cargo hold. Basah shouted across the ship for Roddy to join them in the cargo hold ASAP.

Horris slid to a stop in front of the oversized metal crate from Creedence. A split-second later, Basah crashed into him. There was a brief moment of apologies and scrambling, and in that brief moment, Roddy and Fives appeared in the cargo hold.

"What's wrong?" Roddy demanded. His eyes locked on the crate. "What the hell are we shipping? Something dangerous?"

"Something *alive!*" Basah exclaimed. She was tugging fruitlessly on the lip of the crate. "Oh, for the Matrons' sake–*Fives!* Why didn't you say anything?!"

Fives blinked his big, dark eyes at her. "I did."

"Why didn't you say anything *sooner*?!"

"He didn't want to be found," Fives said. He slipped his headphones over his ears before Horris or Roddy could interrogate him next.

Horris caught Basah's shoulder. He pointed to the clasps on the metal box. "Help me undo these." Roddy came over to help, and with successive *snap-snap-snaps,* the lid was unlocked.

Postal Code Chapter One, Section Four, Horris thought to himself. *Packages are not meant to be opened by United Star System personnel.*

Well. Packages were also not meant to contain living things without proper documentation and paid labeling. With that, he pushed the lid aside and peered in.

Instantly, a black boot connected with his nose. White stars burst across his suddenly-blurry vision; pain, sudden and sharp, drove through his skull and out the other end. Someone caught him before he hit the floor, and through the haze of pain, he heard shouting and a heavy THUMP.

When the wave of pain receded, Horris found himself staring at the ceiling of the cargo hold. Then Roddy's lean face popped into view.

"You good?"

"Yeah," Horris wheezed. He touched a hand to his nose, relieved to find it tender but unbloodied. Roddy helped him sit up right, and when he did, he found the rest of the crew standing around the overturned metal crate. A limp figure sprawled out on the floor.

"What happened?" Horris asked. He took the hand Roddy offered him and got back to his feet.

Fives pointed to Basah. "Basah knocked him out."

Basah shrugged before kneeling beside the prone figure on the floor. She gave their shoulder an experimental poke. "Now what?"

"Are they still alive?" Horris asked.

Basah felt for a pulse. After a moment, she nodded.

The first pangs of a headache began to build behind his eyes. Horris took a deep breath and exhaled. "Let's get them to the infirmary."

So much, he thought glumly, for a quiet route.

2 Proper Postage

United Star System Postal Code, Chapter 3, Section 7: Whoever knowingly conveys any person as a private express is in direct violation of the United Star System Postal Service Code.

The infirmary was a generous term for the walk-in closet repurposed into a first-aid station. The *Silverfish* was not a battleship; the worst injuries its crew saw were bruises and sore backs from lifting heavy packages (as much as Horris lectured them on using the handcart). The biggest luxury the infirmary could afford was a cot for tummy aches.

And that was precisely where Horris dumped their stowaway. The rest of the *Silverfish* crew crowded around the doorway. The infirmary was too small to fit them all at once. Horris glanced back at the crew before he crouched to better examine their stowaway.

Humanoid, male by the look of him, lean and pale with tousled red hair. He wore the slick black uniform of an Imperial soldier. Horris glanced at his boots and noted their make and quality. A well-paid member of the Imperial Army of Creed, then…

"Is he dead?" Roddy asked from the doorway.

"No, he's just…" Horris paused as he turned to Roddy. If Roddy was here, then—"Who's flying the ship?"

Roddy scowled. Before he could reply, a gentle *ding-dong* sounded from above.

BLIP is now your pilot.

"You're not the pilot, BLIP!" Roddy shouted. "You're the autopilot!"

There was a moment of thoughtful silence on BLIP's end.

BLIP has removed all records of Pilot Roderick Marcelo from the 131-C archives. BLIP is now your pilot.

Basah burst out laughing. Roddy flushed even as he pivoted to Fives. "Get your program under control!"

"I didn't teach them to do that," Fives said. He didn't get the chance to add anything else—Roddy seized him by the collar and hauled him off in the direction of the cockpit, muttering under his breath about rogue AIs and their programmers.

Basah watched them go before turning back to their stowaway. Her pupils had narrowed to irritated slits. "What do we do with them?"

Horris had already begun to rifle through the medicine cabinet in search of something that might rouse the stowaway. All he found was Roddy's iron supplements, Basah's herbal remedies, the gummies that Fives liked, and the bandages with smiling cartoon bugs. "Do we have smelling salts?"

"Middle drawer on the right," Basah said. She watched Horris pull on the appropriate drawer with a frown. "What if he attacks you again?"

"I *doubt* that's going to happen," Horris said. He popped open the vial of smelling salts (more of a smelling liquid, really, and pleasantly lavender besides) and waved it under the stowaway's nose.

The stowaway's bright green eyes snapped open.

And then Horris' head snapped backward as a fist collided with his jaw.

"HORRIS!"

Basah caught him as he fell backward—and then both went staggering as the redhead leaped up and sprinted for the door.

"Hey–hey, hang on! *WAIT!*"

Horris' cry went unheeded as he and Basah chased after the redhead. He ran down the length of the corridor to the cockpit, skidding to a halt at the step-down. Roddy and Fives stopped short in their argument as the redhead pinwheeled. He pivoted on his black boots and sprinted back past Horris and Basah, shoulder-checking the latter as he did.

They chased him back down the corridor, past the cabins, and into the mess. By the time the *Silverfish* crew had spilled into the mess, the redhead stood with his back to the wall and a butter knife clenched in his fist.

"STATE YOUR ALLEGIANCE!"

Horris stopped short. He flung a hand out to keep Basah from launching herself at the redhead. That left Fives to hold onto Roddy's wrist as the pilot took a menacing step forward. "I beg your pardon?"

"State your allegiance," the redhead said again. He brandished his dinnerware back and forth, eyes darting wildly from one courier to the next.

Fives winced. Horris didn't have to wonder why: the redhead's panic was palpable. His chest rose and fell in a rapid staccato, and the knife in his hand trembled.

"State your allegiance," the redhead repeated, "or I'll personally have you hauled before Liaison Anaxandros for questioning!"

The effect was dampened by the fact that not one of them knew what a Liaison Anaxandros was. Roddy's small scoff just ruined the sentiment further. "Good luck with that, buddy. We have a *union*."

The redhead blinked. Confusion, by and large, seemed to overtake the fear. He straightened up, studying the motley crew of sentients before him. Then his gaze shifted upwards, noting the small, austere mess, with its small convection oven and the much put-upon coffee pot. The redhead's frown deepened.

"Do you know where you are right now?" Horris asked. He kept his voice low and calm despite the throbbing in his nose and jaw.

"Creedence," the redhead replied.

"Well–no. We left Creedence, and Creed proper, an hour ago. You're in intergalactic territory right now. On a mailship."

"Loaded on, more accurately," Roddy added.

"Mailship?" His green eyes narrowed sharply. For the first time, he seemed to consider them as an entire group: the cerulean blue uniforms, the matching patches on their left breasts. He relaxed just a little. "So we're out of Creed."

"Well out of Creed," Horris said. He hesitated just a moment before stepping forward. "My name is Horris Jensen. I'm Captain of the One-Thirty-One-C, callsign *Silverfish*."

The redhead eyed the hand Horris extended suspiciously before pulling the butter knife to his chest. After a moment, Horris let the hand fall back to his side.

"This is usually the part where you introduce yourself," Basah snapped. Her ears had gone flat, tabby tail twitching from side-to-side. "And explain what the hell you're doing on my ship."

The redhead looked Basah up and down with the pinched expression one usually reserved for rats. "I'm speaking to your captain, *cat*."

Roddy seized Basah by the midriff and physically lifted her as she leaped forward, probably to strangle the Imperial where he stood. Roddy took a full two steps backward as Basah's apoplectic snarling rebounded through the mess.

Horris turned back to the redhead stowaway, who had stepped back into the corner with wary eyes and butter knife at the ready. "You will not," he said, silently reciting protocols about a captain's comportment to keep his anger in check, "insult my crew again."

There was a small ding from above.

OR BLIP WILL FORCE OPEN THE AIRLOCK WITH YOU INSIDE.

The redhead glanced upwards and mouthed the words, 'What the fuck'. Not finding an immediate source of the robotic tone, he lowered his eyes back to Horris. The contempt in his green eyes was clear enough. But beyond that, there was still confusion. Panic. And maybe even a little terror.

Horris took a deep breath and tried again. "What's your name?"

For a moment, it seemed like the stowaway wasn't going to reply. Then—

"Perseus Warden," he snarled, the name ripping out him like some bandage off a wound. "My name is *Perseus Warden*."

"Perseus," Horris repeated. "I'm sure you have a lot of questions. We have a lot of questions, too."

"I've been trained to survive interrogations," Perseus said, lifting his chin in some display of defiance.

"How about interviews?" Roddy said dryly.

Perseus sneered, but his eyes were already back on Horris. The authority in the room. "I suppose you want to know what I'm doing aboard your ship."

"That's sort of the first question we had, yeah," Horris admitted.

Perseus gestured to the whole of his sleek black uniform. "I'm an Imperial soldier. The Imperial capital was being besieged by an army of loons who hate Imperials. Forgive me for not wanting to wait around for the inevitable slaughter."

"So you…shipped yourself out?" Horris asked. "There has to be a better way to leave than mailing yourself."

"Not safer," Fives said from behind them. He stared straight at Perseus, the intensity of his gaze almost piercing straight through the Imperial. "Not without risk of being found."

"Well-spotted," Perseus replied. He stepped to the side, trying and failing to avoid the beam that was Fives' gaze. "Defecting officers rarely hope to be found."

"*You're a deserter*," Basah snarled.

Perseus scowled. "I like my head, and the neck it's attached to. I'd rather not see them separated."

The strength of his sentiment took Horris by surprise. He didn't know much about the civil war that had engulfed Creed—that wasn't what he was paid to do—but execution was a bit of an extreme. "You think the Idolers would do that?"

"I wasn't planning on sticking around to find out. So, I found a decent-sized box, put the label on it, drilled some airholes into the side, and climbed inside."

"You should have made it bigger," Fives observed.

"Yes." Perseus' expression pinched as though he'd just tasted something sour. "I realize that now, thank you." He half-turned away, a subtle gesture indicating that he was finished as far as this round of twenty questions went. The half-turn widened into a proper rotation as he assessed his environment. He looked like a right proper Imperial now: hands folded behind his back, nose in the air, expression teetering on *boredom*. "What manner of vehicle is this?"

"Grummon class," Horris replied automatically. He winced when Basah slapped his shoulder.

"She's a fast ship?"

"Express delivery."

"Excellent." Perseus turned back to the assembled crew. "I expect we'll be in Apollonia by tomorrow, then."

Horris opened his mouth to reply, but Roddy's barking laugh cut him off. "Apollonia is the *last* stop on our route."

For a moment, Perseus didn't seem to comprehend. His thin eyebrows knitted together as he processed what Roddy had said. "*The last stop?* I need to be in Apollonia *yesterday*!"

"Then you should have shipped yourself out *yesterday*," Basah sneered.

Perseus rounded back to Horris. "I assume that I am the only living creature in the cargo hold."

Horris glanced at Fives, who closed his eyes before nodding in confirmation. Not the question he thought he'd have to ask today, let alone feel such overwhelming relief at a negative answer, but huzzah for small miracles. He turned to face the fuming Percy. "You are."

"Then I see no reason why my destination should not take priority!"

Horris perked up, pleased to have an answer for that. "Chapter Five, Section Six."

"I–sorry?"

"USSPS Postal Code, Chapter Five, Section Six," Horris recited, "all courier crafts licensed by the United Star System Postal Service must follow pre-approved routes. Any deviations from the pre-approved route must be cleared by a USSPS supervisor within three-day notice."

A stunned silence followed.

"You're joking," Perseus said at last.

Horris frowned. "I am not."

"You're fucking *joking*." Perseus ogled the *Silverfish* crew. He was aghast. Agog, even. "This is a prank, yes? *Yes?* You're not going to hold me captive on this mailship—"

"Oh, hold him captive!" Basah gasped. She turned to the amused Roddy with eyes wide. "Whose idea was it to sneak an Imperial aboard?"

Perseus, meanwhile, had taken to pacing the small length of the mess, tearing at his hair in frustration. "I am a sentient! I ought to take priority!"

Horris mulled over that before pulling his tablet from his belt. The tablet glowed to life, and Horris tapped through their delivery missive. He scrolled through the list of onboarded items before clucking his tongue. "You're a standard delivery."

Perseus stopped short. "What?"

"You're a standard delivery," Horris repeated. He was pleased to be able to ground himself in this rule, at the very least. "We can't bump you ahead of schedule. You should have paid for expedited shipping if you wanted to take priority."

"I–*what?!*"

Roddy did Horris the favor of echoing, albeit with poorly-concealed delight: "You should have paid for expedited shipping."

Screams couldn't be heard in the vacuum of space, but high-pitched shrieking managed to reverberate through the *Silverfish*. Perseus took a step forward, finger shaking, flushed red with fury and indignation. "I–*you*–you will escort me to Apollonia, or I will commandeer this whole useless ship; I swear on the Emperor, you low-life, postal-pushing *hack!*—"

He stopped short. Percy managed one baffled look before his eyes rolled back in his head. He hit the floor in a crumpled heap.

Everyone whipped around to glare at Fives. Fives stared back, dark eyes wide and guileless. "He was giving me a headache."

There was nothing to be done save gather around their stowaway and consider the options.

"All right. I'll say the quiet part loud. Let's throw him out the airlock," Roddy said.

BLIP volunteers.

"We're not throwing anyone out the airlock!" Horris snapped. "For Pete's sake, people, we're a postal service, not an extrajudicial committee!" He pinched the bridge of his nose, fighting the headache swelling behind his eyes. "Is it too late to turn around?"

Basah nodded. "Creed closed the borders. They're not letting anyone back in there anytime soon. Isn't it illegal to carry people onboard the mail ship?"

"United Star System Postal Code, Chapter Three, Section Seven," Horris replied gloomily. He stared down at the unconscious Perseus. *"Whoever knowingly conveys any person acting as a private express is in direct violation of United Star System Postal Service Code and shall be subject to prosecution from United Star System Postal Service Inspectors."*

Roddy's eyes widened as he plucked the butter knife from Perseus' limp grip. "Oh, shit. We could have the Inspectors on our asses? Can't we just tell them that we didn't know he was onboard until we were space-bound?"

"Good luck trying to square that with a phrenic onboard," Basah muttered. She gave Fives a long look. Fives just shrugged.

Horris continued to study Perseus. He was a young man, in his early twenties at most, and when unconscious the harsher lines of his face softened. He was running from a war. And what was so wrong with that? He couldn't blame someone for not wanting to die. And if the war on Creed was anything like the one that had devoured Ceres…

He remembered the damp and the dark. He remembered the rapid pops of gunfire and the hunger gnawing at his stomach. And the waiting. The endless, quiet waiting. Horris hadn't been a soldier, but he knew war.

"He stays," Horris said out loud. He got to his feet, ignoring the "WHAT"s from behind him. He turned to see the bafflement from his crew. "He's not going out the airlock—"

BOO.

"And he can't go back to Creed. So he stays."

He may have only been captain of a mailship, Horris, but when he spoke with finality, he sounded like a right proper Captain. And when the Captain spoke, the crew listened.

"And *where* is he staying?" Basah demanded. She folded her arms over her chest as her tail thrashed back and forth. "I'm not letting him room in the cabins. *Do not suggest the engine pit.*" Her mouth thinned into a hard line as Horris began to reply.

"We could stick him back in the box," Roddy said. He made a show of inspecting his fingernails when Horris shot him a look.

"No, we're not going to stick him back in the cargo hold." Horris rubbed his hands over his face. This was the correct decision, wasn't it?

A small touch on his shoulder made him jolt. Fives pulled his hand away. Judging by the way Fives frowned, he was forcing himself into the here and now. "He left for a reason," Fives said softly. "We all have our reasons."

Horris considered Fives as Roddy cleared his throat. "There's always that broom closet."

And that was where Perseus woke up about forty-five minutes later.

Horris perked up when he heard the soft groaning. He was sitting cross-legged on the floor beside Perseus. The broom closet was big enough for two once all the actual cleaning supplies had been cleared out. As long as one minded the shelves overhead, it really could be quite a comfortable space. Horris, having learned his lesson about Perseus and personal space, cleared his throat as the redhead sat up. "Hello again! Feeling all right?"

"*Aagh.*"

Perseus rubbed at his temple before glancing at the dim, shelved surroundings. His eyes landed on a bottle of cleaning fluid overhead. "...I'm in a broom closet."

"We moved the brooms," Horris assured him.

"I see." Perseus' lips thinned. "And we are in the broom closet because...?"

"The cabins are full, and it seemed rude to ask you to stay in the cargo hold."

"As opposed to the broom closet?"

"We...didn't have many other options. It's a small ship. I brought you some light." Horris nodded to an egg-shaped night light on one shelf. It filled the room with gently pulsating green light. Perseus' eyes narrowed at the night light before his attention was grabbed by the tablet Horris extended to him. "Here's a spare tablet. It's got games on it if you get bored."

Perseus scowled as he set the tablet aside. His eyes were almost burning in the pale green light. "What are your intentions with me?"

There was a sharp, almost jagged edge to Perseus' voice. Horris cleared his throat. "We've come to a decision."

"Jolly good," was the flat reply.

"We're going to honor your shipment, even if it was improperly labeled. We'll take you to Apollonia. *However*," Horris raised a finger as Perseus started to speak. "Since you didn't pay for expedited shipping, you'll be the last stop on our route. It'll be a week and a half, depending on the state of our next drops. Understand?"

Perseus frowned. But he seemed, at long last, to be coming to the heavy realization that he wasn't going to win this one. He exhaled sharply through his nose. "So...what? I'll just remain in this broom closet for the next ten days, and you'll all leave me in peace?"

"Pretty much, yeah."

The two men considered each other. Then Perseus shrugged. "Works for me."

Horris stuck out a hand to shake. Perseus scowled at the outstretched hand, and when there was no attempt to return the gesture, Horris lowered his hand. He fumbled around in an attempt to save face and produced his second peace offering: a triangle of aluminum foil. "I, uh, brought you some dinner. Ship's pizza, but, uh, I hope you like it!"

It was a handmade flatbread pizza topped with tomato sauce, cheese, and salami. Each crewman made their own according to taste before popping into the convection oven to warm. Horris hadn't known what their guest might like, so he had settled for the simplest toppings. "Be careful," he said as he handed it off, "it's still warm."

Perseus unwrapped the foil slowly. He stared down at the simple homemade fare, and for the first time, something in his narrow face wavered. He sighed and shifted to sit on his knees. He kept his eyes on the floor, almost embarrassed, as he raised the foil to his forehead. "By His Grace, I receive this bounty. By His Grace, I live another day. What is yours has been given unto me. What is mine shall be given unto you until the debt is paid. By His Grace, we are bonded."

Horris blinked. He'd seen his fair share of rites and rituals in his travels, but he never knew what to do when one was performed in his presence. "Uh. Thanks?"

"It's a rite of hospitality among my people," Perseus said. He hissed through his teeth as he unwrapped the piping-hot foil. "Now that the oath has been made, I will not–*cannot*–do you any harm. Even with a butter knife."

Chewing now, he reached into his boot and produced a second butter knife. He sent it spinning over to Horris.

Horris made a mental note to lock the silverware drawer for the time being. "Should I say the oath back?"

"If you want." Perseus shrugged.

It seemed the polite thing to do. Horris shifted to his knees. Perseus watched him with eyebrows arched. Horris didn't have any food on hand, so he settled for lifting the butter knife to his forehead. "By His Grace, I receive this bounty. By His Grace, I live another day. What is yours has been given unto me. What is mine shall be given unto you until the debt is paid. By His Grace, we are bonded."

Perseus didn't say anything. But despite his professed indifference, his shoulders slumped a little in relief.

"There," Horris said as he got to his feet. "So…you stay in here, and we'll stay out there, and we'll be in Apollonia in a few days' time."

"Works for me. Close the door on the way out, will you, Captain Jensen?"

"My name's Horris. And I give the orders on this ship."

"*Please* close the door on your way out, Captain Jensen."

It was a start. Horris tapped a finger to his forehead and left Perseus to his pizza.

❸ The Horrors (Waived)

United Star System Postal Code, Chapter 5, Section 1: In selecting methods of transportation, the USSPS shall give the highest consideration to the prompt and economical delivery of all mail.

Percy woke up back in the box.

Every muscle was dead, one arm floppy and lifeless. His breath constricted in his chest. He couldn't breathe, he couldn't *move*, he needed to get out, get out *now*, but if he flailed against the sides of the box, someone might hear him—if he screamed, someone might find him—stay quiet, stay quiet—slowly, he pushed himself upwards, dreading the moment he found resistance against a padded wall.

But he didn't.

Percy opened his eyes. The first thing he noticed was the soft, red light filling the dark room. His eyes landed on the egg-shaped lamp. He'd figured out how to change the color before he'd settled on the floor to sleep. The captain had given him that egg, along with the tablet on the shelf. The captain of the postal vessel he'd snuck aboard.

No, Percy corrected himself. Not *snuck*. Snuck implied he hadn't paid for passage.

He sat up and rubbed at his deadened arm until pins and needles poked it back to life. His head ached from the two separate knockouts he'd suffered.

Concussions. Was he concussed? Did this ship have a medic aboard? Probably not.

Percy fingered the back of his head with a frown. It would be all right. He just needed to get to Apollonia in one piece. And after that…he was still figuring that piece out.

And wasn't that just deeply irritating?

A knock on the door jerked him out of his thoughts. Percy stood, smoothed out his Imperial uniform, and went to open the door.

The pale, bug-eyed humanoid stood on the other side. He wore a rumpled orange hoodie over his postal uniform and had a massive pair of orange headphones slung around his neck. He didn't say anything, but a small crease appeared on his brow.

A sudden, inexplicable dread seized Percy. It was like being strapped in a dentist's chair, with someone poking at pieces of himself he couldn't see, dissecting things about himself he couldn't fully understand. He froze in place, muscles tensing, bile rising in his throat as he pushed back against the foreign intruder.

No. Get out.

And, as quickly as it came, the sensation receded. The crease in the creepy fellow's brow deepened. And then he extended a protein bar out in a limp grip. "You're hungry."

It was a statement, not a question. A true statement at that, Percy realized. He snatched the protein bar from the creepy bugger's hand and, in the same instant, came to the conclusion that he could never, ever piss this man off. Something about his dark, unblinking stare unnerved him more than any amount of confinement ever could.

"Thank you," he said, "mister–erm–?"

"My name is Fives," the black-eyed bugger said.

"Fives," Percy repeated. Five was a sacred number to his people, but he doubted this pale slip of a thing counted towards holiness. "I don't suppose the rest of the crew is named Ones through Fours?"

"No." Fives finally blinked. Slowly. The process was maddening to watch. "That would be ridiculous."

"Ah," Percy said. "Yes. Quite right."

They stood there for a moment. Fives closed his eyes and tilted his head to the side. Percy opened the protein bar, hoping this was all just an advanced hallucination brought on by hunger. He'd only just begun to eat when Fives reopened his eyes.

"You should come with me," said Fives. "The captain needs you."

Hadn't the agreement been that they would leave each other well enough alone? Percy withheld a sigh, scarfed down his protein bar, and followed Fives out of the closet.

This was his first time on an interstellar ship. He'd always known, on some level, that the tales of galactic jumpers were overblown. Nevertheless…he couldn't help being disappointed by how utilitarian this ship was.

The narrow corridors were gray and undecorated. Sliding doors labeled rooms like 'water closet' and 'cleaning supplies.' Everything he saw was clean and organized. There was no air of mystery about this ship at all.

Fives glanced his way. "It's not very exciting. But we have a nice view."

As he spoke, they slowed to a halt in front of a rectangular window. Perseus stopped short. Outside—outside was *space*.

He'd always been taught it was ink-black. But out here, deep in the edges of the stars, space somehow had more color. The endless expanse of black was speckled with multicolored stars and swirled with oranges and blues from the rolling clouds of a distant nebula. He watched, fascinated, as the clouds of the nebula rose and fell, making the same distorted shapes a child might in wet sand. For an instant, Perseus felt small.

Then Fives looped an arm around his and tugged him away.

Percy allowed himself to be tugged. There was nothing to be done with the current company but to accept that he was at the mercy of a bunch of lousy posties. He wondered if he should attempt small talk–ask questions–*something*–but the sound of raised voices mercifully saved him. Fives winced and pulled those massive orange headphones over his ears.

A side door slid open. Percy jumped as the tall Black man—the captain–Hobber? No, Horcus?—came stumbling out. He clutched a small glass container to his chest. "Fives, have you seen Henri–oh! Good morning, Perseus!" He beamed when his gaze landed on Percy.

Percy considered him warily, wondering what he was needed for and why glass jars were involved. "Morning."

"Where are you two off to?"

Wait. Hadn't Fives said the captain needed his presence? He glared at Fives, who had once more closed his eyes. "Henri is in the mess," Fives said. His shoulders slumped when he reopened his eyes. "Roddy and Basah are sixty seconds away from a fistfight."

The captain—Horris, that was it!—just laughed. "Keep them busy. I'll follow in a moment. Just have to retrieve Henri."

"Yes, sir." Fives managed a sleepy sort of salute. He turned to Percy as Horris strode off towards the mess. "We're going to distract Roddy and Basah for two minutes."

Percy arched an eyebrow. "Is that what the captain needed me for?"

"Yes."

"And how do you know that?"

"You're very good at asking questions."

Fives walked off without waiting for a reply. Percy scowled. He could spin on his heel and retreat back to his little closet. He was more than within his rights. He wasn't about to be ordered about by a bunch of lousy, minimum-wage *posties*. He could go back.

He didn't, though. Not when Fives glanced over his shoulder, and that same invasive, strapped-to-a-chair feeling seized him. Percy threw it off and stalked after Fives.

The sound of fierce arguments grew louder as they approached the cockpit. The pit was the right term for it: one had to step down to reach the pilot's chair and dashboard. A massive window offered a three-fourths view of space, while the cockpit itself blinked with notifications from systems across the ship. It all seemed very technical.

And very ignored, because the curly-haired Elentee pilot was half-out of his chair, the better to argue with the Mefana engineer. The conceit of the argument was lost amid a flurry of insults and scientific babble.

"You're taking us the long way round!" The pilot was saying. He swiveled back to his dashboard and jammed a few buttons. Percy had no idea if that actually did anything, but it looked plenty official. "We'll be sitting ducks on the roundabout."

"I'll take sitting ducks over dead ones," the engineer retorted.

BLIP concurs.

Percy jumped at the tinny voice from overhead. He craned his neck back, scanning the ceiling for some sort of robotic intelligence. If it could manifest, it remained unseen. Probably for its own safety, because the pilot shot his middle finger to the ceiling. "You don't get a say in this, BLIP!"

Your AI microaggression has been noted and processed to SR for review.

"You little sonuva—"

Fives tugged Percy into position in front of the pair. Percy rolled his eyes at the discreet thumbs-up Fives gave him. "If I may," Percy began. He scowled when the engineer and the pilot both swiveled to glare at him.

"No," the pilot snapped, "you may not. What's he doing here, Fives?"

"Horris said to distract you until he got here. He's looking for Henri."

The pilot pinched the bridge of his nose and took a deep breath. "Fine. What."

Percy gathered all the contempt inside him (it was quite a lot) and molded it into what he hoped was a useful interrogation. He folded his arms over his chest and peered down his nose at the pilot. "What's all this debate about anyway? As couriers, shouldn't your route already be plotted?"

His contempt had the desired effect. Both posties were glaring at him now. The pilot leaned forward. "Oh-ho-ho, look who knows so much. How often do you leave your orbit, Red?"

"Never," Percy was forced to admit. He scowled when the pilot snorted.

"Well, let's educate you on that front," said the pilot. He swung back around to the dashboard and tapped a few keys.

"Roddy…" The engineer said in a warning tone.

"Relax, Basah."

In the next instant, a holographic map had materialized in the cockpit. The map mimicked the scene outside of the window: an inky black populated with stars and planets and assorted symbols Percy couldn't even begin to name. Two arrows moved through the black at a steady pace: one blue, the other gray.

"We are here," Roddy jabbed a finger at the holographic map. His fingertip brushed through the small blue arrow hurtling through the projected abyss and then through the inky black of space to land in a small, swirling hole. "We need to get here."

"The bridge, yes." Percy recognized such from his studies. "What seems to be the problem?"

Roddy flicked his wrist, and in response, a ring of brownish dots materialized between the ship and her destination, forming a wide ring like those around gas giants. "All this bullshit."

"Space junk," Basah corrected testily. "Trash from passing ships and satellites, along with natural debris from old moons. It's stuck in the pull of the bridge, which makes actually getting to the bridge more of a chore than it ought to be."

"Not if you're not a coward," Roddy replied in a sing-song tone.

Basah gnashed her teeth before turning back to Percy. "What do you know about jumping bridges?"

"A bridge connects two points in space-time. Interdimensional ships use them as a jump point to different locations in a single galaxy. Useful, if you need a shortcut, but not always advised because of the necessary speed build-up to successfully jump."

Fives gave him another thumbs-up. Basah shrugged. "That's about a secondary school explanation, but we'll take it. The problem is that we can't build up the speed we need in a field of debris like that."

"Sort've like walking through a field of landmines," Percy observed.

"...sure. Dipshit here," she jerked a thumb at Roddy, who flipped her off, "thinks he's an ace pilot who can zip us through a field of orbiting debris at forty-thousand kilometers per Earthan hour."

"It's faster than going all the way up and over!" Roddy said. "We're an expedited delivery service! We ought to *expedite!* Besides, we'll never pick up the speed we need to jump, not unless you want to go at it from the top-down, and I *know* how much you hate faking gravitational pulls with the engines."

The small ship on the screen mimicked Roddy's words. Percy watched as the blue arrow shot vertically and then careened downwards again into the jump point. A ticking number in the upper left corner indicated the projected speed of sixty-thousand kilometers per Earthan hour. He was no expert in space travel, to be sure, but... "Speaking as a customer—"

"Cargo," Roddy corrected.

"As you like. I would prefer not to risk being blown to smithereens by a piece of space junk. It seems to me that the roundabout way is preferable."

Basah threw her hands into the air. "THANK YOU!"

"You can keep thanking him when that ship on our tail turns out to be a pirate," Roddy said. He stretched out his thumb and forefinger, and the gray ship on the map grew correspondingly larger. "The long way around leaves us open to being hooked and cooked."

Footsteps sounded from behind the cockpit. Everyone turned to watch Horris approach. "That's assuming she is a pirate, Rod."

"She's not flying any colors!" Roddy insisted.

"You can't even tell what colors they have from here!" Basah said.

"Sure we can. BLIP, enhance the image."

No response.

Horris grinned. "BLIP, please enhance the image."

The gray ship expanded out further and then switched to a grainy camera image, clearly taken from the *Silverfish*'s exterior. Everyone leaned forward to squint at the blob that was–probably–a ship of some sort. Maybe.

"It's too far to be sure," Horris said. "And I'm not willing to risk our safety on a possibility. How much will going up and over set us back?"

"An hour," Basah said. Judging by her begrudging tone, even an hour was too much for a proud member of the USSPS.

Horris grimaced and rubbed at his chin. "Well, if we make good time on the next few stops…we're due to resupply on Delta Io anyway. We can shave some time off there, too. Up and over it is, Rod."

Roddy grumbled in compliance. He adjusted a few settings on his dashboard. There was a slight shift underfoot, a gentle tug in the stomach as the *Silverfish* adjusted course vertically. Basah nodded and excused herself to check on the engines. Fives slipped out with her, pausing only to give Percy a double thumbs-up.

Percy just stared before turning to Horris, who smiled. "Walk with me? I've got to put Henri back in his cage."

And that's when Percy noticed the giant spider inside the jar Horris held.

In space, they say, no one can hear you scream. But inside the spaceship, all four postal workers heard the shriek loud and clear. Fives subtly adjusted the volume of his music. Basah's ears flattened against her head. And Roddy turned to smirk as Percy scrambled halfway up the wall.

"WHAT THE HELL IS THAT?"

"This...?" Horris blinked and looked down at the jar in his hands. "Oh! This is Henri! He's a giant Targian spider! Don't worry; he's completely harmless outside of mating season."

"AND WHEN IS MATING SEASON?"

"Next Targian month, which for us is..." Horris adjusted his grip to check something on his watch. "Next Tuesday."

Percy was still doing a damn good imitation of a cat halfway up a pair of drapes. He clung to the wall, trying not to stare at the eight beady eyes staring back at him. "And you just let that thing loose on your ship?!"

"Loose? Oh, no! He just got out of his cage! Henri is crafty like that," Horris said, still with that same daft smile.

Percy stared at the Targian giant spider with dawning horror. The last thing he wanted–needed–was waking up to a spider in his closet bedroom. He had half a mind to spin around and tell Roddy full steam ahead, never mind the dangers. The sooner he was off this damn ship, the *better*.

Slowly, he detached himself from the wall to walk beside Horris. Horris shifted Henri to keep him out of Percy's peripheral. "Anyway, I wanted to thank you. Rod and Basah might've started a fistfight if they hadn't had someone to show off their smarts to. So...thanks."

"I'd prefer not to be used as a sounding board for hostile postal workers again if it's all the same to you," Percy said dryly.

Horris nodded. He slowed to a halt in front of a sliding door. "Well. We've got a few hours 'til we jump. You're more than welcome to make yourself comfortable in the meantime—"

Percy kept walking. "I'm going back to my room."

"Oh." Horris had the audacity to seem confused. "Oh! All right, then! I'll come get you before we jump. Standard procedure, all crewmen in the cockpit during a jump."

Percy pivoted to walk backward, all the better to address Horris: "Your pilot was kind enough to point out that I am cargo, not crew. I don't believe standard procedures apply."

"I'm sorry he said that. But for safety purposes, we need everyone accounted for."

"Fine. Leave me alone until then, will you?"

And this time, he didn't wait for a reply. Percy retreated into his little broom closet, closed the door, and slid down into the dark. The next few hours passed in relative peace. Percy tried for fitful sleep, gave up, played a few rounds of solitaire on the tablet he'd been provided, got bored, switched to chess instead, got even more bored, and was left staring at the shifting lamp light to stop himself from going insane.

His mind drifted back to the gray ship on the map. Behind them, he assured himself. Not necessarily following. It was probably just a commercial freighter looking to use the same bridge. It wasn't a pirate. And it certainly wasn't an Imperial war dog. The Imperial Army wouldn't have had time to notice he was MIA–right?

For the Emperor can do all things. None shall ward His gaze or hand. And all the enemies of the Host of hosts will fall.

Percy blew out a sharp breath through his nose. He ran a hand through his hair in a vain attempt at self-comfort. He'd never known a Black Hammer to desert before. Well, no Hammer save for Orestes– but then, Orestes had barely counted as a Hammer. Orestes had barely counted as a man. He was *not* like Orestes.

He reached under his neck collar and pulled a necklace free. It was a very simple chain, and on it swung a very simple pendant: that of the holy falling star, a meteor wreathed in golden flames. He ran his thumb back and forth over the pendant's face, wishing he felt more sure about his leaving than he really did. He needed the answers, didn't he? He needed to know…

He must have closed his eyes at some point because they snapped open again when someone knocked on his door. Groggy, Percy staggered to his feet. He wiped the sleep gunk from his eyes and opened the door to a smiling Horris.

Horris' smile grew before he jabbed his tablet at Percy. "It's time to jump. I need you to sign this."

Percy blinked back the first headache pangs to stare at the scrawl of legal jargon. "What's this?"

"It's a waiver for you to sign. I found it in the archives. It covers all injuries and afflictions related to interstellar jumping, and by signing it, you waive the right to sue USSPS for damages."

"Damages?" Percy repeated warily. He scrolled through the waiver with a frown. "Like what?"

"Common symptoms after jumps. Dizziness, shortness of breath, compressed spine, and feeling like you need to brush your teeth. Oh! And temporary insanity."

"*Temporary insanity?*"

"Hm! Sometimes people report seeing things when jumping. They call the phenomenon The Horrors. My advice? Don't look up."

Horris didn't elaborate on what The Horrors were. Percy, for the sake of his own lasting sanity, didn't ask him to. He read through the waiver carefully before signing off.

After that, it was a brisk walk back to the cockpit. Four seats had appeared behind the lower area, which was the cockpit itself. Basah and Fives were already strapped into seats. Percy hesitated before taking the seat beside Fives. He began to strap himself in, feeling like a small child on their first amusement ride.

"Ready?" Roddy asked from the pilot's chair.

"Ready!" Horris replied. He took the seat beside Roddy in the cockpit proper.

The windshield rippled. And that was when Percy finally saw the jump. It was a swirling, crackling vortex that had punched a hole through the fabric of space itself. Percy watched light and stars and space debris collide and burst around the vortex's mouth, pulled deeper and deeper into a tunnel whose end he couldn't see. An inexplicable dread filled Percy. It was an ancient, soul-deep protest, like being at the edge of a precipice and knowing he could leap if not for his own mind. A bead of sweat ran down his face. He couldn't find it in him to be ashamed of his fear.

A soft whir broke through his racing thoughts. Roddy's seat pulled forward and then lowered, sliding the pilot into a stance on his stomach. Percy was reminded vividly of speeders and motorists back in the city. Roddy even pulled on a pair of goggles to complete the look. Horris' seat shifted downwards as well.

Percy jolted when his own seat shifted, leaving him staring at the floor. A quick glance at Basah and Fives told him this was all according to procedure: they looked bored and unbothered, respectively. Fives had closed his eyes, and his fingers twitched in some pattern.

"Crew secured?" Roddy asked. He began to flip a number of switches.

"Crew secured," Horris said.

"Cargo stabilized?"

"Cargo stabilized."

The *Silverfish* whirred softly as it moved into position, the nose of the ship aimed dead at the center of the vortex.

"Diverting engine power," Roddy said. He clicked another button, and a low roar echoed from somewhere below. "Accelerating to six-hundred thousand kay-pee-ee-aitch. All systems–go!"

The *Silverfish* shot forward with a roar. Percy's inners flung backward, and then forward, and then backward again—they were moving so fast he barely had time to register that they were hurtling through space and straight into a swirling vortex of death.

The *Silverfish* jostled and shook with the force of acceleration. The world outside went black, then gray, then to multicolored strands of purple and yellow, lightning streaking down the narrow tunnel to reveal the path ahead. The lightning illuminated clouds of space debris and dust all around them, roiling together in a never-ending storm—

A massive hand lifted itself from the clouds, skeletal fingers outstretched as lightning danced across sunken gray flesh—

Don't look up!

Blood filled his mouth as Percy forced his gaze away. He screwed his eyes shut, forcing himself to focus on physical sensations: the bile in the back of his throat, the blood on his tongue, how his stomach clenched. And just when it all built too high, just when it all became too much—

Ding!

Bridge jump successful. You may now begin to decelerate.

The chairs shot upright. Percy reopened his eyes, not sure whether he wanted to cry or throw up or piss himself. It took everything he had, every ounce of training, to swallow back the burning vomit in his throat. He began to unstrap himself with shaking hands.

Basah was already out of her seat and helping Fives unbuckle. "BLIP, status report."

All interior and exterior systems functional. Heat shields three and four are loose.

"I'll get on that," Basah said, looking over her shoulder to Horris.

Horris had risen from his seat, and he was pulling a small tin from his pocket. "Thanks. Mint?"

It took Percy a moment to realize Horris was addressing him. He looked at the little tin of mints being offered; now that he was thinking about it, he could feel the layer of fuzz over his tongue and teeth, as though he hadn't brushed his teeth in two days. "No," he said, "thank you."

He finished unbuckling and got to his feet. From the corner of his eye, he could see Fives staring at him unabashedly. "I'm going back to my room," he announced.

Horris blinked. "Okay," he said, around the mint in his mouth. He turned to offer a mint to Roddy, who had staggered up from the cockpit.

Percy wheeled around and stalked off, trying not to feel foolish. They were the insane ones; yes, that was it—acting like barreling through that tunnel had been *nothing*. Temporary insanity–*temporary*!

Well, he supposed, jump enough times, and the temporary became permanent.

❹ Delta Io

United Star System Postal Code, Chapter 10, Section 3: All inbound off-planet couriers are required to seek landing clearance with the depot and/or station of destination.

hoosh!

There was the inevitable rush of blood to his head, the churning of his stomach, and the panic as his feet couldn't find purchase against a solid surface. Horris paused long enough to adjust to the sensation of weightlessness. He allowed himself to bounce out into the open void of space, trusting the tether attaching his Exosuit to the ship not to fail. The *Silverfish* sailed at a steady pace and carried Horris along with it.

He drifted for a moment, pretending he was flying, and then took his tether in hand. He pulled himself back against the side of the ship, turning to land feet-first. Small magnets in the soles of his boots kept him against the shell of the *Silverfish* as he strode along.

Like the insect it had been named for, the *Silverfish* had a wide, rounded bow that tapered to a narrow stern. As a Grummon-class, she was small, fast, and maneuverable, relying on the power of swiveling thrusters to control her direction. All thrusters—plus the interior engines—had been cut while Basah reattached the heat shields. Inertia pulled the *Silverfish* along now, aided by the occasional nudge from Roddy to keep on track.

Horris reached Basah and Fives at the stern where they worked. Well–Basah was working. Fives mostly handed her the tools she needed and kept the rest from floating away. She looked up at the sound of Horris' heavy tread. "Horris," she said, voice crackling over the Exosuit radio. "Good of you to join us."

"Is everything all right?" Horris asked. Basah had radioed him to join them, but everything seemed to be in order.

"I wanted us in a spot where no one could overhear us."

"O-oh?"

Basah looked at Fives, who flinched and lowered his eyes. He tapped out a quick, nervous rhythm against the toolbox he held. "Basah said I have to tell you. Or she would."

"Tell me what?" Horris asked, growing more alarmed as the conversation stalled.

Fives kept his eyes on the heat shield at their feet. Basah's tail whipped back and forth in agitation.

"It's Perseus," Fives said at last. "I can't read him."

Horris stared at him. They'd met a lot of people in the two years since Fives had joined the crew. Powerful people, scared people, people just trying to get by, people who'd shoot a courier dead or try to swindle him out of his valuable packages. You never quite knew who you were delivering to in the deep recesses of space, and Fives' ability to read people had saved their skins more than once.

It was the worst-kept secret in all of the United Star System Postal Service: the 131-C had an honest-to-god phrenic on board. And in all their deliveries, Fives had *never* had an issue reading someone.

"What happened?" Horris asked. "You could read him just fine when we brought him onboard."

"He wasn't aware of me then. Now he is. He told me to get out. He slammed the door and turned down the volume. It's quiet around him now."

"Get out?" Horris repeated, troubled. "He *told* you?"

Fives nodded. The phrenic's hands twitched. Out here, without the protection of his headphones, thoughts and feelings flowed into his head unbidden. The toolbox trembled in his grip.

Horris forced his suddenly-racing mind to slow. He took a deep breath and ensured the words in his head matched the ones coming out of his mouth: "Do you think he's dangerous?"

Fives shook his head. The sound of Basah welding the heat shield back into place cut their conversation short. Both waited for Basah to finish and thrust her tools back at Fives.

"I think he's dangerous," Basah said as she got to her feet. "And rude. I want him off the ship as soon as possible."

"That's not your call to make, Bah," Horris said at once. "We're already agreed on terms of passage."

"He's an Imperial Creed. Do you know anything about Imperial Creeds, Horry?"

"No," Horris admitted warily.

Basah shook her head. "Well, they're some of the most dogmatic assholes in this literal universe. They worship their Emperor like a god. From the moment they're born, Imperials are raised to be soldiers fighting for their Emperor's glory. They've been trying to take over their entire planet for a century now. And they *don't* just look sideways at soldiers who go AWOL."

Horris mulled that over. He remembered the strange rite Perseus had performed when he'd received that slice of pizza and the second butter knife he'd produced from his boot. The oath he'd sworn was one of mutual protection, but did that cover his whole crew or only Horris himself? Postmen were protected by their neutral status. But phrenics were rare, very rare, and if Fives' presence was sussed out…

"By His Grace, we are bonded," Fives murmured. His dark eyes had gone unfixed.

"Do you think his training is why he could shut you out?" Horris asked Fives. "Does he know what you are?"

Fives shrugged.

"I think he should go," Basah said.

"Go where exactly?" Horris fired back. "If he's a deserter, he has nowhere *to* go! We're not just going to chuck him off at the next planet and say good luck!"

Fives gave Horris a sidelong look before turning to Basah. "Horris fancies him."

"FIVES!"

Basah rolled her eyes as she snatched her toolbox from Fives. "*He's hot* is not an acceptable reason to put us all in danger."

"I don't think he's *hot*—"

"You like how his hair falls in his face," Fives said dispassionately.

"*Stay out of this, Fives!*"

"*Don't yell at Fives!*" Basah snapped. Her slit pupils thinned as she glared at Horris. Then she sighed, relaxing her stance back. "Look, Horry–you're a sweetheart. That's what we all love about you. But don't let your goodwill get in the way of your judgment, okay? First sign of danger, and I'm throwing him out the airlock myself."

Horris began to argue but then decided against it. Basah could be as stubborn as her machinery sometimes, and he wasn't about to fight where Fives couldn't block them out. "Okay. Fine. But unless he makes a move to hurt someone, we're not ditching him. We're better than that."

Basah nodded, satisfied, and returned to her work. Horris remained with them, overseeing but not interfering. Both knew how to do their job and do it well. When they finished, though, Horris did not immediately return to the interior of the ship. He walked his way upward to the roof of the *Silverfish*, staring out into the great deep empty that was space.

Space stretched out onto forever ahead and behind. Horris quite liked the sight. Most didn't, he knew. They found the endless expanse horrifying. But space held no special horror for him. He liked the silence, the simple beauty, and how everything seemed to know exactly what it was supposed to do when it was supposed to do it. There had yet to be a city on any planet that offered the same comforting predictability. There were no wars out here. No orphans.

Sweetheart, Basah had called him. That's all anyone would call him. No one became a courier because they wanted to be called strong, clever, or heroic. You did it for the pay, the pension, and the occasional sincere thanks. There was nothing wrong with that, in his opinion. A steady, predictable life, helping where and when you could.

Eventually, his Exosuit beeped a warning. The Exosuit was useful for a great many things, but prolonged sojourns into space were not one of them. The oxygen tank needed to be recharged. Horris followed his tether back to the airlock, keyed in the code, and stepped into the ship's interior.

Basah was waiting for him when Horris emerged from the other side of the airlock. She waited for him to set the Exosuit back on the charger and step out. Once he did, she folded her arms over her chest and set her chin. "Fives won't admit it to you, but he's fascinated." Her tone was begrudging. "He's never met someone he couldn't read before."

"What do you suggest?" Horris asked. Of all the *Silverfish* crew, Fives trusted Basah the most, and she returned that trust with fierce protectiveness.

"Keep Fives away from him. The longer that rat goes without realizing there's a phrenic onboard, the better. Take Fives with you when we land on Delta Io. He needs the delivery experience anyway."

Horris considered the idea. Fives wasn't exactly the friendly, professional courier that USSPS promised. But he did need practice around other people…

"All right," Horris said. "Fives can come with me."

Basah nodded, satisfied, and strode off.

The next few hours passed calmly. The crew of the *Silverfish* took their lunches and did their rounds. Roddy took stretch breaks from the helm, and either Horris or BLIP would relieve him. Basah did regular checks on her engines, and Fives spent most of his time debugging one of the landing programs.

Of Perseus, there was no sign. His broom closet door stayed stubbornly shut.

Three hours out from Delta Io, Horris descended into the hold to sort mail and packages for delivery. It was one of his favorite parts of the job and the one he insisted on doing himself. He would never dare open a package (USSPS Code, Chapter One, Section Four-B: USSPS personnel were to observe and respect the privacy of all packages aboard their ships). Nevertheless, he liked feeling the heft and bulk of different packages and studying the names printed on the mail. Some were stamped, and some were handwritten; some seemed like business notices, and some were a child's eager scrawl. Each told a story. Each had a person behind it and a person waiting for it. There was something magical about that connective tissue, in Horris' opinion, as awe-inspiring and simple as space itself.

When the sorting was done, Horris joined Roddy in the cockpit. Their destination, Delta Io, was a bright blue dot on the horizon, no bigger than a marble. It was a small speck of life suddenly appearing from the nothingness around it.

"Never gets old, does it?" Roddy murmured. Horris agreed softly.

Roddy leaned over and flicked on his comms. "Delta Io Depot Station Twelve-One-Ex, this is USSPS One-Thirty-One-C, designation *Silverfish*, making notice to land at coordinates thirty-seven-twelve-thirty-three degrees north, seventy-six-forty-six-thirty-nine degrees west. Do you copy?"

Crackling silence.

Roddy frowned, checked their manifest, and repeated the message again. "Delta Io Depot Station, this is USSPS One-Thirty-One-C, designation *Silverfish*. Do you copy?"

Static was the only reply.

"Oh, I hate that." Roddy sat back. He frowned down at his communication console.

Horris rubbed his chin. "BLIP, what's the status of Delta Io?"

Delta Io, third planet from the sun star Phoebys. Status: hospitable to sentients. Average climate of destination: slightly above humid. Political status: formerly under the control of Io Prime, it was annexed by the closest sentient-dominant planet of proximity, Creed, in the last decade. Intended use: penal colony. Current use: expatriate colony. USSPS depot status: active.

"Maybe their comms aren't online?" Horris suggested. "If it's a recent colony, their equipment is probably crap."

"Yeah." Roddy scratched at his sideburns. "Yeah. The big cities get all the good equipment, right? Outposts like this got the leftover crap. They wouldn't be the first depot with a shitty radio. Especially if their parent planet is busy with civil war."

It sounded a bit like a justification to both their ears.

"Do we go for it?" Roddy asked tentatively.

"Yes," Horris said. He was thinking of all the packages below: the last words and gifts of loved ones hauled out before the borders of Creed closed. Widows, widowers, and orphans deserved some semblance of closure. He knew what it was like to be waiting for a goodbye.

He leaned forward and flicked on the intercoms. "All hands, report to the bridge for landing."

Basah and Fives came to the bridge in short order—followed, surprisingly, by a bleary-eyed Perseus. "We're not going to jump through another bloody tunnel, are we?"

"No," Horris said. He ignored the way Perseus' tousled hair fell into his face. "But entries are bumpy. Strap in."

Every sentient-dominant settlement—even the backwater out-posts—had a USSPS landing depot. It was one of those things govern-ments and community leaders were required to build. It was usually a few miles outside of major cities or towns, where mail could be sorted and processed. The landing depot of Delta Io was no different in that regard.

It took about forty minutes for the *Silverfish* to finish the entry process (although Roddy grumbled the whole time he could have done it in thirty-five). As such, it wasn't immediately obvious what was different about the Delta Io depot: it was dark and silent.

From the cockpit, Horris and Roddy exchanged another look. The postage depot should have had at least one light on. USSPS personnel were required to have a standard landing crew to help with unloading and reloading. The landing crew in Creedence had been on their way out, but a quiet backwater like this…

"That's it, we're leaving—"

Horris smacked Roddy's hand away from the console. "If some-thing happened to the crew here, we need to know."

"And who's going to investigate us if we wind up dead?" Roddy scowled. "I'm not getting out of this ship to get got!"

"We're not going to get *got*," Horris said. He twisted to meet Fives' wide, dark eyes. Perseus seemed puzzled; Basah livid. Horris forced himself to ignore both their expressions. They needed forewarning of any dangers. And for that…

"You're up, Fives."

5 In the Dying of the Night

United Star Systems Postal Code Chapter 11, Section 2: Postal Captains shall have the power to investigate postal offenses and civil matters relating to the Postal Service.

Fives blinked.

Slowly, regretting it already, he lowered his orange headphones away from his ears. Coltrane faded from the front of his consciousness as he was beset on all sides by thoughts-feelings.

Horris was bound by his oaths; Basah was quick-hot-fury-spitting-poison; Roddy wanted to leave, now-now-*now*. Perseus was a pillar of silence to his left. Fives glanced his way, trying to know his emotions from his expression alone like Other People had to.

Perseus kept his expression neutral, but his green eyes flashed the longer the arguing continued.

Fives could feel Basah's fury rising like a sickness in his throat. He could feel love and fear driving the sickness and her desire neither to hurt him nor to see him hurt.

Horris' oath—do your duty, protect the USSPS—pressed against Fives' temple. Before Perseus, the oaths were the closest Fives felt to silence unguarded. Horris' oaths helped guide him and taught him right from wrong. Roddy and Basah called them rules-regula-tions, always with that hint of disdain. But Fives saw them as Horris did: a way to make sense of the chaos, a path through the swirl of thoughts-feelings.

Never leave another postie behind.

"I'll go," Fives said out loud.

Dimly, he was aware of sudden silence (physical silence, at least). Horris and Basah had been arguing, he realized. Now, they were both staring at him with incredulity. In fact, everyone was. Roddy had half-risen out of his seat. BLIP beeped overhead.

"I'll go," Fives said again. He began to unbuckle himself before the wave of incredulity drowned him.

"Not alone," Horris said. "I'll go with you. Roddy–Basah–you two stay here and keep the ship ready. Engines warm and ready to fly. Perseus—"

"I am not yours to command," Perseus said flatly.

A rancid taste filled Fives' mouth. Outrage, annoyance, should-have-thrown-him-out. Fives pushed his consciousness out-of-body and up against the shield around Perseus. Testing, not hard, like whispers against a cheek. Perseus brushed him off without so much as a twitch in his direction. He was too busy staring at Horris to acknowledge Fives' prodding.

Fives felt a small thrill in his stomach and decided that the emotion belonged to him. He couldn't *feel* Perseus! He couldn't even *touch* Perseus! He had no idea who Perseus was!

The jerk of confusion-annoyance brought him back to the moment. The feeling belonged to Horris, along with a bit of hurt that stung Fives' eyes. Then, the oaths came back to orient themselves.

He can bluster all he likes, Horris and Fives thought.

It was Horris, though, who shrugged. "Do as you like, then."

Perseus' neutral expression flickered. "I'll be staying aboard your ship."

"Very good," Horris said briskly.

He set off, and Fives followed closely, trying to sort Horris' thought-feelings into their proper spots: fear for the stomach and oaths for the chest, anger for the throat, and clear-thinking for the head and hands and feet. After all, that's where the decisions were made, and the actions were taken.

We'll sweep the depot first and look for signs of trouble.

Horris spoke-thought the plan. It was a relief not to hear him word-speak: sometimes, the word-speak didn't match the speak-thought, and it was a headache to figure out what was true-think and true-speak, what he was supposed to hear versus what he really had.

If we find anything unusual, we go back up and make a radio comm for help.

A memory brushed Fives' mind. He reached for it and held it fast against his own. This was like Before, the time right before he had become Fives. The day Horris and Roddy and Basah had found him. The same uncertainty, the same convictions, that helping mattered more than the fear.

Wet heat settled over them like a thick blanket as they exited the ship. The sky overhead was bluish-purple like a bruise, and the red sun had just begun to set over the horizon. The fetid, sickly-sweet smell of stagnant water coated the humid air. There was a swamp nearby; insects and birds filled the late afternoon with their chitters and cries. The whole land thrummed in a feedback loop of feed-fight-breed-survive. Non-sentients like that were easier to listen to than people but harder to parse for true meaning. It sounded like a crowd of people whispering softly in a room over.

"Is there anyone nearby, Fives?"

Fives closed his eyes and spread his mind outwards across the area. "Yes."

"Where?"

Fives pointed back to the ship.

He only realized his error when Horris' disappointment sank into him like a stone. Fives fought the impulse to frown. That was another problem with Other People: they asked you things and then got annoyed with the answers. There were people here! That was what Horris had asked for!

The captain took a deep breath. "Anyone besides us?"

Sorry-sorry-will try to be better. Don't get upset with Fives. He thinks like that.

Fives sighed and tried again. There were no foreign think-feelings nearby, only the patterns of his friends, the feedback of wildlife, and that strange hole in thinking-feeling space shaped like Perseus. "No," he said.

"Okay," Horris said. He licked his lips once. "Let's go look inside."

Relief-nervous rushed into Five's stomach. He decided the emotion fit: relief that there was no one nearby, nervous because there was no one nearby. He trailed after Horris as they started for the depot's front door.

It didn't budge when Horris gave it a tug, and there was no response when they tried knocking. Horris led Fives around the side to the employee entrance. The keypad was still active, luckily, and when Horris typed in his captaincy clearance code, the lock clicked green.

It took a moment of fumbling to find the interior lights, and Fives squinted against the sudden blaze of fluorescent lights. It was an average layout of an average postal office: they stood on the other side of a long counter with sectioned windows. From here, they could see the stanchion ropes that formed an orderly line, posters outlining what was and was not acceptable for shipment (on- and off-planet), and flickering advertisements for the latest stamp designs. All was still, and a fine layer of dust came off the counter when Horris ran his finger along it.

Fives looked at the untouched mundanity and decided the sorrow he felt was shared by both him and Horris. Worry tinged Horris', though, as they made their way into the back.

Through a set of double doors, the post office became a mini-warehouse. The fluorescent lighting bounced off of black flooring and tall sectioned shelves marked for commercial and residential mail. They sidestepped the empty metal carts and untouched courier lockers. A rack of van keys hung by the lockers. One hook sat empty.

The postmaster's office was set in the far corner of the back room. Large glass windows allowed viewing out and in, and while Horris jiggled the door handle, Fives peered through. He could see walkie-talkies on their chargers and filing cabinets, presumably still full of files. It didn't look ransacked. Nothing here did. It was just...empty.

Horris' worry had tripled to a fear that beat against Fives' temple. He pulled on his headphones and flicked on John Coltrane. Smooth, easy jazz pushed back against the acrid fear swelling in his head, drowning it in a joy inherent to music. He closed his eyes to better focus on the music and, as such, almost missed Horris' remark about the bay doors. It took a gentle hand on his shoulder to get him to move.

The bay doors trundled open when Horris keyed in his code. They stepped out into the suffocating heat of the afternoon and into the loading zone.

"Oh, hell," Horris breathed. His horror rose in Fives' own stomach like hot bile.

Deep, black burn marks gouged the cement in long swipes. Two postal vans had been completely upended; a third was a lump of twisted metal and rubber baking in the late-day sun. Fives studied the ruined vans before his eyes swept north to see massive, charred steel pieces crushing the plantlife.

That was—had been—a postal ship.

■

In a Sentimental Mood wasn't cutting it. Fives took out his tablet and swapped to *Giant Steps*, which fit Roddy's frantic pacing much better. Fives settled back on the *Silverfish's* hard tile floor, letting the music wash over him as a battle raged through the cockpit.

Roddy's long legs took him the length of the *Silverfish*'s entryway. He pivoted and started back towards Horris. "All comms are off-line down here. *All* comms, not even just USSPS lines. If we want to send an SOS out, we'd need to get back to the outersphere."

"I'm not sure that's a good idea," Horris said. "Whatever attacked the post office was massive. And we have no idea where it is right now. If it got an alert about us entering, it could be in the outersphere now."

Roddy's blond curls bounced when he shook his head. "So you'd rather have us politely wait our turn to get blasted?"

"Don't put words in my mouth. We need to be cautious. We don't have any idea what we're dealing with—"

"It's obvious, isn't it?" Basah asked. She folded her arms over her chest. "Pirates are the only ones stupid enough to attack postmen."

"But why? It's not like a depot this size has anything of value…"

Basah glanced up. "BLIP, what is the status of settlements on Delta Io?"

Beep-boop! Delta Io has one active settlement, Icene. Home to expatriate citizens of Creed known as Idolers. Former settlements further north were occupied by Vespane prior to annexation. Vespane departed when annexation was complete.

"Guess even they didn't want to deal with the Creeds," Roddy said. "Do you think anyone's left in Icene?"

The fear and uncertainty grew too much for Fives to bear. He stood and left the cockpit. They would sort it out, he knew, one way or the other. None of them had asked Fives for his opinion, but that was all right. Fives knew it was hard to know what his opinions were and what belonged to the people around him.

Thinking-feelings died to a faint buzz as Fives entered the mess. Perseus sat at the table, flipping through an old shipment processing manual and looking bored.

Looking, Fives thought with that secret thrill, but not really *knowing*. He had no idea what Perseus really thought about the manual. Maybe he liked it. He stood across from Perseus, looking him over the way Other People did. Perseus' expression was flat: lips turned down at the corners, eyebrows slightly furrowed. He seemed lost in the manual…until he sighed and tossed it over his shoulder.

"Is it always like this?" Perseus asked.

"What?" Fives replied.

"This…" He waved a vague hand around to indicate…something. Maybe everything. "Mail service. Is it always this disorganized? Do you really have no protocol in place if a depot is abandoned on some backwater planet at the edge of a galaxy?"

Horris would have known for certain. Fives just shrugged. "Your war is interrupting a lot of the usual routines."

Perseus' eyes flashed. He propelled to his feet. "*Excuse me?*"

They were of a height, which meant they were both quite small. But Perseus was lean, and the way he tightened his body reminded him of Roddy before a fight broke out. Quick temper, Fives thought, quick to fight. A sort of absurd pride seized him.

"Your peoples' war," he explained further. "Closing Creed's borders disrupted a lot. This is a Creed colony," he tossed his hands out to mean the world around them, "and, well…you're here too. That's an interruption in our routine, too!"

The absurd sort of pride surged into his head and left him giddy. Fives beamed at Perseus.

Perseus' fist clenched. For a moment, it seemed like he was going to haul off and punch Fives. But instead, he exhaled and straightened up. "Indeed," he said, and when he spoke, it sounded like he had lemon in his mouth. "My war has…more consequences than anyone intended."

He rubbed his thumb over his forehead. Fives wondered if he had a headache.

"When will we depart?" Perseus asked.

"As soon as they made a decision about what to do," Fives said. "Whether we go for the town or the…"

He trailed off, puzzled. The faint buzz in the back of his mind grew louder. At first, he'd dismissed it as the argument across the ship, but no—this was getting closer, getting louder. A humming drone of many small voices moving towards them in a wave.

"Or?" Perseus prompted.

Fives shushed him. "Can you hear that?"

"No," was the flat, automatic response.

"Listen," Fives insisted. He needed to know if this was really real or real only for himself.

Perseus gave him a look (Fives wondered at its meaning) before closing his eyes and dropping his shoulders. Fives took off his headphones, all the better to hear the *bzzzt-bzzzt-bzzzzt* rattling his head like pennies in a jar. The voices spoke of hunger and light and heat, seeking, always seeking. His stomach roiled with the emptiness of their bellies. They were hungry. *He* was hungry.

Perseus stiffened even as he opened his eyes. "What the hell," he whispered, "*is that noise?*"

At least someone else could hear it, too. Fives fumbled for his walkie-talkie as he left the mess. "Captain," he radioed. He could hear the crackly echo of his voice from the cockpit. "Come to the bridge, please."

Perseus followed him to the wide corridor window. Outside, the sky had darkened from that bruise to a deep, winish purple. The last bands of red and pink sank over the horizons of trees and distant mountains. In an instant, the whole world plunged into darkness.

Thunk.

Fives and Perseus both jumped. They watched as something splattered against the window. Another solid *thunk* followed. Perseus glanced at Fives. "Is someone…throwing things?"

Thunk. Thunk!

The others came running to join them. "BLIP," Horris called, "report."

The *Silverfish* is currently surrounded on all sides. Organic lifeforms. Extremely hostile.

Thunk! Thunk! Thunkthunkthunkthunk—

A sickening chorus of sorts rose up just outside: the sickening crunch of small bodies slammed against the sides of the *Silverfish,* accompanied by that low, maddening drone. The thuds came faster now, harder, and the crew could see fist-sized black masses ramming against the windshield. Some left clear streaks behind them as their bodies smeared down the reinforced glass. Basah gagged.

"What the hell," Roddy breathed, "are those?"

"Chrysopsini," Horris replied. He pushed his way forward to watch the hail of black. "But they aren't nocturnal…"

Fives felt the buzz of interest in his stomach. Horris' fascination with insects took precedence over the immediate concern of so many attempting to ram the ship. Insect behavior was familiar, explainable, and if it was something he could explain, then it was something he could solve. Facts about chrysopsini flooded Fives' mind: habitats, feeding habits, mating rituals…then the solution lit up.

"Of course!" Horris said. "They must have been attracted to the engine's heat!"

Perseus squinted at the hundreds of insects racing to die against the *Silverfish.* "What…are they, exactly?"

"A type of deer fly!" Horris beamed. "Of course, we'd have to get a good look at a specimen to know which one."

"Are they dangerous?" Perseus asked. He tore his gaze from the windshield to Horris, eyebrows arched.

"Oh. Well, yes. They feed on flesh—the females do, at least…lay their eggs in living creatures…some subsets will paralyze a host and keep it alive for weeks while the maggots eat their way out through their innards—"

Basah coughed.

"—but that's not important to our situation," Horris cleared his throat. "Point is, once the sun set, they all made a beeline—well, flyline—to the biggest, warmest object in the immediate area! Us! They think it's a massive creature they can feast on!"

THUNK. THUNK. THUNK.

"Ta-da," Fives said softly.

Roddy scowled. He glanced back down the corridor towards the cockpit. "That's all very exciting, Horry, but I don't want to sit here listening to bugs—"

"Insects," Horris and Fives said together.

"—whatever! I don't wanna listen to insects explode on the windshield all night!" Roddy sighed. "Let's camp out in the outersphere until daylight. God, I hate this place—"

Sudden, sharp pain seized Fives by the arms and throat. Hot, jagged knives tore through his exposed skin, and the more he bled, the more knives pierced him—chewing, biting, white-hot burning, biting, make it stop, *MAKE IT STOP GODS HELP*—

"Fives?! FIVES!" "What's wrong with him?!" "Someone shut him up!"

PLEASE GODS PLEASE—

"*FIVES!*"

Fives heard Basah's voice through the whitewash of burning pain. He forced his eyes open. Somehow, he'd wound up in a heap on the floor. His head pounded, and his stomach roiled; it felt as though some of those chrysopsini had found their way into his stomach. He could feel them under his skin: writhing, biting, *gnawing*. Hot blood trickled down his throat.

He needed to tell Basah, needed to tell them all about the screaming, but all he could manage was a soft "it hurts."

"I know," Basah murmured. Her hand combed through his hair. Her mind was empty, devoid of anything except immediate physical sensations. "I know. I'm putting your headphones on, okay?"

"Billie Holiday," Fives whispered.

"Billie Holiday," Basah confirmed.

The worst of the pain faded as the familiar weight of his head-phones came over his ears. Tears still burned hot on his cheeks, though, and Fives was too-aware of the way Perseus stared at him. He didn't need to read his mind to know what Perseus was thinking: he looked at Fives like he was something low and disgusting. Like he was a fly slamming against a window.

"What's wrong with him?" Perseus demanded.

Fives blinked tears away. Billie Holiday's soft, sad voice drowned out Horris' fears and Roddy and Basah's anger. He searched until he found Horris, and he gave him a nod. There was no point in hiding it any longer.

"Fives…is sensitive to certain things. He can figure things out before other people can."

Perseus' eyes narrowed sharply. He took a full step backward. "A phrenic. You've got a bloody *phrenic* working for your bloody mail service? Are you all mad?"

"Maybe," Horris said. He dismissed all the panic and fear with a firm reaffirmation of their purpose. He knelt down in front of Fives. "Is someone hurt, Fives?"

Fives blinked back the agony and shame. He nodded. Now that the pain didn't sear into his mind, he could feel the shape of a stranger in the distance: writhing in the mud, slapping at the swollen black flies crawling under her skin. "She thought it was safe to move after dark."

"But the chrysopsini are active because of the ship," Horris murmured. He looked back out the window, trying to cut a path through the swarm of insects in his head.

Thud. Thud. Thud. Thud. THUD–

Horris exhaled. Fives felt the decision-calm dispel the swirl of panic in his head. "Rod?"

"Yeah?"

"How fast can you sprint in an Exosuit?"

The question earned a small laugh from Roddy, and a little of his delight trickled into Fives. "C'mon, Horry, track and field champion of Eighty-Eight right here!"

"Good. Suit up because we're going to need a runner. Basah, get the engines good and hot. Expel as much heat as you can from the lower thrusters. Hopefully, we can draw more chrysopsini to the back. Then I want you to suit up too. Your vision is better than Rod's by night."

"Much better," Basah agreed.

"Fives, you and I are on airlock duty. Some of the insects will try to get inside."

"What if this person is hostile?" Perseus demanded. He folded his arms over his chest. "You could be opening your door to one of those pirates."

Horris started to reply, but Basah beat him to the quick. She whipped around, eyes flashing, and shoved a palm out towards Perseus. Instantly, he had her by the wrist, twisting her arm so that her knees buckled. Horris and Roddy both shouted, but Basah shook her head as she jerked out of Perseus' grip. "You're a Creed Imperial. I'm sure you'll be able to handle anyone coming through that door."

Perseus said nothing. He eased back to lean against the wall once more.

From there, it all happened very quickly: Roddy and Basah suited up in the Exosuits while the engines roared low and the hailstorm continued overhead. The Exosuits had been commissioned by USSPS for off-world couriers after losing too many agents to hostile climates. Light but durable, they were designed to withstand extreme temperatures and were resistant to slashing and piercing weapons. They would, in theory, stand up to an assault of deer flies.

The *Silverfish* crew met at the airlock. Horris handed Fives a broom for the inevitable carnage when the chrysopsini got through the airlock. Roddy stretched, looking relaxed for the first time in hours, while Basah remained still and poised. The anticipation made the air taste like lightning. Fives shivered and licked his lips.

Horris' hand hovered over the keypad. "Ready?"

"Ready," Roddy replied. Basah took her place beside him.

"GO!"

The airlock doors opened with a roar. Instantly, huge black deer-flies swarmed into the airlock. Roddy and Basah bolted forward into the black. Fives jumped backward, his own fear a knife in his throat as he swung the broom back and forth, smacking aside fist-sized flies as they rushed for warm flesh. Horris yanked him backward into the ship proper as the airlock slammed close.

THUD. THUD. THUD. BZZT-THUD.

A few crippled flies crawled along the floor. Horris picked one up and held it flat in his palm. "BLIP, analyze insect carcasses, and set security scans across the ship. If any of them gets loose inside the ship, we need to know where."

Aye-aye, Captain!

Fives stared down at the dying flies that littered the floor. He could feel their pain—small jolts of pain, distress, light dimming, and dying through compound eyes. No fear, no confusion, but distress—crawling forward, *forward*, until the light went out. Fives died on the floor, ten times over, before Horris pressed a hand to his shoulder.

"Steady, buddy. Steady. Can you feel Basah and Roddy?"

Fives shook his head to clear away the dying. He closed his eyes and swept his consciousness outward: he could feel panic and disgust—whipped by deerflies as they ran, trying not to think about what the crunch underfoot or splat against their chests meant. Basah led, sharp eyes scanning the dark—looking, following, surprise as she finally heard the cries that were loud as a bell to Fives. A shout to a prone figure in the dark—grabbing, lifting, no time to talk, safety, not so far now—sprinting, faster and faster—pain, blistering hot, as deer flies ripped and tore and drank deep, their song one of deep, belly-clawing hunger—

"Open the door *now*!" Fives shouted.

Whoosh!

Another cloud of chrysopsini pushed through, along with three gasping figures. The deer flies dropped like rain—pitter-patter-pitter—as Basah, Roddy, and their new guest were allowed through the second set of airlock doors. They staggered to a halt and then collapsed in a heap together.

Horris moved to Basah and Roddy, the latter of whom immediately began to complain about Horris' fussing. Fives stood in front of the bleeding, trembling humanoid between them. It was a Marquay woman with olive skin and horns curling upwards through dark hair.

She opened her eyes to glare at Fives. Hate, thick as swarming flies, filled his throat.

"We're not pirates," Fives said.

"Worse than pirates," she spat. Her gaze shifted over Fives' shoulder. He could suddenly feel the empty space that was Perseus, standing at the end of the hall. The thick hate burned, and Fives felt a dozen wounds open and bleed.

"*Imperials.*"

6 The Idoler

United Star System Postal Code, Chapter 10, Section 10: Captains shall maintain responsibility for crews and conveyance of mail and perform all duties assigned within their contracts to their fullest ability.

Horris had about ten seconds to process what the woman had said before she sprung up and leapt at Perseus.

They went down in a ball of limbs and shouts and open wounds. In a flash, Perseus had her pinned to the floor, one hand wrapped around both wrists and the other at her neck. The takedown might have been more impressive if the woman hadn't been bleeding from a dozen open wounds on her face and arms.

Perseus snarled as the woman struggled in his grip. "Try it and see how far you get, *witch*."

"*HOLD!*"

Both Perseus and the woman froze. Horris' voice had pitched deeper on the command. He was a big man, Horris, and contrary to popular belief, he knew when to use his muscular frame to his advantage. He glared at Perseus, who glared back. "Perseus, let her go."

"Why?" Perseus demanded. "So she can attack me again?" His grip on the woman tightened as she muttered something under her breath.

Horris rolled his shoulders back so that he was at his full, impressive height. He tolerated a lot of things on his ship, but violence was not—would never be—on that list. He exhaled through his nose, forcing his own pounding heart and racing blood to cool. "I will not tolerate brawling on *my ship. I* am the captain aboard this vessel, and when I give an order, it *will* be obeyed."

Perseus considered Horris. For a moment, Horris thought he might refuse. Then, he relinquished his grip on the woman. He got to his feet and took a full step backward.

The woman scrambled up. Her eyes went from Perseus' rumpled black uniform to the cerulean blue the USSPS couriers wore. She didn't relax, but something in her expression shifted. "What's USSPS doing with an Imp like *him?*"

"It's a long story," Horris admitted. He ignored Perseus' continued glower. Instead, he held out a hand to the woman. "My name is Captain Horris Jensen of the USSPS *Silverfish.*"

She wiped her bloodied palms on her torn pants before accepting his hand. "Olive Zask, teacher in Icene." She took a deep breath before turning to Basah and Roddy, who had finally wrestled free of their Exosuits. Olive did a small little spasm of a bow in their direction. "Thank you. For saving me."

Horris glanced at Perseus. The Imperial was stiff, red in the face, and his green eyes never once left Olive.

"How does a teacher wind up in the middle of a godforsaken swamp?" Perseus asked.

Olive scowled as she pivoted back towards Perseus. "I could ask the same thing of a Black Hammer."

Perseus' ugly red flush deepened. It clashed horribly with his red hair.

"*Civility,*" Horris said, cold and curt. He stepped between Perseus and Olive.

The heavy patter of chrysopsini continued overhead. Olive's dark blood drip-drip-*dripped* on the floor. Horris could feel the headache building behind his eyes. He'd been awake for fourteen hours now, and there was nothing he wanted more than to crawl into his bunk and go to sleep. But he couldn't. As a captain, he had a responsibility to his crew and his customers. He took a deep breath, buying himself some time to decide on an appropriate course of action.

"Fives, please go to the infirmary and get the first aid kit. We need to get your wounds cleaned," he said to Olive. "Are you hungry, Miss Zask?"

"No, thank you. I'll take bandages, though." Olive looked down at her freely-bleeding arms with a start. Whole chunks of skin had been taken from her arms. Olive winced before tucking her trembling hands under her armpits. Her eyes reddened with sudden tears.

Roddy was beside her instantly, wrapping an arm around her shoulder. "Steady, miss. Steady. Let's head to the mess, okay?"

The crew and their guests settled at the circular table in the mess, the only room big enough to hold them all. Fives elected to stand just outside the doorway; Horris could hear sweet, sad Billie Holiday singing softly as they sat down. Olive stretched her arms out for medical attention and only grimaced a little when Horris dabbed an alcohol wipe down her arm. The deer flies had ripped coin-sized chunks from her olive skin, but fortunately, there were no bulges indicating any were attempting to nest inside her.

"Now," Roddy said as he set a cup of tea down in front of her, "why don't we all get acquainted?"

"First things first," Olive said. She jerked her head towards Perseus. "Why is *he* here?"

"To have a cup of tea," Perseus sneered.

"He's deserting," Basah answered. She ignored the look from Perseus and crouched to help Horris wrap bandages around Olive's arms.

A small hiss of pain escaped Olive. She turned back to Perseus. "A *deserter*? A *Black Hammer deserter*? That's impossible."

"What business is it of yours?" Perseus asked. His voice was taut as a bowstring, and Horris could see the way he clenched his fists under the table.

"I need to know whether you can be trusted," Olive said. Her fingers twitched. She might have clenched them if Basah hadn't forced her to keep still. "Or if you mean to bring harm to my community. We Idolers wish to live in peace."

"How strange, then, that your lot is the one fielding soldiers to wage war," Perseus said dryly.

"And whose war was it to start, hm? If you would deny anyone their free will, then you're every bit the zealot—"

Horris caught Perseus by the arm as he jerked upright. "All right, all right, that's enough! If you two can't have a conversation without a fistfight, I'm dumping you both back outside!" Not that he ever would, and judging by Basah's visible amusement, the rest of the crew knew it. But the guests didn't, and he needed the appeal to force to keep the peace. He forced Perseus back down into his seat. "Perseus, answer the question. Are you going to hurt anyone here?"

"No," Perseus said. He opened his mouth to add something else, but the words seemed to choke him. A long moment of silence followed before he could force it out: "I have renounced my place among the Black Hammers."

Olive's dark eyes widened. "You've…*renounced the Black Hammers?*"

For once, Horris wished he'd paid more attention in his Civics classes. It clearly meant *something* to be a Black Hammer, and it clearly meant something even more to be a Black Hammer who had renounced his place among them. He shared a look with Roddy, who shrugged. Roddy had done even worse in Civics.

"Does that mean…you renounce His Divinity as well?" Olive asked. She'd dropped a little of the bite in her tone.

"No," Perseus said sharply.

"Oh." The bite was back in Olive's voice, quick as it had disappeared. "So you're not a sheep. Just a coward."

Horris tightened his grip on Perseus' arm. The redhead strained forward against the grip. Fortunately, something—Horris' prior threat or the oaths he'd sworn against harm—held him just as tightly as Horris did. Perseus sat back in his seat with a scowl.

"The Red Hammer," Fives said in the sudden silence to no one in particular.

Perseus rolled his eyes at the phrenic. "I mailed myself out of Creedence using the USSPS. The crew has agreed to courier me to Apollonia. That we've been waylaid here as long as we have is nothing more than bad fucking luck."

The explanation seemed to satisfy Olive. She turned to Horris, who released his grip on Perseus' elbow. "You were here to deliver packages?"

"Yes, ma'am," Horris said. "The last batch out of Creedence before they closed the borders."

Olive started. "They closed the borders? Oh, hell." She closed her eyes and took a deep breath. Her lips moved without sound; if she said a prayer, no one here was privy to it.

Basah shared a look with Horris. She waited for Olive to reopen her eyes before asking: "Why is the depot here abandoned?"

"Bad fucking luck," Olive said. She managed a small smile when Perseus snorted. "I'm starting to think this whole colony is cursed. We're an expatriate colony from the westerlands of Creed. When trouble first started between the Emperor and Adastra—"

Perseus made another small noise, this one of disgust.

"Who?" Roddy asked.

"The leader of the Idolers. When troubles first started, the Emperor offered us Delta Io as a colony. A place to settle away from Creed, where our so-called blasphemy wouldn't reach more pious ears. And it was all right, at first…we even petitioned USSPS for a post office and got one. But then the war began, and many of our able-bodied answered Adastra's call to arms. But the Emperor couldn't allow His enemies a home base, aye? So they began attacking supply chains from Creed to Delta Io. Then came the pirates and the blackouts. They're trying to kill us all, all the old folks and children and the farmhands who were left behind."

"Are you saying that the Empire sicced pirates on your colony?" Perseus asked, aghast.

"If it wasn't you, then it was more bad fucking luck."

Horris waved Perseus into silence before he could retort. He leaned forward. "What about the postal workers?"

Olive winced. For the second time, something in her defenses dropped. She lowered her eyes to her bandaged hands. "When they realized there were pirates coming, they tried to get off-world, but the pirates grounded them again. There were four of them. Three died. I'm—I'm really sorry."

Horris' heart dropped somewhere into his stomach. Basah closed her eyes, and Roddy swore under his breath. Horris felt, rather than saw, Fives step further back into the hallway, doing his best to distance himself from the too-heavy, too-raw wave of grief. Horris closed his eyes and took another deep breath.

Death was not uncommon in the USSPS. Some couriers had to traverse the New Edge of the United Star System, and not all travel was kind. Sometimes accidents happened aboard ships; sometimes, couriers weren't prepared for the rigors of homeworlds and colonies. Even grounded agents could get sick or injured. But it was rare—very rare, almost unheard of—for someone to *kill* a courier. USSPS was the heartblood of the universe, after all. Everyone understood that.

He reopened his eyes to see Olive's sympathetic expression and the way Perseus shifted uncomfortably. "We'll need names and identifiers," Horris said. "For their families."

"Of course," Olive said gently. She tucked her dark hair behind her ear. "When we saw your ship, we thought, maybe, that a message had managed to get through. And that you were here to help. I volunteered to scout you all out...which is where I ran into all those bugs." She stretched her bandaged arms out with a sigh.

"Insects," Horris corrected absentmindedly. He rubbed his palms over his thighs. "We'll send a message up when we go. The Inspectors won't stand for the death of USSPS personnel."

"*If* you go," Olive said. "If *we* saw you, chances are you came up on the pirates' radar too. They won't let you leave."

"Where are these pirates?" Roddy asked. "What do you know about them?"

"They circle by periodically. Opportunistic bastards preying on undefended colonists. Their leader is a Marquay named Silver." Olive touched a hand to her curled horns. She was a Marquay, too, and seemed to be taking Silver's villainy personally. "They'll want a tithe from you."

Horris blinked. That didn't make a lick of sense. "USSPS is protected by sanctions."

"Pirates like these don't care about sanctions," Olive said. "They'll take whatever they want from your hold and consider that fair exchange."

That was salt on the stinging wound. These pirates, this Silver, had killed USSPS agents, terrorized innocents, and now threatened their cargo. Fury rose hot and fast, boiling away the heavy grief in his stomach.

"We're not going to let that happen," Horris said, low and furious. Fives took a sharp breath.

Olive nodded, bolstered by his response. "You'll need to talk to Estelle, then. She's the leader of the Idolers here."

"We need to deliver packages while we're here anyway," Horris said. He glanced at his crew: Basah looked unhappy but did not voice her objections in front of strangers. Roddy, on the other hand, had sat forward. "First light, we'll head into town with you."

She nodded once before her gaze went to Perseus. "I don't suppose there's any chance you could leave the Imp bound and gagged aboard your ship while we go?"

"No." Horris didn't think twice, didn't so much as hesitate. Multiple eyebrows around the table arched, and only then did Horris realize he was going to need to explain himself. He focused on Olive, all the better to ignore the looks from Basah and Roddy. "We'll need all hands for deliveries tomorrow, and we can't leave non-USSPS personnel aboard the ship without a crewman present."

Olive said nothing. Instead, she picked up her tea, blew away the steam, and took a small sip. Across the table, Perseus rolled his shoulders back.

Tomorrow was going to be hell, Horris thought. Assuming they even made it through tonight.

■

Olive and Perseus bunked down for the evening: Perseus in his broom closet, Olive in the bunk Roddy had graciously yielded to her. If Perseus had a complaint about a crewman being willing to give up a bunk for her and not for him, he did not voice it.

Only when their guests had settled down (and BLIP covertly set to monitor them) did Horris call a crew meeting. They met in the cargo hold. Horris paced while Basah leaned against a shelf, watching him with narrowed eyes. Fives sat criss-cross on the floor, and Roddy had clambered up to a higher shelf to sit above them all. A quiet attempt to catch their collective breath followed.

"This is dangerous territory," Basah said. She kept her tone even, although her thrashing tail gave her away.

"Agreed," Roddy said from above. He stretched his long legs out along a pile of packages. "Look, I know we've got to recover that last depot agent. We can't just leave 'em here. But what if this Silver shows up in the meantime? We're not equipped for a fight."

Horris stopped pacing long enough to look up. "BLIP?"

Analyzing...analyzing...no spacefaring vessels detected within thirty kilometers of the Silverfish. Pilot Roderick Marcelo is paranoid.

Roddy scowled. Horris shook his head. "It's not paranoia if they really are out to get you, buddy." He rubbed his face, fighting exhaustion. He managed to fend off the first wave before addressing Basah: "If a pirate ship gets within thirty kilometers, how fast can we be airborne?"

"Five minutes," Basah replied. "If we ignore all safety protocols."

Horris hated the sound of that. He massaged his throbbing temples. Five minutes with a warning. Five minutes, assuming they were willing to ignore all safety protocols…which they would have to if pirates were bearing down on them. What else could they do? The Silverfish was fast enough to outpace most ships, but if Silver and his crew opened fire…it was better to make it into the outersphere battered and bruised than not make it at all. He cast a gloomy look around the cargo hold, making a mental note to re-secure everything before bed.

"…Horry?"

Basah's voice jolted Horris out of his thoughts. He blinked and looked down at Basah. "Huh?"

"I said, what are we going to do with the Imperial?" Basah said. Her tail continued to swing wildly. "We're going right into Idoler territory. If they demand his head, what are we going to do about it?"

The question didn't make immediate sense to Horris. "Perseus is with us. As a client of USSPS. We already agreed on this."

"They're zealots, Horry," Roddy said from above. Basah snapped her fingers and pointed to Roddy. "All of them. Olive went after the Imperial just for standing there. And if Imperials are as vicious as she's claiming they are…"

"Are they?" Horris asked. At his feet, Fives heaved a sigh.

Roddy rolled his eyes. "Listen, man. No group calling themselves the Black Hammers is doing charitable works to help orphans and widows. If our Imperial is responsible for hurting people, aren't they due their justice?"

Perhaps they were. Horris had to wonder what Idoler justice looked like and whether Perseus deserved it. He had to have fought in battles. The more he turned the thought over in his head, the more jagged it grew. Horris shook his head and looked down at Fives.

Fives looked back at him with guileless eyes. "You want to believe he's not dangerous. It's easier to bring all the threads together if he doesn't hurt anyone."

Basah arched her eyebrows. A soft, amused noise escaped Roddy.

Horris looked back at his crew, trying not to feel like he'd just been backed into a corner. "He's a deserter, right? And if Creed Imperials are as vicious as you keep saying they are, he has to know what happens if he's found out by other Imperials. Maybe the Idolers are his best chance at staying alive. We won't know until we know."

"And the pirates?" Roddy pressed.

"BLIP, set up alarms to sound if any vehicles come within an eight-kilometer range of the *Silverfish* from any direction."

Acknowledged.

Horris lowered his gaze back down to the others. "And the rest, we'll just have to adjust as we go."

Basah sighed as she unfolded her arms. She crossed to Fives and tugged him gently to his feet. "You better put in OT for this, Horry."

After that, the crew managed to bed down for a few hours of sleep. All save Horris, who returned to the mess to make a nice, strong cup of cocoa. It had been his comfort drink since he was small. His mother used to sprinkle cinnamon on top; of course, powder wasn't allowed in space vessels, so he settled for a packet of liquid cinnamon instead. He stood, bleary-eyed, watching the swirl of cinnamon in his cocoa.

"You do realize it could be a trap, yes?"

Perseus slid out of the shadows, grim-faced and pale. He'd taken the time to comb his hair, although nothing could be done about the rumpled state of his uniform now. Horris wondered if he took as much pride in it as he did his own uniform.

He picked up his cocoa and blew on it. "What's a trap, now?"

"Olive. This whole wounded animal gambit. It's a classic trap. Lure you in, lower your defenses with false sympathy and some sob story, and then *snap!*" He snapped his fingers. "The trap closes. She could be an agent of this Silver."

"Fives would have told us if she was lying," Horris said. He took his first sip of cocoa and watched the way Perseus struggled for a comeback.

"Your phrenic," he said at last. "How did you come by him?"

"He's not *my* phrenic. Fives is his own man. He chooses to work for us."

"Phrenics guide governments and economies. They serve as body-guards, assassins, and interrogators. They're advisors, not *postmen.*"

The sudden venom in Perseus' voice caught Horris off-guard. He'd never met a phrenic besides Fives. They existed in whispers, mostly rumors of people who could detect an assassin before they struck or predict the way a world's economy would turn. If an order of phrenics existed, none had ever come looking for their renegade brother. Fives himself had admitted he would have no idea what would happen if he met another phrenic, and the idea of an infinite feedback loop of emotions had almost brought him to tears.

"Have you met many phrenics?" Horris asked.

"One was the headmaster of the military academy I graduated from. Liaison Nabis. A strong, passionate man. Not nearly as off-put-ting as your phrenic."

Off-putting. That was how most people referred to Fives. Those that didn't take the time to get to know him, at any rate. Those who wrote him off immediately as weird and spooky. "You just haven't gotten to know Fives yet, that's all."

Perseus stared at him. He had pale eyes, Horris thought idly, green eyes that burned like the Wreath Nebula. Perseus wrenched his gaze away when he moved to stand at the counter beside Horris. He paused before reaching for the packets of hot cocoa. "Do you always assume the best of everyone?"

"I try to." Horris programmed the espresso machine for Perseus. It was a compact little device made for space-faring vessels and had been one of the first things on the list when the union demanded fair working conditions for USSPS conveyances.

"That sounds exhausting."

"It can be. Sometimes."

Conversation lapsed while they both watched the water boil in the espresso machine. Only when Perseus had his own steaming mug in hand did Horris continue the game of Twenty Questions: "What's a Black Hammer?"

Perseus fixed him with a look. He sipped his cocoa, grimaced at the heat, and then sighed. "The small elite of His Glory's army. I am a commissioned officer. A Lieutenant."

Horris tilted his head to the side. He studied Perseus again, head to toe. He was a small man, more lithe than muscular, and no younger than twenty. He would have fit right in among the twenty-some-things hired by the USSPS. "You seem a bit young for a CO. No offense, of course."

On the contrary, Perseus actually *chuckled*. "Black Hammer training is very intensive," he replied. His expression soured, and he took refuge in the contents of his cocoa mug. "That's why your new friend was so hostile to my appearance. Idolers don't take kindly to the Emperor's elite forces. Even this far from home."

"Are you in danger here?"

The question escaped Horris before he could stop himself. Perseus had abandoned his post, his people, and his position among the Black Hammers. But Olive had still wanted him bound and gagged. And she was only a scout. What would this Idoler leader, this Estelle, want from Perseus?

Perseus blinked. He seemed more surprised by the concern in Horris' voice than the question itself. He shook his head. "Idolers pose no threat to me. Godless masses are no match for His Glory's ordained forces."

"Then…why did you run?"

Perseus opened his mouth. Closed it. For half a heartbeat, Horris thought he would get a mug of scalding hot cocoa thrown in his face. But instead, Perseus just snorted. "You're shrewder than you let on, Captain Jensen."

"Thank you," Horris tried to smile. Something in his expression must have rung true because Perseus managed a little half-spasm of his lips in return.

They stood in silence for a time, nursing their cocoa and their private thoughts. Horris had almost drained his cup and was about to finish it off when Perseus spoke again: "Since I cannot be left unsupervised aboard your ship, I surmise I will be going with you tomorrow. May I borrow a USSPS uniform or plain clothes?"

"I…yes, of course, that's fine." He hadn't put that far of thought into it, but it made sense. Perseus was of a size with Fives, and Idolers would probably react worse to the sight of an Imperial uniform.

"You didn't think I'd go without a fight," Perseus said, now visibly amused by Horris' uncertainty.

"Well." Horris didn't know how to politely tell Perseus he hadn't exactly done *anything* without a fight so far. "Yeah."

To that, Perseus shrugged. "On the off chance that this is a trap, you'll need someone with combat experience with you. I swore an oath that no harm would come to you, and I intend to keep that oath. I am a deserter. That doesn't mean I'm a coward."

"I–if you're sure…"

"I am. Besides, you are my way to Apollonia. I need to keep you alive to get there." He knocked back the last of his cocoa and set the mug aside. "Thank you for the drink, Captain Horris."

Horris inclined his head. "Sleep well, Perseus."

"You as well."

He left Horris standing in the mess, nursing his lukewarm drink and picking through his exhausted thoughts.

7 Customer Satisfaction Guaranteed

United Star System Postal Code, Chapter 5, Section 3: Whoever has charge of a mail vessel is required to deliver all letters and packages brought within their control.

Basah woke first and woke early.

She lay flat in her bunk, staring at the ceiling overhead as the fog of sleep dissipated. A low groan escaped her as she ran a hand down the side of her face. She was halfway down her mental to-do list before she remembered exactly where they were and why.

"BLIP?"

Good morning, Engineer Basah Anasem!

"Is everyone aboard the *Silverfish* still alive?"

Yes! No one died in the middle of the night. Furthermore, there have been no signals of other space-worthy vessels detected in the last few hours.

Basah exhaled in relief. "Thanks, bud."

You're very welcome!

She smiled. BLIP was Fives' brainchild. Whatever he lacked in social graces, he made up for in software engineering. BLIP had been programmed with all of Fives' best manners and could easily communicate whatever Fives struggled with. No doubt their phrenic had also been awake all night, listening for ill intent. It wasn't like Fives slept much anyway.

Basah sat up and stretched. She swung out of her bunk, stretched again, and dressed in one of her many standard-issue cerulean coveralls. She pulled on her boots, standard-issue but sturdy, and zipped up the sides. She paused in the mirror to detangle her chin-length hair. Her hair—dyed teal, tipped with a lurid orange—was a point of vanity Basah allowed herself, and it looked damn good today.

She paused again at her cabin door. She loved Horris too much to deny him, but the day ahead seemed too long to be truly worth it. They were post office workers, Matrons damn it, and their duties began and ended with the mail. Deliver the packages, retrieve the unfortunate depot worker, and get the hell off Delta Io before someone noticed they were here. If they had to leave the Imperial behind, well…his box would still arrive in Apollonia, and Basah would consider that a job accomplished. Political adversaries and pirates were not in their pay grade.

Still…

Still, better to be out here, tripping over political adversaries and pirates, than to remain at home. At home, she would have wasted her days nursing kits while older matrons discussed marriages and diplomacy. She'd escaped that hell, thank you very much. She escaped matronhood as much as Horris and Roddy had escaped Grand York and Fives had escaped his fate. Perhaps that's why Horris was so keen on keeping Perseus onboard. He understood runaways. More than he ever let on.

Basah traced her fingertips along the walls of the *Silverfish* as she walked. No one knew a ship better than her engineer, and no one loved her better, even when she misbehaved. "Good morning, lovely lady," Basah murmured. It was a small ritual of good luck. She poked her head into the engine room and checked the readings to ensure all was well.

Only then did she descend down into the hold. Dim lights hummed to life as she stepped through the rows and rows of secured packages and envelopes. Basah rolled her shoulders back, pulled her tablet off her belt, and got to work.

Basah enjoyed steady, rhythmic work. Scanning labels and sorting packages allowed her mind to drift where it wanted. And now, it drifted back towards the Imperials and the Idolers. She knew more than Horris or Roddy—she took her Civics classes quite seriously, and the matrons always skewed towards more martial peoples for xenomarriages. The Imperials of Creed were one such martial people, although their reverence of their Emperor put them lower on the list of matches than others. Their natural enemies were the Idolers: those who rejected the divinity of the Emperor. They'd been at war for years, although Basah couldn't recall when or why the conflict had escalated to full violence. She couldn't blame Perseus for wanting to get out, even if she did think him a coward. She couldn't even blame Horris for wanting to keep him safe. But none of their baggage had ever landed them in the middle of an active warzone. And none of the *Silverfish* crew had ever killed anyone. Although Fives…

"I don't want to go back there."

Basah jumped. She spun on her heel to smile at the tousle-haired Fives. "Hey. What's up?"

"I don't want to go back there," Fives repeated. He held out a granola bar and a flask marked with an orange. "Breakfast instead."

Thanks, Fiver.

Fives smiled that fluttery, nervous smile of his, the one that meant he really was quite pleased. His fingers fluttered, playing over each other with spidery softness. Basah smiled and ran a hand through Fives' dark hair. He fell into step beside her. The work went quicker with two.

What do you think of all this?

Fives studied the pile of parcels critically. "A lot of packages for one place." He shot Basah a look when he felt her subsequent amusement.

Sorry. What do you think about the Idolers and the Imperials? Perseus?

Fives flicked a lock of black hair out of his eyes. "Idolers want the truth. Imperials think they have it. Either Idolers submit, or Imperials admit they're wrong."

What is the truth?

Fives shrugged. "Whatever it needs to be."

And Perseus? Can we trust him?

"He's too quiet. A hole in the sheet of music that makes the universe. But quiet can be…preferable. You need silence between songs. Or else they all blend together."

In plain words, Fiver.

Fives sighed deeply. "He listens when Horris speaks."

Basah paused in her scanning to stare at Fives. "Are you kidding? He barely follows orders!"

"I am not a goat. I am not a *kid*. And he is not a crewman. He doesn't have to follow orders. But he listens when Horris speaks. When Horris says wait–stop–*no violence*–Perseus listens. That's what soldiers do."

Basah mulled that over for a long moment. Listening and obeying were the same thing as far as Mefane mothers and matrons were concerned, and she herself couldn't find the same distinction Fives seemed to. She shook her head and resolved to put Perseus aside for the moment. "And Olive? What about her?"

"You think she's pretty," Fives said under his breath. A corner of his mouth twitched upwards.

It was Basah's turn to shoot him a look. "Fiver."

His smile grew, pleased with himself before he turned his gaze back to the bin of mail in front of him. "She wants to believe the best of us. USSPS customer service. Best in the galaxy."

Basah thought she detected the slightest edge of sarcasm in Fives' tone. She shared one commiserating look with him before returning to work.

By the time Horris joined them, the sorting had been completed, and now they were loading the pile of packages onto the speeder. Horris glanced over the manifest once before lending his considerable muscles to the loading effort.

One didn't need to be a phrenic to know Horris hadn't gotten much sleep; Basah prided herself on her ability to pick up minute details, and the way Horris kept double-checking the manifest betrayed his sleepy confusion. But Basah held her tongue and surreptitiously double-checked everything Horris loaded.

At some point, BLIP dinged overhead. It cheerily announced that it was now quarter past seven (adjusted for local time), and Roderick was about to be late for work. Fives immediately perked up and volunteered to go to Roddy's rescue. He didn't wait for the okay from Horris—he simply set his package down next to Basah and walked off.

Basah didn't bother looking up from the stack of manila folders in her hand. Roddy liked to blare music first thing in the morning, some bizarre ritual that he insisted woke his brain up for the day. And Fives, ever in need of noise to drown out the rest, was drawn like a saltstone moth to volcanic flame. Basah's attention was fixed wholly on those manila folders. They were marked like most scams and promotions: DELIVER TO SOLELY TO JOHN SMITH and SECOND NOTICE - LIMITED TIME OFFER. Insurance offers, most likely, pushed out the door by the last gasp of Creedence capitalists. She wondered if the offices still stood. Would policies be void if the databases were blown to kingdom come?

Horris' deep yawn roused her from her thoughts. Basah set the manila folders aside and oh-so-casually picked up the stack Horris had been shifting through. "No pirates in the middle of the night. Did you stay up watching for them?"

"Yeah." Horris pinched the bridge of his nose. "Watching the radars. Nothing. I don't know if that's good news or bad news."

Bad news, in Basah's opinion. Roddy had picked up that gray ship on their radar right before the jump; maybe it was nothing, but nothing rarely razed backwater towns and blasted postships out of the sky. It didn't take a mechanical engineer to know that an express ship like the *Silverfish* could outspeed most ships, even allowing for undocking. If Basah were looking to take out a postie vessel, she'd wait until the crew was off their ship, guard lowered, and then rush the poor bastards. But Horris was a frustratingly eternal optimist; he would take the lack of action as a good sign. It would be up to her, then, to stay alert.

By the time Fives clocked Roddy in and dragged him out of bed (in that order), the crew had moved on to loading up the scooters with their packages. The lurid blue scooters were USSPS standard, large enough to fit two riders with flat trays on either side for packages and a crate in the back for envelopes.

Fuel-inefficient and prone to dying at the slightest inconvenience, the cheap piece-of-shit scooters were the bane of Basah's existence. She had spent long hours arguing with Horris over the value of making modifications to the scooters, only to be rebuffed again and again because modifying USSPS property would earn them a fine.

So Basah had gone ahead and done it privately anyway.

She was in the middle of checking the circuit breaker (piece-of-shit little bastard that liked to blow randomly to keep things interesting) when Fives and Roddy finally rejoined them. Roddy was speaking animatedly to Fives about some old Earth musician, flinging his long arms out to conduct an imaginary big band. Fives' dark eyes were wide and round and attentive. "Gershwin," he said.

"Yeah, yeah, you get it! All the greats die young, y'know? It's like some contract you sign when you make it down to reality. You'll be a genius, but you can't live past the age of fifty." Roddy ruffled Fives' dark hair affectionately, causing the smaller man to swat him away and go find Horris.

Basah shot Roddy a look as he meandered over to finally start working. "You better not be putting ideas in his head about dying young."

"Whomst, me?" Roddy pressed a hand to his thin chest. "*Never*. Besides, if anyone present is going to drop dead at the ripe old age of twenty-seven, it's Saint Horris."

"*Roderick!*" Basah hissed. She flattened her ears in sudden fury.

Roddy held up his hands in a gesture of innocence. "Just sayin'. The company you keep and all." He nodded towards the door, where Olive and Perseus had both appeared. They were blessedly unbloodied, although both maintained a pointed lack of eye contact as they stepped down into the hold.

Roddy slunk away to look busy elsewhere. Basah forced her temper down as Olive made her way over. "How're your hands?"

"Bruised and sore," Olive said. She held out her bandaged hands for inspection. "But I still have all ten fingers. I even managed to get a full night's rest in proximity to an Imp."

Even dressed in a striped button-down and khakis, there was no mistaking Perseus for a civilian. They watched him march over to Horris, where he stood with shoulders squared and hands folded behind his back. He didn't offer to help Horris with the loading, but neither did he react to Olive's audible goading. He just lifted his chin and set his expression like the world's worst-disguised bodyguard.

"Maybe there's something to all this *former* Hammer business after all," Olive mused.

Basah flipped the circuit breaker off, moderately satisfied with its performance. "Do you think he would have tried something?" She asked in a lowered voice.

"No true son of the Emperor should have allowed a heretic to live," Olive shrugged as if threats to her life were so commonplace. Maybe they were. "Or maybe he just knows he's outnumbered."

"Maybe it's a miracle," Basah muttered. She grinned when Olive snorted.

Erelong, they had guided the scooters down the gangplank and out into the fresh air. Basah and Horris drove the scooters, leaving everyone else to clamber aboard as passengers. Deerfly corpses littered the landing dock; some still buzzed feebly, while others popped and cracked under the heavy tread of the scooters. Mountains of black ash piled high around the external engines.

Basah swallowed the queasy taste in her throat. Flies. So what? There were plenty more flies in the swamp. And maybe a field of dead insects would deter any would-be looters. It wouldn't, she knew, and she sounded like Horris for even thinking it.

The captain, in all his optimistic wisdom, had deigned they would all go together into Icene. BLIP had full access and authority to the *Silverfish* in the meantime, with the mandate to signal Horris if any other ships came within a hundred kilometers of their own. Basah had done the math. Assuming they dropped everything and ran, and assuming neither scooter crapped out on the road, they *might* be airborne by the time another vessel swooped down.

Olive shared her misgivings, although she also seemed to appreciate the company of others. She gave Basah's abdomen a small squeeze as they barreled down the muddy road out of the swamp. "Are you sure your ship is secure?"

"Better than a Ruckan bank," Basah replied. She maneuvered around a rock in the middle of the road. "Are all Io roads this crappy?"

"Worse than a Ruckan lover," Olive said, and when she laughed, Basah smiled.

As far as backwater planets went, Delta Io was pleasant enough. After a few minutes, the winding, muddy road converged into a proper dirt road. The tree coverage overhead began to thin, and the fetid smell of swamp cleared. Tall sentinel trees towered overhead, and the sky was a marbled pattern of blue and gray.

"How long has the Icene colony been here?" Basah asked.

"Three years, although the deal was in the works well before that. Adastra wanted a place out of Creed where her people could live and thrive, and the Empire wanted the upstarts out of their system. But, y'know, it's a hard thing to ask people to leave their homes and set up somewhere new. So Adastra put Estelle in charge of Icene while she stayed behind to drum up support. Everything was fine at first. Then…everything escalated, the rebellion began, and we had pirates on our doorstep demanding tribute."

"And the Imperials are behind the pirates."

Basah felt Olive nod against her. "Who else? The timing's convenient enough, what with everyone willing and able to fight gone."

"What about you?"

"I'm a primary school aide. Not much use in a holy war for my skillset."

They must have been in dire straits indeed if a children's aide was the closest thing they had to a scout. Basah pushed the troubling thought away. They were here to deliver the mail, retrieve the depot agent, and get the hell out of dodge. That was *it*. Their skillset didn't lend itself well to a holy war either.

"They learn new things now," Fives said sadly.

It took less than ten minutes before the swamp and forest gave way to a clearing, and the first parapets of Icene emerged over the horizon. Icene looked very much like any other frontier town: like crap. Worse than crap, actually–thanks to the pirates, Icene looked like shit. High stone walls had been melted to black lumps. Hastily made wooden flats stood in place of proper gates; the immediate clearing around town had been scorched, leaving nothing but gray ash and blackened dirt.

Basah stared at the ruins and did not think about what it must have felt like to hide behind those melting walls. What it must have looked like—*sounded* like—superheated stone glowing white-hot in the night. Fives made a soft, mournful noise at her back. Roddy had that cool, disaffected look on his face; Horris, bless him, couldn't even pretend to be unbothered. But Perseus…

Perseus looked *troubled*.

Olive scooted off the bike and gave a sharp, three-note whistle. No reply came, but nevertheless, she strode to the makeshift gate and pushed it open. It gave way with a long, whining shriek. The coast must have been clear, for she waved both scooters forward into the village proper.

Icene's interior was no more appealing: their scooters puttered past shells of buildings and shattered walkways, abandoned businesses, and empty homes. Something metallic creaked in the distance. No animals, Basah noted, and even straining over the humming engines, she heard nothing. No birds, no dogs. Life had fled this place.

Icene was not a large settlement. Olive gave directions, turning them down this street and then another until they reached a sprawling green common. Here, at least, the damage wasn't as significant: most of the buildings around the common still had intact windows, and only a few bore char marks. All the buildings had that squat, brick-make of government buildings, and the tallest of the untouched structures seemed to be a church or community center of sorts. It pierced straight upwards into the marbled sky to end in a sharp spire.

Silence reigned when the two scooters came to a stop in the middle of the green. No one moved. Then—

"HOLD!"

Steel flashed from one of the spired building's windows. Basah froze with one boot on the grass. Guns? Here? They had *guns*?

"ANNOUNCE YOURSELF!" The voice demanded.

"Let me handle this," Olive murmured. At a nod from Horris, she slid off the bike and walked around its front. She raised both hands and faced the spire. "Olive Zask! These outworlders are posties! They're here to help!"

The doors of the spired building swung open. A tall, strapping, olive-skinned woman swept out onto the green. Her long brown coat snapped out behind her, making her look larger than she actually was. Her gaze swept around two scooters before landing on Olive.

"Olive," the tall woman's voice was brisk. If she was relieved to see Olive alive, her voice betrayed none of it. "We feared the worst. Are you all right?"

"Fine. A little roughed up, but I could be a lot worse off. This is the crew of the *Silverfish*...and a guest."

The tall woman's gaze searched them again. Her gaze lingered on the plain-clothed Perseus.

Sudden noise and movement sounded from behind them. Basah fought the urge to look. There was no need: it was the sounds of boots hitting gravel, windows and doors creaking open, and the sudden breath of fifty or so onlookers. They were flanked by the remaining residents of Icene. Basah watched as Olive pulled the tall woman to the side and whispered in her ear.

"What's the call, Captain?" She asked in a low voice.

"Smile and nod," Horris murmured back. "And hope they want their mail."

Roddy shifted in place behind Horris. "What's the crowd's vibe, Fiver? Are we about to die?"

"*Rod!*"

Fives shook his head as Basah hissed. He reached up and pressed his hands to his headphones as though trying to force the music through his skull. "Loud," he whispered. "Too many thoughts, too many feelings. Pounding like flies against glass. They don't want to hope...but they have to."

Perseus remained stone-faced and silent. He might as well not have been present at all.

After what seemed like an eternity, the tall woman straightened and approached Horris' scooter. "Captain Horris Jensen, is it?" She stuck a hand out to shake. "Estelle Malornin. Thank you for all that you've done for us already."

Horris accepted the handshake. Then Estelle pulled her hand back and held it up. She splayed her fingers out as though going for a high-five. Perseus made a sharp, sudden noise of disgust.

Estelle smiled thinly and lowered her hand. "Ah. So there *is* an Imperial among you. Or are *you* with *him*?"

Basah bit back a sharp retort. She could see Horris doing the minute calculations, trapped between his own authority as a captain and the fact that he was no longer on his ship. She had no patience for etiquette, no head for the little games one was meant to play in politics. *We saved Olive's life*, she wanted to snap, *shouldn't that be enough for you?*

"I believe we are owed some benefit of the doubt," Horris said at last, "given that we're here with your agent, and we've come unarmed. Perhaps we could speak inside while my crew delivers packages? I understand you've been tending to a depot agent here as well."

Estelle considered his earnest expression. "Very well. But I want the Imperial in chains." She jerked her head, and there was a sudden rush of movement from the surrounding residents. Perseus sat up sharply.

Horris sprang up after him, hands raised in an echo of that high-five gesture. "That won't be necessary," he said.

"I refuse to believe any Idoler is safe with an Imperial present." Estelle retorted. Behind her, Olive's expression twisted.

Stupid, stubborn, brave Horris shook his head. "USSPS by-laws, section eight, subsection three, article three-point-one. All passengers who've paid postage fall under the jurisdiction of the USSPS authority. You cannot confiscate anything of ours. Including guests aboard our ship. I'll vouch for his conduct."

Estelle studied Horris for a long moment before nodding. "With me, then." Estelle turned on her heel and walked back to the spired building.

Basah shot Perseus a sharp look. If he so much as *breathed* imperially, Horris was dead. And the Black Hammer better pray to his Emperor that he was right behind him because if the Idolers didn't get him, she would.

Perseus seemed to glean all that with a small nod.

"Be careful, Horris," Basah muttered. "If you die, then I'm in charge, and neither of us wants that."

"Agreed," Horris said. He unclipped his helmet and held it against his hip. Curiously enough, he didn't look at Perseus, although the redhead now stared a hole in the back of his head. "Let me know if there's any issues."

"Loud and clear."

Even so, Basah didn't move off the scooter until the heavy wooden doors had closed behind Horris and Perseus. Only then did she turn to Roddy and Fives. "You heard him, boys. Time to start scanning."

The crowd had not dissipated. If anything, more seemed to be joining by the moment. They were a decent mix of sentients: lean Men and horned Marquay, willowy Elentee, scaled Sem, and four-armed Gundobad. Disparate as their species were, though, all had that bleary-eyed look of suspicion. Basah began the inglorious task of undoing all their carefully-loaded work. Roddy, meanwhile, grabbed the scanner from his belt and began to scan envelopes. He held it aloft to the crowd.

"I've got a letter here for a Solomon Gurk!" He called out. He adopted that charming, lopsided grin of his. "Solomon Gurk, are you here?"

Silence. Then, the crowd parted. An aged Gundobad lumbered out of the crowd and up to Roddy. He held out a hand big enough to wrap around Roddy's thin waist and snap. Roddy glanced at Fives, who nodded and then smiled up at Solomon Gurk. "For you," he said, setting the letter in the massive outstretched palm.

The dam broke. Suddenly, there were people all around them, forming lines, calling out that so-and-so wasn't here, but they could take the package for them, asking, "Do you mean John Smith from Eleven Apple Orchard Road or John Smith from Fifty-One Main Street?" Children darted between the legs of parents and guardians, excitedly comparing packages from grandparents and relatives. A few

Idolers soberly took it upon themselves to accept mail in the name of the dead.

Basah sank into the task. She let Roddy be the pleasant face while she and Fives did the sorting and the handing off. Grab, scan, sort, grab, scan, sort—she didn't break out of her rhythm until she saw one name printed neatly on a package. It was small and square, no bigger than a music box, wrapped in brown paper and twine.

"Olive–this is yours. Package for you."

Olive had remained nearby, watching the crowd with an anxious air. She started when Basah extended the small package out to her. Basah watched her read the return address and how her expression softened. She accepted the package gently. "Can I open it now?"

"Of course! I just need you to sign here," Basah held out her tablet with her other hand.

Olive signed off that her package had been received in good condition. She began to undo the twine, visibly holding back tremors as she broke the wrapping. She stopped there, just short of pulling the package free from its wrapping. Olive closed her eyes and pressed the small box to her chest. A soft "thank you" escaped her.

Basah, as a rule, did not feel whatever Horris felt when he delivered the mail. But it was hard, in that moment, to deny why he did it. "We're USSPS, ma'am," she said. "It's what we do."

Olive broke away to finish opening her package alone. The crowd had begun to thin now, enough that Roddy could arch an eyebrow at Basah. "I think we're getting in too deep."

"I know," Basah admitted. She wiped her hand across her face. "But we can't leave without retrieving that postie."

"I'm not talking about the postie. *The USSPS takes no part in foreign politics,* remember? If they ask for the Imperial's head, do you think Horris has it in him to say no?"

"No," Basah sighed. She hoped Horris was addressing whatever was happening inside with his head and not his heart. "Good thing

Horris has all the rules memorized, right? By-law whatever-the-hell number it was."

"Section eight, subsection three, article three-point-one," Fives put in. He was flicking through the remaining pile of envelopes idly.

"Thanks, Fiver—"

"It's not real."

Basah pivoted back to Fives, hoping beyond hope that she had heard that wrong. "What was that, Fiver?"

"USSPS bylaws section eight, subsection three, article three-point-one," Fives recited. He blinked at Basah and Roddy both. "It's not *real*. But Horris had to make it real, to be believed. He had to make it real in his heart."

"Horris lied?" Basah demanded, aghast.

Fives' too-dark eyes pinned her. It was one of those terrifying looks he was capable of, the sort that pierced right through you and drained you dry of everything you kept hidden. "How else are we going to get out of here alive?"

🔳 A Promise Made

United Star System Postal Code, Chapter 12, Section 1: The United Star System Postal Service provides workers compensation to employees injured at work for assistance in medical expenses and lost wages.

"Thank you."

It was the first thing Perseus had said all morning, and it was spoken so softly Horris almost didn't hear him. Horris half-turned back to Perseus with a slight smile. "Well, I'm only following protocols."

It was the truth—well, half of it, at least. The by-laws Horris had pulled from his metaphorical back pocket didn't exist, but the spirit of the law was there. Perseus was a guest aboard his ship, a package stamped and paid for, and therefore under his protection.

Besides, only he and the Postmaster General read the by-laws anyway.

"You didn't have to do that," Perseus said, still in that same soft voice.

No. He didn't. Horris could hear Basah in his ear, angrily demanding why they were going out of their way to protect this Imperial, this *Black Hammer*, from harm. What if he was a killer, a murderer complicit in the crimes that had nearly destroyed this settlement? What if he planned to do more harm? What if, what if, *what if*—

But what good were those oaths they'd sworn to each other over pizza if he folded at the slightest resistance?

For Perseus, though, Horris just smiled. "We're bonded, remember?"

Perseus stared up at him. His mouth did that odd spasm thing when he tried to smile.

The building Estelle had brought them into was a community center of sorts, although aesthetically, it resembled a church. Something about the dim lighting and the narrow corridors reminded Horris of the churches back in Grand York, even if the corkboards on the walls were full of notices for community events instead of psalms. Instead of incense, a medicinal smell hung in the air, a sharp smell of antiseptic that made Horris' nose twitch. He pushed the burgeoning memories down to focus on the present.

Estelle led them into an arts and crafts room: the long, low table and carpeted floor could have been used for anything, but the macaroni art taped to the cabinets gave it away.

"Hungry?" Estelle asked. She yanked a cabinet door open and pulled out a box of granola bars. She shook one into her palm and held it out towards Horris.

This, of all things, was not what Horris expected. He took the granola bar cautiously.

Estelle opened a second granola bar. She lifted it in a vague toast towards Horris. "By our grace, we receive this bounty. By our grace, we live another day. What is yours has been given unto me. What is mine shall be given unto you until the debt is paid. By our own grace, we are bonded." She ended by biting off the end of the granola bar.

It was the same oath Perseus had sworn, albeit edited. Horris didn't know what to make of the new version…but even at his angle, he could see Perseus' darkening expression.

"You're a *blasphemer*," Perseus spat.

"And *you're* a deserter," Estelle replied. She was calm, even amused by Perseus' pointless rage. "So let's not throw stones, Imperial. What's your name?"

"Third Lieutenant Perseus Warden," Perseus said. He'd gone very, very stiff.

"Warden?" Estelle's eyes narrowed sharply. "As in, Admiral Warden?"

Horris scarfed down his granola bar on the off-chance they were about to be thrown off the planet.

"We have the pleasure of being related, yes."

"What are you doing in this colony?"

"Waiting to leave, mostly. I've made an arrangement with the captain of the *Silverfish* for safe passage to Apollonia. That we have been detained here as long as we have is a regrettable happenstance."

"Regrettable," Estelle repeated, dubious. "You understand how this looks to us. We've barely begun the process of rebuilding when an Imperial shows up on our doorstep. How can you expect us to believe that you'd leave us alone, vulnerable as we are? How do I know you're not at the head of some fleet bearing down on us?"

Fleets? Surely Horris had misheard. Or Estelle had misspoken. Everyone knew and accepted the politics of interstellar commerce: planetary rivals took potshots at each other, using pirates and mercenaries to sabotage trade routes or waystations, while neutral parties like USSPS filled the needs all societies had. But *fleets?* Fleets were for *oceans.* Large-scale military maneuvers in space were too complex, too time-consuming, and most of all, too *expensive* for even the most united of planets to attempt. Surely Creed, bogged down in its own holy war as it was, didn't have those sorts of resources.

"If I wanted you all dead, I would have come at the head of the fleet," said Perseus, "not as part of a postal convey. There is no subterfuge here."

Estelle's free hand tightened into a fist. "Forgive me if I doubt your assurances. I've yet to meet a trustworthy Imperial."

"And I've yet to meet an Idoler who'll trust the truth before their eyes." Perseus flicked his gaze up and down Estelle's frame dismissively. "And yet."

Estelle took a full step forward. Horris stepped sideways, between Estelle and Perseus, with both hands raised. "USSPS is a neutral entity. We take no part in wars, no part in conflicts. We would never knowingly bring a hostile entity into civilian territory."

"And yet, you did." Estelle countered. Her hand strayed to her hip, to the holster of some barely-concealed weapon. "Even postmen can be bought."

A low rumble of warning sounded from behind Horris. Horris lowered a hand and pressed back against Perseus even as the Imperial pressed forward. Now was not the time for aggression. They were in the minority here, and—unfortunately—Estelle was right. They had brought an Imperial into Idoler territory. A show of good faith was necessary here.

"I understand you have another postman in your care. Someone who was attacked by the pirate, Silver. He's been harassing your settlement."

"Harassing," Estelle scoffed, "that's a word for it. Half our town decimated, off-world communication offline, food and medicine supplies dwindling...and that's without counting our dead."

"What does this Silver want?"

"What does any bully want? Extortion. Protection money. Pay him or his price." Estelle shook her head in disgust. "He's given us time to contemplate our options. Should we accept, he'll drain our resources dry. Should we refuse, he and his crew will finish the work they started." She waved a hand around the room they stood in.

Flowers and lions and curly-haired children danced through the macaroni art. One child had stamped their palm in purple paint in lieu of a signature. Horris swallowed hard. "Is there anything we can do to help?"

Estelle's gaze flicked back to Perseus. They had each other's gaze for a heartbeat too long. Then she sighed. Her hand came away from her waistline. "Your fellow agents asked the same thing. They'd planned to get airborne, get notice back to your supervisors—"

"Inspectors," Horris corrected politely. A small surge of ugly satisfaction ran through him. No one—not even pirates—could escape the Postal Inspectors.

Estelle nodded. "Your Inspectors. Unfortunately—"

"Silver shot them out of the sky," Horris said. He couldn't hide the strain in his voice. In his mind's eye, the depot ship looked a lot like the *Silverfish*. "Is the remaining postman here? Can I speak to him?"

"He's here," she replied. "Follow me."

Horris followed Estelle out of the craft room with Perseus on his heels. It felt a little like having a bristling guard dog at his back. Horris slowed his pace a bit so he and Perseus could walk side-by-side. He tried to think of something he could say to Perseus—one question out of the hundred in his head—but nothing pried itself free. All he managed was a small noise in his throat.

Perseus shot him a curious look before slowing his pace so that he walked a step behind Horris. Horris rolled his eyes and continued on.

The sharp smell of antiseptic grew stronger, and beneath that, the stink of sickness. Estelle flung a door open and led them down a narrow flight of stairs. Typically, in Horris' experience, a community center basement was useful for group workouts or therapy sessions, maybe holiday events and recreational activities. Now…

"Oh," said Horris very softly.

The community center's basement had been transformed into a makeshift hospital: long rows of cots had been set along the walls. Bedsheets and blankets served as makeshift privacy curtains and a cluster of folding chairs made a waiting room of sorts. There were coolers full of bottled water and cardboard boxes full of non-perishable snacks. People in scrubs moved between the sheets with soft reverence. The silence was placid, but underneath it all was the tell-tale smell of hot sick and bodily fluids.

Estelle's face was stone, but her eyes were bright with fury as she turned to Horris. "These are my people. Not all of them have made it."

The refugee camp of his youth had been a lot like this. Clustered around a still-standing building, volunteers doing their best with what remained to them following the bombing. Horris hadn't been injured, but as a small child alone, he'd been made to wait where adults could keep an eye on him. And Horris, a rule-follower even then, had sat and watched and waited.

Horris of the here and now swallowed the bile in his throat and ignored the sudden stone in his stomach. He nodded to Estelle, unable to speak.

Estelle led them over to a privacy sheet. She pulled it back with no ceremony.

An instant wave of sickness hits Horris. The rock in his stomach tumbled, sending him reeling as the sickly-sweet stink of burnt flesh hit him. Horris turned away, lips pressed together to stop himself from vomiting. This left Perseus to study the depot agent with a flat, disaffected expression.

"Is he cognizant?" Perseus asked. Horris could hear him through the sudden pounding in his head; his tone was cool and professional. Horris wiped the hot tears from his eyes and forced himself to turn back.

"We're not sure," Estelle admitted. "Two days ago, he could respond to yes-no questions. Now…" She glanced down, obviously struggling to hide her own horror.

The depot agent's charred face twitched in their direction. A rattling breath escaped between melted lips. Perseus glanced at Horris and nodded subtly toward the depot agent.

Right. He was the captain. He had a veneer of professionalism to maintain. Horris took a deep breath through his mouth, all the better to block out the smell, and crouched down in front of the depot agent. He forced himself to look past the blackened flesh and the trickles of white pus. He forced himself to find the shape of the man, the features of a face. "Hello. My name is Captain Horris Jensen, USSPS One-Thirty-One-C, designation *Silverfish*. We're here to…"

Help? Avenge his crew? Deliver the mail? What were they supposed to do?

"Get you home," Horris said. "We're here to get you home."

The depot agent managed another wheezing breath. Horris lingered a moment longer before standing and turning to Estelle. "Thank you," he said sincerely. "For taking care of him this long. I understand it must have been a strain on your resources."

"We weren't going to leave him out there," Estelle said. Her expression remained guarded. Horris wondered how long she had had to practice that. He wondered where the threshold was, of deciding it was safer not to show how you felt. "But we don't have the resources to care for him much longer. My people…" She trailed off, looking around the makeshift infirmary. "My people are my priority."

"I understand. In your place, I would do the same." Horris assured her. He grimaced as he looked over the depot agent. They didn't have the supplies onboard to care for such a severe burn victim. Nor, he suspected, was this man's odds of survival increased by space travel. They needed the Inspectors here. But to get the Inspectors here, they needed to be able to call off-planet…

"Olive mentioned your communication tower has been disabled. No messages on- or off-planet."

Estelle nodded. "The comm tower is a few miles outside of town. We've sent several teams out there to restore power. No one has come back."

Of course not. Horris fought the instinct to wince. "Any idea why?"

"Pirates, maybe. Or something else. There are…things…in the woods. Things stirred up by the pirates and native things besides. Adastra took all the fighters when she called for aid on Creed. The remnants here aren't fighters, not in the way they've been forced to be."

The request was there, couched between the words of what her people weren't. Well, his people weren't naturally-born fighters either. Except…

"Excuse us a moment," Horris said. Estelle nodded and stepped away to speak to a nurse, leaving Horris free to step across to the makeshift waiting room. Perseus followed.

"No," the Black Hammer said the instant they were alone.

Horris couldn't pretend to be surprised. But there was a part of him that was disappointed nonetheless. "Why not?"

"This—" Perseus swept a hand out towards the infirmary "—is not your problem. This is not *my* problem. We are not here to help them. You are here to deliver the mail. That is all."

"A post agent is dying. The Idolers here have done their best to care for him. They didn't need to, but they did. You're not a postal worker, so you're not obligated to return the favor. I am."

"The only thing they've done for him is prolong his suffering," Perseus said. "They should have killed him days ago."

Fury, hot and sharp, stabbed through him like a knife. Horris exhaled through his nose. Everyone had good in them. Everyone was capable of kindness. He had to keep believing that, even if Perseus was sorely testing his patience. "If we don't do something, they'll be slaughtered."

"Idolers." Perseus shrugged. "Heathens."

"Children." Horris countered. "Innocents."

"No one is innocent in the eyes of the Emperor," Perseus said. "They wanted me in chains, remember?"

"Then maybe you should stop acting like they all deserve to die!" Horris snapped. He didn't realize how loud his voice had risen until Perseus shot a wary look to the side. The Idolers in the infirmary were staring openly at the pair. Estelle was frowning, one hand pressed against her waistline. A shameful heat crept up Horris' face as he turned back to Perseus. "You can wait on the ship if you like. I have a duty to my fellow postal workers and to the customers of the worlds we service. I wouldn't expect a coward to understand."

Perseus scowled. It was a low blow, Horris knew, but there was a crude part of him that burned with satisfaction as he turned away. Perseus could hem and haw and naysay all he liked, but he would be damned before he sat here on his hands while there was something to be done—

"Captain Jensen."

Horris stopped mid-step. He half-turned back to Perseus, watching the minute expressions dart across the Black Hammer's face. His poker face wasn't very good, in truth: you could see the quick downturn of his mouth, the crease that appeared between his thin brows. He opened his mouth, choked on his words, and then cleared his throat.

Finally, without a word, Perseus moved to stand just behind Horris.

Estelle's hand stayed steady on her waistline as they approached. She shifted so that she was between the two outworlders and her infirmary. "Well?"

Horris rolled his shoulders back. "The USSPS takes no part in inter- or outer-planetary conflicts. However," he glanced at the groaning, burnt shell of a depot agent, "these pirates have demonstrated a blatant disregard for standard conventions. As such, I feel it is within my rights and responsibilities as a commissioned officer of USSPS to render aid where I can, as well as provide protection for fellow agents."

It was a lot of jargon, but then again, jargon looked good in the reports. And knowing the union, he was going to have to write a lot of reports after this.

Estelle didn't reply. Horris had just begun to think he'd completely misread the situation when she finally nodded. She held up her hand, palm out, fingers splayed. It was a strange gesture, made even stranger when Perseus curled his right hand into a fist and held it over his heart. The Idoler and the Imperial held each other's gaze for too long, neither willing nor able to break contact first.

"We'll do what we can," said Horris, trying not to feel like he was intruding on a private moment.

"Thank you," Estelle said. But her eyes never left Perseus as she added: "Our lives are in your hands."

❾ The Fist and the Open Palm

United Star System Postal Code, Chapter 12, Section 4: If an on-site injury prevents a courier from earning full wages, the courier's supervisor is required to file a Report of Injury form within 10 days of the actual injury or knowledge of it.

How had his life come to this?

He was—had been—a Black Hammer. He had been a soldier of his God, the scourge of heathens, defender of his fellow soldiers of faith. The Red Hammer, they'd named him, and an entire ceremonial ball had been hosted in his name.

Now, here he was, tramping through swampy undergrowth, swatting at whining mosquitoes with hands that had drawn unholy blood. The boots that had once marched in spectacular formation now trailed after the footsteps of a postie who couldn't leave well enough alone, all in the service of Idolers who would have had him hanging from a gibbet.

The Extraordinaries, Percy decided, had been correct. During his reviews, they'd told him his pride was too easily pricked. All Horris had to do was remind him of the oaths he'd already forsaken, and he'd fallen right behind him. He was an oathbreaker, yes. But not a coward. *Never* a coward.

Then again, the Extraordinaries had been talking about humbling himself before the Emperor's Liaisons. They never said he had to humble himself before some minimum-wage civil servant. He'd missed that memo, and now his pride had landed him in this godforsaken swamp.

They walked just north of Icene. The scooter had been abandoned on the side of the road; the road to the electrical compound was choked with weeds and small rocks, a classic case of Idoler mismanagement. They went alone. The rest of the postmen had been left behind to finish deliveries and retrieve outbound mail. It seemed a mind-numbing, ignominious task. Percy had to wonder if envy was behind the looks he'd gotten from the postmen when Horris told them their mission.

At any rate, he was relieved it was Horris and not another with him now. Horris, at least, had made it overtly clear that he had no intent of doing harm. So he followed Horris into the dense, tangled swamp. Here, the foliage grew thicker and darker overhead, making it seem later than mid-morning. Birdcalls and the drone of insects filled the dead air. Horris clicked on a borrowed torch and plunged deeper into the thicket.

Horris, the great lumbering oaf. He couldn't leave well enough alone, could he? A backwater Idoler leads him into a room full of children's drawings, shows him a half-dead *alleged* postie, and he falls for the entire scheme hook, line, and sinker. Surely, *meddling* was nowhere in his contractual duties. How did he intend to explain this detour on the expense sheet?

Something akin to guilt twinged in his stomach. The Idolers weren't the only ones Horris was bending the procedure for. The Idolers weren't the only ones depending on this minimum-wage civil servant and his bleeding heart.

Horris must have felt his burning gaze because he turned back to Percy with a puzzled expression. Percy stared back. And he very valiantly withheld a groan when Horris cleared his throat.

"So…what's with the hand gestures?"

"What," Percy replied flatly. It wasn't a question.

"Y'know, the…" Horris curled his hand into a fist and pressed it to his heart.

That, at least, was easily answered. Percy folded his fingers to demonstrate. The gesture was comfortingly familiar. Even if he'd lost everything else, he still had his muscle memory. "The folded fist. The symbol of our Emperor."

"Why is it a symbol of your Emperor?"

Horris, Percy decided, was a man who thrived off questions. He sighed loudly to signal to Horris that he was only *humoring* said questions. "What does a closed hand do? It holds tools, it rallies armies, it waves a banner. It brings disparate peoples together." He splayed his fingers out and folded them again, one by one. "One People. One Cause. One God."

"And the Black Hammers are a tool of the closed fist."

"Well-spotted," Percy said, pleased.

"So…the Idolers?"

Horris immediately ruined the goodwill by spreading his fingers out again. He didn't mean anything by copying the Idolers' gesture—Percy understood that well enough—but all the same, his stomach twisted. Only so many friends could die before an open palm made your blood burn. He turned his head to the side and spat out the sudden bloody taste in his mouth.

"An open palm. What does an open palm do? *Nothing*. It holds no tools, offers no worship, and grasps no banners. Who uses an open palm? Beggars. Children. They *wait* for an offering instead of working towards it themselves. An open hand flails against a foe. An open palm marks each finger individually. Divided. Easily broken. The Idolers consider themselves special. They are *weak*."

Percy didn't realize he was proselytizing until he saw the look on Horris' face. He lowered his hands awkwardly. He was no good at preaching the Word, never had been. He'd never been up for consideration as a Trumpeter. This was the first time he'd ever spoken about the Creed war to an outworlder. He'd had a golden opportunity to teach Horris, to *explain* why the Idolers weren't worth his time. The Emperor was the light and the truth and the way. The Idolers had spurned the Word, spurned *Him*. But instead of making that clear, Horris was looking at him like he'd suddenly sprouted a second head.

For the second time in his life, Perseus Warden felt shame.

He cleared his throat and focused his gaze over Horris' shoulder. "So. That's that."

"I see," Horris said.

They continued on. Silence fell between them, save for the crunch of dead leaves underfoot. Percy took a few breaths to cool his temper. It wasn't his fault, he told himself. Horris was too willing to give to an open palm to understand the importance of the Word. He was no Idoler, true, but unless he accepted the Word, he was still a blasphemer.

Like you?

The voice in his head sounded too much like Orestes. Perseus shook his head to clear the murmur. The silence stretched on long enough for Percy to think he'd cleared the gauntlet of Horris' questions.

And then the postie cleared his throat again.

This time, Percy didn't bother hiding his groan. "*What.*"

"Why did you become a Black Hammer?"

Despite his annoyance, Percy felt compelled to answer. Maybe Horris would better understand if he did. "I was chosen."

"Because you're related to an admiral?"

Credit where credit was due. Horris was a good listener. Percy shook his head. "Hammers are chosen regardless of family ties or social background. We are chosen based on merit alone."

"You must have had a lot of merit at a young age," Horris said, in that searching tone people used when they didn't quite believe you.

"Seven," Percy said with a burst of pride.

Horris stopped short. "Seven?"

"Mmhm. The Academy begins scouting at six. Prospective applicants are enrolled in the Academy at seven. We graduate at twenty-one." Under normal circumstances, at least. The war had accelerated the program, and field-based promotions had become commonplace. That was how he had earned his promotion to Lieutenant, bypassing the rank of Extraordinary entirely.

"Are your parents Black Hammers too?"

"No," he heard himself answering. Percy paused as something rustled in the trees overhead. He glanced up to see a flash of luminescent eyes. Leaves fluttered down as the creature—whatever it was—scampered away. "My mother is…well, she's the aforementioned admiral. My father was an adjutant. Pencil-pusher."

"Oh. I'm sorry for your loss."

Percy lowered his gaze to blink at Horris. "Sorry?"

"Your mom *is* an admiral. Your father *was* an adjutant. I'm sorry for your loss."

"Oh. We weren't close. Once I enrolled in the Academy, I only saw them a few times a year."

Twelve, to be precise. Once a month every year for thirteen years. One hundred and fifty-six visits. He wondered if he'd been declared MIA or KIA yet and whether his mother had heard the news. He wondered if they would award Admiral Warden a medal of recognition for the loss of her only child in the Emperor's service.

He wondered, way deep down in a small part of himself, if she would even care.

This line of questioning skirted too close to things too painful to think about. Percy saw Horris opening his mouth for another question and beat him to the quick: "What about your parents? Posties?"

"Oh! No. My mom was a pilot. My dad worked for a non-profit."

"*Was*," Percy echoed. "*Worked*."

Horris winced as though struck. "Yeah. They died in the Helium Wars."

The name struck a dim bell. He'd studied this in the Academy. The Helium Wars had taken place nearly two decades past, some sort of resource-based civil war on the heavily-populated planet of Ceres. Helium had played a major role in life there, as he understood it, until the day the shortages began. Then, it was a mad rush to stockpile, privatize, and politize the remaining helium until countries were finding excuses to invade their neighbors. The Helium Wars had nearly destroyed Ceres.

At the time, Percy had been disgusted by the waste of resources and the bullheadedness of the faction leaders. The Helium Wars had been a very important lesson about the need for one leader. One voice guiding the planet and all the cultures therein. He'd felt a certain rush of satisfaction, a surge of pride that he lived in such an enlightened society, safe in the Emperor's palm.

Something screeched in the gloom ahead. Percy aimed his torch straight ahead. The light shone wider and thinner, out out out into the dark.

"This is usually the part where people say, 'I'm sorry for your loss,'" Horris said.

"What?" Percy tore his eyes from the tangled road ahead. Horris was looking at him with faint amusement. "Oh. I'm sorry for your loss." The faux pas compelled him to add something, if only to distract from it: "You and the pilot—Roddy?—you and he are from the same area. Your accents are similar."

"Good ears. We're both from Grand York. We were taken in together, y'know, one of those programs that pop up after wars to help orphan kiddos. We were the same age, similar enough interests, and as we grew up, we stuck together."

Yes, that made sense. Those who grew up together stood together in the face of adversity. That was why the Academy took in their soldiers so young; the better to make connections and foster loyalty between members of a cohort.

Orestes' wavering smile flashed through his mind, along with his blue eyes. Percy swallowed the rush of bile in his throat. Orestes did *not* count. Orestes had been weak. Weak and foolish and soft. Just like Horris. And Horris would probably meet a similar end.

He nearly walked right into Horris when the postie stopped short. Percy peered around him, aiming his flashlight at the tall spine of metal that looked completely displaced in the middle of this goddamn swamp.

It looked to be an electrical compound, built and then abandoned in a hurry. Thick vines crept up the sides and the front. Swamp flora choked the walkway and rusted chain-link fence. Even the metal tower seemed askew from this angle. It looked like anything else that belonged to the Idolers—like shit.

"What idiot builds their communication tower in the middle of a swamp?"

Horris gave him a look. "Didn't the Imperials build this place as a penal colony first?"

Percy shrugged. "It was on the Idolers to take care of the place." He started forward, all the better to ignore Horris. He scanned the front of the building for signs of disturbance. "What do you suppose happened to those other—"

Crunch.

Something gave way beneath him. Percy lifted his boot to stare at the desiccated corpse under his boot. It had been partially concealed by weed and reed, half-sunken into the soft ground around them. Percy swallowed his initial shock and crouched to examine the remains. He heard Horris gasp and then retch. Percy took the sound, the smell, even the twist of contempt in his stomach with measured breath. He put every sensation he didn't want or need and set it inside a box for later.

The corpse was—had been—a humanoid male. It was almost impossible to tell what precisely had killed him: swamp water bloated his red-green skin, and animals had gnawed at limbs and torso both. Fat white maggots squirmed just under the skin and at the corners of dead eyes.

Somewhere in the brush, two creatures screamed. Percy stilled, listening to the snarls and splashes of a nearby fight, the shriek of the predator, and the wet panting of its prey. The fight seemed to stretch on for too long before silence fell again.

Horris croaked a word.

"What?" Percy glanced his way.

Horris wiped his mouth with the back of his hand and pointed.

A nearby machete stuck point-down into the mud. Percy picked his way over to it, mindful of how the mud rose around his boots. He bent down, wrapped a hand around the hilt of the machete, and pulled. The mud sucked and squelched, loathed to give up its prize, but relented when Percy gave the machete a sharp twist and yanked.

He wished he could say it came gleaming from the swamp. It did not. It was a half-rusted blade, chipped in places and stained with what might have been blood. Nevertheless, a sword was a sword. Perseus murmured a thanks to the Emperor for their deliverance. *And the weapon of the holy will strike off the chains of faithful.*

It was a sign. Wasn't it?

Horris was looking at him warily. "Do you know how to use that?"

"Better than he did. Come along." Percy started for the compound's door. He could almost feel Horris lingering by the corpse. "Come *along*, Horris."

He didn't wait for the postie to follow, instead marching up to the front door. If it had had a lock, it had rusted away long ago. Someone—or something—had forced the door open a crack. Percy gave the door a testing nudge and frowned when it didn't budge. He studied the door, its make, the angle at which it was open. He shifted his weight and raised a boot.

BANG!

Horris winced as the door slammed inward. The screech of rusted hinges reverberated through the swamp. Birds burst from the treetops, and fauna scrambled through the underbrush.

"Something will have heard that," said Horris.

"Good," Percy said. He strode forward into the dark.

A small thrill shivered down Percy's spine. For the first time in three days, he had some semblance of control over a situation. Horris may have had the upper hand while they were among the Idolers, but Perseus had been trained for scenarios like this. He *knew* what to do here: kill anything that got in his way.

The interior of the electrical compound did not offer much in the way of hospitality. The dark corridors were dusty, and when he swept his torch down the hall, something skittered further into the dark. More alarming, though, were the cobwebs that coated the walls. The back of Percy's neck prickled. Spiders. Spiders who lived in massive webs full of dried husks the size of his fist. Those deerflies, Percy supposed, and the occasional unlucky rat.

Horris illuminated one of the webs with his torch. "Huh."

"I don't suppose these spiders are also in mating season," Percy said. He worked overtime to keep the tremor out of his tone; he had already embarrassed himself over an arachnid.

"No. These webs have been abandoned. See?" Horris pointed to one tattered, husk-littered web. "Web-weavers like to keep their homes tidy. They can't catch prey on a web like this."

Percy wiped a sweaty palm against his thigh. "So there are no spiders here?"

"Well—" Horris kicked aside a massive dust bunny "—not *here*, at least."

The electrical compound wasn't very big, and it wasn't long before they found the main control board coated in a thick layer of dust and grime. Percy took to rummaging through nearby drawers while Horris inspected more of those tattered webs.

Percy couldn't fathom what intrigued Horris until he remembered the Targian spider named Henri. He wiped his hands on his thighs again. "Fascinated by spiders, are you?"

"Oh, all insects," said Horris. He shone his torchlight through a dilapidated web. "Well, insects and arachnids. Spiders aren't insects. They have eight legs, not six."

Six legs, eight legs, Percy didn't care if spiders could do a full backflip. They were disgusting little creepy-crawlies. How anyone could be so transfixed by them was beyond him. "Strange hobby."

"At least I have a hobby," said Horris. He aimed the torch at Percy with a small smile.

"I have hobbies."

"Preaching isn't a hobby."

Percy shot him a look. He took a sharp breath—and immediately doubled over, hacking and wheezing as thick dust choked him. Horris burst out laughing, which doubled when Percy shot him the universal one-fingered salute.

He resumed digging through ancient filing cabinets until he found a yellowed paper copy of an instruction manual. He held it up for Horris to see. "Paper? In this day and age?"

"It wouldn't have done much for them to keep the instructions on a tablet, would it?"

Percy hummed an agreement and tossed the instruction manual to Horris. "You're up, postman."

Horris didn't argue. He opened the manual and gave it a quick skim. "Looks like we'll have to reboot the grid. See?" He turned the manual around for Percy to see. Percy couldn't make heads nor tails of the diagrams involved, but he nodded all the same. "The grid is just down the corridor."

"Can you take care of it?"

"Basah could do it faster, but as long as I follow the instructions, yeah."

They left the main control room and started down the corridor for a door marked maintenance. The door groaned open to a flight of stairs leading down into the dark. Percy looked at Horris, who looked back at him, and after a moment, Percy started down the stairs first.

Fortunately, there was nothing to be found in the maintenance room save thicker dust and rodent droppings. Percy stood off to the side, holding the torch while Horris read the manual and flipped switches in certain orders. After a few minutes of doing so, a low hum reverberated throughout the compound. Lights flickered to life, putting them in a low-level gloom instead of total darkness. Horris grinned up at the massive, blinking electrical board on the wall, and Percy found himself impressed.

And then a long, low shadow dipped from the wall behind them. Percy felt Horris stiffen beside him. Instantly, he straightened, putting a hand to the machete at his hip. He stared at the long, appendage-like shadow as it retreated back into the gloom above. And now he could hear it: a soft *tap-tap-tap* of claws against the ceiling. Percy exhaled, readying to pivot and face the horror.

"Don't," Horris hissed.

"What?" Percy whispered back. It felt ridiculous to whisper now, what with the hum of electricity and the distant rattle of machinery filling the air around them. "What is it?"

"It's a hunter spider," Horris replied. He stared straight forward at the electrical grid.

"I thought you said all the webs were abandoned!"

"They were. The web-weaving spiders are gone. This is a *hunter*. It probably…"

"I know what it probably did!" Percy hissed back. The last thing he wanted or needed to think about was a spider large and lethal enough to devour a whole host of other spiders. "And now I'm going to return the favor!"

The *tap-tap-tap* continued overhead. It was growing louder now and much, much closer. Lights around them flickered on and off, twisting and distorting the shadows around them. Were they shadows at all?

"*No*," Horris whispered sharply. "This is a hunter. It's too fast to fight. We just have to make a break for it."

Percy strained to hear the spider over Horris' plea. Shouldn't it have been clicking, hissing, snarling? Shouldn't it have been making the low rumble of a predator? It was quiet, it was so damn quiet... he fought the urge to look up, to confirm whether or not the spider dangled directly overhead. Rats the size of his fist wrapped in thick webs—the Idoler torn and shredded in the mud—he'd fought men before, but not monsters—his blood roared in his ears, drowning out the spider's tapping and whatever inanity Horris muttered in his ear.

"—rely on their eyesight. I'll shine the torch at it, and then we run. They aren't pursuit predators, we should be safe once we get outside. Ready?"

Emperor, guide me. "Ready," Perseus whispered.

"Run–run, now, *RUN!*"

The torchlight swung upwards, right into the black eyes of the massive spider overhead. Percy had just enough time to see a massive spider rear, front legs flailing, before he bolted for the door. Horris was beside him—overtaking him—sprinting up the flight of stairs ahead.

Something heavy thudded to the floor behind them. One moment, Percy was two footsteps to the door—and in the next instant, his head was colliding with the floor. His head rang with sudden pain. The coppery taste of blood filled his mouth as something grabbed his boot and yanked him backward.

The hunter was massive, as wide as Percy was tall, and a soft clicking sound filled the small room. Percy twisted and grabbed for the machete. He slashed backward, striking at the hunter's pedipalps and its soft undersides. The spider shuddered silently as clear liquid dripped from its underside. Its claw-tipped legs jabbed at Percy again and again, determined to beat its prey into submission, and pulled him across the tile floor.

Percy screamed as the spider sank its fangs into his thigh. He reared his free leg back and slammed his boot into one of the spider's round black eyes. Something burst beneath the heel of his boot, and in the next instant, he was free, scrambling backward away from the spider as it wriggled and reared, flinging its front legs out in some threat display.

Piss-poor decision. Percy sprang up and slammed the machete deep through the slice in its abdomen, burying the blade up to the hilt. The spider shivered and sagged, legs and palps twitching in death throes.

Percy staggered back from the dying spider. A small, pinching sensation seized his leg where the spider had bitten him. It was wet where he touched his thigh, but suddenly, that didn't matter. What mattered was what he couldn't feel: pain. He couldn't feel the wound.

He couldn't feel anything in his right leg at all.

Percy collapsed to the floor as his leg gave out. He dragged himself away from the spider's corpse, cursing under his breath—until the tell-tale *tap-tap-tap* sounded from above.

A second spider emerged from the flickering darkness. It clicked softly as it crawled over its dead partner. All eyes fixed on Percy.

Percy threw himself backward. He was scrambling now, trying and failing to get to his feet as the spider skittered towards him. No–no no *no*–no no–not like this, not like this, never like this, he couldn't die in the dark to a fucking *spider* of all things. He dug under his collar and seized his pendant in a white-knuckled grip. Unbidden, unconsciously, the Litany came to his lips: "Savior of my soul, through the shadow of doubt and death, my arm is Your arm, Your heart is my heart, deliver me unto Your breast, deliver me–*please*—"

PSHHAW!

The second spider skittered backward from a rolling cloud of white foam. Horris was suddenly standing over him, in *front* of him, lobbing a fire extinguisher at its head.

Someone was lifting him, forcing his feet to the floor. Someone was telling him to move, to *run*, and a sharp, absurd burst of laughter escaped him. *Running?* The pattern had been established, running never did him a lick of fucking good! He'd just been saved, what did he need to run for?

The world went tilty-slidy-wobbly-wiggly, all the colors swirling together like some child's artwork. Some logical part of his brain knew about toxins and paralytics, and that logical bit sounded a lot like Horris. But the greater part of him had just been snatched from the jaws of death, delivered, and it sang the Emperor's name.

He loves me, He loves me, He loves me, *HelovesmeHelovesme Helovesme*—

Perseus was back in the Academy. He walked upright, alone, in his crisp black uniform with the medals that jingled against his chest. Everything was clean, bright, and well-lit. Everything was as it should be. He lifted his chin, righteously confident of his place in the world.

Someone from behind gripped his shoulder, hard (*Horris*, his mind screamed, but he couldn't know that name here). He turned. And his stomach soured the instant he saw who stood behind him.

"No," he said. "No. *No.* You're *dead.*"

Orestes stared back at him sadly. Thick, dark blood trickled out of his gaping head wound and congealed in his ridiculous sideburns. He didn't say a word. He just looked at Percy.

"You're dead!" Perseus said again. The other part of him screamed louder, trying to drag him back into a world of blood and mud and Idolers and posties. He resisted. Not yet. Not until he'd gotten his answers from the broken Hammer in front of him. "You failed! *It's your fault!*"

"It's going to be all right," Orestes said.

"It is not going to be *all right!*" Perseus snapped. The edges of his vision grayed like old photos. Percy ignored the sensation and funneled all of his fury and loathing at the ghost of the soldier in front of him: "You dragged me down with you! Your curse—your weakness—it's in my heart now! You *infected* me!"

"It's going be all right," Orestes said again.

"*IT IS NOT—*"

His body jerked hard, and pain shot through his chest. Everything went white and still and quiet.

10 A Promise Kept

United Star System Postal Code, Chapter 12, Section 2: Seek medical attention and report all injuries to your captain immediately or as soon as you realize it is work-related.

The dense, tangled swamp seemed even more dense and tangled than it had just ten minutes before. Horris kept his eyes on the path ahead, fighting the instinct to look off the path, to see what watched and waited in the brush. He picked up his pace even as his grip tightened on the convulsing Perseus.

Perseus moaned against his shoulder. Sweat plastered his red hair to his pale skin, and he kept his eyes screwed shut even as another tremor nearly took him off his good leg. The other dragged uselessly, leaving deep gouges in the mud behind them. He muttered something under his breath.

Horris glanced around before hauling Perseus to the edge of the path. He found a dry bit of earth and lowered Perseus to the ground. Perseus flung his head back against the rough trunk of the tree they'd found themselves under. He twisted the fabric of his torn pant leg around his fingers and yanked as though he could pull the poison from his system.

Venom, Horris corrected himself. If something bites you, it's venom.

He crouched down in front of Perseus. The Imperial's eyes were still screwed shut, and he continued with murmurs too soft and fast for Horris to make out. Horris hesitated before gripping Perseus' shoulder. "It's going to be all right."

Perseus shook his head furiously. His shaking increased as Horris tore the hole in his pant leg wider.

The spider had bitten deep, leaving two puncture wounds the size of stamps. Horris felt the first rush of nausea and blinked rapidly to keep the hot tears back. He was no good with blood or fluids or anything else that made up the meat of a body. But there was no one else here who could treat the wound. It had to be him. He closed his eyes, wiped the tears away, and forced himself to focus. He was no good with bodies. But spiders—spiders, he understood.

The puncture wounds were red but not bleeding. The skin immediately around the wound had turned a virulent pink, and a faint red line radiated out towards Perseus' groin. He checked Percy's right leg over for further injury and was relieved to find none besides the initial puncture wound. That likely meant the spider hadn't been able to inject him with liquifying enzymes. There was initial paralysis, yes, but that was easier to deal with than innards turning to juice.

Horris slid his company belt off his waistline and tied it around Percy's thigh, just above the wound itself. He fastened as tight as he possibly dared. It was a poor attempt at a tourniquet, but what else could he do? None of his USSPS-mandated first aid training covered this. Hopefully, they had something on the *Silverfish* that could help. And if they didn't–well, if they didn't, Perseus would just have to work through the paralytic on his own. As long as it didn't reach his heart...

"Hey," he said softly. "Hey. Perce–Perseus. It's going to be all right."

Perseus' burning green eyes snapped open. He stared at Horris, through Horris, with tears in his eyes. His tousled red hair fell across his forehead, and at that moment, Perseus looked his age.

He was young, Horris thought, with all his twenty-four years of wisdom.

"Percy," he said.

Perseus' green eyes snapped to him. A little of the confusion cleared. Horris held up his hand before offering it out to Perseus. Perseus' hand twitched. Slowly, his tight fist relaxed its death grip on the fabric of his pants. Slowly, his fist unfurled into an open palm and slid into Horris'.

Perseus didn't struggle when Horris pulled them both back to their feet. He flopped against Horris' chest, but now his breathing had leveled to a reasonable pace. He flung an arm around Horris' shoulder and squeezed.

Horris squeezed back. He was about to start forward when a small *bzzt* stopped him short.

A fist-sized chrysops perched on the trunk of the tree above. It rubbed its forelegs together as it watched Horris haul Perseus upright. Then it took wing, buzzing off in the direction of the electrical compound. Horris released a breath he didn't know he'd been holding. The deerfly didn't know what was going on. The deerfly didn't care. That was the beauty of an insect, sometimes.

He remembered, suddenly, the mildewy smell of the basement. He remembered the distant rumbles of bombs and the *pop-pop* of gun-shots. He remembered sitting on his father's lap, watching silverfish crawl over a copy of his father's thesis, gnawing on yellowed paper.

Funny little guys, huh? They don't even know there's a war on. They're just living their own lives. It all goes on, Horris. It's all gonna be okay.

Horris swallowed the node in his throat. "Just a little further, Percy. C'mon."

■

The standard-issue scooter saw them back to the *Silverfish*, although it was a struggle to keep the scooter upright as Perseus flopped against his chest. The *Silverfish* crew stood on the lowered ramp of the ship; Basah was in a heated conversation with Estelle, strangely enough, while Olive stood by a worn motorcycle.

"HEY! HEY, HELP!"

All stopped as the scooter skidded to a halt. Horris wrapped an arm around Perseus and flung them both off the scooter. Basah was already off the ramp and sprinting towards them. Roddy seized Fives by the shoulder and shoved him up the ramp and into the *Silverfish* proper.

Basah caught Perseus as he fell forward. "What happened?"

"Spiders—huge spiders—got bit—"

In the distance, he saw Roddy disappear up into the ship after Fives. Between himself and Basah, they were able to drag Perseus to the *Silverfish*'s gangplank. Estelle held up a hand to stop them from entering the ship. "What happened?" She demanded, with far less warmth than Basah.

Horris took a breath to ease his searing lungs. "We—we got the power back on. Comms are back online. But we got attacked—"

"Pirates?"

He shook his head. "Spiders. Things. In the woods."

Estelle frowned. "You saw no pirates?"

"No."

That did not assure her. Estelle glanced skyward. Midday had passed, and the sun was incrementally shifting westwards. The shadows were longer than they had been a minute ago. "Olive, radio back to—"

"Horris!"

Basah had laid Perseus down on the ramp and now knelt beside him. Fives skittered back down the ramp with a first aid kit clutched to his chest. Horris excused himself from Estelle and jogged over to Basah. She had snatched the first aid kit from Fives. Fives stared down at Perseus with his wide, too-dark eyes, but one look from Horris sent him back up into the ship.

"Venom?" Basah asked as she rummaged through the first aid kit. After a moment, she produced a thick plastic tube from the bottom of the kit.

"Paralytic." Horris turned away as Basah snapped the cap off the tube. A spider's fangs he could handle, but the thin artificial sharpness of a needle skeeved him out. He watched Estelle grab a walkie-talkie from Olive, her body language taut.

Perseus shouted a sharp, wordless bellow of pain that forced Horris' attention back down. Basah pulled the tubed needle from his wounded thigh, recapped it, and set it back in the kit. Perseus collapsed back on the ramp, sweaty and breathing hard.

Horris had no idea if he was in or out of it. "Do we have anything else that could help?"

"I'm doing my best here, Horry." Basah's ears flattened against her head. "This will have to do until—"

A low, slow rumble in the distance cut her off. Birds flushed from shaking treetops as the rumble built to a roar, louder and louder. Basah slapped both hands to her ears and shouted something to Horris. When he shook his head, she scrambled back up into the *Silverfish*. The ground around them began to shake with the force of whatever approached. A high whine cut through the bassy roar, and one of the shadows grew longer and longer as a ship appeared over the horizon.

It was a triple-decker man-of-war, three times the size of the *Silverfish*. Two massive cannons sprouted from her bulkhead on either side and just below the cannons, Horris could see the jagged steel of mounted harpoons. A pair of horns and claws had been graffitied onto her flank in lieu of a callsign. The man-of-war rumbled overhead, too close for comfort, before slowing over the modest depot.

Horris jumped when Roddy seized his shoulder. "The engines are hot," the pilot hissed, "let's go, let's *go*—"

Movement from above cut him off. A cable line flung over the side of the man-of-war. Estelle cocked her gun but did not fire as four figures came rappelling down the line. The first of the four leapt a few feet from the ground and landed smoothly. He straightened, smoothed out his jacket, and strode towards the small group.

He was a Marquay with gleaming silver horns. He was handsome in that scruffy way all pirates could be considered handsome: tall and muscular, with black hair tied back in a tight bun. He wore a long scarlet coat over leather armor and carried no visible weapon save the rapier at his hip. The Marquay glanced at the posties with disinterest before turning to beam at Estelle.

"Estelle," he exclaimed, "*darling!*"

Estelle's gun flashed in the sunlight; the pirate sidestepped the bullet just before it careened past. Instantly, the other three pirates drew their weapons.

"Careful, dear," the Marquay said, all with that too-bright smile. A whir from above forced their gaze upwards: one of the ship's cannons was moving into position. "My aim is better than yours."

"What are you doing here, Silver?" Estelle demanded. She had not reloaded her gun, but neither had she lowered it.

Silver. Hot bile rose in Horris' throat. *This was Silver.* He clenched his hands into fists and took a wary step backward. Roddy moved with him until they both stood over the paralyzed, groaning Perseus.

"I'm here to congratulate you! My men and I were taking bets on how long it would take for you to fix the communication system. Although none of us had you getting someone else to do it on our table." Silver's eyes flicked to Horris with visible amusement. "How very clever."

Horris stood up straighter. Roddy's grip tightened into a vice even as Horris spoke: "You have a lot to answer for, Silver."

"That's Captain Silver of the *Scorpion*, thank you very much, Mister Mailman, of the Mail Truck." Silver turned to him fully. His men kept their weapons on Estelle and Olive. "And to whom do I owe answers?"

"To the inspectors of the United Star System Postal Service."

Silver burst out laughing. So did his men. Horris stood stock-still, quivering with rage, and did not flinch when Silver grinned. "And why should I fear some glorified stamp collectors?"

"You've murdered USSPS carriers and endangered the lives of USSPS customers. You've disrupted the flow of mail."

Silver's eyes flicked skyward. Perhaps he was recalling the carnage of a mailship careening down from the sky. "Well, maybe those carriers should have picked a faster ship."

Roddy dug his heels into the metal grate and all but flung himself onto Horris as Silver went back to Estelle. Estelle had shifted her stance slightly, shielding Olive as if that would protect the younger woman should any decide to open fire. "What are you doing here, Silver?"

Silver shrugged. "Any other day of the week, I'd be here to slaughter your little town and collect hands to sell back to the Imperials. But today is your lucky day. Today, I'm here for—" he pivoted "—him."

He pointed past the pair of posties at Perseus. Perseus, despite the commotion, had not moved or spoken. Perseus, who had only just managed to prop himself up on his elbows, now looked back at Silver with green eyes blown wide.

Horris swung back around to Silver. But it was Estelle who gave him pause. She didn't look surprised or confused. She looked *livid*.

"What do you want with him?" Horris asked.

"Money, first and foremost. News travels fast these days, postman. The Empire of Creed has a BOLO for that runaway there. Sixty-thousand credits to the crew that brings him back alive." Silver leaned around Horris to study Perseus before straightening. "Course, they didn't say anything about him being in one piece."

Sixty-thousand credits? That was his year's salary right there. What would he even do with a whole extra year's salary?

Didn't matter. Not against the fear in Perseus' eyes.

"No," Estelle said, even before Horris could shake his head. "You can't have him. We found him first."

"And yet, you don't have him," Silver said, indicating Perseus behind Horris and Roddy's legs. "Curious."

She had known. Horris didn't know how Estelle had known, and he didn't care. But she had known there was a price on Perseus' head. "Go," he whispered to Roddy. "Get ready."

The pressure of Roddy's hand vanished. Horris stepped forward to cover the movement of his retreat. "I thought you were Idolers!" He accused Estelle. "I thought you refused to work with the Imperials."

Olive winced. Estelle, to her credit, did not. She lifted her chin. "If the Imperials want him that badly, they can have him. On the condition they leave my people *alone*."

"A traitor isn't a half-bad bargaining chip," Silver mused. Estelle shot him a dark look when he shrugged. "Anyway!" He clapped his hands together, a teacher getting the attention of his unruly class. "I believe I have a way of settling this amicably for all.

"Give the Black Hammer to me. In exchange, I and my crew will leave your charming little husk of a town in peace. I'll even put in a good word regarding the state of your town to the Imps. The posties," he smiled, "can take their cargo and leave untouched. I'll even let you have that barbequed survivor I know they're hanging onto."

Horris stopped short. The John Doe. The postal carrier clinging to life. "Y-you couldn't stop us from leaving."

"Couldn't I?" Silver smiled thinly.

"I refuse to trust the word of a pirate," Estelle said, sparing Horris the razor-thin smile.

"Then trust the word of a Marquay." Silver pressed a hand to his chest. "I swear that I will leave Estelle's shitty little town to its fate and let the posties go unabated, or else my horns will rot and fall to nubs. That ought to suffice, eh, Olive? An oath made on the tip of a horn means something."

Olive touched a hand to the tip of her horns self-consciously. "Indeed," she murmured, the first word Horris had heard her speak.

Silver nodded. "I'll swear it. All you need to do is hand me the Hammer."

Horris looked back at Perseus. The Black Hammer stared back at him with eyes wide. His chest rose and fell rapidly. He'd curled his good leg in towards his waist, but the paralyzed one remained limp and unresponsive. He was no threat to anyone in this state.

If they take him, they'll kill him.

Horris didn't know how he knew that, but it was a bone-deep certainty. The way Perseus had spoken about his people did not inspire confidence in their ability to show mercy. To surrender Perseus would be to kill him. But if he didn't...

That triple-decker was designed to take down ships like theirs. If he handed Perseus over, Silver would let them go free. They could radio for help and get an inspection squad on the surface to help the Idolers and the injured postie.

We're going to get you home, he promised.

He could protect one, Horris realized with dawning horror. But not both.

Everyone was looking at him, waiting for a decision to be reached.

Horris wiped his hands on his thighs and let go of a promise in his heart. He thought of one instruction—one sharp, crystal-clear instruction, loud enough for Fives to hear—before sticking a hand out for Silver to shake.

Silver's fierce smile widened. He crossed to Horris and accepted the outstretched hand. Silver had a grip like iron, and Horris kept his expression neutral as the pirate squeezed.

"Smart man," Silver purred.

"Yeah," Horris said.

Then he swung his free hand up and punched the pirate in the face.

🎜 Acceleration

United Star System Postal Code Chapter 20, Section 1: In consideration of expeditious deliveries as well as demands of interstellar travel, all Grummon-class accelerators should be regularly tested for performance.

Approximately eight minutes prior to hell breaking loose, Roderick Marcelo had been sitting in the pilot's seat and playing with blue putty.

The putty could be stretched thin or rolled into a ball. You could poke your fingers through it or just squish it in your grip. Roddy may have only been half-Elentee, but that half had inherited all of his mother's tics. Elentees did not sit still, and in fact, it was considered an omen of ill health if one was stationary for more than twenty minutes. Not an ideal trait for a pilot, that, and between his restlessness and his grades, he'd nearly failed out of flight school.

It had been Horris who'd suggested the putty to keep his hands busy. Horris, who'd spent a full week researching Elentee spacefarers and how they adapted to the confines of space. Dependable, soft-hearted Horris, that—

"Dumb motherfucker," said Fives.

The phrenic sat in the copilot's chair, rolling putty around in his palms.

Roddy glanced at him approvingly. "Damn straight, Five-o. Don't let Basah hear you—"

"Call someone a dumb motherfucker?" Basah said dryly. She materialized behind them with the cat-like grace her people were known for. She planted both hands on her hips as Roddy busied himself with the putty. "Better not have been me."

"Nah." Roddy took an enormous interest in how thin the putty could stretch. "Our fearless leader."

"Dumb motherfucker," Fives said again.

Well then. Fives certainly hadn't been echoing *his* thought. Roddy risked a smirk in Basah's direction, and she only confirmed it by rolling her eyes. "He's going to be fine," she insisted, although Roddy didn't recall stating anything to the contrary.

Horris had gone tramping into the woods with the Imperial about an hour ago. He probably *was* fine; the Imperial seemed to tolerate Horris, and in any case, it was in his best interest to make sure they both came back in one piece. Even so, Roddy would have felt better about the whole thing if he or Basah had gone along as well.

"It's not an adventure," Fives said suddenly. He smushed his putty between his fingers, watching the compound ooze out with a sort of grim satisfaction. "He wouldn't go on an adventure without you. It's duty."

Ding-dong! Ship detected!

The crew's eyes shot upwards. "How far out, BLIP?" Basah asked.

One-hundred kilometers due north! Also, there is a ground vehicle rapidly approaching!

An exterior camera on the ship's dashboard flickered on. A motorcycle with two riders rapidly sped towards the *Silverfish* with little care for the mud- and bug-splattered concrete. Basah rumbled low in her throat before heading for the lower deck. "BLIP, drop the gangplank."

Roddy sighed loudly and swung his legs off the dashboard. "Never a quiet moment, eh, Five-o?"

"You like it," Fives replied. He cranked up the volume on the Al Hirt album he was listening to, and the old trumpeter drowned out whatever witty retort Roddy could have given.

Roddy meandered down to the lower deck hold and out onto the gangplank. Roddy would have liked to walk at a reasonable speed, but everyone else was so damn short that a Reasonable Roddy Pace was liable to leave everyone else in the dust. Thus, he meandered, which gave Basah enough time to act like she was in charge and Fives enough time to start lurking in the background.

The motorcycle roared to a halt just short of the lowering gang-plank. Estelle jerked the engine off and swung a long leg around to dismount. Olive followed suit. Basah met both at the end of the gangplank. Estelle nodded at her. "Where is he?"

"The Imperial?" Roddy asked. There was no other 'he' who could have inspired such frantic indignation. "What did he do now?"

"He's not here," Olive said, in the tone of someone who had been saying the same thing for quite a while now. "He and Captain Horris are probably still at the compound." She looked off into the woods.

Estelle exhaled. "We need him. It's imperative we get our hands on him immediately."

Roddy was about to ask why but then thought better of it. You didn't need to ask questions when you had an automatic answer-giver standing right behind you. He turned to Fives with a questioning expression.

Good ol' reliable Fives stared hard at Estelle. "...something happened in Creedence," he said, sotto voce. "Something bad."

Estelle gave Fives a cursory look before nodding. She pulled a tablet from her pocket and handed it out to Basah. "The inner-world communications came back online a few minutes ago. This was the first message we picked up. It's been broadcast galaxy-wide."

Roddy peered over Basah's shoulder to watch the broadcast. In it, some skeletal-looking Imperial in a high-collared black jacket preached the good word: "—has delivered His faithful from the armies of apostates, who sought to break our backs and rend us from His holy sight! We have not been deterred! We will not be deterred! We will rise up against the hordes and—"

Basah lowered the tablet. "The Imperials…*won*? But Creed was under complete siege when we left! Half the city was evacuated!" One ear twitched as a new broadcast began, and she returned her attention to the tablet.

"No one knows what's happened," Estelle said grimly. "All the Imperial broadcasts are talking about is how the Emperor delivered them. None of the rebel cells have received word from Adastra. She was in the city. She was supposed to…it shouldn't have…" She fell silent, visibly troubled by the implications of an Imperial victory.

"We had them backed into a corner," Olive said. "All they had to do was kill…"

Roddy had little and less interest in the politics of living gods. His main focus at the moment was getting off Delta Io in one piece. "So, what's this got to do with the Imp?" He asked. "Rushing to tell him the good news?"

"No, Rod," Basah said. She shoved the tablet at Roddy's chest. "Look at this."

Roddy fumbled the tablet. Fives peered around him as he scanned the latest broadcast. It was a red-alert BOLO for Third Lieutenant Perseus Warden, formerly of the Black Hammers, wanted for questioning regarding high crimes against the Emperor and his holy army. A sixty-thousand credit reward was being offered if Perseus Warden was brought in alive. No reward if brought in dead.

Roddy whistled as he handed the tablet back to Estelle. He couldn't help but be impressed. It had been easy, hell near convenient, to assume Perseus was a coward who wanted out of a losing war. But this–*this* was *much* more interesting. What sort of high crimes did one commit against their god?

"You want to turn him in for the reward?" Basah sounded disgusted. She would be, Roddy thought. As much as Basah pretended she didn't believe in institutions, she did believe in things like honor. Such was the side effect of being raised by queens.

Estelle scowled. "No. I have no interest in their blood money. What I need now is leverage. If this news is true, Icene is now the last safe Idoler outpost in the galaxy. And we're alone. I need the Imperial as a bargaining chip—if I can trade him for some guarantee of safe conduct, or for Adastra if they have her—"

Basah's ears had gone flat against her head. "We don't have Perseus."

"I know. But I need your help to find him, *now.*"

"What's the rush?"

"Silver and his crew," Olive said grimly. "If we saw this, so did they."

"But how would they even know he was here?"

The answer came to Roddy with a jolt. Because only one foreign ship had left Creedence airspace before the borders closed: their own. And any fool with an internet connection and a tablet could look up the flight routes of mailships in the local galaxies. Of course, they assumed this was Perseus' stop. If you were wanted for high crimes against your god, who else would you go to, other than the ones ready to commit deicide?

"HEY! HEY, HELP!"

Horris' hoarse shout went up an instant before he burst from the brush on the scooter. Perseus sagged against the seat with Horris. Something was wrong, very wrong, and the way Horris flung himself off the scooter confirmed it. Roddy grabbed Fives by the shoulder and shoved him up into the ship, partially to protect him from the wave of panic coming off Horris and partially to get a head start on the med kit.

"BLIP," Roddy called as he ascended back into the ship, "how close is that ship?"

Twenty-five kilometers away!

Not good. Really, really, not good. Roddy fought a wave of queasiness. He hadn't felt this mingled sense of hopeless urgency and rising dread since that time he set fire to the toaster while Horris was out of the apartment. This time, at least, there was something he could do to head off disaster. He strode to the cockpit and began firing up the *Silverfish*'s engines. He knew what was going to happen when Estelle asked for Perseus. Horris would never give up someone he thought he could help.

It'd be a noble trait if it weren't liable to get them all killed.

BLIP continued to unhelpfully count down the foreign ship's approach while Roddy raced across the *Silverfish*, checking the engines and fuel gauges, back to the cockpit to set the trajectory and bare minimum speed needed to break the atmosphere. He'd just begun running the numbers when a low rumble shook the ship. It was the roar of some great, big, ugly thing, and BLIP unhelpfully informed Roddy that a man-of-war was just over the horizon.

And despite it all, Roddy's jaw dropped as the man-of-war rose over the treeline. He'd never seen one so close before, and the sheer size and scale of the thing was beautiful in its own twisted way. The engineering alone required to make her space-worthy! A boyish thrill coursed beneath urgency and dread. Pirates, like his favorite games and movies, come true. *Pirates!*

Basah and Fives ruined his private moment by stumbling up into the *Silverfish*, the former rubbing at her sensitive ears and cursing between calls of: "Rod! Rod!"

"Right here, right here! Double-check the engines, we gotta go! I'll get Horry." Roddy rushed down the gangplank, nearly stepping on the Imperial as he did, and seized Horris' shoulder. "The engines are hot," the pilot hissed, "let's go, let's *go—*"

The appearance of the pirate captain cut him short. Roddy did his best not to stare at the handsome Marquay and his effortless swagger. He did his absolute best not to feel excited about his sudden proximity to a real pirate. This man, this Silver, was responsible for killing USSPS agents and did not give a damn about anything except targeting his next victim…but hot damn, how would an Elentee look in a jacket like that? Roddy momentarily lost himself in the vision and only came back when Horris stepped over to cover the paralyzed Imperial.

Horris, Dumb Motherfucker of All Time, was speaking to Silver like he was the hero of the thing: "You have a lot to answer for, Silver."

Silver's eyes fixed on Horris. And Roddy, despite his fascination, didn't like the way Silver looked at his brother at all. His eyes peeled Horris apart layer by layer; he'd seen Horris feed Henri enough times to know what a predator was thinking. "That's Captain Silver of the *Scorpion*, thank you very much, Mister Mailman, of the Mail Truck. And to whom do I owe answers?"

Roddy didn't trust himself to speak, only to hold onto Horris while he and Silver exchanged hostilities. At one point, Horris tensed like he was about to rush Silver, and Roddy nearly flung himself onto Horris to keep him in place. Horris was a big human, stronger than he looked, but no man won a fistfight when the other party brought a gun. Their chances to make a clean getaway slipped through their fingers moment by moment, and by the time Silver pointed to Perseus, Roddy knew they weren't getting out of here peaceably. Now, it was a matter of getting out in one piece.

"Go," Horris whispered to Roddy. "Get ready."

Roddy didn't need telling twice. He bolted back up into the *Silverfish* as Horris stepped forward. He sprinted through the hold and back up onto the main deck, where Basah and Fives both waited. "Basah, get to the engine—we're gonna need to be fast."

"What's the plan?" Basah asked, even as she started down the ladder Roddy had just come up.

"Dunno. Something stupid. BLIP, shields up."

Ask nicely.

"NOW, BLIP!"

The engines purred to half-power, and with a click, the air around the *Silverfish* rippled as the energy shield activated. It was their only countermeasure against a direct attack. Roddy swung into his seat, wishing he didn't feel as sweaty and shaky as he did. He needed to focus. He had no interest in dying on this backwater planet, no interest in dying at all, actually, and he could only hope Horris shared that sentiment. He watched the exterior cameras as Horris stuck his hand out for Silver to shake.

"Fly," Fives said. The phrenic was behind Roddy's seat, watching Horris.

Roddy glanced up at Fives. "What?"

"Fly. Horris says fly. *Now!*"

Roddy turned back to the exterior camera in time to see Horris deck Silver.

A moment of stunned silence ensued. Silver was flat on his back on the ground. Pirates and Idolers alike gaped at Horris.

Roddy slammed a hand down on his dashboard.

ENGAGE!

The engager engine roared; the *Silverfish* jerked upwards, that initial, uncertain wobble as the rest of the engines came to life. Outside, Idolers and pirates alike scrambled away from the sudden heat blasting off the mailship. BLIP beeped a warning about the *Scorpion*'s cannons, and Roddy banked the *Silverfish* hard to the left, nearly rolling her over as a beam of crackling energy fired overhead. The cannon fire hit their shield with a shriek, and warning *beep-beep-beeps* of possible damage filled the cockpit.

That was a problem for Later Roddy.

The *Silverfish* burst through the lower atmosphere, with the rumble of the *Scorpion* behind her. Dimly, Roddy heard the hiss of the gangplank pulling inward, and a moment later, Horris appeared, tugging the Imperial up the ladder with him. Roddy swallowed the rage in his throat to focus on keeping the *Silverfish* skyborne as another blast shook the ship. The energy shields only just held as BLIP rattled off statistics about surviving ship crashes.

The *Scorpion* loomed behind them, both massive cannons readying to fire.

"DROP!" Horris bellowed.

Roddy yanked the helm down, and the nose of the *Silverfish* shrieked downwards to avoid cannon fire. Everyone besides Roddy went tumbling backward, and howls of shock and pain joined the dashboard alarms. The taste of blood filled Roddy's mouth as he forced the *Silverfish* back onto a horizontal path. He fought the awful swooping in his stomach to slam a hand on the dashboard to re-engage gravity. Basah screamed for help in the engine pit, and there was the clatter of someone racing to aid her.

Someone else clambered into the copilot's seat beside him. Roddy glanced over, ready to chew Horris out even if they were his last words—but instead, it was the pale, sweat-soaked Perseus next to him.

"WEST!" Perseus barked. "Fly west, NOW!"

"You're not the captain," Roddy snapped. Nevertheless, he banked sharply over an ocean that glinted with the western sun. Roddy cursed and squinted against the glare. "The sun's in our eyes!"

"It's in their eyes, too, now," Perseus said. He gave Roddy a grim, appraising look. "And we're not the ones trying to aim, now are we?"

"Great. So we can let them fire blindly while they kill us. Maybe they'll hit a cloud."

A roar from behind served as an answer. Roddy called up the rear exterior monitor. The *Scorpion* loomed in their cameras. Both frontal cannons rumbled to life, bright blue pinpricks of light set deep in dark sockets.

Roddy had never thought he'd see his own death closing in. His fault, he supposed, for choosing a career with the post office.

Perseus interrupted his mourning with a sharp shout. "The phrenic! Where's your bloody phrenic–?!"

He flung himself out of the copilot chair with all the urgency of a man who had not yet accepted they were SOL, and in the next instant, Fives was slammed into the copilot's chair beside Roddy. They exchanged bewildered looks before Perseus collapsed on the floor beside Fives. He pressed a shaking hand to Fives' knee, either to steady himself or the phrenic. "Focus! Listen for their orders!"

Fives' eyes widened. Roddy waited for the rebuttal, the refusal, even as he kept his eyes on the monitor, watching those blue lights grow brighter, listening for the sharp whine indicating the blast was ready.

Instead, Fives reached over and grabbed his shoulder in a vice grip.

Silence. The roar of the engines and BLIP's shrill beeps cut suddenly as if someone had clicked off the volume of the world. Even the thundering of his own heart was very far away.

All he heard was Silver's voice, shouting from a distant tunnel: *Fire starboard!*

Roddy banked the *Silverfish* portside so hard they almost went vertical. Crackling, electric blue energy careened past the starboard bow, firing off to explode somewhere across the horizon.

What the hell, Silver breathed in his ear.

Perseus laughed incredulously, and only then did Roddy remember to right his own careening ship. He risked a glance at Fives. The phrenic stared forward without seeing. Blood trickled from a nostril and over his cracked lips, but his grip on Roddy was iron.

Give 'em a shave!

Roddy heard Silver's command and dove without hesitation. This time, the energy fired overhead, just ten feet from where they had been a moment before.

"Good–good!" Perseus cried. "Keep it up! *KEEP IT UP!*"

Incredulity and understanding dawned in equal measure. Somehow, someway, over the noise and chaos of their own minds, Fives had heard Silver. Fives had intercepted Silver's orders even before he gave them. Which meant–which meant–*they had an advantage.*

"Keep it up, Five-o!" Roddy shouted.

Fives didn't reply. His lips moved wordlessly, dark gaze unfocused as the phrenic reached for something only he could hear.

Run out the broadsides! If that fucking mailtruck swoops around us, I want it blasted like salt on a bug!

A delirious sort of giddiness seized him. They were schoolboys who'd just found the cheat code, the hack to winning a game they shouldn't even have been playing. It was hard to hear his own voice over the pounding of his heart: "They want to keep us in their sights!"

Perseus nodded. "Well. Let's not oblige them."

The giddiness bubbled up in his chest and spilled out as a full laugh. *"Let's go!"* Roddy lowered his chair into the prone position, ready now for the challenge.

And the challenge was on as the *Silverfish* and the *Scorpion* raced over the open ocean. The atmosphere burst with the sound of roaring engines and cannonades as the *Silverfish* dodged every shot the *Scorpion* fired. Everything else melted away, even the dashboard, as Roddy dipped and wheeled and dived, his Elentee reflexes faster than a human's or a Marquay's, effortlessly able to counter the commands he heard in his mind. He and the *Silverfish* were one entity, one living, breathing thing, connected like they'd never been before; she responded to the slightest of touches, more suggestion than command, putting leagues of Delta Io beneath them.

"THERE!" Perseus shouted and pointed.

Roddy followed his pointing finger to the right. He could just make out a massive shape in the distance. Another ship, he thought for a moment—no, mountains! He curved the *Silverfish* to the right and gunned it, beelining for the mountains.

"What's the plan?" he asked.

"Lose them in the peaks," Perseus said. "We're smaller, more agile. Use their size against them to gain some distance."

"Do you think they'll fall for that? What're they thinking, Fives?"

"I WANT THOSE POSTMEN DEAD!" Fives roared.

The *Silverfish* soared over the black ocean, the greens and browns of solid land, a forest of petrified trees, until the mountain range grew larger, the peaks jutting up from thick cloud cover like the fingers of some massive earth god.

Roddy flicked on the intercom. "Crew, strap in!"

Distant shouts echoed from the engine pit: "Roddy?!" "Rod, what are you—"

And then the *Silverfish* was weaving between those rocky digits, skirting around ice-capped peaks while the *Scorpion* trundled behind her, blasting the face of the mountain range to pieces, firing wildly now in an attempt to strafe the smaller ship.

Roddy whooped as they soared between mountain passes. "BLIP, bring the wings in, fifty degrees starboard, three-twenty-five port!"

The Grummon-class ship—designed for speed and maneuverability—tucked its wings close to its silver body. Roddy yanked the *Silverfish* starboard, sending the starship and her crew vertical as they passed through a narrow gap between two peaks.

Behind them, the ugly screech of metal on stone sounded as the *Scorpion* strafed too close to the mountaintops. Something burst, followed by a blasting explosion from the *Scorpion*. Percy whooped with him this time, the sheer exhilaration slicing through fear and panic—

Fives relinquished his grip and sagged back in the copilot's upright seat. He wiped the thick black blood covering the lower half of his face with the back of his hand. He paused when he saw the blood smeared across his hand, brow furrowed in bafflement. "Heat missiles," he said, apropos of nothing.

"What?" Roddy demanded.

"Heat missiles," Fives said again.

Roddy looked back to the rear external camera. Onscreen, the *Scorpion* was still amidst the mountains, shrinking as they put leagues of distance between the ships. Then, a swarm of missiles burst from her broadsides, careening through the peaks in pursuit of the *Silverfish*.

"Gun it!" Perseus ordered. "Gun it, now, *GO!*"

"BLIP, calculate the trajectory up and out of the atmosphere at the current position and speed!"

BLIP dinged in acknowledgment, and a split-second later, a dotted line appeared on the dashboard screen. Roddy nudged the *Silverfish* onto the corrected course, speeding over the curve of the horizon so fast the colors of the earth below blended into a sickly brown-blue blur—the number on the speedometer clicked up, up, up, faster and faster—

"C'mon girl, c'mon, you can do it, C'MON!"

The *Silverfish* obeyed like she never had before, even as her body rattled from the sheer force of acceleration. Roddy clung to her helm as though his force of will alone would keep her from bursting apart; distantly, he heard someone with his voice screaming about impact—they were up, up, up, through the troposphere, out of the strato and the meso, all with a swarm of missiles hurtling through the air behind them—

They had broken the exo, they were barreling toward the indigo of space—higher, higher, faster, faster–going, going—

GONE!

Interlude 1: The Scorpion

Xandinho Silver had been an active space pirate for nearly fifteen years. He'd been the captain of the *Scorpion* for six years now, and in the course of his six-year reign, the man-of-war had profited nicely off petty squabbles between merchant companies and rival planets. Silver himself was a four-time raider of Ganymedian meteorite mines, a three-time escapee of Ruckan prisons, and a record holder for deaths faked across the United Star System's satellite cities.

And he had just been outmaneuvered by a crew of minimum-wage civil servants in their outdated mailship.

Silence hung heavy in the bridge of the *Scorpion* as the mailship rocketed off into the horizon. Silver stood at the helm, staring at the speck of a ship disappearing into the distance. His bridge crew shared glances. A few removed their headsets; others slunk down into their seats as though that would spare them Silver's wrath.

"What," Silver said, "the *fuck was that.*"

He spun on his boot to stare at his lead gunner. "What," he said again, "the fuck was that!"

The lead gunner had been mentally composing his last will and testament and a heartfelt goodbye to his wife. He straightened when Silver's burning eyes landed on him. "We—we fired as ordered, sir. Our equipment is fully functional."

"I *know* that. *What the fuck was that!*"

The gunner cleared his throat. "I don't know."

"*I know that!*" Silver snapped. He pressed a hand to the hilt of his rapier. He should have slit the captain's throat when he had the chance; he should have run him clean through and taken the Imperial. This was what he got for trying to be decent—dare he say, *merciful*. Silver rubbed at his sore jaw. That was the last time he decided to play fair.

He decided the lead gunner could live and looked next to his technical engineer. "What was the callsign on that mailship?"

The technical engineer met the lead gunner's eyes before forcing herself to look at Silver: "One-Thirty-One-C."

"They're civil servants. They have public records. Get me the names of that One-Thirty-One-C crew. Names and addresses. I want their families, their friends, coworkers—hell, I want their favorite blazeball players! *AND I WANT THEM NOW!*"

He collapsed down in his captain's seat, ignoring the sudden flurry of piratical activity around him. He massaged his throbbing temple with a finger. There was always something. It didn't matter what day of the week it was or what moon they were raiding. There was always fucking something. He couldn't go a week without something.

He was quiet for long enough that his first mate, Sami, deemed it safe to sidle up alongside him. "We gonna circle back to the Idolers, sir? Blast 'em to kingdom come?"

"Nah." Silver pressed hard against his temple as though he could pop his headache like a grape. "Those posties will squeal. Hell, they're probably squealing right now. The sooner we get off this planet, the better."

As fun as it would have been to go back and stomp Estelle's little colony into a paste, doing so would cost them precious time. Even the most ruthless of pirates paled in comparison to the bureaucracy-perfected USSPS, and he had no interest in dealing with the stamp-pushers unless cornered. The sooner they were in open space, the better.

His gaze flickered back up to the bridge's three-fourths view of the world. Delta Io, beautiful and blue, loomed around them. Silver considered the distant horizon, remembering how that little mailship wheeled and dove among the mountaintops.

"That was one hell of a pilot, though, eh?" Silver murmured.

Sami started. She'd busied herself with her tablet. "Sir?"

Silver shook his head. "Get me the Imperial line. On deck, full screen."

His first nodded. A massive black square appeared on the center dashboard window. Three centered dots rattled in time with the call tone. The flurry of activity on the bridge dwindled as the ringing continued.

Silver settled himself back in his chair. He flung one leg over the arm of his chair and let the other rest at a lazy angle. It was an open, lazily inviting stance, the sort that made stiff-backed Imperials squirm. Negotiations went much faster when your opponent was off-kilter.

The screen clicked gray, and then the stern, stony expression of their Imperial liaison appeared. His eyes were hidden behind a pair of black pince-nez, but the crease in his brow gave him away. He straightened his shoulders. "Captain Silver. To what do we owe the pleasure?"

"Liaison Nabis," Silver said. He smiled knowingly and swung his leg down to sit forward. Body language was all necessary for the show. "I thought you'd like to know that we've located that little lost lamb of yours."

Liaison Nabis stared. It was hard to tell what he was thinking behind the pince-nez. That was probably why he wore them. "Where is he?"

"Not here, alas." Silver spread his arms wide to indicate his deck. "Elsewise, I would have had him on his knees for you. That is how you like them, ain't it?"

Snickers broke out around the deck. Silver pulled his smile tight as a bowstring.

Nabis just continued to stare across the screen. "Where is he?"

"He's stowed away on some postal carrier. We've got their callsign, and we're tracking their route across the star system. I'll have him for you in less than a week. Less than three days if you're inclined to double the payout."

"We are not."

Silver shrugged. It was worth a shot. He was about to hang up when Liaison Nabis spoke again:

"What is the nearest populated satellite to your current position?"

"Taygate, sir," Sami replied before Silver even gestured towards her. "About thirty hours from Io."

Liaison Nabis nodded. "Excellent. You'll pick up a platoon of Hammers there."

"Excuse me?"

"A platoon of Hammers will be joining your crew to assist in your retrieval of Lieutenant Warden," Liaison Nabis spoke with a slow, measured tone as though repeating his instructions to a crowd of morons.

Silver couldn't believe his ears. He stood with a scowl. "Oh, I don't think so! We don't need help."

"It is the Emperor's will. He believes Lieutenant Warden's retrieval will provide a valuable lesson to the younger Hammers regarding disloyalty."

"My crew and I aren't here to teach a bunch of brats about what happens when daddy's pissed! If this is the Imperial way of trying to wiggle out of that sixty-thousand, then you and your Emperor are dead men walking—"

Liaison Nabis never said a word. He simply reached up and removed his pince-nez, revealing a pair of eyes so pale that they were almost translucent.

Silver froze. His headache rushed back thricefold, a throbbing, rapidly-building pressure that threatened to burst behind his eyes. He could hear the blood drumming in his ears as the invisible band wrapped around his forehead, tighter and tighter, squeezing. There was a hand in his brain, in his mind, fingers groping at all the dark corners, yanking all the old and ugly fears into the light. He was weak, worthless, shackled—

The hand withdrew. Silver gasped for air and went slack in his chair. He was dimly aware of his crew staring at him. *Afraid*, the part of his mind that was always aware screamed.

"The Emperor wills it," Liaison Nabis said again. He set his pince-nez back on the bridge of his nose. "And his Hand will see it done."

"F-fine." Silver sat up slowly. "Fine. We'll pick up the goddamn platoon. Just give us the rendezvous point. Tell them to bring popcorn for the show."

Liaison Nabis cut the call. For the second time in only a few minutes, a silence hung heavy in the *Scorpion*'s bridge. This one was heavier, though, laced with a sort of dread no one had the words for. Silver exhaled through his nose before turning to his first. "Sam."

"Sir?" Sami replied warily. She had a white-knuckled grip on her tablet.

"I need the names of those postmen. Now."

■

Half a galaxy away, Nabis turned from his dark screen to the young Hammer standing just off to the side. "Mind the pirate, Lieutenant Mason. Creatures like that will attempt to sway you from your duty."

Lieutenant Electra Mason lifted her chin. Her eyes rested somewhere over her superior's shoulder. Like all Hammers, she knew better than to meet the Liaison's eyes. "Yes, sir."

Nabis considered her. He did not have to probe her mind to feel her anxiety, her doubts, the simmering anger beneath it all. Her cohort had been spared the worst of the war, and there was a growing restlessness among the younger Hammers regarding their place in it. The siege against Creedence had ended. The Idolers had been backed into a corner, and nowhere was a creature more dangerous than in a corner. Sending them to retrieve the wayward Hammer was a good solution: it allowed them experience without risking them against desperate heretics. Even so...

"You do not have to pursue this path," he said gently.

Electra's expression did not waver. "My brother's weakness must be cleansed."

She did look very much like her brother. Orestes had been the elder: a gangly, nervous youth who had never been comfortable in his uniform. Electra had the same blue eyes set deep in a long face, with the same oversized nose and weak chin. She wore her mouse-brown hair short and businesslike under her cap.

Electra had not grieved when Orestes died. She had renounced her brother, his blood, any and all claims to his worldly possessions. There was strength in her, a conviction they'd all mistakenly thought Perseus Warden possessed.

Now that was a lesson, Nabis thought. A good soldier could kill his heretical enemies. A true soldier could renounce her heretical kin.

"Orestes was weak," he agreed. "But weakness originates in the spirit, not the blood."

Electra jumped when Nabis rested a hand on her shoulder. He soothed the rush of uncertainty with a gentle nudge. He pulled a thread from the blanket of the Emperor's love and sewed it into her soul like a secret stitch. "The Emperor sees you, child. The Emperor knows the strength in your heart."

She nodded as Nabis pulled back. "And if we should recover Lieutenant Warden?"

"The Emperor wants him alive," Nabis said. "Bring him home."

"And those postmen with him? Should we bring them back, too?"

"No," Nabis said very softly. The USSPS was a powerful institution worthy of respect. But an individual postman was not special. An individual postman was not important. Assuming they were not directly aiding and abetting the wayward Hammer, there was no need to worry about them. "Now go. You have a long journey ahead."

He dismissed Electra with a nod. Nabris turned back to his massive work desk, considering the mounds of to-dos and paperwork even the Emperor's personal phrenic was not exempt from. He settled down in his seat and closed his eyes. He took a deep, centering breath. Orestes had been a coward, Perseus a reckless fool. The war revealed the rot under the floorboards. One could only hope it continued to weed out the weak.

Emperor guide me, Nabis prayed. Then he opened up his emails.

12 The World Apology Tour

United Star System Postal Code, Chapter 11, Section 1: All incidences of hostile behavior towards USSPS employees should be reported to an immediate supervisor using SR support.

At some point, the *Silverfish* stopped rattling like a bomb about to blow. The engines' scream died to a somewhat-reasonable wheeze, and only then did Horris unclench his aching jaw. He sat up off the engine pit bench—and immediately sank down again. His head swam as blood and brain fluid recentered themselves; muscles quivered as adrenaline slammed through his body like a wasp caught under a glass.

"We're not dead," Basah announced.

"How d'you figure that?"

"Because if we were in heaven, there'd be women. And if we were in hell, Roddy would be here."

Horris snorted. After a moment or two, the buzzing wasps in his system reduced to occasional twitches, and he trusted himself to sit upright. A wild-eyed Basah sat beside him. She'd lost the top half of her jumpsuit in the wild scramble to keep the engines from overheating, and the fingers she carded through her hair left oily black streaks behind.

"What happened?"

"Dunno. Let's go find out."

Retching sounds greeted Horris and Basah at the bridge. Roddy was on his hands and knees, vomiting in a corner. Fives sat in the copilot's seat with hands slammed over his headphones and eyes screwed shut.

"Rod?" Horris started towards him. "Rod, are you—"

"SHUT UP!" Roddy snapped. He propelled himself upright and tucked his trembling hands against his chest. "Shut up, just shut up—what the hell were you thinking? You dumb fuck, you nearly got us killed!"

Horris froze. Any and all assurances died in his throat. He'd only been thinking of one thing, in truth. "I—I couldn't let them take Perseus. They were going to kill him!"

"So the next-best solution was *getting us all killed*? Are you *INSANE*?"

"Roddy, please—"

"The only reason we're alive right now is because Fives is a damn good mind reader! And even that almost killed him!" Roddy snapped a hand out to Fives, who had tucked his legs against his body and began to rock back and forth. As such, it took Horris longer than it should have to see the blood staining his mouth and neck.

Basah gasped and ran to crouch beside Fives. Horris looked back to the seething Roddy, not sure what to do with the foul-tasting lump of guilt in his throat. The sickening truth of his split-second decision was on him: he had just risked his friends—their *lives*—on a gamble they hadn't asked to take.

"I'm sorry," he said in the strained silence. He didn't know what else to say.

Roddy sniffed. He ran the back of his hand across his mouth. "Good. You should be." He glanced down at his puddle of sickness and grimaced. "Goddamnit. Where're the wipes?"

"I'll clean it."

Perseus spoke so softly Horris almost didn't realize it was him. The Imperial stood in the corridor connecting the bridge to crew quarters, clutching a roll of microfiber wipes in a white-knuckled grip. With his other hand, he flicked his limp hair out of his eyes. He seemed to realize something else was needed because he straightened up. "Do not think I do not recognize the enormity of what you've done for me, nor the risk involved. I—thank you. Thank you. Thank you for saving my life."

Perseus' eyes burned that brilliant pale green, and when their eyes met, a sudden heat crept up the back of Horris' neck. A sort of calm washed over him.

Roddy rubbed at the back of his long neck. There was no clever retort to gratitude that didn't make him look like an asshole. "Yeah. Well. You're all right in a firefight, Red."

"He likes you," Fives exclaimed. The phrenic had slowly unfurled from his fetal position and gotten to his feet. It wasn't obvious who he was speaking to, and he left the bridge before anyone recovered enough to ask him. Perseus side-stepped Fives warily as he went by.

Horris shook his head. "Fives has the right idea. Rod, Bah, go get some rest. You've earned it. I've got to call this into central office." The thought did not inspire confidence so much as a low-level dread. Calling the central office meant speaking to the postmaster…and, worse, a postal inspector.

A poke in his shoulder brought him back. Basah stood beside him with tail twitching. "I'll help you make the call."

"That would be a huge help." Horris rolled his shoulders back and cleared his throat. It was better to adopt Captain Mode: "BLIP, set course for next postal destination."

Roger roger!

Perseus stepped past him to start cleaning. He limped as he walked, heavily favoring his left leg, and under the pale lights, he looked ill. But he got straight to work without complaining. The best Horris could do was follow his example.

■

Three hours later, Horris was beginning to think letting Silver take Perseus would have been the more merciful option.

All right, that wasn't true—but the part of his mind that sounded a lot like Roddy complained anyway.

Finding the phone number for Sentient Resources on the cluttered USSPS employee page took nearly five minutes. Then it was calling Sentient Resources, being put on hold, starting a tablet game while they were on hold, having to pause the tablet game when they finally patched through to someone, downloading and filling out the incident report—except the incident report PDF was uneditable, so Basah had to call Fives in to fix it—email back the incident report, play more tablet games until the local postmaster rang them, heard their oral report, and then called her boss, who called his boss, who finally, finally, *finally* got them on the line with *his* boss, who happened the postmaster general of the United Star System Postal Service.

His name was David Kalani, and among postal service enthusiasts, he was considered to be something of a badass.

He was captain of the first postal crew to establish contact with the people living in the New Edge and had successfully negotiated the establishment of the first interstellar postal satellite in the Tutone region. During his term as president of the union, he'd renegotiated dental coverage and the uniform requisition system, led a six-week strike resulting in better pay for carriers and inspectors alike, and introduced Secret Santas into Jolliday parties.

Now, Postmaster General Kalani watched the external video of the *Scorpion* firing on the *Silverfish* with a furrowed brow. BLIP had downloaded their recording of the dogfight and sent it over for review. The Postmaster General folded his hands together. "And they attacked you unprovoked?"

Horris winced. He had been very careful to leave Perseus out of the events preceding up to the dogfight. All USSPS had to know was that they'd been confronted by pirates and attacked. "Well, not exactly, sir. We wouldn't negotiate with their terms."

"Nor should you have." The Postmaster General's eyes tracked the wheeling ship even as he spoke. A low whistle escaped him as the *Silverfish* dove between mountain peaks. "How on earth did you escape?"

"We owe it to Fives," Basah said. "He could read their intent."

The Postmaster General glanced at something by his elbow and nodded. "Right, right, you're the crew with the phrenic." He looked back up and met Horris' gaze. The corner of his mustache twitched upwards as he smiled. "Well, good work, all of you. We'll send a squadron of inspectors out to Delta Io immediately. Reroute back to your postal route—"

"Already done, sir."

"Very good. We'll send a notice out about shipping delays along your route. When do you check in at a USSPS depot station?"

"That's our next stop," Basah said. She had her tablet out and their route open for consultation. "The Franklin-Two Depot."

"Excellent. I'll meet you there, Captain Horris."

The sentence almost didn't make sense. And when it did, Horris almost didn't believe him. "You'll…meet me there, sir?"

The Postmaster General nodded. "You've done excellent—dare I say, stellar—work. I would like to commend you in person for your duty to the postal service."

The sightless eyes of the John Doe stared back at him. *Get you home*, he'd promised. And he'd broken that promise for Perseus' sake. Now, he was lying—omitting Perseus' presence on their ship—from the Postmaster General himself. His stomach twisted into a sharp knot. He hadn't done his duty to the postal service. Not at all.

Basah nudged him for an answer. Horris took a deep breath and nodded. "I'll notify you when we arrive at Franklin-Two, sir."

"Excellent. Have a safe journey, Captain Horris. And don't worry about those pirates."

When the feed cut, Horris was left staring at his own miserable reflection. He pitched forward with a groan, holding his head in his hands. Slimy, sour guilt formed in the pit of his stomach. He'd lied. He'd lied to the *Postmaster General* of all people. He was no proper captain of the postal service. He was no proper postman at all.

Basah clucked her tongue. "Oh, no, you don't. No self-pity allowed in this house." She seized him by the shoulder and hauled him upright.

Horris threw his head back in a groan. "I screwed up, Basah! I screwed up *hard*! When the Postmaster General finds out why those pirates opened fire, we're all *screwed*! I never should have—"

"Oh, Matron, preserve me. Stop it!" She smacked the top of his head lightly. "Just–*stop*!"

"But—"

Basah slapped her hand over his mouth. "You're so *dramatic* when you've got some authority figure in front of you! Horris, please! You were never going to leave Perseus behind, and don't try to argue shoulda-woulda-coulda! Now, I'm going to tell you something, and you're going to shut up and listen. Okay?"

Horris nodded cautiously. Basah removed her hand from his mouth but kept it close, just in case. She eased her hip up against his cluttered cabin desk.

"When I was young, my mother gave me a riddle. Once, deep in winter, a huntress set forth from her starving village to find game. She had a husband and two little ones waiting at home, and she could not afford to fail. After many hours in the forest, she came across a quail and a buck. The quail could be easily killed and dressed, but it would only feed her family. The buck would feed many families, and its hide and antlers could be used by the village. But killing the buck and bringing it back would be a longer and more arduous process. Which should she choose?"

The buck, Horris wanted to say. *The most good for the most people.* But he was no hunter, had never been hunting, and the prospect of bringing one down alone seemed daunting. The quail, then, but what would the hunter's neighbors say when she only returned with one bird? He weighed the pros and cons for a long moment, not wholly satisfied with either answer.

"What did you say?" He asked in lieu of answering.

"The quail." If Basah was annoyed by his lack of answer, she didn't let it show. "If there's one nearby, I told my mother, surely there are others. You could bring more hunters with you next time and get more."

"And were you right?"

Basah shrugged. "Didn't matter. The point of the story was the lesson. You have to make a choice. And if you take too long, the choice escapes. You made a choice, Horry. And now you get to live with it." She clapped him on the shoulder.

"Do you think I made the correct choice?" Horris asked, desperate for assurance.

She waggled a finger at him. "I'm not your mother. You figure it out." She hopped off his desk and left without a word further.

Horris sat alone in his darkened cabin. It had all seemed so simple at the start. A simple yes to a simple request: *get me off this planet, I don't want to go to war.* Who could be blamed for wanting to lend a hand? All they had to do was follow the route. But suddenly, somehow, motives had tangled into a hopeless knot. If the Postmaster General discovered that he'd chosen a passenger over a fellow USSPS agent, a passenger they weren't even supposed to have, who currently had a bounty on his head…

The fallout was going to suck. But when Horris thought about Perseus and his bright green eyes, he couldn't find it in him to regret the choice.

Of course, the choice hadn't been his alone to make, and the fallout wouldn't hit him alone. Horris began his Apology World Tour just outside Roddy's cabin. Before he could even lift a hand to knock, a curt "Come in, Horris" sounded from inside.

Horris didn't have to ask how Roddy knew it was him: Fives rocked back and forth on Roddy's bunk. He had his eyes closed and hands pressed against his headphones as though trying to shove the music directly into his brain. Roddy himself sat at his desk, smacking blue putty around with a frown. Horris winced as Roddy smacked the putty against the desk.

"Hey," he began, "can we talk?"

"Horris feels guilty and wants to apologize for being a dumb motherfucker," Fives said.

"Not the words I was going to use, Fives."

"It's the words Roddy used," Fives said, somewhat defensively. He opened one eye to peek at Roddy. "Roddy wants to keep being angry at you, but being angry gives him an upset stomach."

Roddy shot Fives a look. "Y'know, Fives, you're really ruining the apology I've been waiting for."

"You two give me a headache." Fives retorted. He opened both eyes now to glare at them both. "I can't hear Coltrane over the sound of your angry-sad-guilty-sick."

Horris opened his mouth. Closed it. Exchanged a look with Roddy.

Fives frowned as thoughts flowed unbidden. "Shut up! It's only awkward because you two make it awkward!"

Roddy held up his hands. So did Horris. "Okay, okay! Sorry, Fiver, I'm sorry. Can you give Rod and I a moment alone?"

"Finally." Fives got to his feet and crossed to the door. He stopped on the threshold and pivoted back to Horris. "It was Percy."

Horris blinked at Fives. "Sorry?"

"You already said sorry. You want to know how I could read the pirate's mind. Silver. You're all so *loud* all the time. It was Perseus. I touched his knee, and it was quiet. Like turning down the volume to hear shouting down the hall." He shrugged. "Thank *him*. I just listened."

He left Horris and Roddy to their own apologies. Horris paused, collecting himself, and then gestured to the bunk previously occupied by Fives. "May I?"

"Yeah." Roddy sighed. He stood and moved to sit on the end of the bunk. "Let's get this over with."

Horris sat. He studied his hands for a moment, working up the nerve to repeat what Fives had already said. Roddy squeezed blue putty between his fingers and waited.

"I'm sorry," Horris said at last. The words were still difficult to say. "I made a decision, in the moment, without consulting any of you. I trusted you all to see it through—and thank god you did; otherwise, we'd all be dead. But it's not something I should have put you through without warning."

Roddy didn't reply right away. Such was the natural course of their disagreements; Horris had long since learned to wait the silence out. And sure enough, after a minute or two, Roddy blew out a breath. "Yeah. It sucked. It sucked big time, okay? Next time you're about to do something stupid, just–trust us to have your back, okay? None of us were gonna let them have Red. You should've seen Basah before you got there. She was about to go all interstellar amnesty on Estelle."

"You wouldn't have handed him over?" Horris' eyes widened.

Roddy scratched at his sideburns. "No? I mean, I would've *thought* about it. No question there, I would have for sure *thought* about it. But actually turning him in? Nah. For one, you would've killed me. For two," he paused, evidently struggling to come up with a second reason for his altruism, "he's not *that* bad as far as live packages go. Remember the ducklings?"

Horris would've preferred not to remember about the ducklings. Still, he nodded.

"So, yeah. He's not the worst. Listen, next time, just—*tell us* when you're gonna pull some stupid shit, so we can be ready to make it unstupid. That's what a crew is for."

"I will," Horris said. His shoulders lifted as a weight came off him. "I will. Thank you. I don't know how to make it up to you."

"Oh, that's easy. I wanna be team captain next time we play Survival Horror."

Horris blinked twice. "But I'm always the team captain when we play Survival Horror."

"Well, not anymore. Your judgment has been impaired by that perky Imperial ass—"

Roddy yelped when Horris punched his shoulder. He flopped over onto his bunk and rubbed at his shoulder. Horris let the moaning carry on for a bit before relenting. He threw his hands up. "Fine. Fine! You can be the team captain! But when we have to start the game over because you blew all our resources in the first twenty minutes, don't come crying to me!"

"Bet."

They shook on it. Roddy twisted to watch Horris get to his feet. "Hey, Horry. Since Red is an unofficial part of the team and all…"

"Yeah?"

"Well. I feel bad shoving him back into the closet after he saved our lives. He can bunk with me if he wants."

Horris smiled. "That's really generous of you, Rod."

"See? I'm a better team captain than you already."

"Fuck you."

"Fuck *you.*"

The brotherly love thus preserved, Horris exited. He drifted down the hall, already feeling better than he had ten minutes before. No matter what, he had the crew. And the crew had him. He took a moment to gather himself outside of the broom closet and then knocked on the door.

"Enter," Perseus' muffled voice called.

When Horris poked his head through the door, it was to find Perseus sitting on the floor. He had his injured leg stretched out in front of him. He'd torn away the remnants of his remaining pant leg, leaving the wound exposed as he rummaged through the first aid kit. His eyes flickered to Horris and back to the first aid kit.

It was hard not to feel like he was intruding. "Hey," he said, "how're you doing?"

"Oh, well, you know how it goes. In the past twenty-four hours, I've been swarmed by flies, harassed by Idolers, slogged through a swamp, attacked by spiders the size of a pony, tripped on whatever paralytic they use on prey, stopping tripping in time to be pounced upon by pirates, while I discovered that I'm wanted on my home planet for high crimes against my god, all while in the company of idealistic postmen who'd punch a man in the face before coming up with a solid escape plan. How are *you* doing?"

"I've been better." Horris crossed to sit across from Perseus.

The redhead snorted. He went back to picking through their medical supplies.

The silence was almost comfortable. Then Horris cleared his throat. "Why are you wanted?"

Perseus paused. "Sorry?"

"Before, you said you were escaping Creed because you didn't want to die. And that made sense to me. But why are you wanted?"

"The Imperial Army of Creed isn't one that takes lightly to desertion."

There was more there. Horris didn't need to be a phrenic to sense it. It was in the way Perseus' gaze flickered away and then back again. The Imperial shook his head. "It's–I–there are some things I cannot speak about. Not here. I'm sorry, Captain Horris. You're just going to have to take my word on that."

"Okay."

"Okay?" Perseus drew up. His eyes narrowed sharply, and he tensed like a serpent ready to strike. "Okay? That's it? Just—*okay?*"

"Yeah. Just okay. My crew and I are committed to getting you to safety. We don't have to know your trauma. That's not part of our job."

Horris thought this would have served as assurance. And maybe with any other man, it would have. But Perseus just gaped at him. He was angry, almost, although Horris couldn't tell if he was angry with himself or the crew or the world he'd left behind.

Perseus spluttered his next question: "Why—why are you so *kind?*"

What a question. No one had ever asked it of him before. Horris didn't have a ready answer, no easy quip or riddle that would sum it all up. Why? Because the other option was cruelty, and Horris had no interest in being cruel. He didn't know if Perseus would understand, though, not with the way he stared at Horris as if he had two heads. His thoughts turned to Basah and the simple wisdom from her childhood.

"When I was a kid," he began slowly, "we lived in the city. And there was this street cart vendor who worked on the corner near our condo. He sold all kinds of hot food, but I loved his churros the best. They were pretty much perfect, hot and crispy with cinnamon sugar. He'd even give you this little cup of chocolate to dip them in." His mouth watered at the memory, recalling the way the sugar sparkled on his tongue, the chocolate he licked from his teeth hours after he'd eaten.

"He survived the war. Not much else did. He kept up the street cart business until I was in my teens. And then he retired. And when he did," Horris shrugged, "he took his recipes with him. I tried to find other churro guys, but nobody's tasted exactly the same, y'know? So, I started learning how to make them at home. They weren't perfect—still aren't—but I learned a valuable lesson."

"What's that?" Perseus asked.

"If you can't find it," Horris said, "you have to make it yourself."

Perseus stared at him. His expression didn't change, but something in his eyes softened. Something equally soft and warm bloomed in Horris' chest. He got to his feet before the warmth could spread. "Anyway, I, uh–wanted to tell you that Rod said you could bunk with him if you're interested. You don't have to make a decision right away. I'll check in with you later, Perseus."

"Horris," Perseus spoke only when Horris turned away.

Horris turned back. "Yeah?"

Perseus looked up at him and then away. He fixed his gaze on a shelf full of cleaning supplies before speaking: "You can call me Percy, if you like. My–my friends used to. Back in the Academy."

"Percy," Horris tried the nickname out. He was trying so very hard not to smile like some fool, and somewhere on the ship, he knew Fives could feel his elation. "Take care, Percy. Get some rest."

"You as well, Horris."

13 Survival Horror

United Star System Postal Code, Chapter 13, Section 1: All couriers on extended conveys are required by law to be allowed upwards of two (2) hours of downtime following eight (8) or more full hours of work completion.

He used to dream of space.

He had devoured every book and video on the subject, and his parents had taken him multiple times to see the space exploration exhibits at the Ceres Children's Science Museum. Twice he'd gone to see *Rocket! The Space Dog: The Movie* while it was in its theatrical run. Painted galaxies and planets had swirled across his bedroom walls. It had all been accurate; his father had been an artist, his mother a chemist, which meant they were both sticklers for details. Instead of bedtime stories, they'd curled up together in his bed and counted the stars.

Roddy exhaled sharply. He blinked and shook his head, anchoring himself in the cockpit of the *Silverfish*. The three-fourths view of space stretched out before him. Space was not empty; his parents had taught him that, but it could be very lonely.

Roddy rubbed at a knot in the back of his neck. He hadn't had cause to think of his parents in ages. He wondered if they'd be proud of their son. He'd made it to space, after all. His dream had, in theory, come true.

Footsteps echoed from behind him. Percy strode up with hands clasped behind his back. He still looked pale, and he limped when he walked, but at least he wasn't on the verge of death. They exchanged polite nods.

Roddy watched Percy watch the expanse of space. "Never been off-planet, have you, Red?"

"Red?" Percy arched an eyebrow. He had the right sort of eyebrows for arching: thin and angular and judgmental. "Is that the best appellation you could come up with?"

"I'm not gonna overthink a nickname."

"Fair enough, Blond."

Roddy couldn't help his grin. Percy's lips twitched in an odd spasm of a smile. "To answer your original question, no." Percy turned his eyes back to space. "I've never been outside my orbit."

"How d'you like it?"

"It's certainly not as glamorous as I was led to believe." Percy glanced down at the cockpit dashboard. He lowered himself into the cockpit beside Roddy slowly, as if testing to see whether or not he would be thrown out. "Nor as quickly traversed."

Roddy snorted in amusement. He checked the fuel gauges, pulled up the inter-ship log, and fired off a quick message to Fives regarding the readings. "Yeah, the vids leave out all the uninteresting stuff like travel times."

"I never knew it was so large," murmured Percy.

Roddy swiveled back to follow his gaze out the window. Purple and orange nebulae roiled together in a dance spanning thousands of years. A nova remnant, light-years away by his radar's reading, nevertheless pulsed soft blue light over the *Silverfish* as she sailed. *Revenants*, his father used to call them, *singing dead stars to sleep*. White pinpricks shone far in the distance, stars or planets or satellites assuring travelers that they were not alone. It was all so very far away, stretched out over eons inconceivable to even the longest-lived sentients. And yet—it was all so close, comparatively. Space was good at screwing with your sense of scale like that.

"Welcome to space, Red," Roddy said, proud as a father introducing his child.

Percy tore his eyes off the horizon long enough to look at Roddy. "Did you always want to be a pilot?"

"I wanted to go to space." Roddy shrugged. "This was the best way to get there."

"How so?"

"I wanted to fly, Horris loves the mail, and USSPS is always hiring. Two plus one equals three."

It had been Horris' idea, of course. Get out of Grand York, get off Ceres, get away from the place where they had nothing and no one to return to. Get out into space where the adventures waited. Roddy had despaired at the thought of being stuck as a mail pilot, but what other choice did he have? It took years to work up to captaincy of a cruise starship or a commercial freighter. Horris would never have forgiven him if he had enlisted in the military and there hadn't been any pirates in the bay that week. Mail couriers worked long hours in dangerous territories for little thanks, but at least they had a union. At least they got out and could see the universe.

"They're always hiring?"

"Oh, yeah. Don't let the ship chases and stowaway Imperials fool you. Most of our routes are *pick up cargo here, fly it there, rinse and repeat*. Long hours, rarely on solid ground…most people don't make it more than a year on a crew."

"Why do it at all, then?"

"We get our own ship," Roddy indicated the cockpit all around them, "and we get to see the universe." He lowered his hand back to the controls. "Why did *you* become a soldier?"

"Because I was called to." Percy turned back to the window, staring off into the sea of stars. "Because I was chosen."

Roddy didn't know what to make of that. For the first time, he wished he'd paid more attention to his Civics classes. Maybe knowing a bit more about Creed would explain Percy's whole deal. But he hadn't, so he didn't, and so he cast around for as generic a question as possible: "What did you want to be when you grew up?"

Percy didn't answer. A strange sort of sympathy seized Roddy. After the war, plenty of orphans and displaced youths signed onto the military in search of safety and stability, never mind that it was the military that had destroyed their lives in the first place. If he hadn't had Horris in his ear, begging him not to…well, Cerian or Creed, the fact was very few of them really got to choose.

A notification from Horris flashed on his chatlog. *Dinnertime!*

Oh, thank God. This conversation was veering too far into depressing territory. Roddy engaged BLIP as the autopilot and got to his feet. Percy followed.

"So," Roddy said as they strode towards the mess, "what do you do for fun?"

He expected something like 'drinking the blood of the enemy' or 'wearing all black to hide the blood of the enemy.' So Percy surprised him with: "I studied dance."

"Dance?"

"Yes. I believed the extra physical training would serve me well. Did you take any extra curricula in training?"

Training? "Uh, I ran track, if that's what you mean."

"Track—oh!" Percy's eyes lit up. "Athletics! You're a field man!"

Oh, God. Roddy was beginning to think he liked Percy better when the Imperial acted like he was above them. Listening to Percy put tidbits of information through his Child Soldier Private Education translator was excruciating. He fought the urge to walk faster down the corridor. "I used to run track. Something to do while Horris was on the wrestling team."

Basah was already in the mess, picking through the available options for dinner. Grummons had been designed economically, which meant that space was maximized for packages and minimized for crew. The mess on a Grummon had no fancy cookware or fresh ingredients. Their meals were dehydrated and sealed in space-sturdy packaging. All one needed to dine on the *Silverfish* was a pair of scissors, a few drops of water, and the microwave. Only a few items— cookies, tortillas, granola bars—escaped the rehydrating process.

"Fives called the mac-and-cheese, and Horris wanted soup," Basah said. She indicated the flat, silver packages tucked under one arm. "And I've got the hunter's chicken. Rod?"

"Ah, beef tips." Roddy turned to Percy. "Red, what do you want?"

Percy watched Basah flick through the silver packages. Either he didn't have an answer, or he dreaded giving it. Roddy decided to take pity on the man and ordered the beef tips for him. He set the table while Basah rehydrated and reheated the food.

Percy watched the process with fascination. "You've no fresh food aboard, then?"

Basah shook her head. "It'd spoil. Plus, the weight of everything aboard a ship has to be taken into consideration, especially on an express delivery ship. Our water tank, small as it is, takes up a lot of our non-cargo weight."

Roddy nodded in agreement. "And even then, the geniuses over in the policies and decisions department thought about reducing the size of water tanks on mailships for…ah, what was it, Basah?"

"Maximizing cargo space and reducing unused water resources. For the good of the economy and the budget, of course." She rolled her eyes as she spoke.

Percy's thin, Imperial eyebrows drew together. "Why didn't they go through with it?"

"Because the union raised holy hell," Roddy replied gleefully. The memory of watching the union president rip the board of directors a new one incited a delicious sort of schadenfreude. "We should watch the recordings sometime, Red. Public policy is fantastic entertainment."

Roddy was setting the vitamin supplements down on the dinner table when Horris and Fives joined them. Horris' expression brightened the instant he saw Percy.

Because he was in a generous mood, Roddy did not roll his eyes. Thank God Percy had been raised in a covenant of child soldiers, or otherwise he might have noticed Horris' painfully obvious big dumb crush. Horris had had a weakness for redheads ever since Margot Halsten in their eighth year (they'd dated for about three weeks). Margot had been nice enough, but putting her in the same category as Percy was like putting a poodle in the same category as a wolfdog.

Fives laughed softly at the observation.

They sat down for dinner. It was a funny feeling, sitting down, swallowing their supplements, chatting idly about this and that. Had they really just been flying for their lives a few hours before? This was probably the part where he was supposed to be thankful to be alive. Mostly, he just felt dizzy. At least he wasn't alone: Percy sat between him and Horris, picking at his food without eating it.

"So," Roddy cleared his throat, "what's next?"

"We've got a transfer at Franklin-Two," Horris replied. He tilted his full soup spoon so that soup dribbled back into the bowl. "The Postmaster General wants to meet with me."

Roddy blinked. Horris the Fanboy didn't sound excited at all. "Do you think there'll be a problem?"

"Hopefully not. We didn't take any sustained damage, and nothing is missing from the cargo hold. But…" Horris trailed off.

"But if there's any word of a stowaway onboard," Percy said, "that could mark trouble for you. The Idolers know I'm here, and doubtless, your postal inspectors have already arrived on Io to speak with them. There's a good chance they know I'm onboard already. What happens then?"

"We face some disciplinary action," Basah said, matter-of-fact.

Horris winced.

Percy pushed his food around idly. "And what happens to me, then? Would I be returned to Creed?"

"Of course not!" Horris exclaimed.

"You don't know that, Horry," said Roddy.

"The USSPS is a *neutral* entity," said Horris. "They wouldn't be able to accept any financial compensation for Percy's return."

"It's also against rules and regulations to stowaway on a USSPS ship," Basah replied. She leveled her fork at Horris. "You said so yourself."

"Could I claim asylum?" Percy asked.

Basah shook her head. "Not with a business entity like the post office." She took a quick bite of her hunter's chicken, looking at Percy thoughtfully. "Look, until they ask where we've stowed the Imperial, you can stay with Fives and I in the engine pit. Even if the inspectors search the hold, they won't come into the engine pit. They're all afraid of Fives." She grinned across the table at the phrenic, who sipped his apple juice and did not comment.

Percy's gaze lingered too long on Fives before nodding. "I would appreciate that."

"So," Roddy said, "what *did* you do that pissed them off so badly?"

"I deserted. They do not take kindly to deserters."

"Sixty-thousand credits and a charge of high crimes sounds a lot more dire than *does not take kindly*."

"My people are very good at what they do." Percy tried for a thin smile, but it faltered. He twisted his fork through his fingers. "I thought I had more time. I thought they would be more preoccupied with the Idolers…"

"The Idolers," said Roddy, "who your people curb-stomped in that battle."

Percy looked troubled. Roddy picked at his beef stew. "Why Apollonia anyway?" He shifted as Horris kicked his leg under the table.

Percy must have felt the kick because he glanced at Horris. Nevertheless, he answered: "I have a great-aunt who lives there, from my mother's side. My only off-planet relation."

What then? Roddy wondered. He'd had no family to turn to after the Helium War, but he had had Horris and a system—not perfect, but present—dedicated to getting children sheltered and schooled. Percy didn't have any of that. What did an ex-child soldier do with his life?

He wanted to ask more questions, but it wasn't worth the daggered look Horris was shooting at him. A heavy sort of silence enveloped the table. Fives stood abruptly, took his mac and cheese, and left the room.

"Anyone up for a round of Survival Horror later?" Horris asked into the silence.

Roddy initially assumed he'd heard him wrong. No, he hadn't, because Basah relaxed and agreed. Now, they were both looking at him. Right—Horris promised he could be the Captain on the next round of Survival Horror. This was probably his way of trying to distract them all from the looming specter of Franklin-Two.

And, damn the man, it worked. He *really* wanted to be the Captain. Roddy agreed to a few rounds of Survival Horror during their downtime.

Percy seemed not to have heard any of the exchange. He was staring down at his food, lips moving without sound, but Roddy's sharp ears could nevertheless catch the faintest whisper of a prayer.

■

A knock at the door drew Roddy from his laptop screen. He pulled one bud out of his ear and twisted towards the door. "Yo? Come in?"

Percy entered. Roddy had to hand it to him: the Imperial had the uncanny ability to look out-of-place no matter where he was. Maybe it was the rumpled black uniform, or maybe it was how he held his shoulders stiff and straight. The only place Percy logically belonged was a war room practicing Baby's First War Crime. But here he stood, taking in Roddy's cabin with a pinched expression.

Like the mess, the crew cabins had been designed with the economy in mind: they were just large enough to pace, with a raised bunk and desk fixed against the wall opposite the door. Any other amenities were crew-provided or requisitioned from the company store. Roddy didn't bother with requisitions. His cabin was plastered with posters from his favorite shonen anime, photos of his favorite wrestler (a Gundobad named Boulderfist), and signed paraphernalia from jazz musicians the universe over.

Percy's eyes lingered on famed jazz pianist Malork Nolark. Then he turned to Roddy with hands folded behind his back. "Horris informed me you would be amenable to sharing a cabin."

"Amenable is kind of a big word for it, but yeah."

The Imperial looked around the small space again. "Where will I sleep?"

"BLIP?" Roddy asked.

Say please.

"If you please, BLIP," Percy said, with more pleasantry than any Imperial should have been capable of.

The wall parallel to Roddy's bunk fell open to reveal a secondary bunk. There was less room to maneuver now, but at least no one was sleeping on the floor. Percy arched his eyebrows before looking back at Roddy. "Convenient."

"Yeah. Horry has the big room since he's the captain. Everyone else has to budge up."

Although a Grummon-class ship could fit up to five crewmen, the *Silverfish* had never had need of a fifth member. A secondary technician would have slotted into that role, but Horris had never put in for one. For one, BLIP covered most of the bases. For two, adding someone to a postal route was an arduous, multi-step process that involved the entire crew. It was the end result of having many people working in a small space for weeks at a time; interviews, personality tests, and pressure scenarios weeded out those who did not work well together. Such a vetted process resulted in fewer crew murders on company-time.

Percy sat on the new bunk with knees pressed together. Once more, he looked around the decorated cabin. Roddy shifted. He wasn't one for self-consciousness, but he had no idea what the average Imperial thought about sex, violence, and jazz. Probably nothing flattering.

"What do you do to avoid going mad in here?" Percy asked at last.

Roddy perked up. He grabbed his laptop and crossed to sit beside Percy. "Funny you should ask! We were about to hop onto Survival Horror if you wanna watch."

"Survival...Horror?" Percy repeated.

"Yeah! Here, I'll show you." He booted up the Survival Horror launcher. Once the server opened, he fired off three invites to play. While they waited, his pixelated avatar walked through a stylized dark forest, holding a flickering torch. He angled his laptop so Percy could better watch.

Percy frowned. "Why is your character wearing sunglasses?"

"It's a cosmetic," Roddy replied a little defensively. The sunglasses weren't a particularly rare cosmetic, but that didn't mean they were bad.

The rarity of cosmetic drops wasn't Percy's issue. "It's *nighttime*," he said. "You're wearing sunglasses. At night."

Roddy rolled his eyes. It was a little disheartening to know the soon-to-be rulers of Percy's homeworld hadn't raised their sovereign sons with a sense of humor. A small ding-ding of music caught his attention; someone had joined the server. A dark-skinned avatar with a butterfly perched on his forehead ran onto the screen to walk beside Roddy's (much-cooler) avatar.

"Horris," said Percy, and it was impossible to ignore the warmth in his voice.

Red says hi, Roddy typed into the party chat.

A muffled shout of 'hello!' came through the walls. Two more ding-dings sounded as the final two avatars ran onto the screen: a pixelated Mefana holding a cup of coffee and Fives' modded avvie with orange headphones. The four marched in a row to a jauntily spooky tune.

Percy watched the screen. A faint line had appeared between his eyebrows. "What is the objective of this game?"

"Ah, it's a survival horror. You're a crew that crash-landed in a haunted forest. You've got four roles, and you have to work together for as long as you can. It gets harder as the days go on, monsters start attacking, and resources get rarer..."

Sudden understanding lit Percy's bright green eyes. "It's a resource management exercise."

"Yeah!" Roddy said, excited by the enthusiasm in Percy's reply. Fives had found the game while browsing through F2P online games one flight, and it quickly became a staple in their rotation of downtime activities. Horris liked to think of it as an exercise in teamwork, no matter how many times Roddy and Basah tried to get each other killed. "I'm the Captain, so I get to assign the roles."

"Why isn't Horris the Captain?"

"He lost that privilege when he punched a pirate in the face." Roddy grinned when Percy snorted. His cursor hovered over the available options: Forager, Hunter, and Builder. "What should he be?"

He thought about making Horris the Hunter, if only because Horris hated being the Hunter, but Percy was considering the options with all the seriousness of a cadet in his first round of war games. "The Forager," he decided. "Horris has a good eye for detail, and he's knowledgeable about wildlife."

"Well, okay. I'm gonna make Fives the Hunter and Basah the Builder."

"Seems a bit on the nose to make your engineer the Builder."

"It'd be even more on the nose to make the one Mefana on the crew the Hunter." Besides, Fives' favorite role was the Hunter, and

Roddy couldn't deny Fives anything. He assigned the roles thusly and began the game.

The view shifted to a top-down screen. The avvies scattered in different directions as they sought resources and shelter. The camera remained on Roddy's avvie as he jogged through the woods.

"All right, Red, first order of business?" Roddy was enjoying watching Percy process the established scenario.

"If we were to crash into an unknown land, with little in the way of resources? Find a source of clean water to start."

Roddy wandered for a bit, watching various counters tick up and down as the rest of the team collected or used resources until a pixely blue lake appeared at the edge of the screen. Roddy set a flag down on the spot to indicate the establishment of a base. "All right, let's see what we can build—"

He opened the build menu and scrolled through the available camp options. He'd need Basah to build anything, but as Captain, he could submit suggestions. "Oooh, we could do a treehouse this run…"

"*A treehouse?*"

"What! Treehouses are fun!"

"What good would it serve to spend time and resources on a treehouse?" Percy demanded.

"It's fun, and it looks cool!"

"You've barely enough food to survive the next two days!" Percy said, aghast. "You need to focus on building a defensible position and creating shelter, not *aesthetics*."

"If we go up into the treehouse, nothing can get us!"

"And what if your enemy chops your treehouse down? There's no exits, no fallback points. Just a bunch of broken bodies on the forest floor. You're not taking this exercise seriously, Blond."

"It's a game, Red! It's not meant to be taken *seriously*."

A danger notification blinked onscreen. Percy turned back to the laptop with eyebrows arched. "Oh, look. Horris is being attacked by badgers."

Oh, he was not taking lip from a man who didn't even know what cosmetics were. Roddy shoved the laptop into Percy's lap. "Here! You take it if you think you can do better!"

"I know I will." Percy cracked his neck and then his knuckles and both men settled back onto the bunk. "Now, how do you play?"

🔢 The Postmaster General

United Star System Postal Code Chapter 10, Section 9: The appointment of the Postmaster General is the duty of the USSPS Board of Directors.

To: captaincyall@ussps.org
From: adminall@ussps.org
Re: Postal Route Closure

Captains—

The United Star System Postal Service will be ceasing all operations along postal route 222 for the foreseeable future. Given the currently unstable nature of the societies along that route, postal inspectors have determined courier safety is currently compromised. A squadron of inspectors has been dispatched to the route and will be providing updates as the situation progresses.

Safe travels,
Postmaster General David Kalani

Horris sat back in his desk chair and pinched the bridge of his nose. Closing a route was not unheard of—the given dangers of space always loomed—but it was strange to be on the receiving end of this notice when he knew what the cause of the closure was.

Sure enough, a notification pinged on his captaincy chat. The private server was for USSPS captains only; it was a place to share information and occasional memes. Horris stared at the rapidly-climbing number of notifications. He sighed before opening the chat log.

@vossd: They're closing the 222? I thought the fighting was localized to Creed?

@flambeaux: isn't that @jensenh's route?

@torresf: @jensenh please stay safe!!!

@irvingj: @jensenh are you okay?

@klinep: @jensenh can't you get your phrenic to explode their minds lmao

@fletchneri: {this comment has been removed by a moderator}

Horris ran a hand down his face. He was in no mood to fend off questions and snide comments about Fives at the same time.

A long hairy leg extended over the chatlog. Horris couldn't help but smile as Henri crawled over his monitor. "Hey, buddy," he said softly. He extended his flat palm out, holding steady as Henri climbed on. Henri's tarsus tickled Horris' palm as he padded his way across to his hand. Horris huffed out a laugh to keep steady.

The first rule of entomology: never anthropomorphize. Insects and arachnids didn't think like sentients did. They simply couldn't. Insects and arachnids were not capable of the same complex thought; it was instinct that drove their impulses. Nevertheless, Henri still managed to awe him sometimes. It took trust, or the arachnid equivalent, to climb into the palm of a being that towered over you. To sit in the palm of a giant and know that you weren't going to get hurt.

Henri tapped around his fingers, parting pointer and middle in search of food. Horris chuckled. He got to his feet, cradling his Henri-laden hand to his chest as he crossed to his far wall.

The captain's cabin was slightly larger than the rest of the crew's, but he had fenced himself in with enclosures. Henri had the largest, with a layer of earthy substrate coating the bottom and climbable decor along the walls. There was even a small jeweled tower Henri sometimes admired his own reflection in.

Horris opened the lid on the enclosure and slid Henri inside. Immediately, the spider skittered to one side and then the other. After a brief consideration, he began to fling dirt aside with his front legs.

Sylvia watched from the enclosure beside Henri's. A praying mantis couldn't emote, but nevertheless, she managed a holier-than-thou expression as dirt hit the sides of Henri's case. Her enclosure was loamier, with more dead leaves and debris littering the floor. Sylvia was a member of *Deroplatys Lobata*, a dead leaf mantis, and she liked to camouflage herself in her spare time. She was also, in Horris' humble opinion, the most beautiful mantis in the entire universe.

Horris watched her ascend a twig before turning his attention to the smallest enclosure, covered by a dark square of cloth.

Tim zipped off the instant light hit the interior of the enclosure. The silverfish skittered over the soft substrate and dove under a crumbled bit of cardboard. Jeff, by contrast, sat at the back of the tank with antennae twitching. He didn't move when Horris lifted the lid to sprinkle a bit of fish flakes inside.

Horris squinted at the stationary Jeff. "You molting, buddy?"

Jeff, of course, did not answer.

Horris watched the silverfish for a moment longer before dropping the black cloth back over the container. The silverfish were left to their own devices; Henri had burrowed himself deep into his dirt, and Sylvia now hung upside down from her mesh ceiling. Horris sat back on his heels to watch them.

There were regulations against keeping live animals aboard postal ships as pets: dogs, cats, birds, and the like. But the rules, insofar as Horris had scrutinized them, did not mention insects and arachnids. As long as they remained unobtrusive, these friends could remain as unofficial crewmen of the USSPS 131-C.

A small ding sounded from overhead. *"Horry,"* Roddy's voice crackled over the intercom, *"we're coming up on Franklin-Two."*

Horris sighed and got to his feet. "Wish me luck, fellas."

He slid on his captain's jacket (pressed and ironed) and triple-checked that his shoes shone. His captaincy hat, with its little winged star pin, sat beside his monitor. Horris examined it, picked off a piece of lint, and squared it onto his forehead. It always felt a bit silly, the ceremony that went into captaincy, but when he caught his reflection in the mirror, he couldn't help a burst of pride. He looked *good* in uniform.

The rest of the crew, plus Percy, had already gathered in the cockpit. Basah glanced his way with a smirk. "Looking good, Cap."

Horris fiddled with the brim of his cap. Out of the corner of his eye, he saw Percy staring at him. The Imperial quickly looked away as Horris turned towards him. Instead, he leaned forward over Roddy's chair to watch a distant object. Roddy's external radio crackled with sudden chatter.

Percy squinted. "Is that a moon?"

"That's no moon," said Roddy, "that's a postal depot!"

Percy's guess hadn't been too far off the mark. The massive, spherical Franklin-Two could easily be mistaken for a moon by those unfamiliar, especially since she was caught in the orbit of a small planet named Locar-Four. As they approached, they could see the other Grummon-class ships and larger freighters taking off and docking at different numbered bays around the midsection. She had no external decoration save for a blue, winged star shooting upwards between the bays.

Horris flushed with an odd excitement. He had had no part in building or designing the F-2, but all the same, there was something special in being able to show her off to someone new. This must have been what it felt like to show someone around your home city. "Isn't she beautiful?" He asked Percy.

It was Basah who answered with a snort. "She was, one-hundred-and-thirty years ago. Now she's just a time and resources sink."

"She is not!" Horris replied, stung.

"C'mon, Horry," said Roddy, "you and the old men in charge are the only ones who think that. She should have been broken into smaller depots years ago. The fad in the last century was bigger means better," he added as an aside to Percy. "Hence, F-Two. The only reason they keep her around is otherwise, they would have to admit they screwed up."

"I'm certain Horris has said similar about you," Percy said pleasantly. Basah barked a laugh, and Roddy shot him a one-fingered salute. Percy smirked before lifting his gaze to Horris. "There is value in the historical example. And I think she looks lovely."

Horris smiled at him, feeling absurdly grateful and not at all like the back of his neck was on fire.

Fives sighed loudly as if to remind everyone he was there. "*Romantic*," he said, disgusted.

While Roddy radioed to the depot operators, Horris pulled the rest to the side. "All right, so. Fives, Roddy is going to help you with unloading and reloading. Percy, you're going to stay with Basah in the engine room. And I..." he took a deep breath, fighting the urge to wipe his sweaty palms on his slacks, "am going to speak to the Postmaster General."

Can't someone else do it? He wanted to ask. But of course, no one else could do it. Only he could. That's why he got the uniform and the hat with the pin. He took another deep breath and caught Percy's eye again.

The Imperial looked faintly amused. "Don't vomit on my account. And..." he looked around the small circle they had made. "If it does come about that I am forced back, then...thank you. Thank you all. For bringing me this far."

Horris watched Percy. He looked calm. Relaxed, almost. How could he be so steady, right as they were docking in a postal depot? How could he be smiling right now, not knowing what was going to happen next? He wanted an ounce of that bravery for himself.

Maybe that's why he stuck his hand out in front of Percy. "See you later," he said stupidly, not knowing what else to say.

Percy hesitated a moment before accepting the handshake. "See you later."

Once the outgoing mail had been processed, Horris and Roddy disembarked with canvas carts stacked high with mail. The central depot of F-2 was a site of constant motion: crews of couriers heading towards their ships with canvas carts piled high with mail, while station couriers sorted mail from ships into different sections with occasional input from floor managers. To anyone not in the business of the post, it would have been utter chaos. As it was, everyone knew their job and moved with it, albeit at their own pace, as evidenced by the tired-eyed couriers draining coffee from their tumblers off to the side. A few raised their tumblers in greeting as Horris and Roddy passed.

The depot was budget-friendly utilitarian: massive halogen lights shone over the factory-like floor packed with pallet jackets, forklifts, and rolling carts. Conveyor-belt machines sorted mail into plastic buckets or long trays, which were then snatched up by couriers and moved to a new section of the floor for further processing. Posters on the walls outlined what was and was not safe for mailing, safety reminders, and notices for the next union meeting.

The interior of the Franklin-Two was much more elegantly decorated. High white walls rose overhead in elegant arcs, decorated with art and museum pieces celebrating the long history of the postal service across civilizations. Here and there, holographic maps pointed the way to bays, sorting areas, and the food court. Other signs listed the status of in- and outbound vessels. The trundle of canvas cart wheels mixed with the rapid-fire steps of postal workers with places to be. Roddy expertly wheeled the load from the *Silverfish* in and around the foot traffic. He and Horris gave each postal worker the universal up-nod as they passed. The others nodded back, the accepted gesture of "nice to see you, have a nice day, too busy to talk."

The only exception to the rule of the universal up-nod was the postal inspectors. They stood here and there, stones in the flow of the business river, hands folded in front of them and expressions flat. Even in the safety of F-2, they wore sleek dark blue armor, and long guns—actual, *real* guns—hung at their hips. Horris tried not to feel like their eyes followed he and Roddy down the corridor.

Horris slowed his pace as they passed through the main vestibule. Words hung overhead. Massive words in wrought iron, impossible to miss even by those walking at a brisk pace beneath the arc: *"Neither snow nor rain nor gloom of night shall stay these couriers from the swift completion of their appointed course with all speed."*

He tried to imagine it. He tried to put himself back and back and back, back to the time of myth, riding a steed on a dirt road under a hot sun, a bag of letters slung over his shoulder. Not knowing what dangers lay over the next hill, not knowing where the next message might take you...and walking anyway. They must have been some of the bravest men who ever lived.

The moment was ruined when Roddy scoffed. "You know the guy who wrote *that* never had to deliver a package."

They parted ways not soon after: Roddy down a corridor to a processing center, Horris to the front desk that guarded upper management offices.

He smiled at the secretary behind the desk. "Good—" he checked his watch "—morning. I have an appointment with the Postmaster

General." After a moment, he hastily added: "My name is Horris Jensen, captain of USSPS One-Thirty-One-C."

The secretary took pity on him by smiling. "He's expecting you, Captain. Take that elevator up to the fifteenth floor and head straight through the double-doors."

Horris did his utmost not to feel miserable the entire ride up, even as his lower intestines twisted into intricate knots. He took a deep breath and then another, trying to convince himself that everything was going to be okay. They weren't going to be fired. They had a good case for helping Percy get to his destination. All he just needed to do was stay calm while explaining himself.

The elevator doors opened right into the Postmaster General's office. It was a massive space, as long as three crew cabins put together, decorated in mahogany and gold leafing. A massive work desk and plush visitor chairs took up the center space, but Horris' attention was caught by the enormous fish tank against one wall. He did a quick glance around for the Postmaster before approaching the fish tank.

Bright fish of all color and variety swam in placid circles. Horris couldn't identify a single one, and in truth he was more intrigued by the snails inching over mossy rocks and panes of glass anyway. *Engina mendicaria*, he was fairly certain. He watched one cross the tank before his attention drifted to the wall behind the fish tank itself. It was decorated with photos and certificates, accolades from years of service.

His gaze lingered on one photo, older than the rest, of a five-man crew in front of their mailship: two women, one a Marquay and other Elentee, a tall Black human like himself, a flexing Gundobad, and at the center of them all…

"Do you recognize that ship, Captain?"

Horris jumped and pivoted towards the Postmaster General, who had just stepped out from a side door. He fumbled a salute of sorts. "Yes, sir. That's the *Agoraeus*, sir. Your ship."

The Postmaster nodded. "We took that photo right after we received our commission." He moved to stand beside Horris, looking at the old photo with clear fondness. "Hazel and Elia settled down on Locar-Four and opened a restaurant. Marcus went to politics, God save him, and Maldoro retired to raise a family."

Oh God he's right next to me. It was only with a heroic effort that Horris ignored the pounding of his heart. "You remain, sir."

He was a large man, Postmaster General David Kalani, built more like a wrestler than a public servant. He kept his dark hair in a neat bun, out of a cragged face and dark, intelligent eyes. A scar bridged his nose and ran the length of his left cheek. His thick mustache lifted a bit when he smiled. "Space has always been my place, Captain."

He pivoted suddenly, walking back towards his desk. "What was the name of the first postal ship to leave Earth orbit?"

Horris started. He hadn't expected a quiz upon arrival. "The *Mary-Anne*, sir. It was supposed to be the *Vivian*, but her engine malfunctioned during test flights."

The Postmaster General nodded as he collapsed down in his leather desk chair. "And the first ship to include a sentient-diverse crew?"

"The *Eureka*."

"Chief Architect of the Franklin-Two?"

"Abigail LaMone, but there is evidence her daughter Lillian had a substantial, if uncredited, hand in the design."

The Postmaster General grinned, a wide smile that revealed his teeth. "Y'know, Captain Jensen, most people *this* enthusiastic about the postal service don't actually work for it."

"My hobbies often raise eyebrows, sir," said Horris. A bit of his racing anxiety slowed; if this was the Postmaster's way of easing into a disciplinary hearing, that was fine by him.

The Postmaster snapped his fingers at Horris' reply. He tapped a few keys on his keyboard, pulling something up on his PC, before turning back to Horris. "You're the…bug guy, right? The one who was asking about the rules and regulations about keeping bugs on his ship?"

"Uh…"

"Does your ship have bugs on it?" asked the Postmaster.

"Bugs? No, sir." Horris couldn't help blurting out: "But it does have insects and arachnids."

The Postmaster threw his head back with a laugh. "Well, for what it's worth, the rules and regulations didn't say anything about fish either. I took a look at your record after our initial conversation, Captain Jensen. And I have to say I'm impressed. You've got strong customer satisfaction feedback, your logs are always on-time, you regularly come in under budget on company expenses…well done, Captain. Very well done."

"Thank you. Sir."

"You can relax now, Captain," said the Postmaster. He gestured to one of the empty visitor chairs. Horris would have preferred to stand, but rank was rank. So he sat, removing his hat and balancing it on his knee.

"So, some updates," the Postmaster continued. "Postal inspectors have landed on Delta Io and are working with the community there to restore order. We've identified the fallen postal workers and notified their families."

A heavy, respectful moment of silence passed between the pair.

"And the survivor?" Horris asked softly.

"He's been recovered alive, and is now undergoing treatment at an off-planet facility. He has a long recovery ahead of him…but he has his life, thanks to you."

Horris exhaled a breath he didn't realize he'd been holding. He rubbed his hands against his palms. "It—it doesn't feel like it, sir." *I left him behind*, he wanted to say. *I broke a promise.* Somehow, the words didn't come.

"No?" The Postmaster General arched an eyebrow. "You ought to take your accolades when you get them. There's little glory to be had otherwise in this business. But back to the point at hand, my inspectors were able to interview the leader of the community there, Estelle, and put together a report." '

Here we go.

Horris swallowed the bile in his throat and lifted his chin. He was going to do his best. If the blame came down, he would take as much of it as he could.

"She reports that pirates attempted to apprehend your cargo, and when you resisted they opened fire on your vessel. You then engaged in retreat maneuvers that resulted in the *Scorpion* chasing you off-planet."

Horris blinked, still waiting for the other shoe to drop.

Instead, the Postmaster General leaned back in his chair. "Some would call it stupidity to resist a man-o'-war when you've got no offensive capabilities of your own."

"It wasn't their cargo to take!" Horris exclaimed, before remembering where he was and who he was talking to. "Sir."

Fortunately the Postmaster General seemed more amused by his outburst than anything else. "You weren't concerned about being blasted to kingdom come?"

"With due respect, the *Silverfish* is a vessel built for speed and maneuverability. We were at a stand-still when the confrontation began. Once we built up enough acceleration, the *Scorpion* couldn't catch us. Nothing could." Not even, he wanted to add, the famed *Agoraeus.*

The Postmaster General rubbed his chin. "Having a phrenic onboard and an Elentee pilot must have helped. In any case, Captain Jensen, I'd like to extend commendations to your entire crew for your handling of this crisis, and your continued dedication to the United Star System Postal Service."

Horris almost couldn't believe what he was hearing. Where was the condemnation? Why wasn't the Postmaster General demanding to have the stowaway dragged off a postal service vessel? Had Estelle simply–*not told*?

He realized he'd been quiet for too long when the Postmaster General tilted his head. He got to his feet and extended a hand out across the desk. "Thank you, sir. This is appreciated–more than you know."

The Postmaster General had a grip like a vice. He looked at Horris, *through* Horris, as though trying to understand him from the inside out. But Horris had lived too long with Fives, and the Postmaster's gaze was nothing compared to the way Fives could peel you back layer by layer. He forced all thoughts of Percy from his mind with a smile.

The Postmaster General did not speak until Horris was almost out the door. "Is there anything else you would like to add onto the report, Captain Jensen?"

Stay calm. Calm like Percy. Horris turned back to the Postmaster with hat in hand. "No, sir. Not at this time."

The Postmaster stared back at him with a thoughtful expression. "Very good. Take care on the remainder of your route, Captain."

15 The Lives Left Behind

United Star System Postal Code, Chapter 11, Section 3: All USSPS employees are required to report any and all violations of United Star System law witnessed on their routes.

Basah watched Percy watch Horris walk down the gangplank and out into the depot. Only once Horris had been swallowed by the crowd did Basah deem it wise to nudge Percy's shoulder.

"C'mon, Red. You can help me refuel the Exosuits and check the vitals."

The subtle contact jolted Percy out of whatever thoughts he'd been lost in. "Exosuits?"

"Mm-hm." Basah nodded. "You'll do as a model."

She led Percy back through the hold and down into the engine pit. They were silent as they walked, for which Basah was grateful; even in the *Silverfish*'s hold, her sensitive ears could pick up the distant rumbles and clatter from the depot proper. F-2 was too much: too loud, too bright, too smelly. After days or weeks in the relative peace of the *Silverfish*, the F-2 was hell on her senses. A pity no one but Fives saw it that way.

The phrenic himself was curled up on the bench of the engine pit with his tablet in his lap. Long, complicated lines of code—the sort Basah had no head for—streamed across his screen. Fives jerked upright as they entered, yanking his tablet close as though expecting someone to snatch it. Basah watched his expression shift into a twitching, nervous smile.

Hey, just here to try on some suits.

Fives' smile grew more comfortable, and he relaxed perceptively.

She crossed to the closet of Exosuits (five, one for each prospective crewman) and selected an Exosuit at random. She held it out to the bemused Percy. "Put this on and stand there."

It took some time, longer than it probably would have if she'd used one of the boys as her model. She had to help Percy wriggle into the thin-but-sturdy bodysuit called the pressure layer, show him how to connect the breathing tube to his nostrils, and how the Exosuit cycled oxygen and CO_2 between the tanks installed in the suit. Eventually, her explanations fell silent as she worked the suit over, tightening here and there, checking the gauges in the support systems, and ensuring that each part worked individually and as a whole. Basah didn't realize her stream-of-consciousness was being echoed by Fives until Percy shot him a dark look.

Basah shook herself out of her work and turned to Fives, who lifted one of his headphones away from his ear. He looked between the two before getting to his feet. "Sorry, I can do this somewhere else."

"You don't have to, Fives," Basah said at once.

Although it wasn't aimed at him, her flash of annoyance made Fives wince. Fives' background muttering had never bothered her. If anything, it helped her focus. It was good to hear her own thoughts echoed back to her, and through the course of a conversation with Fives, she could usually break through some mental block. But few saw Fives like she did: different, special, *helpful*. Most didn't know what to do with the way he fidgeted and avoided their eyes. Most did not want their private thoughts echoed back to them. And because their own insecurities won, they treated Fives like crap: something to be shoved away or asked to leave the room because it made them more comfortable.

Fives looked at her with his big, dark eyes. "He doesn't understand, Basah."

Basah's ears flattened. "He doesn't have to!"

"I'm right here, you know," said Percy. He turned to Fives. "What don't I understand?"

Basah grimaced. It was a topic they'd managed to dodge so far, what with all the running for their lives and all. A few days ago, she would have clocked Percy in the jaw just for asking anything about Fives. But now…now she felt more comfortable sighing as she checked the readings on the Exosuit. Where did they even begin?

"Fives is…" Basah paused. It wasn't for lack of an adjective. There were just so many.

"Complicated," Fives answered.

"I'm complicated." Percy's smile was a razor. "Try me."

Basah looked to Fives. It would fall to her, they both knew, but she was not indulging without his permission.

For a long moment, Fives chewed on his lower lip. Finally, he shrugged. "You can tell him, Basah. I don't mind."

He got to his feet and exited the engine pit. Going to his cabin, Basah supposed, or Roddy's, where he would blast jazz and try to block out the feedback from her. She sighed and wiped her hands absentmindedly on her thighs. Another long moment passed before she got to her feet and looked at the suited Percy.

The Imperial arched his eyebrows at her. He was a small man, like Fives, but in her head, he seemed much taller.

"We used to have a stop along one of our routes. A space station, some privately-funded research center, the brainchild of some planet-bound billionaire genius who woke up one day and decided he was going to sort out all the secrets of the universe for himself since all the publicly funded programs weren't going fast enough for his liking—"

Percy stared at her. Basah cleared her throat. Her diatribe on privatized research could wait another day.

"Anyway, it was a research center, studying two bridges in relative proximity. At least, that was the gist we got from the place. We'd usually be dropping off equipment or supplies or some such. Busy place. Lots to do. And then one day…"

Basah trailed off again. She could still recall the look on Horris' face, the glances they'd shared as they'd radioed in for permission to land, and no one answered. She'd known even then, even before they'd docked, that something terrible had happened.

"*And then one day,*" Percy prompted.

"We radioed in for a drop-off. Usual routine, nothing out of the ordinary. But no one answered. And as we got closer, even from the outside, the space station seemed…wrong. Quiet. The lights were on, but no one was home."

"I'm certain Horris was willing to just let that go."

Basah forced herself to laugh. "You know him; he hates to get involved. So, we call the postal inspectors, who give us the go-ahead to dock anyway, to see if we can get more information–maybe there had been an accident or something, or comms had failed."

She remembered the argument, too, between herself and the boys. Roddy had seen enough horror movies to know what happened next, and even from within the *Silverfish,* Basah swore she could smell it: blood, and death, and more blood. But Horris had insisted, appealing to their better natures in that uncanny way of his, saying that if there was anyone in trouble, they owed it to help.

She shook her head. She began to check the thermal heaters on the Exosuit gloves in an attempt to stay productive. "Everyone inside the station was dead."

Percy's brow furrowed. "An accident?"

"No. Well, probably not. They'd been…mutilated. You know, like when someone steps on a bug, and it's flattened, twisted, blood and guts gooshing out?"

"*Gooshing?*"

"It's a word," Basah said. If she could focus on the words, trying to pick the right ones, then she wasn't remembering the remains, or the smells, or the splatters of gore against the floors and walls. She fidgeted with the oxygen tube in her grip. "It was…Matrons, it was awful. Like something out of a horror flick. We searched the place top to bottom, and everywhere we went…"

Security offices. Private offices. Hallways. Labs. No section had been spared. The labs had been the worst part: lights flickering, broken glass crunching underfoot, twitching remains melded with lab coats, splattered over harsh-looking equipment. There had been massive test tubes, tall as Roddy, shattered open. Some still leaked viscous green liquid over the tiled floor. Cages, too, waist-high, although they'd never found signs of animals, alive or dead.

Horris had vomited a few times. Roddy had gone absolutely silent and gray-faced. Basah could handle the sight of blood and remains, but at some point, she'd found herself clutching both Horris and Roddy's hands as they walked, shouting for someone, *anyone,* to answer.

Percy's next question drew her out of the horror: "Had they been attacked by pirates or the like? Some rival corporation setting them up for failure?"

"No, no…it was a massacre, but it was…mindless." It was frustrating not being able to communicate just how total the slaughter had been, but at the same time, Basah was relieved Percy couldn't quite picture what she was describing.

"An animal, then?"

Basah made a noncommittal noise in the back of her throat. "There was a bathroom near one of the labs. And that's how we finally found Fives."

Her sharp ears had picked it up first: the faint sound of sobbing, a high and wild noise that sounded more animal than sentient. They found the long, dragging trail of blood not long after and followed it into the bathroom. He'd been huddled in a ball on the floor in a stall; arms flung over his head, the force of his sobs wracking him to and fro.

He had been small and sickly pale, like a plant grown in darkness, and he'd been drenched in blood. None of it his own. He didn't have a scratch on him, except for a vertical slice through his right earlobe. The scar was still there, hidden now by Fives' shaggy hair and orange headphones.

"The only survivor of the massacre," Basah said softly.

Percy's expression shifted. He glanced overhead and then back down to Basah, looking concerned. And for that, Basah could almost forgive him for his earlier rudeness. Almost.

"Judging by your lack of specifics," said Percy, "Fives never managed to tell you what happened that day."

"No. He was half-out of his mind with terror. We managed to calm him down and get him onto the *Silverfish*, and from there, he went catatonic. He didn't come out of it until the postal inspectors tried to interview him…and it was only when he started reciting their questions back to him that we realized he was…different."

It had all been cause for excitement among postal employees. A *phrenic!* Most of them had never seen a phrenic before. Some refused to believe they even existed. And now there was one in USSPS custody. He had no United Star System ID and no memory of anything from before the *Silverfish* crew found him. He'd refused medical treatment, refused interviews, refused anything that had to do with the space station. The Postmaster General himself had stepped in. He'd spoken with Fives alone for a very long time, and after a few days, he'd been released back to the *Silverfish* crew. He wanted to join them, the Postmaster General explained, and in lieu of memory and ID, the postal service seemed the ideal place to keep an eye on him in the meantime.

"What happened to the space station? Did they ever find the cause of the massacre?"

"If they did, no one's told us." Basah shrugged. "The interplanetary media spun it as some tragic malfunction."

She did not allow herself to wonder about it. There was always the chance that Fives would catch the stray musing, and any reminder of *before* sent him into a spiral of panic and self-loathing. But all the same…sometimes she wondered about what had happened that day and the lengths the postal service could go to keep a phrenic in their control.

Percy, however, had no reservations about wondering: "And after all this time, no one's come looking for their wayward phrenic? And he hasn't remembered anything?"

"No." Basah looked up and sent a silent apology to Fives for putting him through her memories. "Whatever happened on that station, it took something from Fives. Something he was never able to get back."

Perseus was quiet for a long moment. Basah went back to work, testing the oxygen flow from the tank to the nostrils. "The perils of space never end, do they?" He asked.

"Nope." Basah straightened. She and Percy met eyes. He was a strange sort, Basah decided, but in the end, Horris' instincts were correct. They usually were. She nodded towards the ladder. "C'mon, I want to show you something."

She secured the Exosuit and its helmet on Percy before dressing in an Exosuit of her own. Together, they started out of the engine pit, but it was only when they neared the airlock that Percy stopped short. "Aren't we surrounded by post service personnel?" He asked, alarmed. "Won't they see me?"

"They'll see what they expect to see: a Mefana and a human working on the exterior," Basah replied. "No one can see your hair color under that helmet anyway."

Percy made no argument to that. Perhaps he sensed that this was an olive branch being extended in his direction. Basah radioed into the depot station, made some excuse about testing the engines to the personnel in charge of the bay, and got permission to maintain a low-level orbit around the exterior of the F-2. ("Just be back in twenty minutes," said the operator, audibly caught between boredom and 'if this becomes a problem, it becomes my problem, so don't make it a problem'). The BLIP autopilot lifted them into orbit.

Percy squinted as the *Silverfish* hummed into space. "This isn't some elaborate scheme to send me spiraling into the abyss of space, is it?"

"Do you want it to be?" Basah cocked an eyebrow.

"Alone with my thoughts in the black abyss? Now, what have I done to deserve that?"

Basah laughed as she opened the airlock and guided them through the decompression chamber. From there, they stepped through another set of double doors—and out into the vacuum of space.

Percy seized her arm in sudden panic. Basah winced; even through the padded layers of the Exosuit, the Imperial had a grip like iron. But she couldn't blame him. Everyone's first time out of the airlock was terrifying, even within the relative safety of the F-2.

What an experience, though. Stepping out into the floaty nothingness, feeling the laws of gravity shift and bend all around you–and then seizing control, bending reality back into a semblance of shape as your oxygen tank kicked on and heat warmed your fingers. Life was not supposed to *survive* out here. And yet it did. Space was a machine like any other, with gears and mechanisms and springs for an engineer to study and learn from. And once it could be understood, it could be conquered. It was an addicting thrill, stepping into a space you were never supposed to have accessed.

A sharp tug from Percy brought her back to reality. They were drifting slowly upwards off of the *Silverfish*. Percy had too much pride to voice his terror, but it was obvious in his wide green eyes. "Steady, steady, steady! It's okay!" Basah laughed and pulled him along, hop-stepping around the doors and onto the shell of the *Silverfish* itself.

Their magnetic boots locked them against the shell. She explained the particulars to Percy as they walk-hopped towards the engines.

"—and if all else goes tits-up, we have booster packs built into the suit. You can use it to propel yourself back. See?"

She activated her booster, shooting them both off the *Silverfish* and into open space with a small roar. Percy squawked indignantly. *"Emperor's hand!"*

"It takes some getting used to," Basah assured him. She adjusted the booster with a flick of her wrist, lowering them back to the *Silverfish*. "The propellers are no good for long-range. It's meant for a quick jolt in case you lose your footing somehow. C'mon, you can walk with me while I check the external engines."

The external engines had taken some surface damage in their *Scorpion* skirmish, but for a mercy, it was nothing she couldn't handle. Even sturdy Grummons could rack up a tab when it came to repairs, and the last thing she wanted to do was haul the *Silverfish* into a shop. She drifted and bounced here and there, taking notes on the state of the engines to send to Horris later.

Percy, meanwhile, had grown bold enough to bounce off on his own. Basah watched him bound over the *Silverfish*, even testing out the booster pack now and then. He had taken to it quickly enough. Hell, he even seemed to be enjoying himself.

Basah waited until he'd leap-frogged back towards her to comment. "I have to hand it to you, Red—you're pretty level-headed about all this. Poor Horry looked like he was going to vomit everywhere."

"His is the more difficult job now," Percy said. He settled down to watch her work. "Mine is simply waiting."

"Waiting would drive some people off the wall," Basah replied. She thought of Roddy and, admittedly, Horry too. Horris was just as impatient as his brother when it came to getting what he wanted. He was just far, far better at hiding it.

"Anxiety is a waste of energy," Percy said. His voice was flat and disaffected. "And I will need all my energy if I am returning to Creed."

"Why's that?"

Percy didn't reply, but the thin-lipped smile he gave her was more than a little chilling.

Basah shook off the feeling. "Funny. You sound a lot like me when I left my home planet."

She hadn't meant to give that much away. She winced even as Percy straightened up. "How's that?"

Basah sighed. There was no putting the cat back in its carrier now. "Defiant," she flicked a wrist around. "Daring someone to come and drag me back home—and prepared to put up a fight. I ran away when I turned eighteen and spent the first sixteen months looking over my shoulder. So...I get where you're at it. Some of it, at least." She hadn't committed any crimes against any gods, but the way her mother had reacted seemed damn close.

Percy leaned back, resting with palms flat against the humming *Silverfish*. "It seems to me there's a pattern emerging amongst you posties."

"How's that?" Basah echoed.

"War orphans, space massacre survivors, runaways...who else would work these hours while stuck in a tin can of a shuttle, bundled in the United Star Systems' red tape? No sane person with anything worth returning to."

He'd hit something there. Hurt when he did, like some bruise she'd mistakenly supposed healed. Basah snorted to hide her discomfort. "I've had worse performance reviews."

They sat together in silence, watching the hustle and bustle of F-2. Far in the distance, Locar-Four swirled in hues of blue and white.

"Why did you run from your home?" Percy asked.

Basah watched a massive freighter trundle off F-2 in the direction of a nearby bridge. She exhaled. "Why did you?"

Basah didn't actually expect him to answer, but he shocked her by sighing. He raised a hand to his helmet, seemingly having forgotten it was there, and lowered it again. "I had questions. Questions no one seemed able to answer." He did not look at her, choosing instead to stare out across the busy dark around them. "I don't think I'll find the answers out here."

Basah had to wonder what the point of leaving was, then. But she let him have it since they'd crossed the threshold of civil and now danced the line of friendly. "I left because of a girl," she offered.

Tisenna.

That drew Perseus' attention off the distant stars and back to her. "What happened?"

Basah settled down to sit beside Percy. "Mefane are matriarchal," she began, unsure of how much Percy already knew of her people. "Our mothers, and our mothers' mothers, rule. Women are hunters, explorers, priestesses, politicians, caregivers…"

"And the men?"

She shrugged. "They exist."

"Delightful," Percy said flatly. "I can't imagine wanting to leave if that was the case."

A low growl escaped Basah. "The matrons dictate that women have a sacred duty." She flung her arms out to indicate a full moon. It was a familiar, almost automatic gesture. *The feminine divine.* The old echo of the matrons was enough to make her roll her eyes. "To mate with the men chosen for us by the matrons and give birth to the next generation of leaders. But I refused."

"Oh." Percy tilted his head to the side. "Why?"

"I'm a lesbian, Red."

A long, long silence ensured. Basah was deciding whether or not she was going to have to shove Perseus into the dark abyss of space after all when he finally cleared his throat. "What…what does that mean?"

Basah could have laughed. But she knew Percy well enough by now that admitting to not knowing something was a massive tip of his hand. So, she settled for a soft chuckle. "It means I'm attracted to women, and only women. They didn't teach you this in the Academy of Doom?"

"Pleasures of the flesh were prohibited." He lifted his shoulders in a shrug. "As was fraternizing between cadets. Our body and soul were devoted to the Emperor."

No wonder the Creed Imperials were such a mess. Basah shook her head. "So, anyway. I refused to be matched. I didn't want to lay with a man. I didn't want to raise children. I didn't want to sit through endless political conversations. But according to the matrons, that choice wasn't mine to make. I was going to be forced into it, for my own good. For the sake of my people."

"For the sake of your people," Percy echoed. There was an odd, strangled quality to his voice.

Basah didn't register it. She was lost in the memory now, the rage that burned like a low fire in her heart. "Oh, they made some noise about letting me keep a concubine, a woman on the side or something. Some noblewomen do that. But I couldn't..." The indignation rose in her throat as bile. It seared her throat as she swallowed. "I couldn't live that lie. I couldn't smile and nod and pretend to want something I didn't. I would have died screaming on the inside."

"What was the girl like?"

"Her name is Tisenna. She worked in the gardens—she could make anything grow. I'd seen her coax plants back from the dead. She's silly and sweet, and she liked to paint in her spare time. She's an amazing artist. I would bring her gifts, little things I'd learned how to make with my tutors, and she'd trade me her art. I still have some of them in my cabin. She could sing, too. She had the best voice in the palace choir."

"She sounds like someone I knew," Percy murmured. "Where is she now?"

"Still at home, I think. Tisenna, ah…Tisenna didn't come with me when I told her I was leaving." And didn't that burn too, hotter and more painful than the memory of her mother or the matrons? It was that bruised part of her all over again. She still remembered the look on Tisenna's face when she'd pulled her hands from hers. She still remembered how Tisenna shook her head, backing away from her. *We can't just leave! We can't—what will we do? Where will we go?*

Basah blew out the memories in a breath. "She was afraid of having to start over."

"Do you resent her for that?"

"Not on my good days." Basah forced herself to shrug, sliding the old weight off her shoulders and out into space. "So, that's the story."

Percy looked at her long and hard. For a moment, he reminded Basah of Fives. "Not all of it, I should think."

"Sorry?"

"You spoke of gardens and tutors. Noblewomen and a palace choir. Having children for the sake of your people. Who are you?"

"Oh, fuck me." She hadn't meant to give him *that* much. But if she didn't tell him, one of the boys would eventually spill it. She flung her head back in a long, exaggerated sigh. "Basah of House Anasem, second in line to the throne of Pah-Banan. Or, at least, I was. They've probably stricken my name from the record by now—"

Percy's shriek cut her off. Suddenly, he was clambering awkwardly to his feet. Even with movement hindered by the Exosuit, he still managed a clumsy spasm of a bow towards her.

"Oh, *stuff it!*" Basah exclaimed. She tugged Percy back down beside her by the belt. "This is embarrassing for both of us! Matrons preserve me..." She huffed. "Like I said, I was second-in-line. *Was.* No longer. I was a terrible disappointment to my mother, and she had two daughters to spare. So."

"So you're a princess turned postie." Now that the instinctual niceties had passed, Percy's amusement was visible.

"I will shove you off this ship, Red."

"Apologies, apologies." Percy held up his hands in a gesture of self-defense. "Do you ever regret leaving home?"

Sometimes. It was difficult to think about the lives left behind—her mother, her sisters, Tisenna—without thinking about who she could have been or what she could have been. Home. The word inspired many things: an aching sadness, a tinge of relief, the memories of a blissful youth swirled with a bone-deep rage. But even in her darkest moments, when the longing was a knifepoint at her ribs, she could never regret her choice.

"Only when Roddy opens his mouth," she answered.

Percy snorted. "The man isn't even here to defend himself."

"Do *you* regret leaving?"

"I regret the circumstances of my leaving. I couldn't...it was like you said. I couldn't live a lie even if I wanted to. Even if it would have been easier." He fell silent in thought. Basah waited for him to shake his head. "So, how did you meet Horris and Roderick?"

"They put out an ad for a roommate, and I answered. Figured I would be able to handle two boys. And I was correct." They shared a small laugh at that. Basah leaned forward to rest her elbows on her knees. "What was the name of your Tisenna?"

"Sorry?"

"Your Tisenna. The one you said reminded you of her. What was their name?"

Percy shifted slightly, pulling his legs to his chest as best he was able. He wrapped his arms around his legs and stared straight out into space. Only then, it seemed, he was ready to answer: "His name was Orestes."

Basah didn't pry further. There was a raw edge to Percy's voice, and Basah recognized the heartbreak and the fury both. She recognized it, sound and taste. It was bittersweet, like the last kiss she and Tisenna had shared.

Interlude 2: The Kyriakon

The faint scent of sandalwood incense permeated the small kyriakon. Percy's boots echoed against the solid black marble floor. This was the Old Kyriakon, smaller than the one in the main courtyard and built in the old style: a tall, spiraling tower, each landing a series of small rooms meant for prayer and reflection. Mylian Towers like these had fallen out of style after the Second Conquest. These days, kyriakons consisted of large rectangular buildings from which a presbyster could instruct a congregation of the faithful.

Nevertheless, Mylian Towers had their place. Percy passed a harried presbyter and the three chatty Ordinaries accompanying him. He stepped aside to allow the presbyster to pass, and inclined his head as he did. The Ordinaries saluted him in turn; such was the deference due, Ordinary to Midman. The presbyter called sharply after the children, who hurried after him. Percy's lips twitched upwards in a slight smile; no doubt they were climbing the Mylian Tower as punishment for some youthful transgression.

He had not come here to study history, nor due to some punishment. He'd come here because he preferred to worship in a quiet spot, away from crowds and excitable Middies who whispered about their test scores instead of their prayers. He preferred the empty dark to the eyes that would inevitably follow him around the kyriakon. How did the son of Admiral Danae Warden fare in the exams? How did he compare to his fellows?

He had his pick of small, private cells for worship. Percy chose a door at random and yanked it open.

Orestes Mason whirled to his feet.

Percy stopped short. "Oh," he said dumbly. "Oh–I didn't realize this room was taken—"

"No, no, it's all right!" Orestes protested. "You can join me here."

An awkward beat of silence followed.

"If you want to," said Orestes, pathetically.

That was the word for Midman Orestes Mason: *pathetic*. Tall and gangly and doe-eyed, more a dreamer than a doer, the fact that he'd made it this far was either a testament to the Emperor's mercy or a grim reminder that some things were even beyond His control. He and Percy were in the same cohort. That did not make them friends. Perseus Warden had made a point of not befriending men like Orestes Mason.

Nevertheless, it would be rude to slam the door shut on his face now. Besides, on the slim chance Orestes did pass his exams, they would work together. A good leader knew how to work with all personalities, even the ones he detested. Percy cleared his throat. "Thank you," he said.

The prayer room was small and windowless, empty of furniture and comforts save for the thin pillows on which a supplicant could rest their knees. Lit wicks floated in pools of wax around a statue of the Emperor; apparently, Orestes had been here for some time. Percy's suspicion was confirmed when he noted the bloody splotches on Orestes' knees.

"Praying for your exam scores?" Percy asked. He picked up a thin pillow from the box and tossed it down beside Orestes.

"Praying for guidance," Orestes replied. He sank back down to his knees with a wince. "The proctor said I ought to."

"I suppose he meant it as a joke."

Orestes smiled thinly. "No. He did not."

"Dare I ask what happened?" Percy shouldn't have asked. Everyone in their cohort knew that no matter their score, Orestes would still come in dead last. He was asking out of some perverse enjoyment of Orestes' failure. It did not reflect well on him, the better part of him chided, but as long as he did not spread the story of Orestes' humiliation, surely there was no harm done.

Orestes' larynx bobbed as he swallowed. "I, ah, hesitated during the command scenario. I didn't want to sacrifice my men."

He had to have been referring to last night's command scenario; they hadn't been presented with another yet. Because he was a good person, Percy did not roll his eyes. "They're just numbers."

"They won't always be, someday."

"Nevertheless. A good commander understands the necessity of sacrifice."

Orestes did not reply.

Percy settled into his prayers, pleased that Orestes did not drag the conversation out. Orestes was a quiet man, that compliment Percy would allow, and had never bothered him for details about his mother the way other cohorts had.

Unbidden, his thoughts drifted back to the command scenario. He had sacrificed his right flank in a false rout and then overwhelmed the enemy when they plunged too deeply behind his lines. It had been a good plan, and the loss of thirty men was preferable to the loss of three hundred. His proctors had agreed. Sacrifice was necessary for victory. No war had been won without bloodshed, and the Emperor did not bless half-measures.

Orestes was murmuring the first Litany beside him. Percy shook himself back to the here and now to join him: "He hath struck off my chains and risen me to a place of grace, so that I may spread the

Word of His Glory—He hath given my soul wings to soar and hands of blessed fire—"

Together, they recited the five Litanies. The flames flickered and sputtered in their pools of wax, and the smell of incense soothed Percy. It was quiet here, peaceful in a way you could rarely find in the Academy, and when their prayers subsided, a deep contentment filled Percy.

And so, naturally, Orestes had to ruin the moment by speaking. "May I confess something to you?"

"I'm no presbyster," Percy snapped.

Orestes flinched. Percy bit back a further sharp remark as a strange sort of guilt came over him. He considered Orestes and his bloody knees, Orestes and his bloodshot blue eyes, the eyes of a man who'd been praying all night and half the morning. Orestes was not a bad man. And he had been praying for guidance. Perhaps the Emperor had willed this meeting.

"...but in the absence of a presbyter," he said haltingly, "I can hear your confession. Assuming, of course, you don't mind that I cannot absolve you."

Orestes had straightened up a bit as Percy spoke. He even managed a wavering sort of smile. "Thank you. I...I fear I might be a coward."

Percy was thunderstruck. Cowardice was chief among all sins, the root of all evils, and an irremovable mark of shame against a Black Hammer. Hammers were not cowards. They simply couldn't be. "No," he said. Presbyster or not, he had to save Orestes' soul. "No, that's not possible. You're a Hammer. Hammers aren't cowards. You're just—you're being tested, that's all. Faith needs to be tested, or else it isn't faith."

Orestes did not seem comforted by this. "Why?"

"Why, what?"

"Why does it have to be a struggle? Why can't it just *be*?"

The questioning irritated Percy. Questions were for children and Idolers, the foolish and the faithless. Hammers did not question. They had learned the truth long ago as Ordinaries. "Is your heart closed to the Emperor's grace?" He demanded.

Orestes did not answer.

"*Is it?*"

More nervous swallowing served as Orestes' reply. He reached up to fiddle with the necklace around his neck: a simple black chain with a circular pendant of the holy falling star. "No," he said at last. "No, never. I just—I struggle with the demands."

"Explain." Percy's voice flattened, even as his mind raced with the possible outcomes of this conversation. Would he have to report Orestes to the presbysters? Was he sympathetic to the Idolers?

Orestes continued to fiddle with the pendant around his neck. "We love the Emperor. And the Emperor loves us."

"Indeed."

So it was, and so it had been taught. Three hundred years ago, the planet of Creed had lagged behind other civilizations, primitive and earthbound. It had been invaded by spacefarers, and the people were subjugated as slaves. One hundred and fifty years ago, the Emperor had come to them, falling to Creed on a burning star and rising to liberate the masses. Under His guidance, they had thrown off their shackles, ousted the masters, and taken their technology for themselves. He had brought the planet into the fold of the United Star System. Their savior had been crowned as Emperor Eternal, and so it had been. He had reigned, long and well, and in gratitude for His works, the people of Creed spread His Word across the planet. They owed the Emperor their lives and liberties, and the Idolers spat in the face of His courage.

Every Black Hammer knew their history. To deny it was to deny the truth.

"Why not prove to Adastra and the Idolers that He is Divinity, then? Why do we have to fight?"

Percy was aghast. The duty of a Black Hammer was not to question why. Theirs was to do and die, if necessary. They were the holy instruments of His great work, bringing His grace and mercy to the unliberated lands and rooting out the rot where it dwelled and bred. The Idolers did not care if the Emperor was Divinity or not; assuming a mere show of force would placate them was thinking like a child.

"You sound like a child," Percy said, scathing.

"I know," Orestes said softly.

He did everything softly. That was the problem with Orestes. It had been easier to forgive when they were both Ordinaries, untested boys of seven and eight, but harder to forgive now that they were almost men grown. Orestes spoke softly and walked softly, and no amount of beatings had driven that dreamy look from his eyes. He should have been a Trumpeter or perhaps a Chorister; his gentle manner would have served him well as a missionary.

Perhaps his family realized their mistake and were attempting to fix it with Electra. She was two years younger than Orestes but had proven adept among her cohort.

"Thank you," Orestes said into the sudden silence. "Thank you for listening. I–I do appreciate it."

Percy exhaled through his nose. That was the other problem with Orestes Mason: he wasn't a bad sort at the end of the day. Just wildly unsuited to the tasks at hand. And, in an odd sense, that he could admit to cowardice was almost admirable. It meant he was capable of self-reflection and, therefore, improvement.

He lifted his eyes to the visage of the Emperor. *He doubts, my Lord, but he is not without promise. Guide him to a better path.*

"Why do you fight?"

Percy lowered his eyes to look at Orestes. He had the bluest eyes Percy had ever seen, the blue of the sky over the ocean, and it was the most comely thing about him. Otherwise, he was all gawky angles and uneven bits: oversized nose, a narrow chin, and sideburns that crept down his narrow face like thick ivy. Percy could see the gauntness in his cheeks and the heavy bags under his eyes.

"Why do you fight?" Orestes asked again.

"Because I am called to."

"Do you enjoy it?"

The question threw Percy. Well? Did he? He should have answered yes, of course—but somehow, that answer seemed wrong. The Emperor preached love. A hard-won love, the love of a father who needed to correct his children's mistakes. But to enjoy the violence seemed crass. One should see it as duty, as a grim necessity, not something to be enjoyed…

He opened his mouth to rebuff Orestes, but the distant sound of raised voices stopped him. He half-turned towards the closed door. "Do you hear—"

The world exploded into a rush of hot-blasting–searing-pain. Percy flew against the opposite wall, where he lay, crumpled and stunned. The taste of blood filled his mouth, and his head rang with white noise. Someone stood over him, and every instinct screamed danger. *Get up!* His mind screamed through the white noise. *GET UP NOW!*

The world snapped back into an awful clarity. Percy surged upright and caught the wrist of the man standing over him. Brown leathers, an open palm stitched into his vest—an Idoler, here! *Here!*

Percy had no time to ponder the implications. The Idoler swung at him, and he shoved forward, taking them both to the ruined floor. Percy was smaller, faster, but the Idoler had had the advantage of surprise. He pinned Percy, animal eyes flashing as he picked Percy up and slammed him against the marble, once, twice—

Then Orestes was behind him with a chunk of stone in hand, and with a sharp *crack,* the Idoler froze. His grip on Percy slackened. Percy shoved the Idoler off and scrambled to his feet. The Idoler did not fight. He only slumped to the floor, blood and gray bits leaking down his neck and back.

Orestes stared at the dead Idoler with eyes wide. The chunk of marble hit the floor with a heavy *thunk.* "Emperor, forgive me," he whimpered, "Oh have mercy, Emperor, forgive me…"

Percy stared down at the body with an odd sort of detachment. He'd never seen one in real life before. He should have felt something, he knew, but all he could feel was the pounding in his head and how his heart beat double-time in his chest. He could hear more screaming now, wailing alarms, and the *pop-pop* of explosives.

The Idolers were here. The Idolers were attacking the Academy.

Fury and bile rose into his throat. He staggered towards what remained of the door, intent on joining the fray. How dare they attack *here*, of all places—he was going to get to the courtyard, he was going to join the fight, he was going to kill them all—

Orestes caught his arm. He was yelling something, Percy realized, although it was hard to hear over the roar of hatred in his heart. *The Ordinaries*, Orestes was screaming, *the children!*

The children. The Ordinaries. Trailing up the steps after the presbyster…

Together, they burst out of the room and into the smoke- and rubble-filled hallway. Here, the sounds of fighting were louder, and Percy had to force himself to ignore the impulse to join the courtyard. Liaison Nabis was here, somewhere, and no matter how strong the Idoler, they would crumple before the Emperor's phrenic. He took a grim satisfaction in the knowledge as he and Orestes raced for the stairwell, following the sound of children wailing.

Percy took the lead, and at the top of the stairwell, he nearly tripped over the glassy-eyed corpse of the young presbyster. He shouted and staggered back against Orestes. The presbyster was freshly dead, blood trickling out of his mouth, and his expression seemed to reproach the Midmen for not being faster. Percy's stunned horror churned into a blinding rage. He leapt over the corpse and charged forward, ignoring Orestes' cry of warning as he rounded the corner.

An Idoler crouched in front of the three Ordinaries, hands up, trying to say something over their screaming. She wheeled up and around as Percy rounded the corner. Their eyes met for a split second, and before she could draw the knife at her waist, Percy was on her.

They went down in a heap of limbs and teeth, fighting and clawing like animals, all sense of tactics or decorum abandoned. The Idoler bucked her hips to shake Percy off and yanked her knife free from its case. Percy caught her wrist and wrenched it backward, and when that didn't work, he sank his teeth into her shoulder.

The Idoler screamed and dropped her knife. In the next instant, it was in Percy's hand, and he had plunged it up to the hilt into her gut. The Idoler jerked, shuddered, and jerked again as Percy wretched the knife free. He pitched to his feet with hot blood running down to his elbow. The Idoler looked up at him, mouth gaping like a fish, hands grasping at the innards spilling from her stomach.

It *reeked*. The simulations had never included a smell.

Percy caught movement from the corner of his eye. He wheeled to find Orestes with the children. He cradled the littlest in his arms while the other two clung to his jacket. "Are they harmed?" Percy demanded.

Orestes was staring past him, down at the dying Idoler. He jerked his head back up when Percy spoke. His eyes widened. "No–no, they're all right—"

Percy grunted his approval. He considered the knife in his hand before crouching down by the Idoler. He ignored the feeble hands swatting at him as he pulled the holster from her belt. He pulled a second knife free and extended it towards Orestes.

Orestes looked at the knife and then at Percy. Wordlessly, horrified, he shook his head. He sidestepped Percy, taking the sobbing children along with him as he did.

"Coward," Percy spat.

He shoved past Orestes with a knife in each hand. He could hear Orestes speaking softly, *singing*, of all things, here, now, that ridiculous softhearted fool. He glanced back in time to see Orestes kneeling down beside the dying Idoler, taking her hand in his. Singing to her and the children both.

Percy had no time for outrage, no time to process the blasphemy. One of them needed to do something, Emperor damn it! He broke into a run, following the sound of fighting inside the kyriakon, and rounded the corner back towards the stairwell.

"*HAMMERS!*" He bellowed.

That was the only warning he gave them.

He met the next Idoler with a knife to the chest, slicing through the leather armor like a hot knife through butter. He shoved the Idoler backward into the next, slashed at his exposed throat, ducked the blow coming his way, and sliced his second knife from stomach to sternum.

Smoke seared his throat, and blood thundered in his ears. Everything had snapped into a strange sort of clarity; this was what he had been trained for his whole life; this was his purpose, and the holy song sang in his blood as he twisted and slashed and sliced, striking and cutting, stabbing, stabbing, stabbing—it was hot, it was bloody, but momentum propelled him forward, telling him to fight, to destroy, to kill them, kill them *kill them kill them kill them*—

"PERSEUS!"

KILL THEM ALL–

"PERSEUS! *PERCY!*"

The scream wrenched him from the haze of red and black. He blinked and staggered, suddenly aware of the arms around his torso, holding him in place. He was aware, suddenly, of the burning pain in his stomach and shoulder, and of the bodies…

The bodies. All around him, bodies. Young and old, male and female, humanoid and otherwise, all Idolers. Some still clutched at gaping wounds and sobbed for their mothers. Others were dead, dead, throats slashed, stomachs rent, glassy eyes staring, dead. Their blood pooled on the marble floor and splattered the walls. The wet glistened on the pair of knives in his hands. He could taste the coppery sourness on his lips.

Perseus trembled. *I killed them all,* he tried to say, but when he opened his mouth, a sob burst out instead. The knives clattered to the floor as he raised his bloody hands to his pounding head. He couldn't breathe, he couldn't *breathe*; he was too aware of the hot blood trickling down his arms and legs, of the rank smell of loosened bowels mixed with blood. This–this didn't make any sense—this was war, this was victory, this was supposed to be glorious—this was supposed to be *holy*—

—but this didn't feel holy *at all*.

Another sob burst from him, and another, and his knees buckled.

It was Orestes who caught him, Orestes who held him. It was Orestes who made a soft, mournful noise and ran his fingers through Percy's sweat- and blood-tangled hair. It was Orestes who held firm as Perseus' high, quick panting subsided into silent shaking.

That was how Liaison Nabis found them, huddled together in the midst of dead and dying heretics.

16 Delivery Day

United Star System Postal Code, Chapter 3, Section 5: Whoever knowingly impersonates a USSPS courier shall be subject to prosecution from United Star System Postal Service Inspectors.

Perseus woke, alone, in the dark of the morning.

He lay still, riding out the wild beating of his heart as mind and body reconciled. It had been an awful dream: he'd been back at the Academy, overseeing roll call, and the only one who didn't answer was Orestes. He'd searched frantically for the missing Hammer, only for Liaison Nabis to tell him it was his fault Orestes was gone. *No,* he'd tried to say, *no, it's not me*—but in the next instant, he'd been floating alone through the dark abyss of space.

Percy ran a hand down the side of his face. He closed his eyes and took a steadying breath. It didn't matter. Dreams were nothing more than the mind shuffling anxieties into proper places. They meant nothing.

Orestes. He never should have said his name out loud to Basah. He had not allowed himself to think of Orestes since leaving Creedence; aside from that venom-fueled hallucination, he'd had no *reason* to. Even that Perseus had set aside: hallucinations were like dreams,

208

and in the waking hours, dreams were useless. He couldn't afford to dwell on Orestes, even if it was his fault he was out here, searching for answers he didn't necessarily want to find.

Percy ran his hand across the back of his head, massaged his neck, and then ghosted his thumb across his chin. He was in desperate need of both a shower and a shave: patchy, wispy bits of red hair had sprouted over his lip and chin, and he didn't want Roderick poking fun.

Speaking of…

Roderick's bunk lay empty, pillows and blankets tangled together in a hopeless mess. Percy scowled and flung himself out of bed. He crossed to Roderick's bunk and began making the bed. "BLIP," he called.

Good morning!

"Please remind Roderick that a successful day begins with a bed made." Percy leaned down and around to tuck the corners of the sheets back around the mattress.

A moment of silence followed on BLIP's end. When they spoke again, it was with the AI equivalent of glee: Marcelo, Pilot Roderick says, and BLIP quotes, 'bite me Red!'

"Not even if he was the only thing standing between myself and starvation," Percy muttered. A corner of his mouth twitched upwards when BLIP cackled. He pivoted back to his own bunk to make it. "Where is everyone?"

Up and working on morning assignments! Today is Delivery Day for the Hayabusa Mining Base!

The name gave Percy pause. He was passingly familiar with the concept of asteroid mining and the stereotypical asteroid miner: a slouching, uncouth man in brown overalls, clutching a thermos of bad coffee in one hand and a sixteen-month commission in the other. The Middies and the Extraordinaries had liked to dangle the threat of becoming an asteroid miner over the Ordinaries' heads if they failed an exam; he'd done it in turn when he'd graduated to a Midman.

He smoothed a hand over his creaseless sheets. The act of making the beds had left him more restless than satisfied; surely there was *more* he could do. "Is there anything I could do to help?"

Negative. Warden, Lieutenant Perseus does not have USSPS clearance necessary to aid in delivery of USSPS goods.

"Is there anything else?"

A small *click-click-click* indicated BLIP was thinking it through. You could grab a mop.

Percy snorted. He rolled his shoulders back before stretching both arms out. The movement did little to abate the sudden rush of anxiety. He needed to move. He needed to do *something* besides sit and twiddle his thumbs. He hadn't had anything to do for two days now, not since they'd left Franklin-Two.

He still remembered the look on Basah's face when Horris came hurrying back. Basah, Emperor bless her, excelled at saying what everyone was thinking: *"They're just letting us go?"* Roddy had been similarly pessimistic but more concerned with getting out while the getting was good. So they loaded up their cargo and went. And since no one had come after them in the interim, the posties had eventually come to the conclusion that Estelle hadn't said a word.

Percy refused to believe it. She was an Idoler. They were *all* Idolers. They knew he was a Black Hammer; they knew he had Idoler blood on his hands. Even if Estelle herself had not said a word, surely others would have. They owed him nothing. But—why hadn't the postal inspectors hauled him off the ship at F-2? What would the point be in letting him go?

For two days, he'd been gnawing at that point like a dog with a bone. It had been Horris, he'd eventually decided. If Estelle and the Idolers hadn't lied for his sake, they had lied for Horris, who'd gone out of his way to do them a good deed. Reckless, painfully naive Horris, who'd stood between Percy and a pirate and said *no*.

Percy blew out a breath. He reached up and dug under his thin t-shirt for the pendant resting against his skin: a meteor wreathed in flames, one of the symbols of His Glory and His Might. He'd prayed to the Emperor for help when the spider bit him, but it was Horris who'd appeared. It was Horris who'd saved him, time and again.

But if Horris was the answer to his prayer, what did that mean for his questions? Horris was neither Imperial nor Idoler. Horris believed in making his own way. *If you cannot find it,* he had said, *you have to make it.* All well and good for churros, but what about faith? How was he going to make his own faith all the way out here?

Sudden stinging pain brought him back to the here and now. He'd clenched his fist and dug his nails into his palm. Percy relaxed his fist and sighed down at the pendant in his palm. "What did you do to me?" He whispered.

Finding no point in dwelling, Percy got ready for the day. A small mint-flavored strip served as a mouth cleanser and breath freshener, and with one of Roddy's spare combs, he managed to shape his hair into some semblance of order. His Imperial uniform was in dire need of a wash, but water was something of a premium in space, and Basah had tossed his uniform into the laundry bag with the rest of the dirtied clothes. He was borrowing more of Fives' clothes in the meantime (black jeans and black turtleneck, and thank the Emperor, his black jackboots weren't ruined).

Roddy was at the helm, but the rest of the posties were working in the hold, and so it was into the hold Percy descended. He slid down the ladder in time to watch Basah heft a massive box into her arms. "*Matron's teats, this is heavy—*"

"Lift with your legs, Bah, please!" An unseen Horris pleaded. His voice echoed from down a row of shelved packages.

"I *am*, Horry," Basah rolled her eyes. She caught Percy's eye and gave him an up-nod. "Good morning, Perseus."

THUD.

They both twisted as Horris groaned with pain. He emerged from within the depths of a low shelf, rubbing at the top of his head with a free hand. Percy watched him grumble, caught between amusement and endearment. Horris straightened up with a bright smile. "Morning, Perce!"

"Good morning." Percy did a quick scan of the immediate area. The normally-tidy hold was in complete disarray: boxes strewn everywhere, canvas carts and dollies alike stacked high with packages and envelopes. Fives sat amid the mess, scanning everything within reach. A cheery '*doodoo!*' chime rang out from the scanner, followed by:

Please scan flats then—

Pause.

Letters.

"*Please scan flats, then letters,*" Fives imitated under his breath. He picked up a stack of thin, rectangular envelopes (the flats, Percy presumed) and fired his scanner at their barcodes.

Percy arched his eyebrows as he turned back to Horris. "Busy day?"

Horris nodded. "We're going to touch down at the Hayabusa station in a few hours. We only make deliveries there once a month, so it's vital that we're thorough."

"Why do you only deliver once a month?"

"Logistics," Basah answered. She had given up on being the hero and passed by them with a handcart. "The Hayabusa Base chases some of the largest asteroids in the Hirayama Ring. Our route is designed to fire across the circular route." She pantomimed, firing a gun down the hold. "They can spare a half-hour, forty minutes tops, before the base has to be on the move again. Which is why we have to have as much ready to go as possible—"

"And make sure we didn't screw up," Horris nodded.

Percy looked back at the disarray of packages. "I had no idea delivery was this complex."

"We're the lifeblood of the United Star System!"

"Then we ought to get paid like it," Basah muttered. Fives laughed.

Percy remained quiet. He thought back to his average day at the Academy: get up, train, study, train some more, pray, go to sleep. It wasn't that he hadn't worked hard—he had, every day, and he had the scars to show for it—but his hard work had always been oriented towards himself and his cohort. Self-improvement for the individual and cohesion for the group. Oh, the end result would have been in service to the Emperor, of course…but he'd never worked as diligently as these postal workers did now, in service to a public they weren't a part of.

"Is there anything I can do to help?"

The question fell out of his mouth before he even realized it. The posties froze in place.

Percy shifted on the spot and fought the urge to scowl. "What?"

Basah shrugged. Fives glanced at her and then Percy. "Basah figured you thought you were too good to lug packages around."

"*Really?!*" Basah and Percy exclaimed at the same time: Basah to Fives, Percy to Basah.

Horris held up his hands for peace. "We'd love the extra help. *Really.*" He grinned just a little, and against his better judgment, Percy returned it. Horris indicated the massive pile between himself and Basah. "If you could tag in for Bah, she can start inventory for Brose Front."

"Gladly."

The pile of mail stacked almost as high as Percy and twice as wide, a hodgepodge of envelopes and boxes of varying sizes. Horris added onto the pile as he went up and down the shelves, consulting his tablet and then pulling this or that. Fives would scan whatever was sorted and toss it into one of several canvas carts. Percy picked up a package at random and read the shipping address:

To: Piter van Dermeer
Hayabusa Mining Base
Mailroom 55B, 7th Lower Floor
Hirayama Asteroid Ring
USSOS Route 22234-D14

"USSOS?" He asked.

"United Star System Open Space," Basah answered. "Standard notation used for any organization operating outside a claimed political territory."

"And which pile would this package go in?" He indicated the multiple canvas carts around Fives.

"Let me see." Basah looked over his shoulder and made a noise of recognition. "That's for the admin team on the Hayabusa Base. You need to put it in that cart there." She indicated a cart with an orange flag sticking out of it. "Generally, mail falls into two categories: personal and professional. Professional will all go to the same mailroom address. See, here?" She tapped the word mailroom. "Personal will have an apartment number or something similar."

With the parameters set, Percy fell into a workable rhythm. It didn't take long to notice the cart of personal mail was just as full as the cart of professional mail. The professional made sense—a business needed supplies, after all—but what on earth did all these other people need?

Horris stopped to think when Percy voiced the question. "I dunno. Stuff to get by, I guess."

Percy peered at the return label for the package in his hands. "*Model robots?*"

"Sure, why not?"

Horris' response took Percy off-guard. Why not? Because of all the things to ship into the deep recesses of space, plastic models would not have ranked anywhere on his list. It smacked of the sort of thoughtless excess the Emperor preached against. "Surely things like this aren't necessary for survival."

"People aren't robots, Perce. You gotta give them room to breathe. Otherwise, what's the point?"

Percy stared at Horris in bewilderment. These packages were meant for adults, adults who worked some of the grittiest and unglamorous jobs in the galaxy. Surely, they didn't have time for toys. He and his cohort certainly hadn't: toys had been surrendered upon their enrollment into the Academy, and the only games they had played were designed to stimulate their bodies and enhance cooperation as a unit. If he'd abandoned toys at seven, what did grown adults need them for?

What *was* the point?

He opened his mouth to ask Horris, but the postal captain had already gone back to work. Percy grimaced as he turned away. He would ask later when they had a moment alone. These posties excelled at accidentally exposing gaps in his knowledge, and the more it happened, the more frustrated he became. Why hadn't the Academy taught him about things like *survival horror* and *lesbians*?

The floodgates had opened, and the questions were pouring in. With each package Percy sorted, he found himself trying to create a story for the name on the label. Why had Gladys ordered something from HerbalWorld, and would it help whatever afflicted her? What about Jandar and the package that had something heavy sliding from side to side? What were these people looking forward to on delivery day—messages and reminders of home, some tool or toy purchased to pass the time?

What would it be like if he worked on an asteroid base? What would he need to help pass the time?

Music, he decided. High-energy music he could dance to. A decent set of earbuds, some workout equipment, and a set of gym clothes (black). As long as he could keep moving, he would be fine.

He could feel his mood boosting even now through the simple act of lifting packages and sorting them into the correct piles. A pleasant burn had blossomed between his shoulder blades and in the back of his thighs. He hummed a simple hymn to himself as he worked.

Horris caught his eye with a grin. "BLIP, can you pick a playlist?"

Now playing playlist: Music To Sort Mail To.

Something jazzy blasted over the ship's speakers, a sweeping, joyful tune full of brass and woodwinds. A woman's sharp, ecstatic voice rose over the instruments. Basah began to wiggle and bop as she worked; Fives took off his headphones and closed his eyes, fingers moving in time to the beat of the song. Horris sang along as he snagged a package off a high shelf, and after a moment, Roddy's voice crackled over the intercom to hit the high note Horris couldn't.

Percy watched with fascination. He'd never seen menial work done with so much joy. He wanted to join Basah in dance, but something held him back. Perhaps it was a lingering sense of propriety: a Black Hammer did not *dance* with strangers in the hold of a service ship. But there was a twinge in his stomach that felt a little like embarrassment and a lot more like guilt.

It took another ninety minutes and the remainder of Fives' playlist, but the work was done by the time Roddy heralded their arrival at the Hirayama Ring.

Horris tapped Percy on the shoulder as he stood contemplating the completed work. "Come take a look!"

Percy followed Horris back to the main floor and to that large window. Outside, several massive asteroids, some twice as big as the *Silverfish*, soared past. Percy whistled through his teeth. The *Silverfish* cruised at a respectful distance from the asteroids and their orbit, but even so…a stray rock would have easily obliterated them all. Here and there, he could see asteroids with partially-disassembled rigs and drill holes piercing through their exteriors. Hayabusa Base was a just-visible dot in the distance: it was a reversed conical shape, with a flat disk marked for landing and take-off. The base became more industrial the further down the cone one went, with enormous claws and drills poking from the sides. Percy could only guess at the mechanisms of how they worked.

"What are they mining for?"

"Metallics, mostly. Iron and nickel. Ooh, look! That's the Laurel," Horris pointed to the largest of the asteroids sweeping by. "The miners use drones to remotely land on the asteroids and do survey work before they start drilling."

"So, there's no pickaxes involved?"

"Tragically, no. But lots of sorting through chunks that are brought back to the base."

Percy leaned against the glass. He looked left and right, surprised to see that there were relatively few asteroids in proximity. When he heard *asteroid belt*, he'd expected a minefield of space rocks to navigate. But like so much else in space, the asteroid belt was empty. He glanced up at Horris, trying not to feel personally betrayed.

Horris caught his look. "There are more asteroids in the belt. But a ring isn't clustered together. The next closest is probably, oh, a thousand kilometers from here."

"My scale for astronomical features continues to fail me." Percy pushed off the glass. The sight of the asteroids, combined with the burn in his muscles, set a fire in him. He needed off this ship, if only for a little while. He needed to see new things and new people. "May I accompany you when you deliver?"

"No."

Percy blinked. He could count on one hand the number of times he'd been told "no" in his lifetime (the majority now was from Horris). He gaped as the postie turned away. "*Excuse me?*"

"Oh." Horris started to step aside to give him room. "Sorry."

"No, you complete—" Percy tamped down on the rush of indignation. Instead, he took a deep breath. "I need to get off this ship. I'm starting to go in circles!"

Horris stared at him as though he'd grown two heads. "You are not supposed to be on this ship, remember? And you've got a price on your head! We got very lucky with Estelle! If anyone sees you—no. You need to stay here. Your safety is my priority, Percy, and I'm very sorry if that upsets you."

"No, you're not."

"You're right," Horris folded his arms over his chest. "I'm not."

A mutual, frustrated silence lapsed between them. Percy turned back to the window. The need to get off the ship grew like an itch under his skin. But Horris was right (he was going to have to get used to saying that, Percy realized with some despair). There was no leaving this ship unnoticed. Unless...

Percy glanced back at Horris. The taller man had similarly taken to staring out the window. "What if I helped you with mail delivery?"

"You're not a mail carrier. Legally, you wouldn't be able to—"

"I know. But Fives doesn't typically help with deliveries, does he? Or, if he does, he's got those headphones on—he and I are of a size. I could borrow his uniform, wear a hat, just hang back, and watch the rest of you work. Just to get off the ship. Just for a little bit–*please*."

Horris' eyes shot to him. Percy eased back. He hadn't meant to add a "please". As a Black Hammer, he'd never had to say *please* before.

Horris looked away again, lips pursed, fingers fidgeting. "Fine!" He said, at last, so loudly that Percy jumped. "Fine–just, just let me see if it's okay with Fives first. Then maybe–maybe–you can come along. *Maybe*."

Twenty minutes later, Percy was pushing a canvas cart down the *Silverfish* ramp and into the Hayabusa Base loading bay. He lowered the brim of a borrowed USSPS cap over his eyes, both to shield himself from view and as relief against the stark white lights of the bay.

The unloading bay had that stark, utilitarian look F-2 had. The difference was in the stillness. The crowd here had gathered just behind a yellow marking line, and in the first scan of the crowd, his initial stereotype seemed correct. The miners were rugged men and women in varying states of cleanliness, dressed in gray shirts and brown overalls with the company logo on them. They reminded Percy of Idolers, in truth: motley crowds of common people living dreary lives.

Horris skidded down the end of the gangplank, smiling and waving at the woman in front of the crowd.

She returned neither. Instead, she folded her arms over her chest. "You're late."

Her tone had Percy bristling, but Horris just removed his cap and began to apologize. Percy watched the exchange with eyes narrowed. If anyone had spoken to an Imperial officer with that tone, sharp discipline would have followed—and shouldn't the same be true for postal workers?

Evidently, it was not. Horris just continued to apologize and say things like "on behalf of the United Star System Postal Service." Basah and Roddy ignored the scene in favor of their canvas carts. They would reach into the cart, pull out a package, and call a name. The person would step forward, sign for their package on a tablet, and then accept it over the rope.

Percy took a full step backward to watch: some miners took their packages and scurried off, while others only made it a few steps before succumbing to temptation and tearing the package open. Most, though, were ripping it open where they stood using brute strength or pocket-knives.

One had unfurled a poster of some blazeball team to much admiration. Another, teary-eyed and beaming, swapped pictures and handwritten letters with a graybeard, who cooed about grandchildren. A younger miner unearthed the model kit and excitedly pointed out its features to a friend. Ripples of delight made their way through the crowd.

Funny. The more he watched, the less ugly these miners became. Percy's mouth twitched upwards.

"Excuse me?"

A soft voice cut through his thoughts. A young woman stood close to the rope separating them from the unloading dock. She hunched her shoulders when Percy looked her way. "Can I help you?"

"Um…I was expecting a package, and my tracking app said that it was going to be delivered today. But, ah…no one's called my name yet." She looked to where Basah and Roddy were finishing up.

Percy was about to ask why this was his problem…and then he remembered the uniform he was wearing. He straightened up and rolled his shoulders back. Perhaps he wasn't USSPS, but he could damn well act like it. "What's your name?"

"Mei Greenwood."

"I'll be right back."

He crossed to Roddy, who looked up from his tablet with eyebrows arched. "What's up, Red?"

"Do you have a Mei Greenwood on your manifest?"

"Greenwood, Greenwood…" Roddy murmured as he scrolled through the list of deliveries on his tablet. He shook his head. "No dice."

Percy looked over his shoulder at Mei Greenwood. She managed a wobbly, hopeful smile when she noticed him. "She says she ordered a package, and the tracking said it would be delivered today."

"Can't trust tracking apps." Roddy shook his head. He peered over Percy at the waiting young woman and then sighed. "Maybe her package is still on the ship. It could have gotten lost in the shuffle. Want me to—"

"I'll go."

It was important to him, suddenly, that he retrieve Mei Greenwood's missing package. Suddenly, it was his sole mission in life. He wanted to help. He wanted to be a part of it. Roddy blinked but stepped back enough to allow Percy to pass up the gangplank and back into the hold.

"BLIP?" Percy called out once inside.

Present!

"Do you have any record of a package for Greenwood, Mei?"

Click-click-click. An eight-ounce package for Greenwood, Mei manifested at the Salonia Outpost three weeks ago. It was logged onboard the *Silverfish* two days ago after processing at the Franklin-Two Depot.

Percy sighed in relief. "Where is it?"

BLIP is good. BLIP is not that good.

"Any idea on where to start, then?"

Click-click-click. Check shelving units F2 through F7 in the hold. Packages under seven kilograms that have been processed through the Franklin-Two Depot are usually shelved there.

Percy hurried down the rows and rows of shelves in the hold. F2 through F6 had been completely emptied of packages, but his luck held at F7. A small, square package had been pushed all the way to the back, lost amid the hustle and bustle.

Mei Greenwood beamed when he handed her her package. "Oh, thank you, thank you! Thank you, thank you, I really appreciate you checking, thank you!"

"Of course," Percy replied. An embarrassed heat crept up his neck. "It's what we do, miss."

"Thank you! Have a great day!"

"You too," Percy's response was vague and probably not heard as Mei vanished into the crowd. He stared after her, slightly dazed and struggling not to feel like a hero. Such effusive thanks had not been needed. It had been such a simple thing, really, the smallest of all the problems in the universe.

He felt the weight of eyes on him and turned to see Horris grinning at him. He held up a finger to stop whatever Horris was going to say. "Not a word, postman."

Horris held up both hands. "Of course, of course."

"I mean it. It was just—playing the part, that's all. I'd never have heard the end of it from you if I'd just ignored her. Besides, if I had ignored her, it might have raised suspicions about a postman unable to do his job—"

"Thank you," Horris said.

The thanks cut Percy's rambling explanation off at the head. His shoulders sank as he exhaled. He could ignore the swell of pride that Mei's gratitude gave him. But it was a lot harder to ignore Horris and his dark eyes, which danced with delight. So he wrenched his gaze towards the *Silverfish* and focused hard on one of its engines.

"I was happy to," he said.

■

Hours later, Percy woke again in the dark.

This time, he wasn't alone: Roddy was passed out in his bunk, wrapped in sheets and blankets like some caterpillar half-assing its transformation into a butterfly. He didn't stir as Percy swung out of bed and padded out of the room.

The water closet was a small, cramped space with barely enough room to turn around. Percy yanked on the sink and splashed cold water onto his face. He clutched the edge of the sink and breathed hard through his nose.

Another dream. This time he'd been alone in the hold of the *Silverfish*, calling for help as he frantically searched for something he'd lost. He couldn't remember what it was now, but in the dream, it had been urgent that he found the lost thing. They wouldn't let him go back home without it.

Home. Percy shook his head and stared down into the sink. There was no such thing as a *home* for him anymore.

"Are you all right?" A soft voice asked.

"Fine, Horris, I'm fine—" Percy looked up into the mirror.

Orestes looked back at him with eyes wide and sorrowful.

Percy shouted and pivoted, instinctually swinging a fist out to knock the other soldier aside. But his fist only collided with the wall. There was nothing behind him. There was no one in the water closet besides himself, and when he swung back towards the mirror, he only saw his own reflection.

"*Leave me alone!*"

And there he stood, straining to hear an answer in the silence, until Fives opened the water closet door.

🄱🄷 Secrets To Keep

United Star System Postal Code Chapter 5, Section 10: Any and all usage of interstellar wormholes, hereto referred to as 'bridges,' by USSPS couriers must be sanctioned by the nearest sentient-dominate planet, which must also be a member of the USS.

Fives had a secret.

Fives knew all about secrets. Secrets were something you held close to your heart, not your head, and they were not for anyone else to know. Fives had had no secrets Before. Roddy was the one who taught him what a secret was on the night he had become Fives.

"Horris said you might be allergic, but we don't have any other snacks," Roddy had said, passing him a sticky piece of peanut brittle with a small smile. "We'll keep it a secret, okay?"

It was the first time Fives had ever been a part of something as monumental as a "we."

You were not supposed to talk about secrets. Secrets were supposed to be kept private. (Fives knew about *private* from Before, and something about the word made his throat constrict). Some secrets were silly like the time Basah got gum in her hair and blamed her bad haircut on a phase. Some secrets were sad, like how Roddy went hollow when he thought about his family. Some secrets, though… some were dangerous.

Fives knew he was a dangerous secret. That was the only reason he'd been allowed to become a postman after he'd been found. The United Star System wanted a phrenic they could keep an eye on even from afar. Fives was a Never-Should-Have-Been-Allowed secret, a Testament-To-Hubris secret. Fives had never *felt* like any of those things, but nevertheless, that's what strange men in dark suits had called him.

What Fives was, however, was not his own secret.

The *Silverfish* sailed through space in silence. Everyone had bunked down for a few hours, leaving BLIP on autopilot and Fives free to wander the ship alone. Rest time was tricky: the feedback from dreams could be sharp and intense or muddled and strange and faraway, like people talking two rooms over. Sometimes, he would hunker down in the engine pit with Cab Calloway and wait for the nonsense noise to pass. Now, though…

Now, the *Silverfish* passed close to an active bridge. And as they passed, Fives could hear Her singing.

She was Fives' most precious secret. He didn't think the others would even begin to understand if he tried to describe Her. After all, they couldn't hear what he did on a normal day. She was loudest near a bridge: a soft, constant humming, soothing and rhythmic like a lullaby. Even from far away, She drowned out all the other noises. His mind stilled when he heard Her. And for that reason alone, he called her Mother.

Fives stood by the *Silverfish*'s window. The distant bridge was a swirling vortex punched through the sheer fabric of space. As he looked out the window, the bridge was no bigger than his thumbnail. Nevertheless, it was close enough. Fives pulled off his oversized headphones and closed his eyes.

Mmm-hm-mmm, mmm-hm-mmm, Mother sang. Fives' fingers twitched, moving up and down an invisible scale in time to Her song.

Fives loved Her music as much as he loved jazz. Mother's music made him feel bubbly and floaty, pushing him outside of the confining shape of his body. He lifted away from a world that was dark and hard and cruel. A world where he was a mistake.

A sharp, strangled shout sent him crashing back to reality. Fives' eyes shot open. Immediately, he spread out his awareness and counted his sleeping family. Waves from Horris and Basah and Roddy lapped against him in nonsensical images and murmurs. Fives blew out a breath of relief. All asleep, all sound, all safe. Which left only one option.

Fives turned from the window with some regret. Mother continued to sing wordlessly, providing him with a soundtrack of sorts, but her song faded to almost nothing as he approached the water closet.

Percy jumped when Fives opened the door. He had a white-knuckled grip on the edge of the sink, and his green eyes were wild when their gaze met.

Fives watched Percy stiffen. He pushed his consciousness out against Percy and was immediately rebuffed. It had been a fun sort of challenge this past week and a half, learning how to figure out Percy's mood based on expression and body language. Honestly, he didn't know how Other People did it all the time. It was *exhausting*. But he didn't need to be a phrenic to know Percy disliked him: it was in his flat, cold courtesy, and the way his eyes followed Fives whenever they were in the same room.

"What," snarled Percy.

Fives blinked. He had been standing and staring for too long. "You shouted."

"Well-spotted."

"Why?"

"I'm certain you already know. Good night." He shoved past Fives and stalked out.

Fives let himself be shoved. He turned to watch Percy stagger down the corridor. Now, he had a decision to make. The prospect daunted him; he was not the decision-making type and preferred leaving the decision-making to people who liked it, like Horris. But there was no one here to make the decision for him. Did he trust Percy?

Yes, Fives decided. Yes, he did.

"I don't."

He watched Percy stop short. The Imperial wheeled back towards him with brow furrowed. "I beg your pardon?"

"You're–you're different from other people." It was strange being on the other end of this sort of talk. The right words and phrases dripped through his fingers like oil, leaving him sticky and unclean. The lack of feedback from Percy didn't help: he just stared, expression incredulous, fists clenched white. Fives flicked a bit of hair out of his eyes. "You're silent. A hole in the sheet music of the universe. A closed door in a loud house. I don't hear you like I do other people—"

In a flash, Perseus crossed back to him and slammed him against the wall. What little he heard of Mother's song snapped to complete and utter silence.

A nervous giggle escaped Fives. He hadn't anticipated that at all! The giggle helped disguise the twist in his stomach, the twinge in the back of his mind that screamed danger-danger. He rag-dolled as Perseus leaned in; you were harder to hurt that way.

"What are you saying?"

"That I can't hear you." His eyes darted around, trying to look at anything that wasn't Perseus. "No thoughts, no intentions. Nothing."

Perseus' mouth twisted into a snarl. He lifted Fives up and shoved him against the wall again. Fives whimpered. He could cry for help, he knew, or tell BLIP to sound the alarm. Or–or–*or he could tear the little thing apart piece by piece and listen to it die screaming*–

Somewhere far away, Mother sang. The silence in the *Silverfish* stretched on.

"Are you saying," Perseus said, voice quivering, eyes wild, "that I'm some sort of *freak*?"

His tone, more than his words, brought Fives back. He knew that frightened, trembling tone. It was the caged thing backed into a corner, chest heaving and teeth bared. Fives recognized the caged thing as assuredly as he did his own reflection.

"No," he said, matter-of-fact. "You are not a freak."

"Have you ever met anyone else you couldn't dig around inside?"

Fives blinked, annoyed without knowing why. "The odds of being born a phrenic are three in one-hundred million." It had been one of the first things he'd looked up when left to his own devices: was there anyone else like him? Was he alone in the universe?

"So?"

"So," Fives continued, testy, "being a phrenic is rare. We're like… stars. Stretched out over miles and miles and miles. *Lonely* but not *alone.* Maybe you're like me, like that. Most people don't ever meet phrenics, so they don't know if they can block them out. You're probably not a freak. You're probably not alone."

Perseus snorted. He lowered Fives so that his sneakers hit the floor. "So, what would you call someone like me?"

Fives regarded him. He was suddenly too-aware of being inside the bubble of silence around Perseus. And in the silence came a giddiness that was all his own. He'd never known such a deafening silence before or the bliss of knowing a thought was his own alone. He wanted more of it. He leaned into Perseus' space, chasing the high, before remembering he had been asked a question.

"A reinforcer," he decided.

Perseus leaned away as Fives leaned in. "A reinforcer?"

"Reality feels more…real around you. Drawn just a bit sharper, in darker ink. You close the doors and turn down the volume. It's why I could hear Silver from so far away. You blocked out all the noise around me."

"So…I'm soundproofing, is that it?"

"Yes," Fives admitted. "I could hear you a little bit at the start. But then you said *stop* and *get out.* You haven't opened up to me since."

Percy turned away. He folded his arms over his chest and stared at a point on the floor. "Do the rest know?"

"Yes."

"And they didn't say anything."

"It wasn't their place to. We didn't know who you were or what you wanted. Best to play safe until we knew what you were."

Percy nodded a fraction. "And what am I, to you all?"

"A friend."

Percy flinched as if struck. His hand flew to his collar, fiddling with a necklace chain. "I am not the sort of man you want for a friend."

"It's not our choice to make. Whether they look at us and think, *friend.*"

Percy sighed. Fives scooted further up the wall. Old warnings still ached in the back of his head. Percy was his friend. Perseus the Imperial, on the other head...

"I hurt people who try to be my friend, Fives," Percy muttered.

"Oh." What did that mean? He wanted to push and pull and pluck like he could with anyone else, draw apart what Percy said and what he *meant,* like sinew from muscle. Fives tampered down the initial rush of frustration. Other People had to ask the question, and so did he: "Why?"

"Because—because I am naive and foolish and—" A sharp, bitter laugh tore out of Percy. It was a hysterical sort of laugh without any humor. "I think I might be a bad person."

"I don't think so," said Fives. This he could say with some confidence. He had known bad people, and they were not like Percy.

"You don't know what's inside my head. You can't be sure."

"No," Fives conceded. "But you ask questions. Bad people don't ask questions. Bad people don't want to learn."

Percy didn't immediately reply. Instead, he stood still, running his thumb back and forth over a pendant. He took a long, deep breath. "I'm going to ask you a question. And you have to promise to take it seriously."

"Okay."

"Are ghosts real?"

Despite his assurance, Fives laughed. What a ridiculous question. "Of course, ghosts are real."

What little color Percy had drained from his face. Apparently, the answer did not please him. "Can you see them?"

Fives shook his head. "Ghosts don't work like that. They're… impressions. Things left behind. The living drag the ghosts around with them wherever they go." He had sensed the ghosts that surrounded Horris, ghosts called *Mom* and *Dad*, and similar ones around Roddy and Basah. The sensations were always bittersweet and left him oddly empty.

"Does everyone have ghosts?"

"Oh, yes. Everyone."

Percy rubbed his arms before reaching for his pendant again. He looked so miserable that Fives reached for him—only to snap his hand back when Percy jerked away. Percy took a full step backward. "I don't suppose there's a chance I'm just slowly going insane?"

"There's always a chance you're just slowly going insane," Fives said in his very best soothing tone.

"Thank you, Fives."

"You're welcome."

Percy snorted again, and it was only then that Fives realized he was being sarcastic. He hunched down into his hoodie and likewise took a full step away. Next time, he would wake up Horris first. He was useless at this.

"I would appreciate it if you kept this incident to yourself," Percy said curtly.

"I will."

"Good."

Percy's mouth turned down at the corners. Fives could see the two people within, Perseus and Percy, battling it out for dominance.

Percy won because he sighed and turned fully back to Fives. "Why are you up at this hour?"

"I don't sleep."

Which was the truth, or most of it. Fives had long since discovered he could work just fine on three or four hours of sleep. He didn't want any more than that; sleep meant dreams, and he did not like dreams. Dreams contained truths he did not want to face. Dreams reminded him of what he really was beneath the fragile skin.

Percy looked at him. He looked back at Percy. Funny—he really did think of Percy as a friend. They all did. Percy ate and played with him. He helped sort and deliver the mail. He talked and listened. What else was a friend, if not someone who could do all that?

"I have a secret," Fives blurted out.

This, too, was important. The sharing of secrets. Just like Roddy had done all the way at the start. He didn't have Roddy's smile or his winking eyes, but he did have a secret he could share. He outstretched his hand towards Percy. "I'll keep yours," he said. "You keep mine."

This, at least, Percy seemed to understand. He nodded but did not take Fives' proffered hand. "What's your secret, then?"

Fives led him over to the window. Mother's song was still muted, although the proximity to Percy meant the usual waves of feedback didn't slap him either. He existed in a rare state, almost like Other People.

He pointed to the distant bridge. "Do you see that bridge?"

Percy squinted. "Yes."

"When we're close to one," he took a deep breath, "I can hear singing."

Percy opened his mouth. Closed it. A crease appeared between his brows. Fives gauged his reaction and tried not to feel self-consciousness. He shuffled his place, fingers playing over each other in an attempt at self-comfort.

"You hear singing," he repeated at last.

"Yes."

"Who's singing?"

"Mother," Fives said. That wouldn't be enough explanation, he realized, so he added: "She sings."

Percy's jaw dropped. "This is–are you talking about a god? You can hear a *god*?"

"No. I don't think so." Fives knew a little about gods. They were the thing that preceded "dammit" and "fucking dammit." They were also the things you called upon when you wanted revenge or rescue. Mother wasn't like that. She just *was*, like the empty spaces between stars. He pondered a bit more before shaking his head. "No. She isn't a god."

"What is she, then?"

"The universe."

"The universe," Percy repeated again. He spoke slowly, deliberately, as if he was tasting Fives' words. His expression shifted from baffled to interested. Intrigued. "The universe sings to you?"

"Not *to* me. She sings for everyone. But most can't hear Her."

"What does she sound like?"

Fives hummed the six notes Mother always sang. Percy surprised him—pleased him—by humming it back. "It's...pretty," he decided.

Fives nodded in agreement.

"No one else knows about this—about Mother?"

"No one." Fives smiled at Percy. Percy, who was just his size. Percy, who was not quite like Other People, and therefore was his friend. "We'll keep it a secret, okay?"

Percy smiled back. He did not have the face for smiles—he was all hard angles, better suited for scowls and frowns—but nevertheless, he smiled. "Very well. Thank you, Fives."

And this time, Fives knew he meant it.

18 Electra

United Star System Postal Code, Chapter 3, Section 1: All USSPS personnel are required to carry photo IDs on their person during normal business hours.

Soft, agreeable music played through the elegant coffeehouse on the Taygate satellite. Sparta sang along under her breath, tapping her hands against the table's smooth surface. She froze when Electra shot her a cold look.

Electra couldn't stand the music. Even the innocent *tap-tap-tap* of palms against a table set her teeth on edge. She needed silence to think and work. And more than that, the music reminded her of her brother.

When she had been very little, seven, and newly admitted to the Academy, she'd cried herself to sleep every night. Foolish and selfish child that she'd been, she could only think of the creature comforts of home, not the glory that enrolling into the Academy brought her family. To have not one but *two* children deemed worthy was an unusual honor.

Orestes was—had been—two years her senior. At nine or ten, he'd stolen into her barracks and slipped into bed with her. He'd held her while she cried into his bony shoulder and sang soft lullabies to lull her to sleep. She'd thought the world of him then, a foolish, naive child that she'd been. Her big, strong brother with his voice high and clear as a kyriakon bell.

It hadn't taken long, though, for her to learn better. To be the sister of *Orestes Mason* was its own special source of shame. To the rest of the world, he was not a big, strong brother. He was an indecisive, doe-eyed weakling, and his reputation cast a long shadow over hers. The instructors and tutors expected less of her; the older Ordinaries snickered behind their hands at her. Even the Mids and the Extraordinaries—older still, supposedly above such behavior—regarded her with a sort of strained-smile pity. Electra had to work harder, fight better, and think faster to claw her way out of Orestes' fumbling shadow. So *he* could be called *Electra's brother* and not the other way around.

She still remembered the look on his face when she told him she didn't need him anymore. *Leave*, she'd said. *Get out, before I call the prefects.*

He'd ruined music forever. Ever since that night, even the lightest hum made her stomach clench.

"What are you thinking about?" Sparta asked conversationally.

Electra looked at her. Sparta was a member of her cohort and had been her dearest friend from day one. She was the eldest daughter of Liaison Anaxandros and, as such, had immediately been held to a much higher standard than the rest. Perhaps their mutual misery had been their initial starting point, but over the years, their friendship had grown. As such, Electra felt she could be truthful, even here:

"Orestes."

"Oh." Sparta sipped her tea. "What about him?"

"This is all his fault. If he'd just listened and done his job, then he wouldn't have blown his own brains out. And then, whatever he did to Percy—because he did *something*, he must have; Percy isn't the sort to just snap and go rogue. It's his stupid fault we're sitting here at this stupid table listening to this stupid music."

Sparta stabbed at the little pearls floating in her drink. "I sort've like it."

"You would," Electra grumbled. That was the thing she both loved and despaired over when it came to Sparta. She would have done very well for herself as an explorer or an adventurer if she hadn't had the very good fortune of being the daughter of a Liaison. Sparta was bright and curious, and although she was a fierce fighter, she preferred a diplomatic approach. Electra could easily see her featured in some article someday, working as a Liaison to distant stars.

Sparta had the look for it: tall and lean and tan, with messy dark hair and dark, intelligent eyes. Next to her, Electra cut a less-than-impressive figure. But that was all right—the Imperials valued ability over appearance, and when it came to hunting heretics, Electra considered herself second-to-none.

Taygate was full of heretics. It was a resort satellite lazily orbiting a life-friendly planet. It served as a vacation destination for the planet of Tay, as well as travelers through this leg of the system. Everything had been designed with *allure* in mind. Water splashed from marble fountains as people passed, arms laden with shopping bags and over-priced drinks. They moved in clumps, oohing and awwing at window displays of glittery shoes or signed blazeball posters. Electra was too aware of the excess of this place and how the vanity of the individual was celebrated above all the common good. *What do you live for?* She wanted to scream. *What will you die for?*

She missed home. She missed feeling like a part of something greater than herself. She hated sitting here in street clothes, feeling the weighing eyes of these–these *individuals*–on her.

Something of her discomfort must have shown because Sparta leaned over and punched her shoulder. "Relax, Elle. I can hear you grinding your teeth from here."

"I can't afford to relax. This is my mission, remember? Liaison Nabis put *me* in charge."

Sparta frowned but did not answer.

Electra shifted. She knew Sparta well enough to know that she had been expecting command of this mission. It would have been a massive favor to Liaison Anaxandros. Instead, the honor had gone to Electra. The decision probably caused no small discourse in the capital, but Liaison Nabis had been firm. He had seen no sign of Orestes' weakness in her. *It was in the spirit, not the blood.*

She still remembered it. If she closed her eyes and took a centering breath, she could put herself back there in the courtyard. Thick black smoke curled up into a storm-gray sky. Perseus, soaked in heretical blood, standing beside Nabis on the stone steps. The line of Idolers on their knees. And Orestes, Orestes saying *no.*

She still remembered her shock, her dread, her mortification. And then—as the others gave her sidelong, judgmental looks—her blistering rage. How it tasted like hot, coppery blood on her tongue.

She *needed* this chance. More than Sparta needed glory.

Electra shook her head. "I won't relax until Perseus is back in Imperial custody. Then…"

Then what?

Sparta nudged her under the table. "Then," she said, "with the Idolers dead, and before the Emperor begins his next campaign, we should go somewhere nice. Just you and me."

"Somewhere nice," Electra repeated dubiously.

"Mmhm! My father has this villa overlooking the southern sea. We can spend a few days there. We'll have earned it, after this goose chase." Sparta cast another look around the little cafe. It was just she and Electra as representatives of the cohort; the others had been ordered to stay behind on the Creed shuttle. Less was more, in this case.

Electra blew out a breath. "Indeed," she said, "indeed. That would be…nice."

The tingling of the bell broke their conversation. A small, scaley Sem stepped through the door into the coffeehouse. She looked around, caught Electra's eye, and gave her a small nod of acknowledgment.

Electra nodded back. Her gaze tracked the woman to the counter and did not leave as she ordered a drink.

Sparta had popped open the lid of her drink and began to shake the pearls into her mouth. "Is that our contact?"

"Yes."

Electra sat up as the Sem approached with two iced drinks in hand. She smiled at the two Imperials. "Hiya! I'm Sami."

"Good to meet you," said Electra, while Sparta chirped a "hello!" Sami looked between them. "Are you two ready to meet with the captain?"

Sparta opened her mouth to answer, but Electra beat her to it. "Why couldn't he come himself?" she demanded. She disliked Silver on principle, but she especially disliked being handed off to a subordinate. This was not how one treated Hammers.

"He's had a bit of, *hm*," Sami tilted her head to the side in thought, "historical trouble with the shopping district of Taygate. He's at a bar downcity."

Electra swallowed her noise of indignation. She and Sparta got to their feet and followed Sami out of the coffeehouse.

Taygate was the sort of satellite that had been designed with walkability in mind. There were no 'rough' places in Taygate, so to speak, but downcity appealed to a different clientele. The chic shops and outlets gave way to clubs, bars, and lounges. Signs and ads left little to the imagination. Electra's skin crawled. Sparta stared at everything they passed with wide eyes.

Stop it! Electra shook herself. Silver was doing this on purpose. He was trying to discomfort them, put them on the back foot, so he could dominate their arrangement. It was a petty maneuver. Electra would have gladly run him through and taken his man-of-war for her own, but Liaison Nabis had insisted on using a go-between.

Silver was repulsive, Nabis agreed, but necessary. The call for bounty hunters kept the full Imperial strength out of the eye of the USS.

Sami led them to a dive bar thick with smoke. Their shoes clung to the sticky floor as they walked, and Electra made a note not to touch anything unless she could wash her hands after. Space shanties crackled over an old sound system. Electra's gut twisted, which was the last thing she needed as Sami led them through the bar and into a backroom.

The backroom struck Electra as obscenely masculine: dark wood and red accents, two billiard tables, dartboards, and several worn leather chairs. A cursory sweep of the room revealed Silver: he slouched in one armchair, blowing darts through a small blowgun at one of the dartboards.

A picture of a handsome Elentee with curly blond hair had been pinned to the board. Several darts punctuated his wide grin, and as they watched, Silver fired another–*PWHUNK!*–into the Elentee's forehead.

"Hope he earned that one," Sparta commented.

Silver twirled to his feet with an obnoxious flourish. Gold chains clattered against his horns as he did. "Well, well, well! If it isn't our auspicious guests!" He gestured to the remaining armchairs. "Come sit, come sit."

Sami crossed to him with drink outstretched. "Matcha latte for you, Cap'n."

"You're a gem, Sam." Silver accepted the latte with a smile. It vanished the moment he turned back to Electra and Sparta. His silver eyes flattened. "Sit."

Sparta made to comply, but Electra bristled. "You don't give orders here."

"Oh, but I do." Silver collapsed back into his armchair. He flung one long leg over the arm of the chair.

Electra ignored him. Instead, she looked at the dartboard. "Who is he?"

"Roderick Marcelo." Silver scowled and fixed his daggered glare on the dartboard. "Pilot of the One-Thirty-One-C. The mailship that is currently transporting your little wayward soul."

Electra's pulse jumped in her neck. The 131-C. She filed that information away as Sparta arched her eyebrows. "What did he do to you?"

"He outmaneuvered me." Silver picked up a dart and flung it at the pilot's head. It missed the mark and landed with a clatter on the floor. "It's not going to happen again."

"On that, we can agree," Electra said. She rolled her shoulders back and folded her hands behind her back. "So, what's the plan?"

"That's an excellent question. But I thought I wasn't giving orders here." Silver widened his eyes, all innocence, even as his shit-eating grin grew.

Electra swallowed her bile, even as she dug her nails into her palms. Steady, she told herself. Comport yourself like the Black Hammer you are. "How do we apprehend Perseus?"

"I'm so very glad you asked." Silver leaned over to a table and snatched up a tablet. He swiped open a page before flipping the screen towards them. It was an itemized list of sorts, but Electra couldn't make sense of it. She glanced at Sparta, who shook her head. Silver looked between them. "This is the manifest of the One-Thirty-One-C. Crew, cargo, and scheduled routes. One of my men snatched it right from the USSPS database. Not bad, eh?"

"I'm not here to praise you." Electra snapped. She snatched the tablet from Silver's limp grip and began to scroll through the manifest.

"A thank you would have sufficed." Silver took a long, loud sip of his latte. "Take a look at the second-to-last destination. You know it?"

Electra couldn't help her start when she found it. "The Brose Front."

It was familiar, inasmuch as a cautionary tale could be familiar. The Brose Front was a small desert planet on the Old Edge of space, but what had made the Brose unique in the region was its survivable atmosphere and plentiful oases. When exploration had just begun to push into wilder territories, the Brose had served as a base of sorts for adventurers, explorers, and scientists. Then, as the sentients pushed further and further beyond the Brose, came the sellers, the capitalists, the architects, and, after them, the tourists. Now, the Brose was no better than Taygate: packed with shops and casinos and skyscraper pools. The Brose transformed from a desert haven to a testament to profit.

"Very good. It's the perfect spot to pounce on a mailship. The Brose has so many ships going in and out that we won't flag on their system until we're almost on them. You'll get your man, and we'll get some plunder." Silver winked at Sami, who broke into a wicked grin.

"How can we know where the mailship will be?" Sparta asked. She lowered herself into a seat across from Silver.

"It'll be in the depot, of course."

"What sorts of defenses can we expect?"

It was Sami who answered. She had pulled out her own tablet for review: "There's one postal inspector stationed there."

"Only one?" Silver whipped his head towards her, genuinely surprised. "Really?"

"Aye, Cap'n. Obella Rofon. Age forty-five. Postal inspector for the past fifteen years."

Silver turned back to Electra. "Well, there you have it. Think you can take a forty-five-year-old woman in a fight?"

Postal inspectors were some of the fiercest fighters in the star system…allegedly. But one alone was nothing compared to an Imperial cohort. Electra lifted her chin. "Easily."

Sparta gave Electra a sidelong look. Electra did not acknowledge it.

Silver was chattering on: "We'll fly in by night, strike hard and fast, grab your Imperial and a decent amount of booty, and then get out. This ought to be fun. Never struck at the Brose or its postal depot before. It'll be a nice feather in my cap."

He and Sami high-fived. It took all of Electra's training (and a prayer to the Emperor) not to roll her eyes.

"How do we know the mailship will still be there when we arrive?" Sparta asked.

"What an excellent question. They *do* teach you well in that Academy of yours." Silver took another longer sip of his latte. He shifted, folding one leg over the other. "I've taken the liberty of sending some men ahead on a shuttle. They'll do a bit of gentle sabotage and ensure the postmen are delayed."

"You're certainly going out of your way for us," Sparta said. She tilted her head to the side.

"A bounty is a bounty." Silver shrugged. "And beyond that, I've seen the way the wind is blowing. The Empire of Creed is not an entity I want to make an enemy of."

"You would be correct," said Electra.

Silver studied them over the rim of his latte. His flat, calculating eyes reminded Electra of Idolers. Always testing, these heretics. Always seeking weakness. "One ambitious man recognizes another. Your Emperor won't be content with one little planet, will he?"

"And if He is not, what of it?" Electra demanded. "He deserves the star system."

Even as the words left her mouth, she regretted them. A corner of Silver's mouth twitched upwards, and Electra had a sinking feeling she had just given something away without realizing it. She took an abrupt step backward.

"We'll return to our shuttle and retrieve the rest of our cohort. Thank you for your time."

Silver lifted his latte in a mock toast. "'Cha."

A Black Hammer did not run from heretics. But she could walk, fast, out of that disgusting bar, through the crowded streets of nattering, vapid tourists. The more she walked, the faster her pace became until she was almost running. It was the only thing to do with the blood running in her veins. Stupid, stupid, stupid, *useless*—she wasn't strong enough for this, she wasn't clever enough for this—her lungs were burning, and something sharp pricked behind her eyes.

"Elle–ELLE! *ELLIE!*"

"WHAT!" Electra rounded on Sparta with fists clenched.

Sparta stopped short. She raised both hands in a gesture of innocence. "Emperor's hand, calm down! I'm not the one you're upset with, all right?"

"Sorry. I–sorry." Electra turned away to discreetly wipe her eyes. She took a centering breath before turning back to Sparta. "He makes my skin crawl."

It was a blessed relief that Sparta was not looking at her with pity. Instead, there was a fire shining in her dark eyes. "Mine too. But you can't let him get to you, all right? You're stronger than that. You are the sword by which He cleaves the horde. You are His strength. You are the proof of His conviction and mercy." She seized Electra by the upper arm and pulled her close so that they could press their foreheads together.

Electra relaxed into the touch. She could always rely on Sparta as her anchor, no matter the storm raging in her head. "As you are mine."

"Flatterer," Sparta teased as they pulled back. Her small smile dwindled. "The Red Hammer won't surrender without a fight."

Electra tightened her grip on Sparta's arm. There *was* a path for her through this storm; she was a warrior, after all. She knew her purpose. "I know. I'm looking forward to it."

Orestes, damn him, had escaped his divine punishment through his own hand. But Perseus—well, Perseus would not be so lucky.

19 The Survivors

United Star System Postal Code, Chapter 3, Section 11: It is illegal to keep domesticated animals aboard USSPS-sanctioned vessels for the purpose of companionship. Examples of domesticated animals include, but are not limited to, canines, felines, parrots, and rodents...

Horris pushed back from his desk and rubbed the bridge of his nose. He'd been at his desk for the past few hours. At first, he'd only meant to answer a few emails, but before long, he found himself fending off more questions about the 222 closure and filling out overdue supply and restock forms. Then, while clearing out his inbox, he got caught in the middle of a fierce email chain between captains about enforcing a new uniform policy in depots, and as a result, fourteen captains were being called into a video conference next Tuesday to resolve the issue.

It would last three hours, Horris thought glumly, and go exactly nowhere.

Horris rubbed at a knot in the back of his neck. He needed to relax. In less than six hours, they'd be unloading their cargo at the Brose Front. After that, it was a two-day trip to Apollonia. In less than ninety-six hours, Percy would leave the *Silverfish*.

Which was good, he reminded himself, which was right. Percy needed to go where he was safest, and the *Silverfish* crew could not afford to dodge any more regulations. Percy would depart at Apollonia, the *Silverfish* would go back to its routes, and only luck would bring them together again.

Which, again, was *good*.

After all, Percy seemed to be mentally prepping for a goodbye. He'd been quiet and withdrawn for the past day: not joining in on downtime fun, taking meals in his cabin—well, Roddy's cabin, but the point remained. Any response to a comment or a query had been polite but curt.

Horris had spent several hours wrestling with his anxiety, which had sprinted to the forefront of his mind and boldly announced Percy was mad at him. Basah and Roddy had both called him ridiculous when he'd confessed the fear, and Fives had just shrugged.

"He has a lot in his mind," the phrenic had said, and then he pulled his headphones over his ears before Horris could sort out his sudden flurry of questions.

Which, again, was *fine*. Percy was allowed to have a lot going on in his head. It wasn't Horris' place to pry.

Horris pitched backward and stood. His own mind was a swirl; he needed to calm down.

Henri and Sylvia watched him exit the cabin. The ship's lights were dim for downtime. He could hear jazz playing from behind Roddy's door and the low murmur of voices. Basah laughed at something. Horris crossed to the door, making to join them—then paused.

Another piece of music played from somewhere else on the ship. It definitely wasn't jazz or blues; it was more aggressive, electronic, and almost steely. It was nothing like what his crew enjoyed. Which meant…

He found Percy dancing in the space of the mostly-empty hold. The Imperial had his back to the entrance and, therefore, didn't notice Horris as he spun and kicked his way across the hold. He wore a borrowed pair of sweatpants, socks, and nothing else. Horris watched, stunned less by Percy's state of undress than by the way he moved. Because Percy–Percy could *dance.*

Percy quick-stepped, spun, and flipped before doing a full split down to the floor and back up again in time to the music. He dropped again in a full-body arch, kicked a leg out, and then swung both legs under his arms so he lay on his stomach against the floor. Instantly, he was back on his feet.

It occurred to Horris that this was how Percy fought: fast, fierce, and fluid. His lithe, muscular form had been hidden beneath pressed uniforms and turtlenecks; combined with his small stature, Percy had cut an unassuming, almost unimpressive figure. Not so, Horris thought, not when Percy struck at the air with fist and foot like lightning.

Fascinated, he watched Percy repeat his routine: down to the floor, somersaulting to his feet, spinning, building momentum to pirouette, flinging one leg out—

—and accidentally kicking Horris clear across the face.

"EMPEROR'S HAND–*HORRIS!*"

Horris found himself flat on his back. Bright stars sparkled across his vision, and winged envelopes flapped around his head. They scattered to the four winds when Percy popped into view with eyes wide. "Are you all right?!"

Horris groaned. "We have to stop meeting like this."

Percy laughed, incredulous, and extended a hand out to Horris. "Sorry. I didn't see you. Are you all right?"

Horris accepted the hand and allowed Percy to haul him to his feet. The world swam as his body adjusted to being upright again, but the sparkles faded as he blinked away tears of pain. A dull heat bloomed in his temple. Fingertips brushed against his temple, and he flinched away from the painful contact.

"You'll have a bruise," Percy said matter-of-factly. "Tell someone if you feel nauseous."

"I will." Horris took a step backward out of Percy's grasp. He looked the sweaty, red-faced Percy up and down. "I didn't mean to interrupt."

"It's fine." With that curt politeness, Percy pitched forward on the balls of his feet and fell into push-ups.

Anyone else might have taken that as a dismissal, but Horris was not about to be dismissed on his own ship. Instead, he looked up. "What were you listening to?"

"BLIP found me a playlist," Percy replied between push-ups. "Some modern dance nonsense."

"Did you like it?"

Down. "It was all right." Up.

An awkward beat of silence passed between the pair.

Horris cleared his throat. "You're an excellent dancer."

Up. "Thank you." Down.

Silence lapsed again. Horris could almost feel BLIP watching with mechanical schadenfreude only an AI was capable of. He let a few more beats of silence pass—one, two, three—before exploding: "Are you mad at me?"

Percy paused mid-push-up. His tousled red hair fell into his eyes when he looked up at Horris. "Am I—*what?*"

"Are you mad at me? You've been miserable and avoiding everyone all day. Did I do something?"

Percy rolled to his feet in one fluid action. He fixed Horris with a withering look, the one that always made him seem taller than he actually was. He wiped a trickle of sweat from his brow. "No," he said flatly, "I'm not mad at you."

Horris' relief was momentary. He'd opened the can of worms now; nothing left to do but feed the fish. "Then what's going on?"

"Nothing that concerns you." Percy turned from Horris and crossed to a small bowl with a sponge in it. He ran the sponge over his face and shoulders. "Why are you so nosey?"

"Why are you so defensive?" Horris snapped, irritated now. He'd gone above and beyond for Percy consistently by now—one would think that meant he was worthy of trust, but apparently not. "You *can* trust me, you know."

The sponge hit the bowl with a wet smack. Percy rubbed his hands over his damp face. "I know!" He had the audacity to sound irritated. He must have regretted his tone because he added a softer: "I know." He sighed, shoulders sinking, and turned back to Horris. "Fives told me about what I am. How he can't read me because I'm a–a *reinforcer*."

Oh. That was the last thing Horris had expected. Immediately, he was annoyed with Fives; surely, he could have taken two minutes to tell Horris about a conversation with Percy. Then again, would it have even occurred to Fives? The phrenic had the strangest definition of privacy…

Percy continued: "So, as it turns out, I'm a bit of a genetic anomaly. Perhaps I could handle that. I already do, I suppose—" he gestured to his red hair "—but the fact is you all *knew*. You all *knew* something about myself I didn't, something beyond my control. I—" Percy cut himself off and shook his head. "Perhaps I am a bit mad at you."

His annoyance with Fives gave way to sharp, sudden guilt. Horris tried to tell himself it was justified and necessary, but at the same time, he found himself in Percy's position. It was impossible not to. And how would he feel if something about himself was known to everyone but himself? Scared, defensive…and betrayed.

"I'm sorry," he said, already mourning their friendship.

"I understand it was a tactical decision," he said, "It's just…I just…"

Once more, he turned away from Horris. This time, he started to pace in a small circle.

"I was top of my cohort at the Academy. I excelled in every area: history, religion, science, tactics, combat. I *knew* how the world worked. I knew my place in it. I knew my purpose. But since I burst out of that box…I've been *wrong*. I don't know anything about space travel or meteor mining. I'd never met survivors from a war that wasn't my own. I didn't know how to spot hunting spiders. I didn't know about survival horror or lesbians or ghosts…I didn't know I could reinforce reality. I didn't know how important the mail service was. The more time I spend with you posties, the more I realize that I–I don't know *anything*."

Percy collapsed down on a large metal box. The same one, Horris noted, that he'd shipped himself out of Creedence in.

Horris didn't reply immediately. What could he say? He hadn't grown up in an iron bubble like Percy had. Quite the opposite, in fact. All he'd wanted since high school was to be anywhere but Grand York. All he'd wanted was to see as much as there was to see while he was alive to see it.

Percy didn't look up when Horris sank down beside him. He stared down at his hands.

"You know more than you give yourself credit for. You're the one who saved our asses against Silver, remember?"

"Fives did that."

"And who thought to get Fives? Not any of us. Who helped me restore power in that plant? Who earned us a three-week streak in Survival Horror, and who noticed a package was missing from the manifest? Not any of us knowledgeable posties."

Percy continued to stare at his hands.

"You're an amazing dancer," Horris added.

A flush crept up the back of Percy's neck. He finally glanced up at Horris. "Flatterer."

"So what? I mean it! You're incredible!"

"The end result of years of training."

"That doesn't mean it doesn't belong to you. I mean, what, you think I was born with a volunteer card from the Hobbyist Entomologist Society of the United Star System?"

"Ah." Percy finally leaned back. "And here I was thinking you were born with an encyclopedic knowledge of bugs."

"Insects—" Horris caught Percy's smirk too late. He jabbed him in the shoulder. "My point is, you know a lot too. There's things you could teach me."

"Like what?"

"How to dance like that."

For a moment, he thought Percy was going to laugh at him. Percy did snort, but all the same, he shook his head and got to his feet. "I'm not going to be able to teach you how to pirouette down here."

"Something simple, then," Horris suggested. He'd hit on a passion of Percy's, and he wasn't about to back down now. He watched Percy blow out a breath before extending out a hand. Horris accepted it and allowed Percy to lead him to the clear spot that served as the dance floor.

Percy looked him up and down critically. "You're taller, so you'll lead."

"Oh, well. I'm very good at leading. They gave me a pin for it, you know." Horris grinned, all the better to hide his sudden rush of nerves.

Percy smiled. He hoisted their arms up and rested them at an angle that initially felt silly, like his elbows were jutting out to fend off invisible dancers trying to cut in. "Start with your left foot," Percy instructed, "and take two steps forward."

"Left foot," Horris said, looking down. It was a good excuse not to look at Percy's bare, muscular chest, which was suddenly a lot closer than it had been a minute ago.

Percy coughed and squeezed Horris' hand. "Don't look down."

"I wasn't looking down."

"You were *absolutely* looking down."

"I was making sure I didn't step on your feet."

"That counts as looking down. Eyes on me, Captain Jensen."

"Are you giving a captain orders, Lieutenant Warden?" Horris looked back up with a grin.

"If my captain is looking at his feet instead of his partner? Absolutely." Percy's eyes burned brilliant green. When Horris took two steps forward, he mirrored the action, starting with his right foot and taking two steps backward.

BLIP popped on of their own accord, playing light, upbeat music that was neither Horris' blues nor the electronic music Percy had blared before. Percy guided him through the remaining steps, the quick one-two to the side, repeat, repeat, diagonal cross, repeat, repeat, cross until the steps were automatic. Eventually, Horris stopped looking down at his feet. Bit by bit, he relaxed into his stance, and so did Percy. Before long, they were flying across the hold in time to hear the upbeat music.

"When do I get to dip you?" Horris asked.

Percy laughed. "You don't."

Still, the more they repeated, the easier it became to put their own spin on the steps: they swung their hips as they walked and pulled chest-to-chest as they spun. Percy even spun under his arm when Horris hoisted one hand up. They caught their hands together again, laughing like children at their own ridiculousness. The hold and its remaining cargo melted away; they could have been anywhere in the universe, anywhere at all, in each other's arms.

As the round of songs ended, Horris pulled Percy out of a dip and against his chest. They stood together, breathing hard to catch their breath as the music faded out. Percy stared up at him, bright-eyed and beaming.

Say something! Now's the moment, c'mon, say something, anything, c'mon—

"Do you want to see my insects?" Horris blurted out.

A few minutes and a couple of mental kicks to the head later, Horris opened the door to his cabin for Percy. He was suddenly aware of his unmade bed, the sprawling catastrophe of his work desk, and the fact that his closet door didn't shut all the way. Fortunately, Percy ignored the messes and went straight for the dresser. He pointed to one of the framed photos on top. "This is you?"

"Well, I wouldn't have a picture of some random kid, would I?" Horris followed Percy.

The picture in question was one of him and Roddy as teens, grinning and showing off medals from their respective sports. Roddy had worn his hair long then, swept up in a ponytail, and he'd had the first wisps of facial hair clinging to his upper lip. Horris hadn't fared much better, what with the acne and the glasses he'd since ditched in favor of contacts. Roddy constantly complained about Horris keeping this photo on display, but he refused to take it down. The memories were worth the embarrassment.

He watched Percy's eyes light over the rest of his dresser: his captaincy pins, contacts case, and cleaner, facial moisturizer, a well-worn teddy bear, and his volunteer card from the Hobbyist Entomologist Society of the United Star System. Finally, Percy's gaze landed on the array of cages on the floor. He stiffened.

Horris tried not to feel slighted. He understood most people didn't react with the same awe when it came to insects (or arachnids or bugs). To most, they were creepy and repulsive. Squishable and unimportant. He struggled not to immediately leap to his insects' defense; after all, Percy had agreed to see them. The curiosity was there.

Percy stared at Henri. "Why insects?"

What a question. Few ever asked it of him; most just took it for granted that Horris was the weird kid who loved insects. You weren't allowed to stomp on a spider when Horris was nearby.

Henri tilted his head to the side. He made eye contact with Percy before waving his pedipalps in the air. The uninformed would have taken it as a friendly hello; Horris recognized the body language as simple curiosity, something new but non-threatening in Henri's territory. Sylvia ignored Percy entirely in favor of a grub Horris had dropped in her container hours ago.

"You've studied history, right? You know all those stories of what it was like when sentients first came in contact with each other—all those debates over what it meant to be alien and who to take seriously?"

"Yes."

"Well, I always thought it was silly. Everyone already lived with aliens and never complained." He crouched down in front of Henri and Sylvia. Percy joined him. They both watched Henri wave his pedipalps as Horris continued: "Invertebrates are the most populous type of living being out there. They've adapted so successfully to so many different environments, and yet—we'll never fully be able to understand how they see and process the world, how they talk to each other. Even though they're like us, in many ways. Did you know that bees dance?"

Percy smiled. "Do they?"

Horris nodded. "They'll dance to tell other bees of new food sources. Petra spiders are capable of spatial reasoning. There are ants that farm aphids for food and weevils that cooperatively raise their young. Insects have lived through millions and millions of years of evolution and upheaval, and they've found so many ways to adapt. They've survivors. I admire that about them."

As he spoke, he lifted the black square of fabric off the front of the silverfish enclosure. Jeff and Tim both zipped away from the light. Percy peered down at the burrowing Tim. "Aren't these pests?"

"Well, they wouldn't consider themselves pests—but yes, *Lepisma saccharinum*–silverfish–are considered pests. Their diet consists of starches and sugars, so they like things like glue and paper. Things people need."

Percy sat back on his heels. His face twisted in thought. "You... nicknamed your vessel...after a pest."

"Yes." Horris fought the rush of embarrassment. One would think he'd be used to the disbelieving remark by now. "They're my favorite insect."

"Not your Giant Targian spider?"

"Nope."

"The *silverfish*?"

"Yep."

"Why?"

Horris rubbed his hands together. Very few knew the whole story (they were all on this ship, in fact). Normally, he would have given a vague answer about the silverfish's ancient origins or its physical properties. But for Percy...for Percy, he could tell the truth.

"You know both my parents died in the Helium Wars. My mom was a pilot, and she died pretty early on in the fighting. That left my dad and I when, uh, they started bombing Grand York."

His throat closed over. It was difficult to put himself back there, even now. Even though a part of him had never really left. He fought the tremor in his voice and the *danger-danger* pulse in his neck. He was not trapped in this small, dark room. He had the choice to leave.

"My dad and I bunked down in our basement. We—well, he—had been prepping for this for a while, so we had supplies. Food, batteries, lanterns, stuff like that..."

His father had carried Horris and his favorite teddy bear into the basement. He'd made jokes about camping in the basement and sung some silly song as if that would drown out the whistling shrieks of bombs in the distance. It had taken Horris years to truly appreciate the level of calm that must have taken, to remain soft-spoken and smiling as hellfire rained down.

"We were there for a few days. At some point, my dad noticed that there were silverfish in the basement. They were eating copies of his thesis."

C'mere, Hor, take a look at these guys. S'all right, they won't bite. Silverfish. What a silly name, huh? They're down here safe like we are. Living and thriving. They don't even know there's a war on.

"The silverfish didn't know there was a war on. They were just living their small lives. And, um, after a few days, all the bombing stopped. My dad decided to head back up, see what the damage was, and see if he could get us out of the city. And, um..."

Wait here. I'll be back in a few hours, okay, buddy?

He remembered nestling under his blankets with his teddy bear, eating crackers, and waiting. And waiting. Listening to pops of gunfire and wails of sirens. And waiting. Watching the silverfish placidly crawl along the cardboard. And waiting. The silverfish were the only friendly living things left in the world, and his child mind took them as proof Dad would come back. He just had to wait.

"He was killed in street fighting. I didn't find that out until much later, but…I guess a part of me knew, when he didn't come back."

Horris swallowed the node of grief in his throat. There was nothing he could do for that little boy now.

"How long were you alone in that basement for?" Percy murmured.

"I don't know. A while. Me and my silverfish." Horris smiled sadly down at the silverfish container. "Eventually, a disaster relief organization came through, searching house to house. They had our mailman with them."

"What good was a mailman in a war?"

"He knew the neighborhood, the families. He could tell the organizers what houses had been where and who to look for."

He still remembered that too, vivid as the day: the flash of a cerulean uniform, his friendly mailman staggering down the steps of the basement to see him. Being scooped into his arms and told it was going to be okay. And he'd believed him. How could he not? He trusted the mailman to bring mail and packages and offer rubber bands to the neighborhood kids. The mailman would deliver him to his dad.

Horris shook his head to clear it. "Silverfish have no natural defenses. They aren't fighters. But they're exceptionally fast. And hardy. They're my favorite because they survive, no matter what. They're proof that life will just keep going if the world ends…even if it's not life as we know it."

He had refused to look at Percy this whole time. Now, he felt compelled to look up, struggling to retain his composure as he did. He had had years to process what had happened, years to make his peace with it. So why did it all feel so fresh and raw, like a knife in his chest?

Percy stared at him with an inscrutable expression. It wasn't pity, thankfully, and it wasn't disbelief. It was like horror and sorrow and a deep, terrible sympathy all at once. Slowly, awkwardly, he reached up and around Horris, pulling him into a one-armed hug.

"How old were you?" Percy asked.

"Seven."

A moment of silence passed.

"I was seven, too," Percy finally said.

Horris remembered. But he didn't see the point in telling Percy that the number had stuck in his mind ever since Percy had proudly announced he'd been enrolled in the academy of child soldiers at that age. He didn't sound proud now.

Horris nudged Percy. "Hey."

"Hm?"

"We survived, didn't we?"

20 The Brose Front

United Star System Postal Code, Chapter 5, Section 21: Shore leave may be offered to qualifying USSPS couriers in the event of delays or catastrophes along USS routes.

Percy stared at Horris, stunned.

He'd been called many things as the result of his training, and not all of them kind. But he'd never been called a survivor. He wasn't a *survivor*. Survivors lived through the unimaginable, the unthinkable, the horrific. He hadn't—

His training hadn't been—

A small huff of breath escaped him. He would have time and space to process what his training had been later. In the meantime, he stared up at Horris. The postman would never cease to surprise him with some innocuous statement. He leaned into Horris and was both surprised and delighted when Horris returned the gesture. A few breaths passed between them in silence.

Beep-boop-beep! Call incoming from Brose Front Central Post Office!

Horris drew back sharply. "Oh, what the fuck!" He got to his feet with a groan and turned towards his computer. He motioned for Percy to stay out of sight.

Percy sidled up against the wall. He watched Horris roll his shoulders back and assume his captaincy face; the soft edges of his face hardened, and his jaw tightened. He clicked a button on his computer.

"Apologies for the late notice, Captain Jensen," said a flat, matter-of-fact voice from the monitor.

"It's all right, Inspector Rofon. I was awake. To what do I owe the pleasure?"

"A courtesy call. One of several that I'm making to ships en route to the Brose Front."

Well, that couldn't be good. A crease appeared in Horris' brow. He glanced up, met Percy's eye, and then turned back to his monitor. "Is something wrong, Inspector?"

"Yes." Inspector Rofon's voice was crisp and curt. In other circumstances, Percy would have appreciated her straightforwardness. "Unfortunately, vandals broke into our facility a few hours ago and wreaked havoc. Our main sorting machine is down, and all mail delivery has been delayed by six hours."

"SIX HOURS?!"

Percy jumped at the outburst. Rofon cleared her throat. "I'm no more pleased than you are, Captain Jensen. It is my facility they've destroyed."

"I—yes, Inspector. I apologize."

"Customers in the Brose Front have already been notified about the situation and subsequent delay. You are responsible for issuing delay notices to customers further along your route."

Percy winced in sympathy. Horris, bless his heart, just sighed the sigh of the despairing and accepting. "Okay. I'll have that done in the next few hours. Is there anything else we can do in the meantime?"

"No."

"Are you sure? My engineer could help take a look at the sorting machine—"

"Are you in the habit of ignoring answers, Captain Jensen?"

Horris blinked, physically taken aback by the sharp retort. Percy tensed but didn't realize he was on his feet until Horris shot him a warning look. Percy swallowed his bile and rush of indignation both. Horris looked back to his monitor. "No, ma'am."

"Very good. Be advised that you and your crew will have authorized shore leave when you arrive. Try to make the most of it."

"Yes, ma'am," said Horris, expression and tone carefully blank.

"You and your crew will be required to check in when you arrive."

"Yes, ma'am."

Percy waited for the call to click off before crossing to Horris. He'd fought the tide of fury unsuccessfully; his blood was boiling, the bile churning in his throat. He slammed his hand against Horris' desk, making the postman jump. "You shouldn't have let her speak to you like that!"

"She's my superior, Perce, she sets the tone—"

"You were just trying to help! And she questions your capacity as a captain—"

"Percy—"

"It was unspeakably rude!"

"I *know* that—"

"You know what your problem is, Horris?"

"What's my problem, Percy?"

"You're too patient with terrible people. They don't deserve your patience; what they deserve is a swift kick in the arse!"

"Like you?" Horris asked. He was amused now, dark eyes dancing.

Percy stopped short. He opened his mouth, closed it, and fixed Horris with an amused look of his own.

That's when Percy heard the faint whispering from behind the cabin door. Horris' gaze snapped to it. All amusement faded from his expression. He walked over to the cabin door and yanked it open.

Roddy and Basah fell through the door in a heap of limbs. Fives stood just behind them with hands tucked into his sweatshirt pocket. He locked eyes with Horris before immediately turning and leaving.

"*Oh no, you don't!*"

Basah sprang up and seized Fives by the hoodie, cutting his retreat short.

Horris took a full step backward. "What the hell are you doing?!"

"We were going to ask you the same thing," Roddy said. He remained on the floor, chin in his hands, kicking his feet back and forth. He met Percy's eyes with a wide grin and a wink.

Percy was suddenly aware of himself and his shirtlessness. He didn't know what to make of Roddy's smirk. Nor could he fight the sudden clench of his gut or the inexplicable heat creeping up his neck. He glanced around for something to cover himself and settled for a crumbled sweatshirt poking out of Horris' closet.

Roddy's smirk didn't diminish as Percy finished pulling over the sweatshirt, which had three wolf spiders posed in front of a bright white moon.

Horris scowled. "This isn't what it looks like."

"Is it worse?"

"NO!"

Horris yanked Roddy to his feet again. Percy watched, caught between annoyance that they'd been interrupted and the smug satisfaction of listening to Horris scold Roddy's pointed ear clean off. But why had they been listening at the door in the first place? Surely, nothing he and Horris had to discuss was new information. He turned to Basah. "What are you doing here?"

Basah kept her firm grip on Fives' hoodie. "Fives picked up on some unusual emotions, and when we came to investigate, we couldn't help but overhear your call from the Front."

"Oh really?" Horris switched his hard captain's gaze from Roddy to Fives.

Fives shook himself out of Basah's grip. He straightened up to the fullest of his ability. "It's not *my* fault. I can't decide what you're feeling...or how loud your speaker volume is."

Horris frowned. Percy tugged at the ends of his borrowed sweat-shirt. *Unusual emotions?* Fives couldn't get into his head, thank the Emperor, which left Horris as the instigator. He was annoyed, suddenly, for Horris' sake. He certainly didn't need Fives digging around in his head as he relived old trauma.

Roddy flung a hand in front of Horris to get his attention. "So, are we going to talk about that call or what?"

"I don't see what needs to be discussed," Horris said. He folded his arms over his chest. Percy moved to stand beside him and copied his stance. A united front against an unruly crew.

"The call you just got from the Front. About the six-hour delay. And our authorized shore leave. On the *Front! The Brose Front*, Horris!"

Basah clapped her hands together, giddy as a schoolgirl. Percy had never seen her in such a state—indeed, he hadn't thought her capable of it. She grabbed Horris by the arms and began to shake him back and forth. "When are we going to get a chance like this again?!"

"She's right, Horry! We have to plan an itinerary!" Roddy exclaimed. He joined Basah in trying to rock Horris back and forth. "We're going shopping! We're going clubbing! We're going gambling—"

"We are not going gambling," Horris said flatly.

"But the *CLUBS*, Horris!"

"I heard you about the damn clubs!" Horris wriggled free of Roddy and Basah's grip. He exhaled and pinched the bridge of his nose. "You two are forgetting something important!"

"What?"

"Me," Percy said. He exchanged a look of long-suffering with Horris.

Roddy deflated like a pointy-eared balloon. "Ah, right, right. Well…well—I mean, look at yourself! With that five o'clock shadow and some new clothes, no one will clock you for an Imp!"

Percy chanced a glance at the wall mirror beside Horris' closet. Roddy, annoyingly, was not wrong. Over the past week and a half, he'd grown a patchy, stubbly beard of sorts, and without access to his usual grooming kit, his hair stuck up in tufts, longer and looser than he'd ever worn it on Creed. He didn't know the man in the mirror, although he did look familiar.

"There's also the issue of five people leaving a four-man ship," Horris said. He looked between the three members of his crew. "Look, if you three want to blow your paychecks on the Front, that's fine. I'll come back to the ship after we check in."

Percy straightened up, oddly flattered. Being alone had never bothered him before, but he liked Horris. He liked that Horris chose to spend time with him over the famed Front. He grinned up at Horris as Roddy and Basah high-fived.

Basah did a little wriggle dance of delight. "Six hours on the Front! This is going to be—"

"Hell," said Fives.

The phrenic had been so quiet Percy had almost forgotten he was in the room. Now, Fives shuffled and scowled. One hand fluttered to his headphones. "Hell," he said again, "*other people.*"

"You don't have to go into the Front, Fiver," Roddy said, in a tone more sympathetic than annoyed. "You can stay here with Horry and Red if you want."

"I don't want to go into the depot. They never like me in the depots."

"Fives—"

Fives jerked back as Basah reached for his shoulder. "I don't want to hear them call me a freak. Take Percy."

"Fiver—"

"They will see four postmen leaving the ship. One-two-three-four. It worked at Hiyabusa. Take Percy. Let them think he's *weird-scary-freak-creep.*"

"Do they call you that, Fives?" Percy asked very softly.

Fives met his eyes, black on green. "In their heads. Where they think it's safe." He looked to Horris, who studied him with a contemplative expression. "You don't want me to hear those words either.

You're angry that people called me those words. Angry that I didn't tell you before." He shook his head. "It happens at every depot. But it doesn't have to. Take Percy instead. Dress him in my clothes."

Horris glanced at Percy. "Would you be okay with that, Perce?"

It wasn't a terribly tactical decision, trying to pass off a wanted man as a phrenic, but it would be nice to get off the ship and really stretch his legs. He didn't have the same interest in the Front as Roddy and Basah did, but as he mulled the plan over, an excited sort of curiosity seized him. He wanted to see what else was out there. He wanted to learn all he could, while he could.

"Yes," he said. "We should be fine, as long as I wear a hat and we stick together."

Fives smiled a twitchy, relieved sort of smile.

Four hours later, Percy watched over Roddy's shoulder as the pilot dropped them into the atmosphere of the Brose Front.

Twilight spread amber sunlight over a brown-red desert. Percy had never imagined a desert this expansive could exist anywhere in the galaxy, let alone support life. The first signs of civilization appeared as the *Silverfish* flew over a large set of mountain peaks: buildings lined neat, gridded roads, which eventually gave way to an artificially green field and a spherical stadium. Bright city lights pierced through the twilight gloom like a beacon. The Front, Percy realized with awe and disgust both, was massive. Leagues and leagues of the former desert had been transformed into gleaming white roads, towering skyscrapers, glowing hotels and casinos, and a massive observation wheel—all enclosed within a valley encased by mountains.

"There it is," said Roddy, proud as if he owned it. "The Nocturnal City!"

"Nocturnal City?" Percy repeated, unfamiliar with the appellation.

"All the good stuff starts by nightfall. The temperatures get too extreme by day."

Percy scanned the city below as if he could see the city come alive in real-time. "I wonder what they did in the days before such a raucous nightlife."

"They would find shelter under the fig and palm trees," Fives said, tone oddly sad. "But they're all gone now." He pulled his headphones over his ears before Percy could question him further.

Basah appeared from behind, tugging Percy up and out of the cockpit. He was already dressed in khakis and one of Fives' oversized orange sweatshirts, but the black beanie Basah tugged down over his ears completed the picture. "There. Now all you have to do is keep your head down, mumble—"

"I don't mumble," Fives insisted.

"Yes, you do." Basah kept her attention on Percy. "And then pray to the Matrons that no one notices your scruff is the wrong color."

"And easy detail to miss, I'm sure," Percy said dryly. He gave his stubble a self-conscious scratch.

"You'd be surprised, Red." Basah gave him a light, affectionate punch on the arm.

It took another forty minutes of low-level flight to arrive at the Brose Front Mail Depot. Percy spent the full forty minutes gawking at the maze of neon lights blinking on below. Horris sidled up beside him to watch the Nocturnal City sweep along far below.

The depot jutted up out of the edge of the Brose Front, a three-story warehouse that had been tastefully decorated to match the city's aesthetics. A neon welcome sign blinked on and off in the deepening gloom.

The depot stretched out on either side of them, dominating the entire length of the block. Three other mailships were parked at gates along the depot, and on the other side of a fence, he could see a parking lot full of mail trucks. Distantly, he could make out signs for the Brose Front Water Authority and the Brose Front Energy Company. The quiet was broken only by the electric hum of the signs and the chitter of nighttime insects. Percy closed his eyes and took a deep breath, savoring the sounds of a hot summer night and the scent of a real atmosphere.

He reopened his eyes when Horris stepped off the gangplank beside him. "Are you ready?" He asked, visibly concerned.

Percy didn't reply. Instead, he pulled a set of borrowed headphones over the black beanie, rolled his shoulders forward into a slight slouch, and fixed his eyes on the cracked pavement.

Horris snorted before leading the way into the depot. He signed himself and his three crewmen in at the front desk. The friendly woman at the front desk waved them through, and Horris waved back at her as they went.

This depot looked much like the ones he'd seen before, save that the disarray here was not productive in the least. There were no couriers or sorters at work. Carts and trays had been overturned, and their contents scattered across the black floor. An office window had been shattered into pieces.

Two people stood by what Percy could only assume was the broken sorter, what with the wired guts and bolts spilling out of the machine. One was a blond, curly-haired Elentee, taller and more wiry than even Roddy; the other was a Devinthal, a humanoid with broader shoulders and a wider nose than humans like Horris and himself. The Elentee paused in their argument, pointing at the approaching *Silverfish* crew. The Devinthal spun on her heel, dark eyes narrowing as they landed on Horris.

"Captain Jensen."

Horris doffed his captain's hat. "Inspector Rofon." He looked at the Elentee with a polite, quizzical smile. He extended a hand out for a shake. "I don't believe we've met."

"I'm the new depot master." The Elentee's voice was high and reedy, and his eyes darted around the mess of the depot station. Eventually, his gaze landed on Horris' outstretched hand, and he took it in a loose grip. "Alfred Koss."

"Which of you is the phrenic?" Inspector Rofon demanded.

A stunned, anxious pause followed. Percy swallowed hard but had no choice but to raise a tentative hand. He kept his gaze to the floor and so only caught the sharp, sweeping motion Rofon made out of the corner of his eye.

"Out," she said sharply. "I want that man out of this depot."

For a moment, her words didn't compute. Then came the outrage, the fury, and he didn't realize he'd taken a full step forward until Roddy grabbed his shoulder. Basah stepped in front of him with hackles raised. And when Horris spoke, his voice was cold and curt as he'd ever heard it: "Fives is a part of our crew. He has every right to be here."

"No. He does not. A phrenic is a walking violation of privacy laws, and with the depot in this state, I will take no chances."

"He can't read the mail's mind," Roddy muttered.

"We have opened packages and mail scattered across this depot. His notion of privacy is skewed. I won't have him here until it's been restored." Rofon pierced him with a daggered look, and it took every ounce of Percy's training not to tackle her right there. He settled for a scowl and clenched fists.

"Inspector Rofon, please—"

Rofon rounded on Horris, and this time it took both of Roddy's hands to keep Percy in place. "I have enough on my plate, Captain Jensen. I suggest you do not add to it, unless you want to spend your shore leave detained."

Horris stared at Rofon dumbfounded. He glanced at Depot Master Koss, obviously looking for backup, but found none when Koss just shrugged his shoulders.

A low, furious growl rose from Basah's throat. She fished backward for Percy's hand and held it tightly in hers. "We'll step outside. I'm sure you have some paperwork to attend to." Venom seeped through every courteous word Basah spoke, and Percy was seized by the notion that if Basah hadn't made a damn good engineer, she would have made a damn good politician. She didn't wait for an answer, instead wheeling around and dragging Percy out the door. Roddy followed. Percy had just enough time to twist around and meet Horris' eyes before the door slammed shut behind them.

Percy waited a good three beats before exploding: "Who the HELL does she think she is?!"

"Inspector Rofon, that's who," Roddy said. He shot the exterior door a dark look. "She's been the terror of this depot for years. She runs this place like she owns it."

"And the depot master does nothing?" Percy demanded.

Basah's ears flattened against her head. "No. They're all toadies."

"If we were back on Creedence, that woman would have been detained for misconduct and disrespect ages ago." Not knowing what else to do with his fury, Percy began to pace. "Is she always like that to Fives?"

"She's pretty brusque with him, yeah. That's why Fives didn't want to go in." Roddy said. He frowned in thought. "But she's never told him to just *get out* before." He started an oath under his breath, but Basah stopped him with a look of her own.

"If Horris were here, he'd be giving her the benefit of the doubt. Something about the mess and the stress and all that jazz." Basah flicked a hand around in annoyance.

"Horris gives too many people the benefit of the doubt," Roddy muttered. He caught the eyebrow Percy arched at him and shrugged. "I said what I said, Red."

"Point taken."

Basah ran her hands through her hair. When she dropped them again, her ears sprang back into their usual upright position. "Well. At least Fives didn't have to actually endure that woman. Horris should be out in a few minutes; he just needs to clear some paperwork for the leave. Then we can actually enjoy the Front."

"Let's think positive, then, huh?" Roddy said. He pulled his tablet from his belt and held it out to the rest. "I took the liberty of putting together an itinerary for the Front. Everything we can do in six hours and still make it back here to sort like good little postal workers."

Basah snatched the tablet from his hand, shifting to let Percy read over her shoulder. His eyebrows arched as he did. Yes, Roddy had everything here—fine dining, a few nightclubs, a walking route of the Front's most desired sights…but first on the list, chief above all was…

"*Shopping?*"

21 Prophets Alley

United Star System Postal Code, Chapter 2, Section 1: All personnel of the USSPS will demonstrate respect and regard for the people and cultures that make up the customer base of the United Star System.

orris stood stockstill and stared at himself in the boutique mirror. Roddy had wrangled him into a sleek, dark blue suit, and Horris himself had added an orange pocket square for a pop of color. It was an overpriced outfit, from new shades down to the stylish brown Oxfords. Overpriced and ridiculous, something he'd never have another opportunity to wear. Except...

"You look *damn* good," Roddy declared. He flung aside the privacy curtain in the changing room to saunter inside. The pilot had already ditched his uniform. Now he wore an eye-searing button-down shirt of pink and yellow smiley faces and a pair of yellow booty shorts with the word 'HATER' rhinestoned across the ass. Roddy had topped the gaudy array off with a pair of pink heart-shaped sunglasses that were useless at night.

Roddy was clearly enjoying the opportunity to go all out. He sashayed around Horris. "You look damn good. And don't try to give me any lip about not needing this. You do. You can't go around looking like you have a package to deliver all the time."

"At least I don't look like someone vomited pink lemonade and then put a shirt on it," Horris said flatly. Nevertheless, he tugged on his lapels and twisted back and forth on his heel. He *did* look damn good. And that observation clashed hard against the impracticality of such a purchase.

Roddy arched his eyebrows. "You wanna look good for the Front, man. And anyone else who might be visiting for the first time." He nodded towards the privacy curtain.

"I don't know what you're talking about."

"C'mon, Horry. You're not fooling me, you're not fooling Basah, and you definitely didn't fool Fives. You have a thing for Percy."

"That thing is respect and regard," Horris said with a sniff.

"Oh, you've been regarding him all right. You were *regarding* him with *his shirt off* in *your room*."

"That's not—we were looking at the insects!"

"Is that what the kids are calling it these days?"

"Fuck you, man."

"Fuck you too. Look—you like him. It's obvious. The least you could do is tell him while you're looking good."

"I'm not telling him anything! He's going to live on Apollonia, remember? It wouldn't do any good. Besides, I don't think he—I don't even know if he likes guys!"

"How d'you figure that?"

"Rod, he's still reeling over lesbianism!"

"Wait until he finds out there are many kinds of lesbians."

"Rod." Horris dropped his tone into something low and warning. "Don't push it, okay?"

"Fine!" Roddy exclaimed. He flung his hands into the air. "Fine. Let's change the topic. Have you heard from Fiver at all?"

"Yeah, he checked in with me. He's got some snacks and he's watching some anime called Princess Venus Hyperstar Go."

"Oh, hell yeah! That was on my to-watch list. It's a spin-off from Princess Venus, do you remember me showing you that one…?"

Eventually, Roddy cajoled Horris into purchasing one suit and a sensible pair of Oxfords. Together, they rejoined Basah and Percy, who had found their own suitable looks in the boutique. Basah dressed in the asymmetry that was all the rage on Mars: long bell bottoms and a tight black cut-off layered with a puffy green jacket that only had one sleeve. Percy, by contrast, was classically and empirically conservative: black jeans, black boots, and a black tank top under a black leather jacket. Strands of his red hair peeked underneath the black beanie.

"Whose funeral are you going to?" Roddy asked cheerfully.

"Still deciding," Percy replied. He cast a thoughtful look around the mid-city boutique. "I'm sure we'll find trouble before the night is out."

"Amen to that!" With that, Roddy pulled out his tablet. "Okay, first we carbo-load at this Earth-themed restaurant, and then we hit Superego, and maybe the Scarlet Lady if we have time."

Horris hadn't been looking forward to a night on the town, but Roddy's enthusiasm and thoroughness was admirable. He grinned when he locked eyes with Roddy.

"What are those establishments?" Percy asked.

"The CLUBS, Perce! Not downcity clubs, but still! Clubs!"

"And what does one do at the clubs, perchance?"

"Drink, listen to music," Basah said. She pulled a pair of Mefana-customized earplugs from her pocket and gave them a shake. "And dance!"

Percy's expression lit up, and Horris couldn't help it when his grin grew wider.

Ninety minutes later, the *Silverfish* crew found themselves on the ground floor of the Superego Night Club. Lights flashed in blues and purples and greens across a crowded dance floor that puslated with more multicolored tiles. Dancers of all species and genders swayed hips on raised platforms across the crowd. Pop music swelled and dipped, and the movement of the crowd rose and fell with it.

Horris stood by the bar with an almost-empty screwdriver in hand. Percy stood beside him, nursing his second lemon lime bitters.

Basah and Roddy danced amid the sweeping lights and pounding music. They lacked Percy's grace and training, but they more than made up for it with pure enthusiasm. Basah danced into the arms of a raven-haired human woman, who spun Basah back out and in again with a laugh. They twirled off together into the crowd, past the sweat-soaked Roddy who danced chest-to-chest with a stripe-skinned Sem.

BOOM-BOOM-BOOM, went the music.

Horris sipped his screwdriver for courage. He liked this sort of dancing, the kind you could do without worrying about making a fool of yourself, and ordinarily, he might have joined his family on the dance floor. Instead, he cleared his throat and summed up his courage. "Would you like to dance?" He called over the din.

Percy hesitated, and then shook his head. "No," he called back, "No. I've never–I've never danced like this–like *that*–with anyone. It is—" he grimaced, shook his head again, and clarified: "It would *feel* obscene. Imperial Creeds don't dance like that. It's not...accepted."

Percy stood too stiff, too tense, shoulders and chest drawn up in a soldier's stance. Horris recognized the stance. It was the same one Percy had adopted the entire time they were on Delta Io. It was a coping mechanism, Horris realized, a fallback for when he didn't know what to do or how to comport himself. He wasn't having a good time.

"Wanna get out of here?" Horris called.

Percy looked up sharply from his lemon lime bitters. "Yes."

They left, weaving between the press of bodies to find the exit. Horris found Basah in the crowd and shouted something to her about leaving. Basah, still in the arms of the raven-haired woman, gave a nod of understanding. Horris gave her date a polite nod before following Percy out.

The Superego entrance spilled out onto a side street. A few happy drunks trailed after them, roaring with laughter. Horris sidestepped them to find Percy leaning against the Superego's exterior and breathing hard.

"Hey. Are you all right?"

"Fine." Percy pinched the bridge of his nose. "Fine. I suppose I–I am not a fan of crowds in addition to public dancing." He flexed his hands before taking another full, gulping breath. "But I wanted to try, at least."

Horris tucked his hands into his pockets and leaned against the wall with Percy. "Well, now you can say you did. Did you like dinner, at least?"

"I'm not a stranger to pasta, you know." Percy managed a wan smile. "But I did enjoy the garlic bread."

The din of the club still rang in Horris' ears. Gradually the sound faded into a soft ringing, and then silence. He loosened his tie a little. He liked clubs better in theory than in practice, he supposed. "Wanna go for a walk?"

"Gladly."

Together they set off for the Front. They were nowhere near the heart of the city, but even mid-city there were still sights to see: art installations and street musicians, vendors and hawkers selling wares both genuine and counterfeit; eventually they joined the throng of couples, bands of teenagers, and families with children who strolled along under the bright lights of the Front. The night was calm, the weather balmy, and Horris soaked in the atmosphere like a warm bath. After weeks aboard the *Silverfish*, it was nice to be with people without the expectation of service.

Food cart vendors had set themselves up on strategic corners. Horris bought churros for himself and Percy. Percy did a generous swoop of churro into chocolate sauce and took a bite. "Are these as good as the churros back home?"

Grand York wasn't really his home. It hadn't been for a while. But Horris didn't want to play semantics. Instead he bit into his own. The churro was sugary-sweet perfection: piping hot without burning his tongue, crisp dough coated in a sparkling cinnamon-sugar…ecstasy, or close enough to it.

"No," Horris said once he swallowed the bite. "But it's close enough to it."

They walked aimlessly, chatting about this or that as it caught their eye. Occasionally, Percy would offer an insight into what life had been like on Creed, like how a pair of street performers reminded him of how his parents took him to holiday pantomimes when he was small:

"—and we'd all be on our feet shouting BEHIND YOU, but of course, the hero would never hear us until it was too late…" Percy trailed off in the middle of recounting one such panto. He cocked his head to the side. "Do you hear that?"

Horris slowed to a halt. He copied Percy's head tilt. Yes, he could hear something: music, not too distant, of many clashing styles that didn't even try for harmony. Beneath the music, a cacophony of voices shouted and cheered and hailed passersby. He exchanged a look with Percy. Together, they started off again, following the music and voices a few blocks down, turning onto a massive, vibrant festival space.

At least, Horris thought it was a festival: multicolored banners and streams crisscrossed the rooftops overhead while the flags and signs decorated the alley walls. Tables and displays crowded the street, and in the press of bodies, performers competed for passersby's attention. Hawkers and demonstrators competed with them in turn, and here and there, people carried picket signs. Someone shoved a pamphlet into his hand, and that was when it clicked.

"This is Prophets Alley!" He exclaimed.

"This is a bloody mess," Percy said. He stared into the alley with disbelief. "No one is making a profit here."

"No, no–Prophets Alley is a pretty famous street in the Front. A place for different religions to gather and preach. And argue, I guess." He waited for two men in clashing styles of robes to pass before continuing: "It started out small, y'know, debates among the chaplains who came with all the scientists and adventurers. At some point, it just…exploded."

Percy rolled to the balls of his feet and craned his neck in search of something. Horris didn't have to guess what. All sorts of religions were represented here. Each had its own symbols and signs: a full moon, a crescent moon, a six-pointed star, a stylized fish, a crown set against the sun, a heart engulfed in flames, a diamond engulfed by stars, a rising halo over a cross…but the fist of the Imperial Creeds was absent.

Percy took a tentative step forward. Horris followed, and before long they were swallowed by the festival-like atmosphere. Prophets and priests shouted and waved talismans at them, while others were too caught up in singing and dancing to directly proselytize. Some booth neighbors were caught up in debates both serious and friendly. Prophets Alley was home to all sorts of people, from all corners of the universe and walks of life, come to spread their own word.

Horris had never trucked with religion. In truth, he'd never understood it, and if pressed could admit he was uncomfortable with all the promises of a blissful afterlife so long as you followed someone else's rules. He preferred the certainty and security of the here and now. But as Horris strolled along with Percy, letting the sights and sounds wash over him, he could see appeal. There was a sense of community here amid laughter and mysticism, as religions swapped food and trinkets and texts.

They paused at the edge of a knot in the crowd. In the center, two Sem danced in time to pounding music. Brightly-colored frills billowed behind their heads, and the impressive display was only heightened when both produced knives. They called out to their god before twirling and juggling the weapons to roars of approval from the crowd. A whoop went up from the booth next door, and three human women joined in the dance. It was less of a challenge, Horris thought, and more of a collaboration. His observation was confirmed when one of the Sem tossed his knife to the other in order to dance with the women.

Horris watched the solo juggler with eyebrows arched. "He's good, not to get hurt."

"He wouldn't get hurt," Percy said. He shrugged at Horris' questioning look. "The blades are dull. They wouldn't pierce skin unless you were terribly careless."

One of Percy's feet moved subtly, imitating the quick footwork of the religious dancers. He was smiling, but it didn't quite reach his eyes. "I never knew there were so many," he said. He raised his eyes to the banners overhead. "Back home, they would all be called Idolers and forced to submit. None of this dissent would be lawful in Creedence."

"Everyone follows the Emperor?"

"The Emperor is law." Percy closed his eyes as he spoke. He reached up and tugged at the pendant he wore around his neck. "Why does it have to be a struggle? Why can't it just *be*?"

Horris had no answer to that. He had a feeling he was missing part of a conversation here; without it, how could he convince Percy not to carry the weight of an entire religion? He cleared his throat, readying to say something—

When Percy pivoted sharply, attention caught by something else. He started off at a brisk pace, ignoring Horris as he called after him. Horris cursed under his breath and started after Percy. He kept his eyes locked on the black beanie as it weaved through the crowd. Together they pushed through the crowd and towards the far end of the alley. There, just before the Alley spat tourists back into the Art District, Percy stopped in front of a marble building.

Horris slowed as he approached. He could hear it now: a high, sweet chorus of voices singing in unison. Percy staggered into the marble building as if compelled. Horris had no choice but to follow.

Within, a congregation sang in a language Horris didn't know, although he found it beautiful nevertheless. The song was soft and comforting, almost like a lullaby, and the many voices reverberated through the church they'd stepped into.

The church itself was lit by low blue lights. More light played over the ceiling and walls, and it took a moment of study before Horris realized the origin was a deep pool of water at the apse. An elderly, dark-skinned Elentee woman stood in front of the pool. She was the one leading the congregation in song, and her deep, melodious voice carried over the crowd.

With a word, the parishioners rose from their seats and formed a single-file line down the aisle. Horris and Percy watched as the leader dipped a white cloth into the pool and wiped it across each parishioner's forehead. Once she did, the parishioner would step out through a side door. And all the while they sang the same simple song.

Horris felt Percy brush against him and join the line. Horris remained where he was, caught between wanting to be by Percy and not wanting to get tangled in a religious ceremony he knew nothing about.

The singing faded as the last supplicant disappeared through the side door. The church was suddenly darker and lonelier than it had been moments before.

The officiant smiled warmly as Percy stepped up to her altar. Horris followed a few cautious steps behind. "Welcome, travelers. Are you here to seek peace?"

"Are you here to offer it?" Percy asked. His question carried the faint hint of a plea.

"No," The officiant said very gently.

Percy swallowed hard. Horris stepped into place beside him. "Why not?" He asked. It was a hell of a selling point, he thought, not being able to offer strangers peace.

"If peace were so easily offered, or found, more would have it by now. And someone would have found a way to sell it. All I offer is a place of rest and contemplation." The officiant gestured to the cavernous church around them. The ceiling was made of shimmering lapis lazuli; the sound of splashing water and the rich smell of incense permeated throughout.

Horris gestured to the pool behind her. "Why the water?"

"To wash the burdens and cares away. As well as the dust from the long and terrible roads."

Percy fell to his knees in a smooth, practiced motion. He didn't have to speak; the officiant just nodded. She dipped her cloth into the water and wiped it over Percy's brow, murmuring something in that unknown language as she did. Percy closed his eyes and slumped his shoulders. He remained kneeling, even when the officiant stepped away. She turned to Horris with a questioning look.

Horris consented to having his brow wiped, although he remained standing. The water was warmer than he'd thought. It dripped down his temples and nose, and he fought the instinct to wipe his face dry. He didn't feel any different...but all the same, he inclined his head. "Thank you," he murmured.

"Stay as long as you like, outworlder." The officiant looked down at Percy as she spoke. "I hope you find the peace you seek."

She exited through the same door as her followers. Horris and Percy were left alone in the quiet sanctuary, with only the distant sound of dripping water to break the silence.

Horris settled down criss-cross beside Percy in front of the pool. "What's going on?"

Percy opened his eyes. He shifted so that he could face the pool better. His brow furrowed, and a ghost of a smile crept across his face. "There's a silverfish."

So there was. It scurried along the edge of the pool, antennae quivering as it sought its next meal. Horris couldn't help a smile. Silverfish had managed to establish themselves even on the desert-dominated Front; truly, the wonders never ceased. "We ought to tell that priestess she has an infestation."

"Perhaps they're sacred to the church."

"If it was my church, maybe. I doubt anyone else thinks that highly of them."

"I do," Percy said very softly. He continued staring into the pool when Horris glanced at him. "May I confess something to you?"

"Uh, sure. I'm not, like, a priest or anything."

"I know. But I trust you."

Horris couldn't help the flush of pleasure in his chest. He knew Percy trusted him, but even so it was nice to hear it out loud. It felt–privileged, almost, to be able to sit so close to a man so guarded and prickly. I can sit here, he wanted to say to the water and the silverfish and the lapis lazuli. I can sit here because he trusts me to sit here.

Then, he pulled himself back into the seriousness of the moment. "What's going on?"

"I'm a bad person, Horris."

"You're not—"

"I am. I'm a murderer. I've killed people. Many, many people."

That brought Horris up short. Of course, Percy had killed people; he had been a soldier, and they didn't hand out nicknames like the Red Hammer for nothing. But he'd never really given thought to the fact that Percy had blood on his hands. It had been an abstract. Something he didn't have to think about, or confront, in this quest to get Percy to Apollonia. But now Percy had said it frankly, and Horris didn't know what to say or do. Should he get up and leave? Should he condemn Percy? Forgive him?

Percy continued: "At the time, I thought I was justified. I thought I was holy. That is what we are taught at the Academy—that murder is right, so long as you're murdering the right people."

"Idolers."

"Idolers. I never wondered why they fought so hard to keep their own faiths. As far as I was concerned, they were just stubborn and stupid. Not worthy of living if they would not live in the light of His Grace. Now, though…now I understand. I finally see what they stand to lose." He cast a look around the church. His burning green eyes landed on Horris, and his whole expression crumpled. "I regret every moment of it. I wish I wasn't–that I wasn't—"

"You got out," Horris said immediately. He couldn't absolve Percy, but he could damn well remind him that he wasn't that person anymore. "Remember that, okay? No matter what you did before, you got out. You're not a killer anymore."

"It doesn't change what I did, or who I hurt."

"No," Horris conceded.

A moment of silence followed. Then the question fell out of him, natural as breathing:

"Why did you leave Creed?"

Percy stared into the pool of water. Slowly, haltingly, he began to speak. Horris listened, without interruption, as Percy spoke of a man named Orestes and an attack on the Academy. He spoke of the fierce, frantic fight that followed, the Idoler woman he killed, and how it felt to kill in the moment…and in the aftermath. He spoke of awkward Orestes' soft questioning of doctrine and how, even in the fight, he had sung to keep others calm. How Orestes had held him while everything else fell apart.

"—but the worst part came after."

Horris couldn't see how it could possibly get worse. But all the same, he asked: "What happened after?"

Light from the pool played off of Percy's face. When he spoke this time, his voice was flat and faraway, as if his soul had stepped out of his body for the time being.

"After the attack, we gathered the remaining Idolers in the court-yard. The day had been ours. Their dead outnumbered our own. They had gone after the administrative buildings, the kyriakons, and the officers' wards…but it was the children Liaison Nabis said needed to be avenged. The Ordinaries all lined up to watch and listen and see. Liaison Nabis said that a hand would be taken from every remaining Idoler. The righteous punishment, he said, for raising a hand against the children of the Emperor. And the Midman, those on the brink of graduating, would complete their ascension by taking those hands.

"I was on the steps next to him. Exempt, on account of my demonstration of bravery and devotion. I'd already received my promotion on the battlefield. Third Lieutenant Warden, the Red Hammer. They wouldn't let me change out of my clothes. They told me I had to wear them. For everyone to see what devotion looked like."

Horris swallowed hard. He could see the scene in his mind's eye: lines of shocked, hollowed-eye children and soldiers gathered around kneeling Idolers, this Liaison Nabis roaring into a microphone with Percy beside him. In his head, the sky was a charcoal gray, and the air reeked of smoke, and all the buildings looked like Grand York had after the bombings. In his head, Percy had been drenched in other peoples' blood.

He wanted to reach back in time and save Percy, save the Idolers, save the children. But he couldn't, nor more than he could save seven-year-old Horris. All he could do was listen.

"They called Orestes up first. They wanted to make a man out of him. His very last chance to become a man, an Extraordinary, and all he had to do was take a hand from an Idoler. They handed him a cleaver from the kitchens." Percy's thin eyebrows knitted together. "I remember thinking how strange it was that someone had found the time to get that cleaver from the kitchens. It couldn't ever be used for food prep again, I thought. That's what I was thinking about. I was standing there, the hero of the hour, and all I could think about was how someone had to go and find that cleaver. That someone would have to order a new one. That's what I was thinking about when Orestes said *no*.

"I don't think any of us understood him at first. Not even Liaison Nabis. We all just stood there staring at him. Then he said it again. He said *no*. He said he wouldn't do it. And he spoke so quietly at first that you thought maybe you misheard him. Then he says it again louder and *louder*—louder than you'd ever heard him speak, *shouting* at Liaison Nabis. He's saying that it wasn't right, that enough blood had been spilled that day. To save the children. He wasn't going to hurt anyone else in the name of the children. He drops the cleaver, and he's standing all alone in the middle of this crowd, shouting, and you think—he's a *fucking idiot*. He's a bloody fucking idiot; he's going to get himself killed, that *fucking moron*, all he had to do was swing the cleaver, and he could just walk away—

"But he never could, never would. He was the only one who would say it wasn't right. He was the only one who asked if you were all right after you were done killing all those Idolers. He was the only one who didn't tell you to stop crying like some child. And you think, maybe, you could admire the balls it took to stand up and say no, but even as you think that, even as he's shouting about how he wouldn't do it, Liaison Nabis holds up a hand like this, and he just—"

Percy lifted a hand and flicked his wrist sharply, curling it into a fist as he did.

"And Orestes screams, and drops. And then two of the officers are on him, *hurting him*, and you want to scream *stop*, you want to tell them to let him go, but you can't. You can't, because you're the Red Hammer, you're the *symbol*, and you're standing right beside Nabis, and what if he hurts you like that too? So you stand there, like the fucking coward you are, as they drag Orestes off. You stand there, and you look without seeing, and you let your mind go anywhere but that poor boy and the children—"

Horris had heard enough. He touched a hand to Percy's shoulder. The Imperial jolted as if shocked. He blinked rapidly as he turned to Horris, as if he had forgotten that Horris was there. Tears streaked down the narrow planes of his face and into the rough patchwork of his beard.

Horris, by contrast, had gone curiously calm. Even as his stomach twisted for all those hurt that day, even as the hot tears built behind his eyes, he was calm. It was the sort of calm that settled over you because it had to, because someone had to say it was going to be okay.

It wasn't, though. It was too late for *it's going to be okay*. All he could think of instead was *I'm here. I'm not going anywhere.*

Horris reached up and brushed the tear tracks from Percy's face. "Was that the last time you saw Orestes?"

"No." Percy closed his eyes and shuddered. "No. It was not."

Interlude 3: A Damn Unfortunate Business

The weight of the handgun pressed against Percy's chest. He had it tucked in the inner pocket of his new coat, secured and out of sight. He had requested it from the requisition officer, and she had given it to him without comment or complaint. He was finding, more and more, that people did things just because he asked them to. The thought was as intoxicating as it was terrifying.

His destination was the gaol: an old-fashioned and low-tech building on campus, mostly meant for graduating Extraordinaries and officers to sleep off drunken rowdiness. It rarely, if ever, held actual troublemakers. Ordinaries would scare each other with tales of being locked in gaol for misdemeanors, and Midman would brave nights in a cell on a dare or for a lark.

Now Perseus approached the two officers who'd been posted at the gaol's front desk. *Lieutenants*, he thought, despairingly…until he remembered that he was a Lieutenant now, too. What's more, both officers stared openly at him as he approached the desk.

"I'm here to see Midman Mason," Percy said. His voice was crisp and businesslike, and inwardly, Percy was impressed with himself.

Lieutenant Wayne shook her head. "Liaison Nabis ordered he be kept in solitary confinement until his trial. No one is allowed in."

"Liaison Nabis sent me. I'm to interrogate Midman Mason regarding his Idoler sympathies."

"We should have been notified."

"And I apologize for that. The Liaison has been very busy since the Idoler attack—no doubt it slipped his mind. I could bring the matter back to him, but that would result in…delays." He let the word and its implicit threat hang in the air. He watched the Lieutenants shift, caught between proper procedure and not wanting to invoke the Liaison's wrath.

Finally, they stood aside. "Be quick," said Wayne.

Percy's boots echoed along the long concrete hallway of the gaol. Flickering fluorescent bulbs provided dim light, and the dank, damp air sent gooseflesh up and down his arms. Each cell he passed was empty, save the last on the right.

Orestes looked up as Perseus stopped in front of his cell. The worst of his beating had faded in the intervening days since the scene in the courtyard, but one eye remained swollen shut, and yellow bruises dotted his face and chest. He still wore his uniform from the day of, torn and bloody and reeking of sweat. Percy wrinkled his nose as Orestes limped to the bars of his cell.

"You came," Orestes said. His voice was hoarse. He reached a trembling hand between the bars.

Percy took a step backward out of his reach. "I came. At great personal risk, mind you." Part of him still wasn't sure why he'd come. The distance of a few days had afforded him some clarity. Orestes never should have disobeyed. His imprisonment was his own damn fault.

And yet, here he stood.

Orestes withdrew his hand, wrapping it around the bars of his cell. He licked his bloodied lips. "Thank you for coming. No one else would. Not even Electra. I don't think the Liaison passed my message along to her. But he promised he would."

Electra was a Midman, a full two years younger than Percy, and her existence had always been on the periphery of his life. But even he had heard her loudly and hotly denouncing her brother and his treason in the mess hall. Orestes had ruined her life and reputation in addition to his own. But telling Orestes that would have been kicking a man while he was bleeding out. Instead, he glanced around before leaning in.

"Why did you disobey?"

Orestes stared at him with one blue eye. "Because I couldn't hurt anyone else. I'm not like you, Percy. I'm not strong enough to do that."

"You're a damn fool."

"I know."

"They're calling you an Idoler."

"I know."

"If you had just...I could have saved you, vouched for you, protected you! No one can touch me now! But instead, you–you throw it all away, in front of everyone!" He tossed his hands into the air to better illustrate Orestes flinging his life away. "I can't save you from that!"

"I know."

Percy wanted to hate him. He almost managed it. Then, the fury ebbed. He sighed and reached into his jacket for the hidden gun. "The least I could do was bring you what you asked for."

They would trace the gun back to him, he thought, even as he passed it through the bars to Orestes. He still had no idea what to do about that.

"I still don't see how one handgun is going to help you escape," he said critically.

Orestes looked at him as though he were an idiot. "I'm not trying to escape."

The look on Orestes' face was so unusual that, for a moment, his words didn't register. Then it clicked.

Percy lurched for the cell door. "NO! No, you can't—"

"Says who?" Orestes asked. He was unnervingly calm, spinning the barrel of the handgun so that small *click-click-clicks* filled the air.

"Says the Word, you utter fucking—you're condemning yourself to hell!"

"I'm bound there anyway." Orestes' voice cracked. "There is no hope for me."

"That's not true! Please, just let me—"

"Talk to Nabis?" Orestes asked. His voice twisted with a bitterness that brought Percy up short. "I've already spoken to Nabis. After my trial, they'll take my hand. Maybe my head, if I'm lucky. If I'm not, then I'll be used as an example for all the Ordinaries who ever pass through this place. I'll be a cautionary tale to children about what happens when you say *no*." His lips thinned into a hard line, and a strange fire lit his good eye. "Do not ask me to endure that. Please."

The world tilted one way and then the other. Blood roared in Percy's ears, and he clenched his trembling fists. No, no, this wasn't right, even if Orestes was an Idoler—if he killed himself, he'd never earn his redemption. The Emperor preached about the cowards who burned hot in hell, perdition for denying the sacred flame they'd lit at birth. He should have shouted for the guards or sprung at the bars to wrestle the gun back. But his legs were lead, and when he spoke again, his voice was a cracked whisper: "Please don't do this."

Orestes ignored him in favor of studying the gun. "I've had a lot of time alone to think. And I think the Idolers might be right. Maybe the Emperor isn't a god. Otherwise, why would he have made someone like me?"

He set the gun on the floor before reaching around his neck. He unclasped the pendant and chain he wore before extending it out to Percy. "Take it. You're a better soldier than I could ever be."

Percy fumbled for the necklace. He clenched the pendant tight in his fist, so tight it ached. "I'll pray for you," he said, not knowing what else to say. Something pricked the back of his eyes, and his vision went blurry. He did not want to lose gentle, dreamy Orestes, who sang with a beautiful voice. He did not want to lose the only one who had held him and not chastised him for his tears. "Orestes, *please*. Please don't do this. I don't want you to die."

"This is war, Percy. People die all the time." Orestes extended a hand through the bars, and this time, Percy took it. Funny–although Percy was fighting tears, Orestes was calm. This was the most relaxed Percy had seen him in the thirteen years they'd known each other. "If you do meet the Emperor someday—tell him I did my best. Man or god, I never wanted to disappoint him."

"I will," Percy said hoarsely. He reached up and secured the necklace around his own neck. "I swear it."

Orestes smiled. "You were always kind to me. Goodbye, Percy."

Orestes turned away. Percy backed up slowly as if Orestes had the power to dismiss him. After a few steps, he pivoted, forcing himself to feel nothing, do nothing. He had to look calm and disaffected for the guards at the front. What was one more dead Idoler in the end? But his heart thundered all the same, and the pendant around his neck felt like a noose.

He retreated to the kyriakon to pray. Before the day was out, he had been summoned to Liaison Nabis' office, where the Liaison informed him that Orestes Mason had been found dead in his cell.

"You were, of course, the last to see him alive," said the Liaison. He peered over the rim of his pince-nez at Percy.

Percy forced himself to think of nothing, feel nothing. Block it out, he ordered himself. "Yes, sir. I gave him an ultimatum."

"He should have stood trial," Nabis said. He shook his head. "Under ordinary circumstances, there would be consequences for acting outside of protocol. However, given the circumstances under which we find ourselves…"

He leaned forward, peering at Percy with those translucent eyes.

A faintly unpleasant sensation seized Percy, akin to ants crawling across his skin. He swatted the sensation away and redoubled his efforts to stay in the here and now. He didn't care how strong a phrenic Nabis was. He would not get those final moments with Orestes.

Nabis sat back. He looked disconcerted, and then sat forward again with fingers steepled. "These are *extraordinary* circumstances. Consider this your only warning about acting out of line."

"Yes, sir."

Nabis nodded. He adjusted the edge of his pince-nez, and for a moment, he seemed older than he really was. "Well. It's an unfortunate business, Lieutenant Warden. A damn unfortunate business."

Sixty days later, Perseus found himself standing alone in a wing adjacent to the main hall of the Imperial Palace. It had been sixty days since Orestes died, and the cruel march of time had lessened the blow. Somedays, he could hate Orestes as assuredly as the rest of them. Somedays, he could believe the rumors spoken about him, how he had executed the traitor privately. That was what they called Orestes now—"the traitor." His name had been unofficially stricken from the record.

They called Percy the Red Hammer. For his hair, of course, and for the stories told in the aftermath of the Academy Attack: how heretical blood dripped from his fingers, how it had stained his skin and clothes until he was nothing but a red specter of judgment.

It had been sixty days of shaking hands and receiving commendations, sixty days away from the actual fighting, as Imperial and Idoler traded blow for blow.

Now, here he stood, in full parade dress, readying to be introduced to a ball thrown in his honor. Clergymen and officers and other distinguished dignitaries would be present. He would be blessed by the five Liaisons themselves. And after that…the Emperor Himself. Percy had almost refused to believe it when Liaison Nabis told him that. The Emperor should have been north of Creedence, leading his army against the heretical Adastra.

"The ceremony is an opportunity," Nabis had said. "Why?"

Percy thought it through. "To goad Adastra and her ilk into the heart of Imperial strength. Do you think they'll attempt anything during the ceremony?"

"It is a possibility, however remote," Liaison Nabis admitted. "We are ready to meet them, Lieutenant, when and where they appear."

Percy straightened his cap over his combed hair. Tonight was the night every Academy student dreamed of: a ceremony celebrating his bravery and devotion, a personal blessing from the Emperor Himself. He fiddled with the pendant around his neck.

The night was his. So why did he feel like he wanted to die?

"There you are. Everyone was wondering where you'd hidden yourself away."

Percy jolted. He turned to see his mother striding down the hall towards him. Admiral Danae Warden was in full dress and had tucked her graying red hair into a bun. It had the additional effect of making her appear older and more severe. But the hard planes of her face softened as she smiled.

Percy reached for her. The Admiral caught him and pulled him to her chest in a fierce hug. Percy buried himself against his mother's chest. For a fleeting, foolish moment, he pretended he was six years old again; he wanted nothing more than to stay here, safe in Mother's arms, and never come out.

The Admiral drew him back. She cupped his face in her hands. Her smile grew, and her brown eyes shone with joy. "I am so proud of you."

"Thank you, Mother," Percy murmured.

"I know your father is too, Emperor rest his soul."

His father had passed when Percy was twelve, already entrenched in the Academy. He'd been half a stranger, and Percy didn't know how to miss a stranger. So he just nodded.

"Are you ready?" asked the Admiral.

"As I'll ever be," Percy replied. He rolled his shoulders back, grateful for the extra height his boots gave him, and extended an arm out to his mother. She accepted it most graciously, and together, they walked into the wide, high-ceiling main hall to thunderous applause.

Most of the evening passed in a blur. There were speeches, more speeches, lots of polite clapping, and donations to the Academy to help rebuild and repair. The five Liaisons—Nabis, Anaxandros, Alecto, Castor, and Polluxa—were present on the stage with Percy and his mother. At some point, Liaison Anaxandros pinned yet another medal to his chest. "Nabis tells me you have the making of a Liaison someday, Lieutenant," he said. He'd smiled down at Percy, but his eyes did not warm until he looked at the Admiral.

Then came champagne and a light dinner, followed by the only non-Emperor part of the night Percy had been looking forward to: dancing.

His mother received the honor of the first dance, and as they swept along the ballroom floor, Percy broached the subject of Anaxandros.

The Admiral sighed. "I swear, that man could conquer nations, but he lacks all subtly. Yes, Anaxandros and I have been discussing a marriage match."

"Oh," Percy said, not sure how to feel about that. His father was eight years dead, and the Admiral could do no better than one of the Emperor's personal aides. "How did you two meet?"

"We've been working together on an assignment for the Emperor. I can't say more than that."

"Not even to your war hero son?" He spun her, out and in again, and his mother looked amused when they came together again.

"Not even to my favorite son. It would be an advantageous match—I could use his connections, and he had four daughters in need of a mother figure. It would set you up for success as well. Anaxandros has a daughter about your age. Sparta."

It took some thought before Percy could call her to mind: a dark-eyed woman, always with a smile and a jape, never seen without sour-faced Electra Mason. "You would match us?"

"Yes. Your children would have the advantages of both our lines."

Percy had never given thought to a future marriage and children. For some reason, the idea made him queasy. But for his mother's sake, he smiled. "I hope all goes well."

"As do I." With that, they twirled off together across the dance floor.

He danced several more times that evening, including a slow waltz with the elderly Liaison Alecto. He accepted her tottering gait and overpowering peppermint perfume with as much grace as he could.

After the dancing and before the final ceremony, Liaison Nabis pulled him aside. The phrenic wore a larger pair of shades than his usual pince-nez. Percy assumed it was to better block out the feedback of the crowd. He found himself looking at his reflection even as Nabis asked: "How are you feeling?"

"Well, sir." Slightly buzzed from the free champagne, but no need to mention that.

Nabis nodded before clapping Percy on the shoulder. "The Emperor is most excited to make your acquaintance."

"He is?"

"Most excited." Nabis nodded. "Remember your courtesies when you approach the throne."

"I will, sir."

"I know you will. Seldom have I ever been so proud of a student."

Percy smiled. "What's it like, sir? Being near the Emperor?"

Nabis was silent for a moment, expression contemplative. "Radiant," he said at last. "Like the first burst of springtime sun. You are filled with purpose and clarity. Love. A deep well of love that leaves your cup running over. It is hard to describe, Perseus…but you will understand when you kneel before Him. Everyone does."

"I'm looking forward to it," Percy said. He thought of his promise to Orestes and wondered if he would have time for a fuller conversation with the Emperor someday.

When the time came, he stood on a dais with the Liaisons. A long set of marble stairs extended above them to a gold-leafed throne's landing. Behind the gold-leaf throne was a pair of marble double doors.

Liaison Alecto rose from her seat to lead the faithful in prayer. She led them through the five Litanies and a reading from the first chapter of the Word. The crowd—officers, clergymen, politicians, scientists, and scholars—bowed their heads as Liaison Alecto preached submission before the Emperor. She spoke of His victories against their so-called masters, of hordes vanquished, of his blinding Radiance. She spoke of the virtues of obedience and gratitude and how they should all nurture the flame within:

"Let His holy fire engulf the heretics! Let His holy fire sustain the hearts of the faithful through the darkest night! Let His light be as a second sun, a second moon, a blazing path through our lives until their ends! Praise the Emperor!"

She slammed a curled fist to her heart. The faithful copied the gesture. A cry of "The Emperor!" went up. Percy, caught in the passion of his people, joined the growing chant:

"The Emperor! The Emperor! The Emperor! THE EMPEROR! *THE EMPEROR!*"

The double doors behind the throne burst open. A blinding, dazzling light, strong as the midday sun, flooded the hall. Percy looked away, bowing his head against the Radiance.

The crowd fell silent. There was the soft rustling of hundreds of people kneeling. Percy fell to his knees as well. Tears pricked his eyes, and he tightened his hands into fists to keep them from trembling. *You were wrong, Orestes. He is a god.*

But then—if Orestes was wrong, where had his soul wound up?

Percy didn't want to think about that here, now, at the apex of his triumph. He had earned this audience, earned it through his own courage and the rivers of unholy blood.

You were protecting the children.

Orestes whispered in his ear. Percy jolted in place. He glanced around for some hint of his presence. Nothing. Nothing, despite the clarity with which he had spoken, the clarity with which Percy had heard him.

He was still looking for Orestes when the Emperor spoke. His voice was higher than Percy expected, with an accent he couldn't quite place:

"Approach the throne, Perseus Warden."

Percy lurched to his feet. He cast his gaze around once more. He was flanked by the faithful: his mother, the Liaisons, the officers of good standing. He climbed the steps slowly, keeping his eyes fixed on the red carpet that led up to the throne. He stopped when he saw the tips of black boots.

"Well met, my son," said the Emperor. "Kneel."

Percy knelt. His heart raced, pounding so hard he thought it might burst from his chest. He screwed his eyes shut. A hand touched his shoulder, and Percy felt—

Nothing.

He waited to feel something. Anything. Any of what Liaison Nabis described. But the hand on his shoulder was just a hand. It could have belonged to anyone. There was no rush of love, or peace, or purpose. There was nothing.

The Emperor was speaking, saying something to the crowd, but Percy didn't hear it. His mind raced alongside his heart now. Was this some test? Was he supposed to stand up and denounce this imposter? Or—the dawning thought was horrific, but he couldn't shake it—or—*or*—

He summed up his courage and peeked up at the Emperor. Strangely, the light was less intense up close. The Emperor looked down at him with a still, golden face. A mask. And just beneath the mask, Percy could see the wisps of a red-gray beard.

Perseus did not feel love, or peace, or purpose. All he felt at that moment was a deep, unspeakable rage.

22 The Red Hammer

United Star System Postal Code, Chapter 11, Section 4: In the event of hostile encounters along postal routes, it shall be the priority of USSPS convoys to flee, not fight.

"And that," Percy said, "is why I left."

He swallowed the bile in his raw, burning throat. Tears streaked unchecked down his face. He was exhausted in a way he'd never been before, mind, body, and soul. Percy forced himself to look at Horris, ready for his judgment.

Horris had the dazed expression of a man who'd just been punched in the face. "He's managed to fool everyone else?"

"Somehow, yes. Even Nabis. I–I now suspect it has something to do with what I am. A reinforcer." Percy flexed his hands for lack of anything else to do with them. "I didn't know that at the time, of course. So, I put myself in a box and mailed myself out. Because I needed to know. I needed to know what lay outside Creed. I needed to know if the problem lay with the Emperor…or with me."

He'd lain awake for hours after the ball, replaying that exact question over and over in his head. If the fault lay not with the Emperor—and how could it?—then the fault lay within him. But if it

294

was *his* fault, how could he have knelt before the Emperor in the first place? Wouldn't the Emperor have known that he wasn't worthy?

No one else could know these doubts. They were dangerous, blasphemous. The Red Hammer did not doubt. It was not his place to.

So leave.

He'd seized on the idea half-asleep, and in the dark of night, it had seemed like a brilliant plan. Leave and find proof of the Emperor's will beyond the borders of Creed. A holy mission of sorts, even.

"What did you find?" Horris asked softly.

"You."

The answer fell out of him unthinking. Percy watched Horris blink before continuing:

"You were a textbook Idoler. You were this–this *nobody* postman who knew nothing of the Word and didn't care to. But still, you protected me. Even when I was at my worst. At first, I thought perhaps that my prayers had been answered, that you were proof of the Emperor's providence. But...somewhere along the way...that stopped being the case. You were just *you*. A man. Stubborn and excitable and with his own set of principles. Enamored of things no one else cared about. But that's sort of what I like about you. You find value in the littlest lives. You're an Idoler, but you showed me that life outside the Emperor was still one with meaning. I just..."

His voice cracked. All his loneliness and self-loathing came seeping through.

"All my life, I was told I would live and die for the Emperor. That my purpose was to fight for the Emperor. That's not true anymore, but even so...even so, I wish someone would tell me why I'm alive." He tilted his head back to control the flow of tears. "I wish someone would tell me what the point is."

He pitched forward to bury his face in his knees. He didn't care how juvenile it looked: he wanted to hide here forever, out of the way of heavy questions and decisions. He didn't want to face whatever Horris thought of him now.

"Well...have you ever thought...maybe there is no point?"

Horris' hesitant answer jerked Percy off his knees. He blinked at Horris as the other scratched his cheek. Horris shrugged and turned towards the water. Soft blue light danced over his face, making him look younger than he already was.

"Look—you've only been with us a little while, but you've seen how awful life is out here. People die all the time in terrible ways. Wars or pirates or animal attacks, disease and disasters...and that's without getting into all the dangerous bullshit out in space. Most of us work long hours in cramped places, and we don't see our families for months or years. A successful crew probably doesn't have family waiting for them, and how sad is that? It sucks. Life *sucks*. And I don't think if anyone was really in charge, they would have designed it that way."

Horris' words sank like a stone into Percy's stomach. His grip on his legs went white-knuckled.

Then Horris continued:

"But...I mean, no one ordained me to be a mailman. I don't think I was born to deliver the mail. But that's okay. It makes me happy. And when I'm delivering, I feel like I'm doing something, just a little bit, to make someone else's life easier. And I think that's all we can do, really. Do things that make us happy, and try to make the shitty world a little less shitty for each other. Right?"

He turned back to Percy, and when their eyes met, an electric jolt coursed through Percy's system. Some last lost puzzle pieces clicked into place. He sniffled and wiped the last of his tears from his eyes. "If you can't find it," he said hoarsely, "you have to make it yourself."

Horris smiled, a broad, dazzling smile that brightened the dark chapel. He leaned forward and took Percy's hand in his. "Perce—look. There's nothing we can do to change the past. Neither of us can save the people back there. And I think you'll be paying for it, in different ways, for a long time. But you're trying. And as long as you're trying, we'll help you. All of us."

Percy stared down at their conjoined hands. He squeezed, trying to convey all the pain and gratitude through the action. Horris squeezed back.

Exhausted and emotionally spent, Percy collapsed against Horris. "Orestes would have liked you," he murmured. He scanned the immediate area for the ghost. He was mercifully absent.

"I think I would have liked him too," said Horris softly.

The water lapped against the edge of the pool. The silverfish scurried off in search of a meal. Somewhere in the distance, music played.

"Thank you," Percy said into the soft silence. "For everything."

"USSPS customer service. Best in the galaxy." Horris' laugh was a rumble in his chest.

They remained there for a long while. Percy drifted in and out of alertness, dimly aware of his body stiffening the longer they sat on the floor. Every once in a while, Horris would shift. At some point, he pulled out his tablet and fired up a crossword puzzle. Percy watched him play and offered occasional suggestions ("Thirty-four across is croquembouche").

A blaring alarm shattered the tranquility. Horris and Percy both jolted upright as Horris' tablet rumbled. Text burst onto the screen:

URGENT—IMMEDIATE SHELTER-IN-PLACE WARNING BY ORDER OF THE AMBROSE FRONTIER SECURITY ADMINISTRATION.

THE AMBROSE FRONTIER SECURITY ADMINISTRATION ASKS ALL VISITORS AND PERSONNEL TO SHELTER IN PLACE. A SHIP HAS ENTERED THE AIRSPACE WITHOUT AUTHORIZATION OR CLEARANCE. UNTIL THE SITUATION HAS BEEN ASSESSED, SHELTER IN PLACE IS IN EFFECT FOR THE ENTIRETY OF THE AMBROSE FRONTIER.

*PLEASE DO NOT GO OUTDOORS AND REMAIN
AWAY FROM WINDOWS OR ANY OPEN DOORS.
PLEASE STAY TUNED TO MEDIA OUTLETS
FOR FURTHER INFORMATION.*

Faint screams sounded from without. Percy jumped to his feet and crossed back across the chapel to the entrance. Horris followed. They shared one look before Percy yanked the door open.

Pandemonium greeted them: Prophet's Alley was rapidly emptying of tourists and preachers. People sprinted for cover, heedless of stalls, props, and each other as a massive man-of-war roared through the skies. Crew flung themselves over the sides of the ship, rappelling down ropes or slowing their descent with booster packs. They landed in the middle of the chaos with steel flashing.

Pirates.

Percy's gaze locked on the closest pirate, who advanced on a stunned, bleeding dancer. Percy didn't think; he sprinted forward and tackled the pirate from behind. They went sprawling onto the pavement, rolling against an abandoned stand. Percy pinned the pirate by the back. He seized him by the neck as he tried to rise and slammed the pirate's face once, twice, three times into the pavement. Blood pooled from beneath the still pirate as Percy staggered to his feet.

"PERCY!"

Horris had an arm around the dazed dancer. He led the dancer into the relative safety of the chapel, but both their eyes remained on Percy.

Percy shook his head. He could afford to feel horrified and guilty later when the sound of cannonade didn't shriek overhead. He stepped to the side, his back to a brick wall, and assessed the situation. There were only a handful of pirates here, but a handful was enough to send most of the civilians running. Some held their ground, fighting the invaders with makeshift weapons and fists. Gods, Percy noted bitterly, had yet to appear to save their faithful.

The downed pirate had a knife in his limp grip and another in a sheath at his waist. Percy worked the scabbard free and clicked it around his own waist. The weight was at once comfortingly familiar and terribly heavy.

Horris had tucked the dancer inside the chapel and now fought his way across the street to Percy. He looked down at the still, bloodied pirate, swallowed, and back to Percy. "That was the *Scorpion*."

"Then they're here for me." A new, different sort of guilt seized Percy. This one was harder to set aside: it was the guilt born of those families who'd just been trying to enjoy a night out. All ruined, now, because of him. They were doing this—hurting these innocents—because of *him*.

Every inch of him was suddenly aflame. He scanned the skyline for the man-of-war; it wasn't hard to miss as it roared south of the city. He lowered his gaze back to Horris. "They're going for the postal depot."

"*Fives*," Horris breathed.

They broke into a sprint. Percy took the lead as they weaved through the panicked, stampeding crowd. Horris was on his tablet with Basah, telling her to stay with Roddy, wherever they were, he was with Percy—

There was a shove, a scream, and Horris went down. His tablet slipped from his grip and went skittering away into the swarm of people. Percy stopped short. Blood roared in his ears as he pivoted back to Horris and the pirate who had knocked him to the pavement. No—*no!*

He yanked his knife free and shoved people aside with his free hand as the force of the crowd threatened to sweep him from Horris. He screamed Horris' name, even as Horris twisted up out of the pirate's grip. Percy watched, stunned, as Horris flung an arm over the pirate's neck, slid the other under the pirate's arm, and shoved them both to the pavement. The pirate landed on his back, pinned chest-to-chest with Horris. Horris looked over his shoulder, shouting for Percy.

Percy was there. He slammed the heel of his boot into the pirate's temple. A sharp *crack* followed. Percy gnashed his teeth with satisfaction before yanking Horris to his feet.

"Are you all right?" Percy demanded. And, before Horris could answer: "How did you *do* that?"

"I told you," Horris panted, "I wrestled in high school."

Percy managed a grim smile. Then they were off again, tearing through the tourists and Front personnel in their bid to reach the postal depot. Here and there, they could see private security engaging with pirates as they smashed through shop windows and vendor stalls. Some went down in the fighting; most got away, arms burdened with loot. Percy forced himself to ignore the pirates. They couldn't afford to stop or slow.

His heart leapt into his throat with every pump of his legs. His chest tightened as his lungs burned for air, and there was a sudden stitch in his side. He forced himself to push through the physical sensations and focus on the mission: *get to Fives. Get back to Fives.*

The air burned acrid with the smoke, and the heat of a fire brushed his back. Weaponry screeched, and people screamed. It didn't matter, Percy told himself. There was nothing he could do for those people. He could only push forward, forward, *keep going!*

It seemed at once forever and no time at all before he and Horris collapsed against the Ambrose Frontier Water Authority building. The *Scorpion* hummed just overhead. The postal depot was at the other end of the street; from here, they could see orange flickering light, and the next breath they inhaled was smoky.

"*Those bastards,*" Horris coughed. He doubled over, hands on his knees, sucking in what air he could. He waved Percy off when he crouched to check on him.

Together, they sidled down the street towards the depot. The commotion within the depot offered them cover as they moved; no one noticed them as a knot of figures descended from the *Scorpion* to confront Inspector Rofon.

She stood in front of the depot with her weapon drawn. She shifted her stance as the group approached her. Words were exchanged, but Percy couldn't make out what. Instead, he focused on the black-clad, square-shouldered pirates.

No. His eyes narrowed sharply. *No.* Those weren't pirates.

"Horris," he breathed, "those are Imperials."

Horris stiffened beside him. "We need to go."

"No."

Percy stared ahead as he spoke. He didn't move until Horris seized him by the shoulder. "No? What do you mean, *no?*"

"If we run, they will follow. I have my answers. I'm not running anymore. Go around to the other side, get to the yard. I'll distract them here."

"They'll *kill* you!"

Percy had no grand reply to that. Yes, they would kill him. At least he wouldn't burn in the Emperor's hell. He turned fully to Horris, drinking in the sight of him: his dark eyes, his strong jaw, the dip in his chin. He took Horris by the hand and folded their fingers together. Their palms were hot and slick with sweat, but still, Percy held on. He needed to commit Horris to memory. He needed to hold on, just a moment longer.

"Don't do this," Horris whispered.

A part of him—and it was a stronger part than Percy cared to admit—didn't want to. A part of him wanted to run with Horris back to the *Silverfish* and into the sky. But he'd run for long and far enough. His people had made it perfectly clear: wherever he went, they would follow.

"If they do not find me there, they will tear the Front apart," Percy said in a low voice. "And the first place they'll crush is the Alley. Do not ask me to be responsible for that. *Please.* Do not ask that of me."

"Percy…" Horris' voice cracked even as his grip on Percy tightened.

Horris wouldn't let go. Not first, anyway. So Percy yanked his hand free and took a step backward. "Thank you, Captain Jensen. For getting me this far."

Horris stared at him in clear pain. He looked to be on the verge of saying something else…and then shook his head. He turned and ran back around the other side of the building. Percy watched him go before turning back to the scene at the entrance. He still couldn't make out words, but voices were rising. Rofon had been surrounded on all sides by Black Hammers.

Percy took a deep breath to pace his racing mind and body. He needed calm for this. Absolute calm. He slid his hands across the hilts of his knives. He'd never raised his hand in earnest against another Hammer before, let alone a cohort of them. There was no way he was walking away from this fight.

If he did not do this, though, what would become of the *Silverfish* crew? What would they do to the ones who saved him?

The calm he sought settled over him like a layer of armor. He could do this. He would do this.

Percy exhaled again as he pulled the twin knives free from their sheaths. Firelight danced off the honed steel as he turned the corner out onto the street. He strode towards the depot unhurried, conserving his energy for the moment he needed it. He had nothing to fear. He was the Red Hammer, and they were about to learn why he'd earned that name.

His pace picked up as he neared the depot, and the roar of challenge rose in his throat:

"HAMMERS!"

It was the only warning he gave them.

Percy saw a Hammer pivot and bring his sword down to strike. Percy met him on the downstroke, catching the steel in the cross of his knives. He snapped a leg up, kicked the Hammer away, and spun to slash at the one coming up behind him. His knife caught against thin armor. Percy swung his leg out again, caught this Hammer behind the knee, and sent him sprawling.

A third tried to rush him. Percy went to one knee, ducking the obvious swing of her warhammer, and slammed the blunt hilt of one knife into her stomach. She heaved, making a godawful choking noise before Percy slammed his elbow into her chin.

He used the momentum to spring himself back to his feet. He twirled the knives through his hands and shifted his stance as the Hammers encircled him. From the corner of his eye, he saw a bloodied Rofon stagger to her feet. "GO!" He bellowed.

He didn't wait to see if she obeyed. Instead, he turned on his heel and snarled at the Hammers approaching from behind. They shied back. There was a palpable hesitance among these Hammers; they adjusted their grips on their weapons and shuffled their feet into offensive stances. Their eyes were prey eyes: wide and watching. Afraid.

"HE'S MINE!"

A section of the circle broke. And out strode—

Orestes?

Percy took a full step backward from the approaching ghost. Then the ghost reached for its weapon: an iron-tipped short staff. No—not Orestes. Orestes would never, ever have reached for a weapon. This was the sister, the younger sister...

Electra leveled one end of her staff at his chest. "We'd heard you'd turned traitor, Lieutenant Warden, but none of us wanted to believe it. You were the arm of the Emperor!"

"He is my Emperor no longer," Percy replied.

Flames illuminated Electra's hardening expression. "So you are an Idoler."

"I suppose I am," Percy said. And the declaration filled him with a bizarre sort of pride.

Electra's lips curled back in a sneer. She spun her staff once and settled into a fighting stance. Percy shifted his grip on his knives and slammed his fist to his chest twice.

Electra swung at the challenge, moving hard and fast and fluid. Percy slid away, dodging left and right as she swung. The staff had been an intelligent choice against his blades; she was denying him close range. It was all he could do to evade her strikes and watch for an opening. Occasionally, he would force a blow back with the edge of his blade, and when he did, the ugly sound of metal on metal screeched into the night.

Electra was full on the offensive and deadly quiet. They all were, in fact. Percy could hear nothing save for their grunts and the beating of his own heart.

Finally, he feinted left, saw Electra's swing go wide, and dove in. He dropped his knives and tackled her across the midriff. They went down together on the pavement in a desperate struggle. Percy squeezed his knees into the sides of her abdomen and held fast when she tried to buck him off. He flung himself forward, seized her wrists, and pinned her down.

"GO HOME!"

The demand escaped him without thinking. Electra stared up at him, seething and hateful. Percy raised his gaze from her blue eyes to the Hammers around him.

Young, he thought in horror. They were all so young for this.

His eyes found Sparta. Blood seeped from her mouth where he'd hit her. "Please," he said, "*please*. You don't have to do this. Go home—"

PHWUNK!

Something sharp and stinging pierced his shoulder. Percy jerked, one hand flying to his shoulder without thinking. *Spider bite*–but no, that didn't make sense at all. Not when his fingertips brushed a small, cylindrical object. The world went wiggly, watery, and his body failed to respond when he tried to move.

He slumped off Electra and onto the pavement. There was a crowd gathering at the edges of his vision. He needed to get up…he needed to move…he needed…Horris…

Percy saw Silver approaching, twirling a blowgun through his fingers. Electra's face filled his vision. She cocked her fist back for a punch.

Everything went black.

23 The Letter of the Law

United Star System Postal Code, Chapter 3 Section 8: Whoever, having taken charge of any mail, voluntarily quits or deserts the same before he has delivered it to its next destination shall be subject to prosecution from United Star System Postal Service Inspectors.

"Fives! *FIVES!*"

Horris' shout echoed across the shipyard. He could hear shouting from within the postal depot, more furious than afraid. The shipyard was devoid of people, and in the growing dark, mailships loomed overhead like misshapen sentinels.

The illuminated *Silverfish* stood out amid her fellow ships. Her lights were on, and her ramp had been lowered. Fives stood at the end of it, staring at a dark patch on the pavement. His gaze shot up as Horris sprinted towards him, and he flinched when Horris enveloped him in a fierce hug.

"I'm fine," said the stiff Fives before Horris could even ask. "Let go now."

Horris held on a beat longer. For Fives' sake, he tried to focus on the relief of finding Fives all right, and not on everything that had led up to this moment. He needed to focus on the good news. He needed someone to hold onto, for just a little bit.

Fives wriggled free of his grip. He wiped furious tears from his eyes and glared up at Horris accusingly.

"I'm sorry, Fives, I'm so sorry, I don't mean to be—"

Horris was doing his best to keep from unraveling, but the edges were beginning to fray. His legs ached from the sprint to the shipyard, his lungs burned for air, and his heart twisted every time he thought about Percy. He wiped at his own eyes, and that was when he truly saw the massive dark patch on the pavement.

It was splattered still-wet blood.

Immediately, Horris stilled. "Fives, did anyone try to get aboard the *Silverfish*?"

"Yes. Two men tried to enter the *Silverfish*. I told them they couldn't come aboard without proper authorization." Fives' eyes were two dark bruises when he raised his gaze. "They didn't like that answer."

The back of Horris' neck prickled. "Then what happened?"

"I gave them a warning." Fives shrugged. "They didn't like that warning either."

"Did you—did you kill them?"

Fives scowled, clearly affronted by the question. "No. I just made sure they wouldn't come back."

The shipyard was dark and quiet. In the near distance, Horris could hear the grunts and sounds of a fight. He turned back and took a step forward. Now that he knew Fives was safe and the *Silverfish* remained untouched, they could help Percy. Hope lifted a massive weight off his chest. There was a way out, they could all still make it—

Inspector Rofon limped into the *Silverfish*'s pool of light. She held one arm at an awkward angle. "JENSEN!"

Horris snapped to attention. "Sir!"

"Jensen, move your ass! I don't know where your phrenic learned to fight like that, but he's alone—we need to move, now! Call the F-Two for backup and…"

She trailed off as her eyes found Fives standing just behind Horris. Her brow furrowed.

Shit.

"Shit," Fives echoed.

Horris stepped fully in front of Fives. "Inspector, I can explain—"

A sudden blast of heat and a sky-shattering roar took them all off their feet. Overhead, the *Scorpion* rose above the depot and shipyard. The pure force of its ascension kept the posties pinned to the ground. Dust and pebbles skated over Horris' skin and stung his eyes. It was an effort just to twist facedown out of the way.

The heat and noise subsided as quickly as it began. Horris struggled upright to see the *Scorpion*'s jets belching blue fire into the night sky. It lifted higher and higher as its bow turned back across the city.

"No! No, no, no, no–*PERCY!*" Horris was on his feet, screaming as he ran the length of this shipyard again. He hit the chain-link fence with a scream. *"PERCY!"*

His scream echoed out across the city, but it was just one more in the chorus. Here and there, he could see figures rising into the sky, aiming their jetpacks for the *Scorpion*—pirates, laden with loot, rejoining their ship.

Horris spun and raced for the front of the depot. He found scuffed and bloodied dirt and an abandoned knife. But no body. No body. Maybe they took him alive—maybe he was still alive—

They never found your mother's body either, some terrible voice within whispered. *Maybe she's still alive too.*

An invisible knife pierced between his ribs. A sob burst from him as his chest constricted. His breath fled, his vision blurred, and he collapsed against a wall as his legs gave out. He wrapped his arms around his head to muffle his keening.

Someone was calling his name. Calloused hands wrapped around his wrists. Someone was trying to pull him back into the world. He opened his eyes to stare at the wide-eyed Basah. Her ears were flat against her hair, and her tail had puffed. A red-faced Roddy slowed to a halt just behind her.

"Horris," Basah whispered, "what happened?"

"Percy." The name burned in his throat. He tried to force more words up and out, but his throat had swollen over. He choked and shook his head. Basah hushed his next sob before bunting her forehead against his head.

Roddy knelt beside him and slid an arm around Horris. "Hey, man. Hey, it's okay."

His grip on Horris tightened as Rofon came around the corner. She still cradled her arm close to her chest. *Dislocated*, some dim, detached part of Horris thought. Or broken. Fives trailed just behind her.

"Captain Jensen," Rofon stopped after saying his name. She glanced at Basah and Roddy and then refocused. She took a short, sharp breath. "Captain Jensen, this man has informed me he is your phrenic. Who in the five hells was taken by those bastards?"

There was nothing to be done save yank the knife in his chest free. Basah and Roddy helped him to his feet. Horris gave each a small squeeze before letting go. "That man was our stowaway, sir."

He watched the disbelief, the shock, and the fury cross Rofon's face in turn. "Your *stowaway?*"

"Yes, sir." Admitting the truth was like lancing a boil. It hurt to do it, but at least it was done. "His name is Perseus Warden, and he stowed away during our run to Creed."

"*Creed?*" Rofon repeated, incredulous. "You've had a stowaway onboard since *Creed*? And you didn't report him? USSPS Postal Code states—"

"Chapter Three, Section Seven," Horris answered for her. "Who-ever knowingly conveys any person acting as a private express is in direct violation of United Star System Postal Service Code and shall be subject to prosecution from United Star System Postal Service Inspectors."

That just seemed to infuriate her further. "You know the law! And still, you did not report him?"

"No, sir. I did not feel that was necessary at the time."

"Did not feel? This is the Postal Code, Captain Jensen! It is the foundation of our credibility as an institution! *Feeling* has nothing to do with it!"

Horris grimaced. He could feel Basah and Roddy at his back, and Fives now, too. They were the only things keeping him from flagging against Rofon's outrage. "I understand that, sir, but Perseus Warden was in need of aid, and I decided—"

Rofon cut him off by holding up her good hand. "Wait. Wait. Warden. I know that name. An all-call bulletin went out on him across the USS. Creed wanted him back for criminal charges."

"False criminal charges," Basah said. She lifted her chin in defiance. Once a royal, always a royal, and now she looked at Rofon with the sort of naked contempt only a princess was capable of.

"And *yet*, you chose to stop here. And yet, you allowed him to impersonate a member of the postal service and have access to the postal depot. *And yet.*" Rofon's voice hadn't risen, but all the same, the scorn made Horris want to die. "Did you stop to think what would happen if bounty hunters discovered his trail? Do you know how much damage you've done, not only to this depot but to the entirety of the Front?!"

Horris could feel himself shrinking against the questions. It took Roddy planting a hand on his back to force him upright again. "Inspector Rofon, this is all my fault. I take full responsibility—"

"Your entire crew will take responsibility!" Rofon snapped. "You've just cost USSPS and the Brose Front thousands—if not millions—in credits! You and your crew are *grounded*, your ship is impounded starting *now*, and you'll each be serving eight to ten years in an off-planet cell—*if* you're lucky!"

Horris stared at her dumbfounded. A low growl rose in Basah's throat, and beside him, Roddy had gone rigid. Fives looked at Rofon with brow furrowed.

"Easier to blame us," Fives said into the silence. "Easier to explain away. You didn't check credentials. You didn't scan the ships. Koss is useless. Get him fired, too."

Rofon looked at Fives with the same utter loathing that some people looked at insects. "Get that thing back on your ship."

"Don't talk about Fives like that!" Basah snarled. Horris and Roddy both had to catch her before she flung herself at Rofon.

Fives stared back at Rofon with equal loathing. "You don't like that I'm in your head," he said in a low voice. "I don't like being in your head either."

Rofon curled her lips back into a snarl before rounding on Horris. "Get back aboard your ship and stay there. I will be putting an external lock on your ship before calling the F-Two. The Postmaster General can decide what to do with you."

That was like a punch to his chest, right where the knife had slid in. Horris gasped. But still, still, he had to try. He took a step forward. "Inspector–please. We–our friend–"

"Your stowaway."

"His name is Percy. They're taking him back to Creed. They're going to kill him. If there are more Inspectors coming, they can help rescue Percy–they could take on the *Scorpion*–"

Rofon's eyes were flat and cold. "The USSPS takes no part in politics."

"But–"

"Back to your ship, Jensen. Or do I need to show you the way?"

The *Silverfish* smelled faintly of popcorn as her silent crew boarded. Basah ran a hand across the wall of the hold and murmured something under her breath. The ominous, tell-tale click of the *Silverfish* being remotely locked sounded through the mostly-empty hold. Half her depot in disarray and her postmaster MIA, and Rofon still prioritized locking them down, Horris thought bitterly.

The *Silverfish* crew stood in the hold and stared at each other.

"All right," Roddy declared, too loudly, "what's the plan?"

Horris hated him at that moment. He hated Roddy's blithe optimism, his full-speed-ahead cavalierness. "We're not going to do anything."

"What the fuck is that supposed to mean?"

"We've been grounded. We're locked down!"

Roddy flung both arms out. "So what? Rofon doesn't know about BLIP. I bet Fives and BLIP could bypass those remote locks in a minute!"

BLIP could do it in forty-five seconds.

"And then what?" Horris didn't know if he was demanding an answer from Roddy or BLIP, but it felt good to yell. It felt good to give shape to everything ugly in his chest. "We're a postal carrier! The *Scorpion* is a three-deck man-o-war! We'll be dead before we can get within a hundred yards of her!"

"Then we come up with a plan!" Roddy retorted.

Something deep and dark and ugly inside Horris exploded. "WHAT PLAN? Do you want to ram her broadside? Pull up to her and ask nicely if we can have Percy back? Or do you just want to die so you don't have to spend a decade sitting in a cage?"

The force of his fury took Roddy a full step backward. Basah stepped between them. She glared up at Horris with the same contempt she'd had for Rofon. "You're giving up."

It was a statement, not a question, and Horris knew it. He scowled as Basah continued:

"Just like that—when met with the *slightest* resistance—you're giving up!"

"Slightest resis—Rofon is a goddamn Inspector! The Postmaster General himself is on his way here, and who knows what he's going to do with us!"

Roddy sidestepped Basah to be beside her. Sweat had plastered his curls to his face and forehead. "Who the fuck are you, and what have you done with Horris? You're just going to let Percy die? After all this—after everything—you're just letting him go?"

"You told me not to get us involved in dangerous shit anymore!" Horris snapped.

"Without our consent, you semantic fuck! And now that we're standing here telling you we want to help, now—*now* you decide it's too dangerous?"

Suddenly, he and Roddy were nose-to-nose. "It's IMPOSSIBLE! Even if we had the cannons, how are we getting Percy out? Where is he on the ship? Are we fighting our way through a horde of pirates?"

"So what? You're just going to give up? You get one scolding from one superior, and suddenly, Percy's not worth it?"

"That's not it!"

"Then what the hell is your problem?" Roddy shoved him hard. "Inspector boot can't taste that good!"

The deep and dark and ugly thing surged forward again. Horris tackled Roddy to the floor, and they went down fighting. It felt good, in a visceral way, to get physical. It felt good to hurt someone else, to let the roar from his chest as he did. In an instant, he had locked Roddy in a wrestling pin. Roddy slammed his fist against Horris' arm in a feeble attempt to break free while Basah screamed at them both. Fives was nowhere to be seen.

Horris yelped as Basah dug her nails into his arm in a vain attempt to break Roddy free. He shoved Roddy off and surged to his feet to glare at Basah. He wanted to do more. He wanted to hurt more. He wanted to give into that easy, sadistic pleasure and make everyone as miserable as he was. He wanted to turn the hurt outwards so he didn't have to carry it alone.

Don't. There was a new voice in his head, and it sounded a lot like Percy. *You're better than that.*

Horris pulled himself back. He dragged both hands through his hair. His nice, fancy suit was soaked with dirt and sweat and tears, and it was suffocating him. He undid a few of the buttons to get air against his burning skin.

"*My problem,*" he spoke deliberately and slowly, picking over his words like they were shattered glass. "My problem is that we tried to help Percy, and we failed. Percy got taken because he threw himself in front of Imperials, so no one could get to Fives. He put himself in front of them for us. So what happens if we go after the *Scorpion* and we fail? Percy has to watch us die for nothing."

He rubbed his hands over his face next. It gave him time to gather more of his argument.

"Somehow, they found us on the Front. And they tore the Front apart. There were families there. *Children.* How many of them got hurt? How many of them lost someone tonight? How many of them are waiting for someone to come back?"

His throat closed over. He had to fight not to put himself back in the basement, listening to the sounds of fighting. He had to fight not to think about little ones waiting for someone to come back.

"It's my fault," Horris said. He looked at Roddy and Basah without really seeing them. "It's my fault. I made a decision. And I have to face the consequences."

Silence. Then–

"You're a goddamn coward," Basah said. She yanked Roddy to his feet and left without a word further. Horris had to wonder where she was going to sulk on a ship this size. At least he had a cabin to himself.

The cabin in question shook when Horris slammed the door shut. He managed to cross to his insects before crumpling, heartsick and overwhelmed.

Horris tucked into himself, trying to breathe, trying not to let the massive hole in his chest suck everything into it. Percy wouldn't want him to collapse like that. Percy had admired his openness, his earnestness; he'd said so himself. He ought to stay optimistic and keep his head up, but it was too hard. It was too hard.

He'd lost everything. His ship, his job, his family–Percy. He'd broken the rules. Maybe everyone would have been better off if they'd dropped Percy off at a populated planet or come clean at F-2. He wanted to disappear. He wanted to shrink into a ball and vanish.

His door clicked open and shut again. Horris didn't move until he felt someone slip down to the floor beside him. Only then did he glance to his left.

Fives looked at him with eyes red and puffy. He touched a hand to his own tear-streaked face before speaking: "Don't go away."

"Why not?"

"Because I'm here. And so are Basah and Roddy."

"They hate me."

"They don't. They're angry with you. And they love you. They just have the emotions confused right now. They don't know what to do, seeing you like this. They're trying to fill the space you left behind. Horris would have a plan, Roddy thinks. Horris would appeal to our better natures, Basah thinks. But they aren't Horris. And Horris isn't a Basah or a Roddy."

There was a faint disapproval in Fives' tone. Horris didn't want to face disapproval from Fives of all people. He focused on the insects instead. Henri crept the length of his enclosure. Sylvia remained still and placid in hers. One of the silverfish zipped across the container and burrowed into mulch. Horris watched them and allowed his thoughts to drift.

Fives sucked in a sharp breath. It must have been causing him some pain, sitting here, but to Horris' surprise, Fives did not retreat. Instead, he slipped a pale hand over Horris'. He closed his dark eyes and listened.

"It's easy to feel good when you follow the rules. Show up, do the job, smile and nod, and don't complain even when it's hard. People say nice things about you when you follow the rules. Dedicated.

Loyal. Good. Follow the rules, and you're a good person. Simple. It makes sense.

"You can bend the rules, sometimes. Keep a spider or a phrenic because there's nothing that says you can't. And when asked to break a *real* rule, a big one, you thought maybe there was a way around that, too. So you broke the rule. And then another. And another. And it was easier each time. Because…"

Fives was quiet for a moment. A soft sigh escaped him.

"Because he asked you to. Because it made him smile and wonder and care. You didn't follow the rules, and still, he thought you were good. He looked at you like no one else ever had."

It was odd to hear Fives speak his thoughts so flatly, so frankly, but it was comforting, too. Fives was putting his scramble of thoughts through a filter and making sense out of them. Fives was giving him clarity. Yes. He had broken the rules for Percy. Because Percy made him feel important—special even—because Percy thought he was *good*. Percy thought he was good without trying.

Fives audibly swallowed. He listened to Horris' flowing thoughts, nodded, and continued:

"Percy lived his whole life following rules. He lived thinking the rules made him good. But the moment he knew that wasn't true… he left. He didn't care what the rules said anymore. You think he was strong for that. You think…oh."

Fives' voice cracked. He reached up and gave Horris an awkward pat on the shoulder. "You don't think you're strong enough to do the same."

Horris nodded. "I don't know what to do, Fives."

Fives nodded. He lowered his hands to plant them on the floor, shifting his kneeling position to a criss-cross. He looked between Horris and the insects. "What would an insect do? Against something bigger?"

"Fight or flee," Horris said. He rubbed his hands together as facts sprang into his exhausted mind.

Fives jumped forward as if physically seizing an idea. "Apis cerana japonica. Honeybees."

Horris couldn't help but elaborate: "If a hornet approaches a nest of apis cerana japonica, the honeybees will attempt to warn it away. If it persists and gets into the nest, the bees will send out a signal to attack. They'll swarm the hornet. They can't fight it, but they use numbers to their advantage. They pile on and overheat the hornet to death."

"Many small things can destroy a big thing," Fives noted.

"Yeah. But we're not a honeybee, Fiver. We don't have a hive. We're a silverfish. We're on our own."

Fives hummed thoughtfully. He leaned down and peered into the silverfish enclosure. He glanced back at Horris with eyebrows arched. "A silverfish can't fight a scorpion," he spoke slowly, as if trying to make Horris understand. "But it doesn't have to. It's *faster*."

Something clicked.

It wasn't like a light going on all at once, per se. It was more like the creeping light of dawn. A silverfish was fast. A silverfish was a survivor.

Fives smiled. He stood and held out his hand for Horris to take. Horris accepted it. His captaincy hat sat by his PC, and Horris snagged it as they went out the door.

Roddy and Basah both waited in the corridor. Roddy looked apologetic; Basah, defiant. Horris just waited. And sure enough, after less than a minute of silence, Roddy stepped forward. "Look–Horris, look–it got heated back there, and I'm sorry for what I said—"

"I'm not." Basah planted her hands on her hips. Her tail slammed against the wall with rapid *thump-thumps*. "And I'm not taking it back. You're a goddamn coward."

"We're going after Percy," said Horris.

That brought her up short. Horris watched the quick flash of her eyes. She was still pissed, he knew, but it was anger now tempered with satisfaction. She tossed flyaway hair out of her eyes. "It's about time you came to your senses," she snapped. "The *Scorpion* is halfway back to Creed by now."

Fives looked at her, baffled. "No, it's not. It's *not* that fast."

Roddy snorted.

"We're going after Percy," Horris said again, pulling attention back to him. "I have a plan. Sort've. An outline."

"An idea," Fives clarified with a smile.

Fives' reaction seemed to bolster Basah and Roddy. They both looked at Horris expectantly. Horris straightened the brim of his hat over his forehead and rolled his shoulders back. "It's going to be incredibly dangerous. We'll all have to do our part, and do it well. And even if everything goes according to this idea, we'll still face prosecution from USSPS. We'll face fines, jail time…and unemployment."

He swallowed the lump in his throat. Sure, he never considered himself meant to deliver mail. But he liked it. He was good at it. And without the security of a job, what would happen to them all?

Roddy cut through his worry with a cavalier shrug. "It's just a job."

"And it wouldn't be the first time I pissed off someone in charge," Basah added. She allowed him a small, crooked smile.

A sudden, dizzying gratitude seized Horris and nearly knocked him off his feet. He beamed, too happy for words. Fortunately, Fives was there to translate. The phrenic rolled to the balls of his feet. "Happy. Chest-filling happy, balloons-over-clouds happy. You're my family happy."

Horris coughed before looking up. "BLIP? What about you?"

BLIP would like the chance to commit violence against the sentients who took Warden, Lieutenant Perseus.

"Concerning," Roddy muttered.

Fives grinned. He stuck his hand out. Horris put his palm over it. Roddy followed. And then Basah layered her hand over his. Finally, a shimmering display of a disembodied hand completed the pile. For a moment, they held it.

We're coming, Percy.

Horris eased back first. "BLIP," he said and surprised himself with his authoritative tone. "I need you and Fives to override that remote lock originating from the depot."

"Rofon's going to notice," Basah warned.

"I'll take that call in the cockpit. Basah, ready the engine. Rod, at the helm."

"Aye, Captain!"

It took a few minutes to ready everything. Horris took the time to change back into his postal uniform. It also gave him time to refine his idea as well as what he would say to Rofon.

Finally, there was a soft *ding* overhead. The locks had been bypassed. The *Silverfish*'s engines purred as Roddy roused her to life. Horris sat beside him in the co-pilot seat. The brothers shared a commiserating look as the video call screen rang.

Incoming transmission from Brose Front USSPS Depot.

"Onscreen, BLIP." Horris sat back as Rofon's outraged face filled the dashboard display.

"Captain Jensen, what the hell are you doing?"

"We're going to save our friend, sir," Horris replied.

"You are in direct violation of a superior's orders—"

"We have weighed the risks, sir, and the consequences. And we have decided to act anyway."

Rofon was silent. Her expression had gone steely flat, but Horris thought he saw an involuntary twitch of her lips. The slightest bit of admiration, no matter how begrudgingly given. "And may I ask," she said, "what is worth the consequences?"

Horris had thought long and hard about that. There was only one response he could think of, only one that might earn his crew a reprieve when all was said and done. "The *Scorpion* holds a loyal customer of the USSPS captive. He boarded our ship as our package. We have a responsibility to his well-being and to see him safely delivered to the destination he paid for. We are going to fulfill that responsibility to the best of our ability."

Rofon looked at him for a long moment. Horris stared back, unflinching. "He is a fugitive from justice," she finally said. "USSPS takes no part in politics."

"He is a customer of the USSPS," Horris said. "And we have the best customer service in the galaxy. BLIP, end transmission."

The call screen went dark. He had sealed their fate with a click.

24 The Value of Small Lives

United Star System Postal Code, Chapter 2, Section 3: The United Star System Postal Service does not discriminate against customers on the basis of race, ethnicity, religion, planetary citizenship, gender, disability and/or medical condition, or military status.

Consciousness came back in fits and bursts. So, too, unfortunately, did sensations. One arm lay stiff and deadened beneath his aching chest. His mouth felt stuffed with cotton, and there was a thick elastic band around his head, squeezing his brain to juice. The worst, though, was the lick of fire against his shoulder every time he moved.

Percy was no doctor, but all the same, he diagnosed himself as well and truly fucked.

Crusty bits clung to his eyes as he forced them open. Three walls around him were made of undecorated gray steel, while the fourth was made entirely of iron bars. In the distance, he could hear an engine thrumming. He was aboard the *Scorpion*, then. In the brig.

A low groan escaped him as he sat up. Everything *hurt*. He rubbed his deadened arm back to life, remembering a similar wakeup in the *Silverfish*'s broom closet. At least this box was bigger. Percy waited for the pins and needles to prick his skin. He tested each digit and limb before getting to his feet. He was stiff and sore and achy, but at least he could still move. He paced the length of his cell three times. He needed to keep fit. He needed to keep alert. He wasn't dying without a fight.

What had happened to Horris and the rest? Were they all right? They had to be, of course, they were, postmen were of no interest to Imperials. But the pirates…

A prayer sprung to his lips. Percy swallowed it back with some effort. They were all right. Between Fives' abilities and Roddy's skills, between Basah's practicality and Horris' insight, they were all right. They were probably detained at the depot, that was all…

He rubbed at the back of his neck, and when he did, his fingers brushed the chain of his pendant.

Percy stopped his pacing. He pulled the chain off his neck and held it against the cold fluorescent light.

The sight of the holy falling star filled him with fury. He closed his fist around the pendant and cocked his arm back, readying to chuck it through the bars of his cell. But that was all. As much as he wanted to throw it away, as tempting as it was, he just couldn't. Not when it was the last gift from Orestes. Percy sighed as he slipped the necklace back on.

When he looked up again, Orestes stood in front of him.

He looked exactly as he had in life: tall and gangly, holding himself like he didn't know what to do with his too-long limbs. He had the same narrow face and oversized nose. He still had curly brown hair and thick sideburns. His eyes were as blue and sad as ever when they found Percy. For a moment, they looked at each other. Just looked.

"Go away," Percy finally said. He scowled when Orestes just shrugged. "It's your fault we're in this mess, you know. If you hadn't questioned, then I wouldn't have looked. And if I hadn't looked, I'd still be at home. I'd be happy."

Orestes cocked an eyebrow. Without a word, he looked up, and Percy was compelled to follow his gaze.

A decent-sized spider crawled along the ceiling, heading for the bars. Black, eight-legged–that was all Percy could say for it. Horris would have known its proper name in an instant. Horris would have immediately shared some useless-but-fascinating fact about the arachnid and its world. *See? It's all still here*, is what Horris would have said. *They're just living their small lives.*

The thought filled him with a bizarre sort of comfort even now. Percy ran both hands through his hair before looking back down at Orestes. "Point taken," he muttered. Something in his heart gave way when Orestes smiled. Yes, he and Horris would have liked each other very much. "It should have been you, you know."

He turned away. It was easier to confess to the steel wall than to the ghost. "It should have been you. *You* were the one who deserved to leave. You were the one who should have been on the *Silverfish*. You would have loved it out there, Orry. You would have found good people—"

"Who are you talking to?"

Percy spun back around. Orestes had vanished. Electra stood on the other side of the bars with fists clenched. "Your brother," he replied.

Electra jerked as if struck. "You've gone mad."

"Possibly." He scratched his patchy beard and shrugged. A spiteful sort of calm seized him. If Electra was here seeking answers, she would find them. And he doubted she would like any of them.

Sure enough, her next words were: "Why did you run?"

"Because I couldn't fight for something I didn't believe in anymore. War isn't what they promised." He stepped closer as she looked away. "But perhaps you're beginning to discover that for yourself. Why are *you* out here, Electra?"

The use of her name snapped her face back towards him. Perhaps she thought he didn't know it, or hadn't remembered. Her eyes were the same shade of blue as her brother's. "Liaison Nabis sent us to retrieve you. He didn't trust the pirates to do it."

"So why hire them in the first place? Why not just let one Hammer go?"

"Because—"

"Because they're afraid of what one rogue Hammer would say? They're afraid of what I would tell the star system about His Holiness?"

"Because you need to be punished!" Electra snapped. "You're not supposed to run from your duty! You are–you are *supposed* to be the Red Hammer! You killed scores of Idolers! You're supposed to be a hero!"

"*Orestes was the hero!*" Percy crossed to the bars. He continued as Electra shook her head: "He saved my life, he protected the children, *he* was the hero! And he got nothing! Nothing save scorn!"

Electra shook her head faster as if that would dislodge his words somehow. "He was an idiot! He was a traitor!"

"Orestes was the only one who saw clearly!" And he hadn't even been a reinforcer to do it. He'd figured it out on his own. Percy didn't know if Orestes was there or if Orestes could hear him, but it didn't matter. What mattered was convincing Electra. "He knew there was more to living than dying for the Emperor."

"No, there isn't. This life is temporary. The eternal life afterward is the only one that matters."

"It's not! There is so much out here, Electra; there is so much more than what we were taught! Did you know that bees can dance?"

He didn't know why he said it, but he did. Perhaps because it was his favorite fact of everything Horris had told him. Electra looked at him as though he'd grown a second head. How could he make her understand? How could he make her see what he had seen? The words left him in a torrent:

"Did you know that aphids raise their young together and that asteroid fields are actually leagues apart? Did you know that adults can play games, too? Some of them are even strategic games—educational games—and they just play them for fun! Some people choose to leave their homeworlds and their cultures, and they're even happier for it. Did you know that you can dance with whoever you want to, and there are no rules against it? There are so many different sorts of people beyond Creed! I've met so many in two weeks alone—I met a man who can hear the universe singing!"

He was suddenly panting, gripping the iron bars for support as pain wracked his body.

How could he impress it upon her? The great crowds of people all living their own lives, and what it felt like to be among them, not having to worry whether they were the *right* sort of people? How could he make her feel what he felt, staring out into the vast emptiness of space–how infinitely, comfortingly small you were in the great expanse?

Electra just scoffed. "The Emperor can hear the universe singing."

"Can he?" Percy demanded. He rested his forehead against the bars. "Where is that written in the Word? The Emperor does not exist beyond Creed, Electra–*and that is all right*. Look. See that spider?"

The black spider had passed through the bars and now crawled on the wall beside Electra. She narrowed her eyes.

"We can't think like it, and it can't think like us. But that doesn't mean it's life isn't valuable to—"

Electra spun on her heel and smashed her fist into the spider.

"*NO!*"

His scream echoed down the corridor. The mangled spider fell to the floor when Electra drew her fist back. A smear of blue blood remained on the wall.

"Why—" His breath caught in his throat. "Why would you do that? It wasn't bothering you!"

"It was just a spider," Electra looked him up and down with disgust. "Grow up."

Percy slipped down to his knees. He didn't see Electra leave. All he had eyes for was the spider as it twitched in death throes. She had killed it. *He* had killed it. It hadn't even known it was doing anything wrong. Hot tears burned his eyes. He hadn't meant to—he had never meant to—

Orestes crouched down beside the dead spider and scooped it into his hands.

"I'm sorry," Percy whispered. He didn't know who the apology was meant for.

２５ The Scorpion
and the Silverfish

The United Star System Postal Code, Chapter 2, Section 2: The United Star System Postal Service takes no part in interstellar politics, and will be regarded as a fair and neutral entity by all political bodies.

Fast and maneuverable, no longer burdened by packages, the *Silverfish* sped through the stars at top speed. BLIP broadcast a USS scanner through the ship; the radio chatter between triangulated ships confirmed the *Scorpion* as it raced for the Creed bridge. The *Scorpion* moved at a good pace, but the *Silverfish* engine and its four thrusters had been designed for expedient deliveries. They were gaining. Bit by bit, they were gaining.

Horris watched the pinpricks of stars zip by. Despite the urgency, he couldn't help the thrill that went up his spine. Without the need to follow USSPS speed regulations or zig-zag between stops, the *Silverfish* had hit her top speed effortlessly, and outside the window, space had become blurs of light and color. Every once in a while, the ship shuddered as Roddy corrected course.

With some effort, Horris turned away from the window and descended into the engine pit.

Basah was there alone. She knelt on the floor with her head bowed, tracing her fingers across the floor to write invisible glyphs. Horris leaned against the wall, not interrupting as she murmured unintelligibly. After a few seconds, one of her ears flicked in his direction.

Basah twisted to frown at him. "What?"

"Are you...praying?" Horris eased up off the wall, trying not to sound incredulous as he did.

Basah's ears flattened. She rubbed at the back of her neck. "You know how the saying goes. No atheist in a black hole."

Horris didn't say anything. He just cocked his head to the side.

Basah lifted her shoulders and dropped them. As she did, the disaffected facade crumbled. "Maybe I figured I ought to hedge my bets. I doubt I'll be welcomed into the Moon Mother's silver halls. But..." she sighed, "turns out I remembered more of the prayers than I thought."

"How'd you feel about that?" Horris asked softly.

Basah made a face. "I don't know whether I want to be annoyed or relieved. Both? Both. Some part of me always manages to get back there, whether I want to or not. Still..." she traced her hand across the *Silverfish*'s floor. "The Moon Mother protects all women. And the *Silverfish* is a reliable lady. She deserves a place beside the Moon Mother." She was quiet for a moment. Then she cleared her throat and got to her feet. "Did you need something, Horry?"

"No. Just checking in. How're the engines running?"

"Clean and clear. The Exosuits are charged and fueled." The last was added even as Horris opened his mouth to ask.

"Thanks." Horris' eyes wandered to the poster Basah had slapped on the engine pit wall in their first week as postmen: *Through Rain, Sleet, and Snow, Bitches!* "Is there anything else you need from me right now?"

"Nah. Thanks for checking in, Horry."

"Thanks for all you do, Bah."

He found Fives next in Roddy's cabin. He sat cross-legged on Roddy's bunk and typed rapidly at the laptop on his lap. Like Basah, he muttered under his breath as he worked.

Fives' head shot up as Horris neared. "I'm not praying," he said flatly. "I'm asking for help."

Horris arched an eyebrow.

"There is a difference." Fives did a few quick strokes across his keyboard. "Mother will help us. I think. No," he added, as the question formed in Horris' mind. "You do not know who Mother is. That is preferable."

Horris blinked and thought his next question carefully.

"Might," Fives agreed. "Mother *might* help us. I don't know. I've never asked Her for anything before. So it's good to have our own plan." He flipped his laptop over to show Horris what he had been working on.

Horris had no idea what any of the lines of code meant, but he liked the gif of a cartoon dancing frog in the corner.

Fives smiled. "BLIPware. It's a worm. Worms aren't insects, so it doesn't match the theme. But they don't name malware after insects. Maybe they will when I'm done."

"You're going to use BLIP as a computer virus?"

BLIP is not a virus. BLIP is a malware worm.

"Okay. You're going to use BLIP as a malware worm," Horris said. He was caught between admiration at the audacity, the twelve different ways it could go wrong, and the conviction that Roddy could never, ever know BLIP could be used as malware. "How are you going to get them onto the *Scorpion*'s software?"

Subterfuge! BLIP chimed in excitedly.

Fives' smile thinned to something bitter. "People are stupid."

He spoke with such sudden conviction that Horris was compelled to sit down beside him. He didn't take it personally when Fives shied backward. "People are all we've got, you know."

Fives continued to stare at his laptop screen. "That's what you tell yourself. That's what you say so you don't get left behind again."

Just because Fives felt it didn't mean he had to say it out loud. Horris fought the surge of annoyance. "If Mother helps, what will she do?"

"Dunno. Never asked before." Fives tossed his head to get his black bangs out of his eyes. "But it was important to try. You taught me that."

Horris got to his feet with a silent thanks. Fives nodded once. His gaze never left his laptop.

Horris walked at a slow pace down the *Silverfish*'s corridor. She wasn't a very big ship, the *Silverfish*, and she was dreadfully utilitarian. Those who didn't know her would think her less than impressive. That was their mistake.

He pressed his forehead against the wall. Small vibrations from the engine rattled against his forehead. It almost felt like the rumbling purr of a living creature. Horris remained there for a long moment, trying to convey to the *Silverfish* how much he loved her and how he knew she could do what was going to be asked of her. There was no response, of course, and with a sigh, he pushed himself upright again.

Roddy was waiting for him in the cockpit. He looked up as Horris stepped down and took the co-pilot's chair.

Far in the distance, bright pinwheel arms burned through the dark. They weren't far from the bridge now. Which meant one of those points of light just ahead was the *Scorpion*. They were close now, very close.

Roddy shifted in his seat. Horris watched him squeeze blue putty between his fingers. "Looks like you're going to get your preferred bridge course after all," he said softly.

A corner of Roddy's mouth twitched upwards. He twisted the putty into his palm and rolled it into a ball. His eyes fixed on that distant spiral. "Hey."

"Hm?"

"Don't tell Bah I was afraid."

Horris grinned. "Never."

BLIP beeped overhead. Proximity to ship detected. The Silverfish is one thousand kilometers out from the ship.

Roddy confirmed BLIP's assessment on the radar. "That has to be the *Scorpion*."

Horris flicked on the intercom. "All hands, report to cockpit for…" he trailed off, not sure how to term what they were about to do. "Uh, extraction mission."

"Extraction mission," Roddy repeated. "I like it. Makes us sound like we're actually supposed to be doing this."

"Okay," Horris took a deep breath. He'd expected to feel afraid or, at the very least, jittery. But all he felt was calm. They had their plan. All they had to do was follow it. He could almost see the steps laid out before him, as simple as scanning and sorting the mail.

"Ready?" He asked Roddy.

"Nah. You?"

"No. Let's do this."

Basah and Fives joined them presently. Fives had a flash drive clenched in one hand and his orange headphones over his ears. Something loudly brassy blared loud enough for Horris to hear. "What're you listening to, Fiver?"

"William Tell," Fives replied as he took his seat. "It'll make us go faster."

Basah just shrugged when Horris looked to her for an explanation.

The *Silverfish* pierced through space at an accelerated clip. The chorus of her four thrusters rose from a hum to a roar. Over the course of an hour, the *Scorpion* grew from a distant blot to its proper massive size, almost twelve times the size of the *Silverfish*. Before long, the *Silverfish* cruised along her portside.

Even from a distance, Horris could see growing activity inside the ship. Good–they had the pirates' attention. "BLIP, signal the *Scorpion*."

As Horris spoke, Roddy began making mechanical adjustments to their speed and course. He didn't look up as a baffled Silver flashed onto their dashboard.

"Sami, set this down over there, thank you, darling—what the hell do *you* want?"

He scowled at Horris as the video call stabilized. Horris lifted his chin. "Captain Silver."

"Mailman Punk."

Horris' mouth felt as dry as the Brose Front, but somehow, he found the words he needed: "My name is Captain Jensen, and this vessel is the USSPS One-Thirty-One-C. We are here to formally request the return of stolen goods."

Silver cocked an eyebrow. "Pardon?"

"We are here to formally request the return of stolen goods," Horris repeated. The words came easier now. "In light of your attack on the Brose Front."

Silver slumped down in his captain's chair and crossed one leg over the other. "Let me guess. You want the runaway Hammer back."

"Yes."

A harsh bark of laughter served as Silver's reply. More jeers echoed just off-screen. "You've got balls, mailman, I'll give you that. What have you got in exchange for our meal ticket?"

Horris swallowed back the sudden rush of rage. It took every ounce of Customer Service Training to keep his voice level and polite. "In exchange, you will not face the full fury of the United Star System Postal Service."

This time, the laughter was full of howls. Silver leaned forward with a wide grin. "You do know you're alone in a Grummon, right, mailman? You can't be that stupid."

"The size of our vessel has nothing to do with this. We are representatives of the USSPS. Perseus Warden paid for delivery to Apollonia, and we intend to see that passage through to completion. You have attacked and pillaged a USSPS depot and stolen goods protected under interstellar law. This is your final warning to comply with authority, or face the consequences."

The tracking camera followed Silver as he got to his feet. "Look, mailman, this was cute for the first forty-five seconds. Now, I'm giving you a chance to turn your mail truck around before I blast you into that bridge."

He pointed off towards the swirling hole in reality. From here, Horris could just make out the vortex of space debris surrounding the bridge. He made a show of studying it before turning back to Silver.

"Fuck you," said Horris.

It felt good to say it out loud. It felt *really* good to watch all the smug condescension drain from Silver's face. His smile soured, and rage seeped through his next word: "Pardon?"

"I said, fuck you." Horris looked Silver up and down before wrinkling his nose, an additional act suggested by Roddy. "And your ugly ass coat."

Silver purpled. He struck an arm out, and with the gesture, the video feed cut.

The *Silverfish* crew exhaled a collective breath. A bit of the tension in the cockpit eased, even as the *Scorpion* began running out her broadsides. The massive swiveling cannon at her stern stirred.

"He fell for it," Basah said, almost in wonder.

"Yeah." Roddy's voice was grim as he yanked his seat into a prone position. The other seats followed suit. "BLIP, engage shield, set all systems to maximum efficiency." He glanced at Horris as the *Scorpion*'s stern cannon whirred and the *Silverfish*'s shield rippled across her frame. "Now?"

"Not yet. They have to strike us first for it to count."

"Well, let's not make it easy for them." With that, Roddy strapped on his goggles, seized the helm, and blasted off. "*Silverfish*, ENGAGE!"

The *Silverfish* shot off with a crack like thunder, just dodging the first blast of cannonade from the *Scorpion*. She darted forward and careened to the right, dancing almost tauntingly at the *Scorpion*'s bow.

The *Scorpion* roared in response, and Roddy yanked the *Silverfish* vertical as crackling blue energy exploded across the *Scorpion*'s bow.

The *Silverfish* climbed now, rising over the *Scorpion*, leaving herself vulnerable to another blast. Sure enough, the *Silverfish* rocked as a second shot connected with her stern. The dashboard flashed orange and yellow, and bleeps of warning filled the cockpit.

Shield integrity 91%.

"Now?" Basah demanded.

"Now!" Horris agreed. He flicked a switch on the dashboard, watching the indicator light flash three times to indicate a connection. "This is Captain Horris of the One-Thirty-One-C! We are currently under attack in the Third Quadrant of Sector Eight, near Bridge Creed-Locar! Coordinates are—"

He rattled off the coordinates as the *Silverfish* ducked and wheeled and dived around the larger, more cumbersome *Scorpion*. The *Scorpion* fired haphazardly as the smaller *Silverfish* danced from spot to spot. She stayed atop of the *Scorpion*, out of reach of her broadsides. The stern cannon had a tell-tale whir as its windup, and Roddy timed each swing of the *Silverfish* like a last-second jerk from the jaws of death.

The Elentee whooped, and a similar laugh bubbled out of Horris' chest. Blood swooped through his ears with each wild swing of the *Silverfish*, and it felt as though his heart bounced freely in his rib cage. It lent him a sort of dizzy giddiness as they soared through space. The cacophony of the chase blended into a strange chorus: the cracks of gunfire, BLIP rattling off data on their shield, Basah demanding data on the engines while Roddy laughed and Fives muttered under his breath.

"I think you pissed him off enough!" Horris called over the din. "Ready?"

"READY!"

Roddy adjusted course, and the *Silverfish* went into an abrupt dive towards the bridge. The force of their acceleration shoved them all against their seats. Basah yelped as air popped into her ears. Fives shot her one worried look before unbuckling himself. He dropped onto the floor and crawled forward to seize Roddy's wrist.

"FIRE STARBOARD!" Fives bellowed.

Roddy pulled port, hard, and the *Scorpion*'s next shot shattered against distant debris. Horris gaped at Fives. How had he done that? How could he hear Silver's orders without Percy present as a conduit?

That was the least of his worries, though, as the *Silverfish* careened into the bridge's event horizon at 600,000 kph. The vast, swirling bridge loomed over *Silverfish* and *Scorpion* both, threatening to pull both into its storming mouth along with the debris flinging wildly around it. Satellites and abandoned ships wheeled through space alongside organic matter: comets endlessly chasing their tails, asteroids pried loose from their orbits, stardust, and gasses released from remnant stars.

An almost-sentient scream rose from the mouth of the bridge, and streaks of yellow and red flashed from within like lightning.

The *Silverfish* tucked her wings into her body as she wheeled through space trash. Then she switched course, jettisoning upwards at ninety degrees as the *Scorpion* burst into the debris field behind her. Ugly screeches filled the vacuum of space as the *Scorpion*'s hull rammed through chunks of dead ships, brute forcing through what the *Silverfish* could dodge.

Sweat trickled down Roddy's face even as he grinned. "I got it from here, Fiver." He waited for Fives to slide back into his seat before jamming a few buttons on the dashboard. "Do you all wanna do something cool?!"

"Temperature has nothing to do with it." "NO!" "Rod, what are you—"

Horris almost swallowed his tongue as Roddy yanked them out of their vertical climb–upside down, speeding backward towards the *Scorpion*. All the blood rushed to Horris' head as Basah screamed bloody murder, and Fives made a strange noise between terror and thrill. Roddy hollered wordlessly as the upended *Silverfish* banked another round of fire. With a sharp jerk, she passed into the narrow space between an asteroid and an engine and pierced through the lingering trail of a comet.

"ROD, RIGHT THE SHIP! RIGHT THE SHIP OR I SWEAR ON THE MATRONS I'M GOING TO FUCKING KILL YOU–!"

The *Silverfish* spun a full one-eighty, right side up once more, and as she did, a sharp BANG sounded from below. A sickly sweet smell filled the air, and the entire ship shuddered and slowed. Roddy swore and tucked the *Silverfish* into a nosedive, relying on the bridge's gravity to help her keep pace.

Basah beat the air black and blue with her curses. "Rod! You blew the engines, you complete—Horris, with me!" She was out of her seat and sprinting for the ladder without waiting for a response.

Horris raced after her. He stumbled a bit as a shot from the *Scorpion* rattled the whole ship.

Shield integrity 78%.

"KEEP HER OFF OUR TAIL, ROD!" Horris called.

"WHAT DO YOU THINK I'M DOING?!"

Horris didn't have the breath to reply as he slid down the ladder and into the engine pit.

Here, the strange, sweet smell was stronger, and the air in the engine pit shimmered with heat. Green liquid pooled on the floor in front of the engine. Basah tracked through it as she yanked on a pair of gloves. Hot steam burst from the side of the engine as she twisted knobs and opened valves. The engine hissed, and Basah echoed it as she stepped back. "He blew the IEHS! I'm going to kill him—Hor, get me a bottle of coolant and the block sealant from the locker, third shelf!"

Horris hastened to obey. He flung open the locker, seized both bottles and sprinted back to Basah. She had yanked her jumper over her nose and mouth as her hands flew across the engine, working it on the fly as another shot shook the *Silverfish*.

"BLIP, raise *Silverfish*'s internal temp by four degrees!"

Caution: all sentients aboard will be sweaty.

"DO IT, BLIP!" Horris bellowed. He passed the sealant to Basah. "Is it fixable?"

"Everything is fixable, but not quickly—I can slap something together, just *help me*—"

BOOM!

Another blast, another shudder. Shield integrity 68%.

Horris pulled on a pair of gloves and dove to help. Together, they released what built-up heat they could from values and exhausts and got the sealant poured. The excess heat seared through their lungs, leaving them breathless and sweaty as they worked. Basah muttered under her breath the entire time, though Horris didn't know if she was praying to the Moon Mother or cussing Roddy out.

All at once, something above stopped beeping. Horris and Basah both staggered as the *Silverfish* jolted forward and from the cockpit, Roddy crowed in triumph.

Basah exhaled even as she added more coolant to the thirsty engine. "Atta girl."

"Bah, I could kiss you," Horris said. He grinned when she snorted.

With the coolant topped off, they sprinted back to the cockpit. They flung themselves back into the seats as Roddy pulled them out of their nosedive. The *Silverfish* narrowly missed a massive chunk of space debris coming for them—

—and suddenly, blue lightning shot clean across their bow. The *Scorpion* loomed over the *Silverfish*, too near to veer away from. Horris swallowed hard as the *Scorpion*'s shadow fell across the cockpit. He fought the urge to look at his distress signal readout.

Call incoming.

Roddy swore under his breath. Basah closed her eyes. Fives just stared straight forward at the bridge. Black blood dripped from his nose. Horris wiped a sheen of sweat from his brow. "Onscreen, BLIP."

Silver smirked as he popped back onto the screen. "Well, I must commend you lot. Those were some entertaining little flips and dips you did just now. Hell, for that, I might even keep your pilot alive. Now–this is your last chance to surrender."

"No," Horris said, fully aware of how small they were, how alone in the expanse of the universe.

"Your funeral." Silver shrugged. Once more, the stern cannon whirred to life, aiming dead center at the *Silverfish*. "One…"

Horris dug his nails into his palms.

"Two…"

Please. Please. Anyone–please–

Fives jerked his head up. "They're coming."

"Thr—"

The crackle of the radio cut Silver short. A male voice sounded over both their communications: "USSPS One-Thirty-One-C, this is USSPS Interceptor One-A. Distress signal received, aid dispatched to the immediate area."

Silver's smirk slipped as the wormhole churned and thundered, and from that ripped hole in reality came not one, not five, but *fifteen* USSPS Interceptors, each a war dog armed to the teeth. There was no preamble, no warning; they leapt on the *Scorpion* like bees on a hive intruder.

The *Scorpion*'s stern cannon spun and fired wildly as the Interceptors' guns blasted her hull and bow. They zipped around the *Scorpion*, small and maneuverable like the *Silverfish* but with all the cannonade needed to mount a proper defense. The *Silverfish* herself was suddenly forgotten, left to maneuver amid the debris without issue.

Horris didn't know whether he wanted to vomit or kiss someone. As it was, he wiped a few tears away with a shaking hand.

"I can't believe that worked!" Basah exclaimed. She was gasping as though suddenly remembering she was supposed to be breathing.

"USSPS Code, Chapter Eleven, Section Five. Postal Inspectors are required to answer all carrier distress calls in a timely fashion." A laugh bubbled up out of Horris' chest. "Good work, everyone!"

"Don't thank us yet." Roddy swung the *Silverfish* around as he spoke. "We still have to get Red out of there."

Together, they watched the intensifying firefight. An Interceptor dove at the *Scorpion*, setting her exterior deck aflame, and spun out of the way of returning fire. Horris studied the burning *Scorpion* grimly. Somehow, outlasting the *Scorpion* had been the easier of their two tasks.

"Phase Two. Everyone, suit up."

26 Open Hands

United Star System Postal Code, Chapter 11, Section 5: Postal Inspectors are required to answer all carrier distress calls in a timely fashion.

"C'mon, do somethin'."

Percy remained still as a paper triangle bounced off his forehead. He sat cross-legged on his cell floor with hands resting in his lap. He took another calming breath as another folded triangle hit him.

A brutish, scarred Gundobad paced back and forth in front of his cell. His burning yellow eyes never left Percy. "I thought them Creeds was all killers? I want to see one fight!"

The human beside him shrugged and adjusted his grip on his weapon. "He's a Hammer, Drex. He's not a berserker."

Drex leaned against the bars. "I saw the way he was fightin' them other Hammers. Like a man possessed. You woulda killed them all if the Captain hadn't been there."

Percy kept his eyes fixed on his palms. He had never invested much time in meditation, but now it was all he had. Drex was nothing more than another rumble in his ears, no more worth his notice than the distant chugging engine. He was dimly aware of Orestes leaning against the wall beside him with arms folded over his chest.

"Saw that girl you were fightin' leave the brig. Saw her tryin' not to cry her eyes out. That your girlie, Hammer? I can comfort her if you want; make her less lonely after they take your head."

His concentration shattered. Percy shot his gaze up to glare daggers at Drex. An implacable, almost foreign rage filled him. He looked to his left to see Orestes glaring at the pirate. It was strange to see him angry. Perhaps this outside world affected even ghosts.

"When I get out of here," Percy said aloud to Orestes, "I'm going to kill him first." He smirked when he heard the heavy slam of fists against bars.

"Say that without the bars between us, you little—"

Whoop-whoop, whoop-whoop!

All heads jerked up as the brig lights flashed yellow. Silver's voice boomed over the intercom: "Look lively, crew! We've got a Grummon that thinks she can match us! All hands to combat stations—let's earn ourselves some fireworks!"

A Grummon? A *Grummon*? But that could only have been—No. No. No. They wouldn't have. They couldn't—they shouldn't—*those dumb motherfuckers!*

The two pirates were distracted, and Percy took the moment to rise to his feet. He slid his belt out from around his waist and wrapped one end around his palm.

"Can't go a minute without something," the human said. "Drex, stay here, and for the love of the gods, don't antagonize him." He left the brig as the engine suddenly roared, and the whir of cannonade rose in the distance. The ship tilted, and Drex instinctively leaned back towards the bars to keep his balance—

Percy's legs burned as he launched himself against the bars. In one quick motion, he slid his belt through the bar and around Drex's neck. He held fast as Drex choked and tried to flail forward. When that failed, he slammed his back against the bars, trying to knock Percy loose.

Percy grit his teeth and ducked his head into his elbow, letting his arm take the brunt of the jarring impact. Pain radiated up his left arm, but still, he held fast, focusing on Drex's mounting desperation and not the ringing in his head. Liquid fire seared his muscles, and the white-hot pain almost made him drop. Not yet–Drex first–

And drop he did, all at once. Percy relinquished his grip on the belt, hissing at the purple-red indents in his hands. His head still swam, and his left arm tingled with fresh pain. Percy forced the sensation to the back of his head as he knelt. He stuck his hand through the bars, fishing into Drex's pockets for anything useful. Gum, paperclip–keycard!

His head swam as he got back to his feet. Percy paused. He had to take a moment to breathe and assess. No amount of raw violence was going to get him out of here. He took several gulping breaths as he massaged his tingly arm.

Orestes side-eyed him before looking down at Drex.

"I didn't kill him," Percy snapped, irritated by the ghost's judgment. "But I should have."

He keyed himself out of the cell and stepped out into the brig proper. The other cells in this block were empty, and by the sliding door, a terminal beeped. The *Scorpion* listed again, this time to the right, and Percy stumbled as he made for the terminal.

Drex's keycard gave him access to emails, pay stubs, and work schedules...but what about a map? He needed a map! How was he going to get out of here without a map?

All around him, the *Scorpion* groaned. Silver was back shouting orders over the intercom, demanding his gunners to fire and hit the "goddamn little ship." Percy's heart leaped into his throat. He couldn't think about the *Silverfish*, tiny and utilitarian, trying to outgun the *Scorpion*. Horris wouldn't have raced here without a plan–right?

Focus!

Percy's chest constricted, and his palms were itchy with sweat as he tore through the terminal's documents in search of a map. He finally found one in the employee information folder. The brig was on the lowest level, amid a bunch of utility rooms and corridors. The bay was on the second level, and the bridge was on the first. Could he take on the bridge and try to wrest control of the entire ship? What other choice did he have? His head pounded, and Percy tried to blame it on collision with the cell bars.

The hiss of the sliding door had him wrenching upright. The human stopped short on the threshold, and for a split-second, they stared at each other. Percy reacted first, tackling the human to the floor. He slammed his elbow into the human's stomach before rearing back and punching him in the face. The human went limp beneath him.

Percy shook his hand out with a small hiss. He yanked the human's sheathed knife free and buckled it around his own waist. Their leather armor was too large, but he took their keycard in any case. He got back to his feet and darted out of the brig.

There were two more pirates coming down the hall, and both yelled a warning when they spotted him. Percy dropped to a knee as they rushed forward. He slammed his fist into one's stomach before springing back to his feet, spinning around the wheezing pirate so that he took the next blow from his partner. The second pirate jumped back with an apology. Percy shoved the retching pirate aside and slammed his knee into the groin of the apologizing one.

He didn't wait as the second pirate dropped; he just pivoted and sprinted down the hall.

The world became a blur of gray corridors and violence. Percy sprinted across the lowest deck, flinging himself at any pirate who tried to stop him. The stolen knife slid in and out of armor, and the hilt served as a blunt weapon of sorts as he dropped pirates around him. He lost what little sense of the map he had had, and pure instinct set in as he barreled forward. At some point, he found himself in a knot of pirates, twirling to avoid their blows as years of training took over. He slashed at one, kicked another clear across the face, and stabbed the other through their armor. One by one, they dropped, and when the next door slid open, Percy wrenched his knife free, spun on his heel, and flung it towards the door.

It landed quivering on the wall beside Horris' head. Horris stopped short on the threshold. "*Whoa!*"

Percy froze. "Emperor's hand–Horris?! What are you doing here?!"

"We're here to rescue you!" Horris exclaimed. He peered over Percy's shoulder at the line of injured and unconscious pirates. "Oh, wow. You did all that?"

Percy didn't reply. He was too busy staring at Horris dumbfounded. Of all the asinine–irresponsible–unbelievable–

"I'm not in need of rescuing, you *complete*–!"

"Found him," Fives declared as he squeezed past Horris. He gave Percy a vague wave before his attention fixed on the knife in the wall.

"How did you find me?" Percy demanded. His head reeled from the sudden shift in fortune. He crossed to Horris and took him by the arm to convince himself that this was real. Yes, Horris was flesh and muscle and bone under his vice grip. Yes–he was really here, really real, and in his awe, Percy almost missed Horris' explanation:

"Fives tracked you down. Apparently, you're—"

"Quiet in the chaos." Fives studied the knife as he yanked it free. "A growing blanket of silence that mutes the noise. Like playing hot-cold." He held the knife out to Percy, who sheathed it.

Horris touched a hand to Percy's forehead. "You're bleeding."

"I am?" Percy followed his touch and frowned when his fingertips came away bloody. "Oh."

"Let's get back to the *Silverfish*, quickly—" Horris poked his head into the room he'd just come from. "Found him!"

Percy gaped as Basah and Roddy both spilled into view. Roddy had his pilot goggles still attached to his head, and Basah wore a strange-looking backpack. Both greeted him with a cry of hello, and Percy was too stunned to react when Basah pulled him into a one-armed hug. "What–but–if you're all here, *who's piloting the bloody Silverfish?*!"

"BLIP," Roddy shrugged as Percy turned to him. "I didn't want to miss this. Did you do all that?" He pointed down the corridor at Percy's passage of violence.

A massive BOOM sent them all staggering, and for the first time, Percy caught a whiff of smoke. Silver's bellowed orders had gone silent for the moment. There was a tell-tale groan of bending metal, followed by a distant screech of gears.

"*What,*" Percy said as dust sprinkled down, "*did you all do.*"

Basah grabbed his wrist, and he didn't resist when she tugged him along. "We'll explain as we go. C'mon, run!"

They took off at a run. Percy could hardly believe it. They had come back for him. They had taken on the *Scorpion* for him. "How did you get on board?"

Roddy tapped his chest, and for the first time, Percy realized each postie wore a helmless Exosuit. "The inspectors started blowing holes in the Scorpion's hull. We jumped through the MHD field and right in!"

"Ant nest beetles," Horris interjected with glee. "They just walk right into ant colonies, and they aren't attacked!"

Another boom burst sent the *Scorpion* rolling to the right. Percy cursed as he slipped, shoulder jarring against the wall. "The inspectors? You've got postal inspectors blowing this ship to pieces?!"

"Oh, it wasn't hard. Postal inspectors are sworn by oath to respond to any USSPS vessel under duress. All Silver had to do was not open fire. And we goaded him into firing." Horris shrugged as though this were the simplest thing in the world. He gestured to Basah, who hoisted her backpack a little higher. "We're going to have to jump back out again. We have an Exosuit for you, too."

Percy stopped short. "You're mad! You're all insane!"

"And thank goodness for that, or else we wouldn't have gone after you!" Basah snapped.

Together, they rounded the next corner. Fives pointed to the terminal by the door. "I need to use that."

"Here." Percy fished Drex's keycard out of his pocket. "What are you doing?"

He followed Fives to the terminal as the phrenic keyed in and began to type away. He jammed a flash drive into one of the ports. "Giving the *Scorpion* a tapeworm."

"Well, now, that's just adding insult to injury." Percy glanced at the others, who each shrugged. "What, exactly, is giving the *Scorpion* a tapeworm meant to accomplish?"

"Something funny." Fives stroked the keys a few times, opened a program, and let it run. "All right, BLIP is in."

"BLIP is here too?"

Fives shushed him as the program reached 100%. A flashing thumbs-up appeared on the terminal screen, followed immediately by a gif of a laughing devil. Everything Fives had opened suddenly force-quit. The placid default desktop filled Percy with an ominous feeling.

Fives cracked his neck as he turned back to the group. "All right. I'm ready to go."

"Okay." Horris nodded towards the door. "We're not too far from where we came in; we just need to get through another service hallway and then–"

"TRAITOR!"

The shout froze everyone in their tracks. Electra stood at the other end of the hallway. Sparta stood beside her, and more Hammers crowded the corridor behind her. Percy's heart broke anew at the sight of her. Her eyes were the same color as Orestes but so much *angrier*, and she scowled when their eyes met. Then, her gaze shifted to Horris. Her staff was in her hand, and she aimed the end straight at the postman.

"Nabis wants Warden alive. Kill the others."

"DON'T YOU DARE!"

Percy's roar took everyone off-guard, himself included. He found himself standing in front of Horris with a knife drawn. The younger Hammers had frozen. Still wary of him, perhaps, or too well-trained to ignore the bark of an older Hammer. But the stupefaction would not buy them time. There was only one way Percy could think to reach them.

"Listen to me–*LISTEN*!" He raised his voice over Electra as she began to speak, startling her back into silence. "You all know who I am, what I can do. The only thing you have against me is numbers, and numbers are no good in a corridor like this. If you try to hurt these postmen, I will kill each and every one of you."

Horris made a noise of protest, but someone else hushed him.

"Then we will do so gladly!" Sparta exclaimed. "In the name of the Emperor!" The others took up the rousing cry, and the remains of Percy's heart ached.

"No," he said. "No, you are not meant to die here. That is not a fate you must assign yourself. If not for my sake, then your loved ones, your families. They would not want you to die here, between pirates and postmen. They would want you to live–Sparta!"

Sparta jumped as she was singled out.

"I've met Liaison Anaxandros. Your father. I know what future he wants for you, and it's not your death. He wants you to marry, have a family, be happy. And he can't be the only one!" Percy looked at each young Hammer in turn now, wondering how effective this speech was against children raised away from their families. He understood, now, why it was done. "*Please*," he said, softer now. "Please. *Go home.* You don't need to die here. Tell them I was killed in action. Tell them I died. I don't care what you tell them, just—don't die *here*."

A heavy moment of silence followed, broken only by the distant sounds of fighting.

"Nabis will know if we lie to him," Sparta said. Her voice shook. "Nabis will know."

"Nabis is not as omniscient as you think he is."

Electra scowled and took two steps forward. Percy raised his knife, already loathing himself for doing so.

BEEP-BOOP-BEEP! BLIP HAS SEIZED THE BRIDGE.

Chaotic, high-energy jazz blasted from the intercoms. Another boom followed, and then the world went topsy-turvy as the entire ship banked hard. Floor was wall, wall was floor, and everyone was suddenly tumbling ass-over-end. Percy flung his arms over his head to protect himself as he collided with a solid surface.

He surged to his feet as the world stopped spinning. He was now standing on the wall with a crumbled Roddy at his feet. Roddy hissed as Percy helped him stand. Blood trickled over his goggles from a new gash on his forehead. Then Horris was beside him, taking Roddy's other hand. Together, they got him through the door as Basah and Fives jumped down through it.

Percy looked back. The last he saw of Electra was her helping Sparta back to her feet. Their eyes met. And then Percy jumped through the door.

It slid shut above him. Basah stood up from the sparking control panel at their feet. "BLIP! BE CAREFUL!"

"Your program has gone mad with power, Fiver." Roddy winced as he wiped more blood from his forehead.

"Yeah." Fives mirrored the action, touching a hand to the same spot on his forehead. "I know."

Horris handed Roddy a handkerchief. "At least they bought us some time. Bah, backpack. Are you all right?"

Percy didn't realize Horris was addressing him until he touched his shoulder. He jumped a bit at the contact. "Yes, why?"

"That was really brave, what you just did."

"That was common sense." Percy looked up at the sealed door above them. "Hopefully, they have it."

Basah, meanwhile, was already shrugging off her backpack. Out came the Exosuit. Without a word, she and Horris helped Percy dress in the Exosuit. Fives tore Horris' handkerchief into strips to wrap around Roddy's head.

"Do you remember how to use the boosters?" Basah asked.

"Engager here, don't rely on it for long range."

"Good," said Horris. "If you miss the jump, don't panic. One of us will catch you."

"Just, y'know, try not to miss." Roddy grinned as he slipped his helmet on.

"Everyone—"

Percy didn't know what possessed him to speak, but his throat closed over as the readying crew all paused to look at him. His heart swelled with a thousand sentiments, but the only thing that rose out of his swollen throat was: "Thank you."

The crew exchanged looks. Roddy nudged Horris, who cleared his throat. "You don't have to thank us. You're one of us, Red."

With that, they started for the next door. Here, the sound of cracking gunfire and roaring engineers was louder. There were other, softer sounds, too, like the faint hiss of air and rumbling thunder that had Percy's hair standing on end.

Torn, twisted metal indicated the hole blasted through the hull just ahead. Percy frowned. "Why aren't we being sucked into the vacuum of space?"

"MHD field," Basah answered as she led the way. "All larger ships like these have them. But it's failing. Hear that hissing noise? That's the atmosphere leaking out. Just breathe slowly through your tubes, and you should be okay."

Percy stepped up to the breached hull. The immediate space around the Scorpion had a slight waver to it–that must have been the field–but beyond that was nothing short of hell. Debris and dead ships circled a thundering, multicolored wormhole. Silver bullets of ships shot past in dizzying runs, dodging crackling energy bursts from the *Scorpion* and returning fire. Bile rose in Percy's throat, and that ancient, screaming instinct held him back from the edge.

Horris tapped a finger on his radio. "Bring her in, BLIP."

The *Silverfish*, gray and inconspicuous amid the more graceful ships, soared into view. She hovered just outside of the MHD field, keeping pace with the *Scorpion* as the larger ship barrelled forward.

Basah shooed Percy away from the edge. She and Roddy exchanged nods, backed up, and took off at a run. Together, they leaped through the breach and dove through space. Percy watched them twist mid-leap, magnetic boots aimed at the *Silverfish*'s hull. They landed, and when they did, Percy heard Horris sigh in relief.

He gave Horris a sidelong look. "This is the safest exit you could find?"

"No. But it's the fastest."

"I still think you're mad."

"I can live with that. Besides, you're one of us now." Horris grinned, and Percy couldn't help but return it.

Fives coughed from behind them. He looked between the two with eyebrows arched. "I'd like to leave now."

"Right, right, sorry, Fiver." Horris stepped back and gestured to the breach. "Perce, you and Fives are up."

"What about you?"

"Captain brings up the rear. I'll be right behind you."

Percy didn't like it, but there was no room to argue. He took a few steps back beside Fives. "Ready?"

Fives nodded.

No doubting or overthinking. Percy burst into a full sprint and leaped through the breach. There was the jolt of weightlessness, the gasp of air leaving his lungs, and then he was through the shield. Percy engaged his booster as he left the shield. The rush of terror and exhilaration pulled everything into a sharp focus as he flipped, aiming feet-down for the *Silverfish*.

Impact against the ship jarred his legs, and he stumbled. Roddy was there to steady him, and a few feet away, Basah did the same for Fives. He and Roddy exchanged wild grins, and he accepted the slap on the shoulder.

"Now what?" Percy asked. He looked up, scanning the looming *Scorpion* for Horris.

"We make for Apollonia, fast so no one can catch us. Rod, get the airlock open. Here comes Horris now."

Horris had taken the leap and was now soaring towards them. Percy's grin widened, and for the first time, hope bloomed in his chest. He relaxed his shoulders—

And just as Horris passed through the MHD field, an ear-piercing *crack* echoed across the stars. One of the postal ships swooped down, raining fire on the breached hull. Hull and shield both shattered, superheated metal and plasma exploding out into the debris field–

And the force of the explosion blasted Horris clear off his course, sending him spiraling out into the void of space.

"*HORRIS!*"

"PERCY, NO!"

Percy barely heard Fives' cry. Suddenly, he was sprinting the length of the *Silverfish*, launching himself off of the bow and diving into space. He engaged his boosters and shot off after Horris.

The world snapped into a strange, sudden clarity. All fear and doubt, even exhilaration, had been replaced by laser-focus calm. No–he was beyond even calm, driven only by his objective. It felt as though he had been training his whole life for this, as if each round of combat and training scenario had been meant exactly for this moment. He was hyper-aware of the universe around him, weaving between debris with reflexes he didn't know he had.

He could see Horris up ahead, struggling to regain control of his flight. A massive asteroid swung on its ellipses towards Horris, nearer, nearer—

Percy tucked his arms against his body and accelerated as best he could, trying to go faster, faster, faster!

Out of the corner of his eye, he saw movement. Something within the bridge was stirring, lightning streaking across phantom clouds, and once more, he saw that massive skeletal hand. It rose up with fingers splayed, palm out, reaching, reaching—

And finally, finally, *finally*, Perseus Warden understood what an open hand was for.

REACH!

He flung his arms out and tackled Horris by the midriff, flinging them both out of the way of the asteroid. "PERCY?!" Horris hollered. Blood splattered the interior of his helmet, and he gaped at Percy as they spun. "What are you doing?!"

"I don't know!" Percy replied. A ridiculous laugh bubbled out of him.

Horris burst out laughing, too. Together, they spun through space, crashing through the tail end of a comet as they tumbled without direction, clinging to each other as the only living things in this cosmic graveyard.

It was only as Percy's booster gave out that a larger USSPS ship flew past, and an inspector perched on her bow snatched them out of freefall.

Even as their boots hit solid metal, Percy did not let Horris go.

27 The Law of the Letter

United Star System Postal Code, Chapter 1, Section 1: Reliable, friendly service shall be the highest priority of the entirety of the United Star System Postal Service.

Awareness came in fits and bursts. Chief among them was the sharp, sterile smell of a hospital room. The pain followed. Everything hurt, in that dull way all recovering injuries did. The worst of the pain bloomed along the right side of his face, which felt stiffer and heavier than usual. None of these were encouraging signs. Horris groaned as he opened his eyes.

Sure enough, he was stuck in a hospital bed, with an IV in the back of his hand and crisp, impersonal bedsheets pulled to his chest. Horris winced as he raised both hands. He flexed his fingers and counted out all ten. Then he did it again, just to be absolutely sure. His mind seemed to be three steps behind his body.

"Feeling all right?"

Horris jumped at the deep, semi-familiar voice. He turned as best he was able.

Postmaster General David Kalani sat in the visitor chair beside the hospital bed. He set aside a magazine on tropical fish and sat forward. "Captain Jensen. It's good to see you awake."

Crap. Crap, crap, crap, crap, crap. Horris struggled into an upright position. "Sir—" his voice was little more than a wheeze "—Sir, I can explain—"

"I've no doubt you can. But drink first."

Horris accepted the small paper cup the Postmaster handed to him. He downed the crisp, cold ginger ale in one swallow. When he spoke again, his voice sounded marginally more his own: "Thank you."

"You're welcome." The Postmaster said, even as he studied Horris. He didn't seem angry, which somehow terrified Horris more.

"Where am I?" He asked.

"Emergency Health Services Satellite Q-Seven."

Horris closed his eyes to try to picture the address. "We're on the Two-Twenty-Two route. Orbiting Tay."

The Postmaster nodded. "Do you know why you're here?"

Horris touched a hand to the swathe of bandages covering the right side of his face. "Unplanned exposure to the forces of a bridge."

"Among other things. You rattled your head good there, Jensen, and nearly took your teeth out. As it was, you cut your cheek clean open." The Postmaster dragged a finger along the side of his own face to illustrate. "It'll scar." He must have taken pity when Horris swallowed hard because his finger drifted the scar bridging his own nose. "It's nothing to be ashamed of. Work in the post office long enough, and you'll have plenty of scars to talk about."

Horris tried to take refuge in the assurance, but it was impossible. Maybe a few weeks from now, after he'd had time to look at himself in the mirror... "How long have I been here?"

"Only a day." The Postmaster sat back and folded his hands on one knee. "Do you know why I'm here?"

Well. There was nothing else he could do to avoid it. Horris lowered his face away from his hand. "United Star System Postal

Code, Chapter Three, Section Seven. Whoever knowingly conveys any person acting as a private express is in direct violation of the United Star System Postal Service. We were transporting someone as private express."

"Among other offenses, including knowingly disobeying a direct order from a superior, abandoning your mail route, stealing a mailship from its locked position in a depot, allowing someone to masquerade as a member of the USSPS and have access to private mail…and then there was picking a fight with a pirate ship, which damaged seven out of fifteen USSPS Interceptors and one Grummon's engine." The Postmaster ticked off fingers as he spoke. He peered at Horris through his fingers. "You endangered a lot of lives, Captain Jensen."

Horris had shrank against his mattress as the list of charges was read. It was much, much harder to justify everything he'd done when it was laid out like that. He was going to have to get used to his scarred expression from a prison mirror.

"Now," the Postmaster lowered his hand, "what's your side of the story?"

The question jolted Horris out of his slide into self-pity. "Sir?"

"Jensen, I've pulled your performance reports as well as customer service reviews. You've consistently rated as friendly, professional, and courteous, with a passion for your job. Your excellent recall of USSPS history and law suggests you have regard for both. So, if an employee with such a strong record throws everything away…I have to wonder *why*."

He studied Horris with that same piercing, soul-searching look from before. And this time, Horris knew there was no couching his reasons in the language of the post office. When he spoke, his voice was low:

"If we had turned around and taken him back to Creed, they would have killed him. If we'd surrendered him to Silver, the Idolers, or the inspectors, he would have been taken back to Creed. And they would have killed him. We couldn't. I couldn't. I know the code, but…Percy was right there in front of us, asking for our help. I couldn't put the code above his life. I didn't want to put that blood on my hands. So we agreed to help, and I had to come up with lie after lie...until it all blew up in our face."

"You do realize that by aiding and abetting a fugitive, you put other lives at risk. Silver wouldn't have attacked the Brose Front if Perseus Warden hadn't been there."

An unpleasant lurch soured Horris' stomach. Still, he nodded.

"Not to mention, you couldn't guarantee that cockamamie scheme of yours at the bridge would actually *work*."

"No. But the laws of the postal service and nature were on our side, sir. Silverfish are faster than scorpions, and inspectors are required to answer a mayday from a postal ship in distress."

The Postmaster snorted. For some reason, he still wasn't angry. "The fault is mine, I suppose."

What? How did the Postmaster General factor into any of this mess? Horris looked at him questioningly, waiting for him to elaborate.

"You didn't really think Estelle would leave Warden out of her explanation of events on Delta Io, did you?" The Postmaster shook his head. "But she vouched for you and told us that you had done everything in your power and then some to protect her people and your fellow postman. She told us that she regretted forcing your crew's hand when the BOLO went out on Warden. You had done the best you could in a bad situation, and because of you, everyone had walked away alive."

A pleasant, warm feeling blossomed in Horris' chest. That was one hell of a review. But...even so...

"So, you knew about Percy? All the way back when we stopped at the F-Two? Why didn't you say anything then? Why didn't you *do* anything?"

"Well, Warden was already out of the box, so to speak. And you were correct in your calculation—returning him to Creed would have killed him. I did not want that blood on my hands, no more than you did. Better, I thought, to look the other way, just this once, for a crew that consistently excelled at their job. I didn't anticipate Silver tracking you down…nor the Imperial Creeds taking their own initiative. And for that, I apologize. For putting you, Percy, and your crew in harm's way—I apologize."

Horris had no idea what to do with a direct apology from the Postmaster General himself. He rested his head back on the pillow, trying to blame his spinning head on exhaustion. "What happens next? Where do we go from here?"

"An excellent question." The Postmaster leaned forward. "We've had a very busy thirty-six hours while you recuperated. I'll try to go in order of importance. First, the Imperial Creeds have pulled their BOLO on Perseus Warden. He is no longer a wanted man." He smiled when Horris started. "A cohort of Black Hammers was arrested aboard the *Scorpion*. The BOLO was pulled shortly after they were extradited back to Creed. "

"What happened?"

"Internally? I'm not sure. However, the Emperor received a firm reminder that the USSPS is a neutral entity, and the presence of his personal army on a ship attacking postmen was in direct violation of that neutrality. It's not a good look, especially for a planet that already struggles with interstellar politics. The Emperor may be a god to his people, but even he is not above the laws of the United Star System."

The finality with which the Postmaster spoke filled Horris with disquiet. He thought of the Emperor he'd built up in his head, the Emperor that haunted Percy so. That god—that man—was not some-one who would take a "no" magnanimously. But the Emperor was grounded on Creed, half a galaxy away, and there was nothing a mere postman like him could do. So Horris tried to put the Imperials out of mind.

"What about Silver?" He asked instead. "And his crew?"

"All arrested, and much of their plunder recovered, thanks to you and yours."

"Thanks to my crew," Horris emphasized. "They were amazing. I couldn't have done it without them. Whatever repercussions are coming, please, sir, let it land on me. They just followed my orders—"

The Postmaster held up a hand to stop him short. "They told me you'd say that. And I'm very sorry to tell you that your crew was adamant that I ignore you, and include them in whatever the consequences were."

Annoyance came first, and was abruptly swept away by overwhelming gratitude. Horris wiped the corners of his eyes with his bedsheet. "So," he asked, voice nearly cracking, "what will the consequences be?"

The Postmaster had gone back to looking at the tropical fish magazine for the moment, perhaps to give Horris time to compose himself. "Inspector Rofon and I have been in talks. You're not fired—but you are grounded. You and your crew will be grounded on the Brose Front for one hundred and twenty days–"

"One hundred and twenty days?!"

"Should I make it one hundred and fifty?"

Horris ground his teeth and tried not to stew. They had earned this grounding, and they weren't fired. Bright side, bright side, always look for the bright side…

The Postmaster was visibly amused by his frustration. "It will go by quickly. And you may even learn something valuable in the meantime. The *Silverfish* crew has a unique penchant for finding trouble. Keep your eyes and ears open on the Front, Jensen."

"Sir?" The order was like a full jolt to his system. "Do you expect trouble on the Front?"

"Did I say that?" The Postmaster got to his feet and stretched. "Take the day to rest, Jensen. You'll finish your run to Apollonia tomorrow."

Horris cleared his throat as the Postmaster turned away. There was one last matter on his mind, and he had to voice it before he lost his courage. He waited until the Postmaster met his eyes. "Fives has something to do with it, doesn't he, sir?"

The Postmaster paused. He tucked his thumbs into the pockets of his khakis. "What do you mean by that?"

"Fives isn't loyal to the post office; he's loyal to the *Silverfish*. He'd follow us if you fired us, no matter what you offered him. And the USSPS wouldn't want to lose their phrenic."

For a long moment, the Postmaster just looked at him. The ghost of a smile lifted his mustache. "You're starting to sound like management, Jensen. Rest well."

He must have, because the next thing he knew, soft whispering stirred him awake. Horris opened his eyes once more to blink blearily at his crew.

Basah and Roddy sat on either side of him. Fives had taken the visitor chair with tablet in hand and knees drawn up to his chest. And Percy leaned against the wall with arms crossed.

"Hey," he said hoarsely. He and Roddy exchanged lazy grins. "All good?"

"All good," Basah answered. She took his hand in hers and squeezed.

Horris squeezed back. "We're not fired."

"Nope."

"Looks like we got more shore leave on the Front."

Basah laughed under her breath. "Yeah, Rod is thrilled."

"Fives is building us a one-hundred-and-twenty-day itinerary as we speak," Roddy said, nodding to indicate Fives.

"No." Fives' eyes flicked up over his tablet. "I'm watching murder confession videos."

Roddy rolled his eyes with utmost fondness. Basah snorted.

Horris looked past them to the silent Percy. They locked eyes before Percy's gaze flicked away. Horris was too tired to wonder why. He was just happy to have everyone here, safe. Together. "You're a free man now, Perce."

Percy started as though Horris had drawn him out of his thoughts. "Indeed. You have clearance to bring me to Apollonia. You'll be able to finish your route after all."

"USSPS customer service—"

"—best in the galaxy," Percy finished. He smiled. "So you've proven time and again, Horris."

28 Sign for Delivery

United Star System Postal Code, Chapter 1, Section 6: All oversized packages must be signed by the recipient or representative party, indicating the package was delivered in good condition and in a timely fashion.

Their destination was District 7 of the province of Kalikos, located on the centralized planet of Apollonia. District 7 was, by and large, a gray-hair community populated by former USS officials and other affluent retirees. It was a quiet, lushly green province: sentinel trees lined well-maintained roads, and flowering bushes formed a low wall all the way down Broad Garden Road.

The standard-issue USSPS scooter zipped down the quiet road. Horris kept his eyes forward. Percy sat behind him with arms wrapped around Horris' torso. Every once in a while, he would rest his forehead between Horris' shoulders, but his gaze fixed on the idyllic countryside without really seeing it.

The goodbyes at the District 7 depot had been mercifully short. Basah had wished him luck before bunting her forehead against his. Roddy had enveloped him in a crushing hug while lamenting that no one would make his bed anymore.

His longest goodbye had actually been with Fives. Percy had drawn Fives to a private corner of the hold and taken a deep breath. Fives had just watched him with muted curiosity.

"There's something I need to tell you."

"Okay."

He'd been chewing on it for the past two days in some sorry attempt to convince himself he hadn't actually seen what he'd seen. It was to no avail; his heart knew what he had seen, no matter how his head wanted to reject it.

"I saw Mother. When Horris went flying, and I dove after him." He watched Fives' dark eyebrows knit together. "I saw a massive hand, larger than any ship, rising from the bridge."

Percy had imagined all the ways Fives could react to such monumental news: glee, fury, sympathy. But he had not accounted for Fives simply saying "huh."

He'd waited. When no other response was forthcoming, he frowned. "Huh? That's it? That's all you have to say–huh?!"

"Well, I've never seen Her. I only hear Her. That's one of the reasons we fought near the bridge. She silenced everything…except for you. You and Mother made it quiet so I could concentrate. But I never saw Her. Did you hear Her?"

Percy had thought back. It had all happened so fast, but–no. Everything he'd heard was his own thoughts. "No," he said.

Fives nodded. "The universe is different for all of us."

"Don't you think that odd?"

"No?" Fives had tilted his head to the side, staring at Percy as though he'd grown a second head. "It'd be boring if the universe were the same for everyone."

Fives' voice echoed in Percy's head as he and Horris sped down the long country road. Here and there, Percy could see elongated, flying insects dart around the walls of hedges. "What are those?" He called.

"Huh?" Horris looked over his shoulder at Percy and then at the flying insects. "Oh! Dragonflies! Or maybe damselflies? I'd have to get closer to be sure."

Percy half-expected Horris to pull over. But he didn't. They just continued on their way down the length of Broad Garden Road.

At last, the scooter puttered to a stop outside a pair of wrought iron gates. Beyond, low one-story houses stood in maddeningly identical rows. It was early morning yet, and the only sound to be heard from within the gated community was the growl of a lawnmower.

It occurred to Percy, properly, that this might very well be the place he spent the rest of his life. So long as Great-Aunt Sophia—who he had never met—agreed to take him in. And she would, wouldn't she? They were kin. Here, he could rest and recover until he was well enough to…

Well enough to…

Horris slid off the scooter as it powered down. Percy followed suit. He turned to face Horris, trying to ignore the sour guilt when he saw the pad of bandages covering the right side of Horris' face. He tried to focus instead on Horris' smile.

Horris slung Roddy's tablet off his belt (he had requisitioned a replacement for his own) and held it out. "Sign here, please."

Percy signed off to indicate the package had been safely delivered to its destination and within a reasonable time limit. "Thank you, Horris."

"Anytime, Perce. Just, uh, make yourself known sooner next time. Take care, okay? You have my number, our emails. Keep in touch. If you ever need anything, ever, the *Silverfish* is just—"

Percy cut Horris off by pulling him into a hug. Horris didn't resist; he tucked his arms around Percy and folded over him. Percy buried his face against Horris' chest and inhaled the scent of sweat and cologne. For a selfish instant, he wanted to stay hidden there.

Horris sighed in his ear. He pulled back out of the embrace and stuck a hand out. "See ya, Percy."

"Take care, Horris," Percy said softly. He accepted the extended hand. They shook.

Percy turned to the iron gates, all the better to pretend he didn't see the last wistful look Horris gave him as he powered the scooter back on. He did not look back as Horris took off back down Broad Garden Road.

He was alone, save for the chitter of insects and the rustle of wind through the trees. Percy stared through the bars at the gated community. He tried to imagine living here, waking up every day at nine to enjoy a cup of coffee. Maybe play a game of canasta.

A pair of black boots stepped into place beside his own.

Percy tried not to sigh. "I'm never going to be rid of you, am I?"

Orestes smiled and shook his head. He looked from Percy to the gate.

"Well, you ought to find someone new to haunt," Percy said. He raised his finger to the buzzer that would announce his presence at the gatehouse. "I'm about to live a very boring life, and you deserve better than that. There's so much more out there to see, you know."

He tried to press the buzzer, but for some reason, his finger wouldn't move. Percy stared down at his finger, at the buzzer, at the halcyon little community beyond them both. This had been his goal, hadn't it? This was where he'd meant to go.

But there was so much more…

■

"Horris, let's *go*."

Horris ignored the impatience in Roddy's tone. He lingered by the *Silverfish*'s gangplank. The outgoing packages had been processed and loaded; they would need further sorting once they were airborne.

Still, Horris lingered. A chain-link fence separated the District 7 depot from the lush forest around it. Horris couldn't take his eyes off the dark shapes between the trees.

"Horris."

"Five more minutes."

"No more minutes." Roddy skidded down the gangplank to touch Horris' shoulder. "Hor, we have to go. We can't give Rofon more reasons to be pissed at us."

Basah gave him a sympathetic look when he and Roddy arrived in the cockpit. "I know you were hoping."

Horris shrugged in a futile attempt to offload his disappointment. "Well, we'll still be able to—"

Fives shushed him. He stood at the cockpit window, looking out at the chain-link fence. The others crowded around him to stare out at the forest below. It took a moment, but then it was audible:

"HEY! HEY, WAIT!"

Horris watched, stunned, as Percy appeared at the edge of the depot yard. He flung himself up the chain-link fence and dropped to the lot on the other side. "BLIP, lower the gangplank!"

BLIP obeyed. And a red-faced, sweaty Percy appeared in the cockpit. He tried to speak, shook his head, and doubled over for breath.

Horris crossed to him. A thousand questions sprung into his mind, and it was a fight to put them in order: "Percy! Did you run here—are you all right—what happened—what are you doing here?"

"Take me with you!" Percy straightened on the exclamation.

The cascade of questions ceased. Only one question came tumbling out of Horris' mouth: "What?"

"Take me with you!" Percy said again. He seized Horris by the hand. "Please–I want to be a postman. I want to see everything—everything that's out there—I want to come with you!"

Horris gaped at him. Percy's hand in his was the only confirmation he had that this was not a dream. "Well–well–yes! Of course! But you have to go through admissions and training, and the rest of the crew has to vouch that you'd be a good fit—"

He looked over his shoulder at the said crew. Fives gave them a double thumbs-up. Roddy, however, was sighing as he dug a hand into his pocket. Basah held out her hand to accept the fistful of credits Roddy withdrew.

"You were betting on Percy coming back?!" Horris exclaimed, aghast. Percy made a noise of equal offense.

"Oh, we knew Percy was coming back." Basah grinned as she pocketed her new wealth. "But Rod is a cynic. He thought we'd have to turn around and come get you."

"I didn't know you could sprint that fast!" Roddy protested. He clapped his hands together, spun on his heel, and made for his seat. "All right, people, places for launch!"

"BLIP," Horris said, "please change Percy's designation within the logbook."

Acknowledged. Warden, Lieutenant Perseus is now registered as Warden, Postman Perseus. Welcome aboard!

Horris looked down from the ceiling to meet Percy's brilliant green eyes. They shone with a sort of joy he'd never seen before, and that warm, shining feeling radiated through his own chest. He squeezed Percy's hand and got a firm squeeze in return.

"Not every run is going to be as exciting as this one, you know," he warned.

Percy laughed. "I could do with a bit of monotony, actually."

And then they were airborne, speeding for the expanse of stars and all that lay within it.

About the Author

EMILY FISHER is not a postal carrier, although she is married to one. She is an educator who lives in Coventry, RI, with her husband, her cat Greyjoy, and the spiders who live rent-free in her bathroom. The Silverfish is her first published novel.